'It has opened my eyes to the injustice done to so many . . .
A thought-provoking and interesting read'
Shaz's Book Blog

'*The Oceans Between Us* truly pulls at your heartstrings. With
themes of salvation, longing, self-preservation, inequality,
betrayal, forbidden love, friendship, loyalty, the search for
justice and a place to call home, along with human endur-
ance, this novel will touch your soul'
Mrs B's Book Reviews

'I flew through this emotional book. I raged at just what
some had to endure. But I also felt their bravery in finding
justice for all children who suffered. Highly recommended'
Between My Lines

'A story that will touch every reader's heart. An absolute
must-read'
By The Letter Book Reviews

'Heart-wrenching debut novel. A story based on actual
events which will have you glued to the pages'
Waggy Tales

'A heart-wrenching and heartwarming novel . . . this book is
impossible to put down'
Discovering Diamonds

Gill Thompson is an English lecturer who completed an MA in Creative Writing at Chichester University. Her first two novels, *The Oceans Between Us* and *The Child on Platform One*, were both digital bestsellers and have been highly acclaimed. She lives with her family in West Sussex and teaches English to college students.

🐦 @wordkindling

By Gill Thompson

The Oceans Between Us
The Child on Platform One
The Lighthouse Sisters

The
Lighthouse
Sisters

GILL THOMPSON

HEADLINE

First published in Great Britain in 2022 by
HEADLINE REVIEW
An imprint of HEADLINE PUBLISHING GROUP

First published in Great Britain in paperback in 2022 by
HEADLINE REVIEW

2

Cataloguing in Publication Data is available from the British Library

ISBN 978 1 4722 7995 8

Typeset in Garamond MT by Palimpsest Book Production Ltd,
Falkirk, Stirlingshire

Printed and bound in Great Britain by Clays Ltd, Elcograf S.p.A.

HEADLINE PUBLISHING GROUP
An Hachette UK Company
Carmelite House
50 Victoria Embankment
London EC4Y 0DZ

www.headline.co.uk
www.hachette.co.uk

To Joshua,
With love from your adoring Grandma.

Prologue

November 1996

Some days, when the wind is soft and southerly, she fancies it carries the faintest trace of salt, like the briny breezes she once knew so well on the island. And at once she's transported back to St Aubin's Bay, where the late-afternoon sun turns the wet sand silver and stars of light burst on the waves. Yet she knows that's impossible. They live too far inland now for the smell of the sea to reach them. Too far even to be visited by seagulls – unless a dire storm is on the way. But if she closes her eyes, she can still see them swoop and dive and hear their plaintive calls. Then the memories crowd in: William burying their father up to his neck in sand, save for one grit-caked hand, which still clutches his book; their mother perched on a deckchair pouring tea from an old tartan-patterned Thermos; her sister screaming as she runs into the sea in her blue hand-knitted costume, jumping at the shock of the cold waves. Did the sun always shine in those heady pre-war days, or is it just imagination that bathes her memories in mellow light?

She always sits by the window and the window is always open, even when the catch is crusted with hoar frost and the panes are opaque with ice. The wind scalds her face in winter and sunlight pools on it in summer. It's her only contact with nature these days – unless you count the garish chrysanthemums their daughter sometimes brings that fill the room with their earthy aroma.

She stands up stiffly, grasping the polished arms of the high-backed chair and pushing up as she's been taught, then shuffles over to the dresser, discarding the rug as she does so. There are the smiling photos that she talks to each day, running her finger down their smooth glass, willing the figures to come alive once more. The ones from the past are monochrome, faded over time, their owners wearing the formal clothes of a bygone age. There's her father in a jacket and tie, grinning into the camera, the ever-present book in his hand as though he's only just looked up from the page. A photo of her mother stands next to that of her father. She wears a neat trilby, perched slantwise on her head, as was the fashion. Her suit is dark, calf-length, with a froth of cream at the neck. She's impossibly thin, her body still recovering from those terrible months at the end of the war when the food supplies were cut off and the islanders feared they'd starve to death.

Then come photos of their own three children, in colour now, next to those of their ten grandchildren at various ages and stages.

But the picture she loves best is the one Dad took of her and her sister at St Catherine's Tower. The one that gave them their name: the lighthouse sisters. She smiles at their innocent faces frozen in time, and the moment of joy from nearly seventy years ago catches her again. That childhood closeness has waxed and waned over the years, but their love runs deep.

They were there for each other during the war, and they are there for each other now. Just like the lighthouse, a source of hope and protection over the years. It guided her home once.

Today it will light up her life again.

Part One

June–July 1940

1

Jersey, the Channel Islands

They were all in the back garden when Alice got home from her shift. The ward had been stuffy, the fans whirring noisily in a vain attempt to dispel the thick air. She'd looked forward to walking home with a fresh breeze on her face. But if anything it was hotter outdoors. The sun still blazed and the humid atmosphere wrapped itself around her like a woolly blanket.

She pushed open the side gate and made straight for the patch of stippled shade under Dad's old apple trees.

Mum was deadheading a clump of snapdragons by the kitchen window, their colours vivid in the sunshine. 'Don't sit on the grass, love. There's a deckchair in the shed.'

'All right.' Alice retrieved the chair, set it up under the tree and took off her tightly laced shoes. 'That's better.'

'How was your day? Do you want some tea?' Mum put down the trug and secateurs.

'Hot, tiring . . . and yes, please!'

'Coming up.' She went inside to the kitchen.

Alice peeled off her stiff cuffs and cap, then placed them on the grass beside the deckchair. She tipped her head back and closed her eyes against the glare. Dad and Jenny were murmuring from the bench by the back wall as they pored over a maths textbook – they'd been too absorbed even to greet her when she arrived. William was tearing up handfuls of grass and posting them through the criss-cross wires of Binkie's cage. She didn't bother saying hello to him. He was bound to ignore her.

A pompous voice blared out, announcing news of German bombing raids on Paris. Mum must have switched the wireless on. Forty-five people had been killed. It was terrifying how quickly the Germans were advancing: they'd stormed down from Dunkirk and had already crossed the Somme. It was clear France would soon fall. And then where would that leave the Channel Islands? A dribble of sweat ran down the side of Alice's face. She wiped it off with the back of her hand.

'Here you are, love.' Mum plonked a cup of tea down beside her. Some of the liquid sloshed over the top. 'Are you all right? You look a bit pale.'

Alice picked up the cup and took a sip. 'I'm fine, Mum. Just a long shift. And the news about Paris.'

'I know, love. I wish I hadn't turned the wireless on now.'

'We can't ignore it. There's no doubt the Germans are coming closer. Rebekah's getting really anxious.' Alice frowned as she remembered her close friend's strained expression when they'd met briefly earlier on the ward. Rebekah had only married her husband, Thomas Liron, just before war broke out. He'd enlisted a month later in September 1939 and she hadn't seen him since.

Mum wiped her hands down her apron. 'Poor girl. I can imagine how I'd feel if it was William fighting.'

Alice looked over to her brother, so caught up in his own world. 'I certainly hope this war will be over before William's old enough to join up.'

'So do I.' Mum turned. 'James . . . Jenny . . . Do either of you want tea?'

'No, thanks, Mum.' Jenny glanced up from her textbook. Dad didn't reply.

Mum rolled her eyes and stomped back to her gardening.

Alice leant back again. She really ought to go in and change. There were probably grass stains on her cuffs already, and doubtless the back of her dress was creased from the deckchair. Another load of washing and ironing. But maybe just a few more minutes' rest first to regain some energy.

It was still stifling. She swept a couple of storm bugs off her arm. Sure sign of thunder to come. There was an irritating buzzing in the distance too, like a swarm of angry flies. She sat forward in the deckchair, shading her eyes against the brightness. A line of black dots was inching across the sky over towards Fort Regent.

'Dad?' She got to her feet.

'Mmm?'

'What's that?' She heard the shrillness in her own voice.

Each sound detached itself from the next. The chomping from Binkie's cage. Mum clattering in the kitchen. The creak as Dad stood up from the bench. Then the sky screaming.

The dots had become planes, one after another, flying low in single file like a dark arrow. Alice's chest contracted and the dense air clogged her throat.

'*Dad!*'

'Get down, all of you!'

Alice threw herself to the ground, her pulse accelerating until it was one long blast of fear.

Another clatter from the kitchen.

Jenny shrieked. Alice twisted her head and saw Dad reach out an arm to shield her as they lay side by side on the grass.

William continued to mutter to Binkie, and Alice realised he was still crouching by the rabbit cage. 'Will! Down!' she shouted.

William froze.

'William! You must get down!' yelled Dad.

William didn't move.

Mum raced out of the kitchen and shoved him onto the grass, pinning him down, her hand clamped to his back. William whimpered.

The noise was deafening now as engines roared across the sky. Alice didn't dare look up. There'd been no warning. No siren. No time to take cover from the bombing they'd feared for months. The Germans had launched a surprise attack and were going to murder them in their own garden. She braced herself for the explosion, an agonising pain, the red stains spreading across the grass . . .

'It's all right. It's our lot.' A familiar voice, near at hand.

Alice hadn't heard the click of the garden gate above the boom of engines, but Pip Marett, one of her father's ex-pupils, was striding across the lawn. How on earth could he be so casual? She felt her face colouring.

Dad and Jenny stood up and brushed themselves down. Mum helped William to his feet.

The planes were right above them now, the metal bodies glinting in the sunlight. Pip tipped his head back, chanting under his breath as he counted them. It seemed to take an age as they roared past. 'Wow. Eighteen!' he said eventually. 'Whitleys!'

'Whitleys, eh?' Dad walked up to him. 'Never seen those over here before.'

Pip had to shout to be heard. 'Yes, see the triangular nose? A bit like the roof of a greenhouse.'

As the last plane thundered past, Alice caught sight of the strange-shaped cockpit Pip had described. Despite the clear RAF markings on the side of the fuselage, she still felt weak with fear. It could so easily have been Germans. They were constantly on the watch for them now, expecting to be attacked at any time. 'Do you know what's going on?' It was hard to keep her voice from wobbling, and at first she wondered if Pip had heard her.

He continued to watch the planes as they disappeared into the distance, before turning back. 'Looks as if they're heading out to St Peter. They'll approach the airport from the east.'

'Any idea what they'll be doing there?' Dad asked.

'Refuelling probably. I'm going to sail round to St Ouen's on the *Bynie May* and see what I can find out. Would any of you like to come with me?'

Alice felt a surge of excitement. How wonderful to be with Pip on his boat. Just the two of them. She hoped no one else wanted to go.

'I'm not good in boats,' said Dad.

Pip smiled. 'Mrs Robinson?'

'Thank you, Pip, but I need to get on with the dinner. This has put me all behind.' Mum made it sound as though the planes had flown across deliberately just to delay her food preparations.

Pip cleared his throat. 'Um . . . William?'

'I don't think so, Pip,' said Mum. 'He might be a bit frightened.'

Will had opened Binkie's cage, and had the rabbit in his arms, his face buried in its fur. It was what he always did when he needed reassurance. Mum was right.

'Alice . . . Jenny?' Pip's expression was eager.

Jenny stepped forward, but Dad held up his hand. 'Not Jenny, I'm afraid,' he said. 'She has an exam tomorrow.'

Jenny shrugged at Pip. 'Sorry.'

Pip ran his hands through his light-brown hair. He'd grown taller since Alice had last seen him. When he was cramming for Highers last year, he'd often been round to the house for Dad to tutor him. Jenny had sometimes joined in the lessons, although she scarcely needed to. He'd been in the year above Jenny at school, a year below Alice. Alice couldn't remember when her crush had first started, but she'd found herself thinking about him more and more in the last two years of school. She'd always been too shy to say anything, of course, or even hint at it. Maybe the proximity of being in a boat with him might help accelerate things.

'I'd love to come,' she said, then felt immediately embarrassed, as though he must be able to read her thoughts.

'Aren't you tired after your shift?' Jenny asked.

'No, I feel fine now. A boat trip will be a good way to relax.'

Pip swallowed and smiled, a little awkwardly, Alice thought, but perhaps she imagined it. 'All right. I'll cycle down to the harbour and get the boat ready. You know where she's moored?'

'I think so.'

'We need to be quick. D'you have a bike?'

12

'May I borrow yours, Jen?'

Jenny kicked at a loose stone with her foot. 'I suppose so.'

'I'll get changed and follow you down.'

'See you later.'

Pip disappeared back through the gate. Suddenly no longer tired, Alice rushed upstairs to put on some casual clothes. She was going to be on her own, in a boat, with Pip Marett.

2

Twenty minutes later, Alice walked down South Pier towards the forest of masts, watching the boats bobbing on the water, nudging each other whenever they were jostled by the low waves. She peered over the edge of the jetty. Pip waved up at her from a small yacht. The name *Bynie May* was written on its side in swirly letters.

'Hello there!' His eyes were the same shade of blue as the sea.

'Hello.'

'Come on board. You'll be safe. I've got a spare life jacket.'

She made her way down the steps at the end of the pier and grasped Pip's warm hand. Her body tingled. Almost before she knew it, she'd stepped onto the boat, which lurched at the impact. Still holding her hand, Pip steadied her and laughed. Alice laughed too.

As he navigated their way out of the harbour, then tacked across the mouth of St Aubin's Bay, she perched on one of the low benches that straddled the boat – a 'thwart', Pip had called it – trying to keep out of his way and moving to the other side of the boat whenever he shouted 'Ready about!' in order to avoid the boom. He was so confident, pulling on ropes, drawing the tiller backwards and forwards, peering out beyond the sail to check the route ahead, all the while chatting away. Alice felt a little self-conscious in the bulky life jacket. It was hardly flattering. Now that the wind was a bit stronger, she wished she'd put on a thicker jumper, although the slowly sinking sun still gave off some warmth. She'd always longed to go sailing with Pip. They hadn't seen so much of him since he left school. She missed his visits.

'How are Jenny's exams going?' he asked.

'Fine, I think,' she said. 'Last one tomorrow.' She wasn't looking forward to witnessing the inevitable post-mortem on the maths paper, with Dad hanging on Jenny's every word and ignoring the rest of them. Sometimes she wished she'd been clever like Jenny. They'd been such good friends as children, but as they'd grown up, it became more obvious that Jenny had inherited Dad's sharp maths brain, and Alice had felt increasingly left out of their conversations, which always seemed to revolve around some theorem or other. Mum was much too busy with William and running the house. Thank goodness her patients appreciated her.

Pip's hands on the tiller looked brown and strong, the nails neatly clipped. The sun picked out a few golden hairs on his forearm. 'Thanks for offering to come out on the boat with me,' he said.

'It's a pleasure.' She looked him in the eye, smiling, then turned away. Her throat tightened. Was that too forward?

He smiled back at her. 'It's good to have some company. I've been getting so frustrated, knowing there's a war on and not being able to help.'

'You decided not to enlist?'

'I'd have enlisted like a shot, but Dad was adamant that he wanted me to stay here. I've just started working in the office

15

with him. Helping with the paperwork and such.' He ran a finger round the collar of his shirt.

'That must be interesting.'

Pip laughed, a short bark. 'Not very. But it will do for now. I'm keeping up my sailing skills – you never know when they might come in handy.'

'You manage the boat very well.'

'I was taught by one of the best. The old fisherman, Jack. Do you know who I mean? Dad wanted me to be more than a gentleman sailor. I had to learn the ropes properly.'

'I don't know Jack, but he's obviously done a good job.'

Pip pointed out the Martello tower at Noirmont. 'How many times were we told about that in history lessons? Built to protect us from the French during the Napoleonic wars,' he said. His eyes had a faraway look. 'Let's hope it'll protect us from the Jerries too.'

Alice felt a stab of anxiety. Being here with Pip, on the sea, had allowed her to forget the rumble of war momentarily. 'Do you think the Germans will make it as far as us?' She was still churned up from seeing the Whitley bombers earlier. Even if they were British planes, they made the prospect of fighting on their shores feel all the more real.

Pip shrugged. 'Dad doesn't think so.' Pip's father was high up in Jersey administration. He usually knew what was going on.

'That's some comfort.'

'S'pose so.'

The conversation ceased as Pip navigated his way under the cliffs to avoid a reef of rocks out at sea. The water was choppy now and Alice could sense he needed to concentrate.

But once they were through the tricky part, he seemed keen to talk again.

'Tell me about your day at the hospital,' he said.

Alice stretched out her legs in their navy slacks and crossed them at the ankle. The boat wouldn't be turning for a bit, so she could relax without having to worry about avoiding the boom. It was nice to be asked about her job. No one at home was ever that interested. She recounted the events of her day, trying to make them sound fascinating, but Pip was staring up at the sail, his hair lifting in the breeze, and didn't react. She decided he wouldn't want to know about the less glamorous tasks she had to perform – emptying bedpans, giving blanket baths, mopping up vomit – so she skirted over those and told him about dear Mrs Perchard. When she'd last seen the old lady that afternoon, she'd been a little pale, and had only managed a few spoonfuls of soup before turning her head and closing her eyes. Alice hoped she wouldn't deteriorate overnight. She hated to think of her struggling without anyone to hold her hand or talk to her. Luckily Rebekah was on duty. She'd look out for her.

She cleared her throat. Perhaps she'd tell Pip about Rebekah. But just as she was trying to work out how to steer the conversation towards her friend, Pip interjected.

'So Jenny's okay, is she?'

'Jenny?'

'Yes.' Pip pushed the tiller away from him, then tugged on the rope. Alice ducked towards him as the boat tacked and the boom swung across. She caught a whiff of cologne. 'Did you say tomorrow is her last exam?'

Alice stared curiously at him. Hadn't he listened to a word

she'd said? 'Yes, I told you that earlier.' Did she sound a little petulant?

'I see,' he said distractedly. 'That's good.' He looked up at the sail. 'She'll be fine for a while.'

For a moment, Alice thought he meant Jenny, then she realised Pip was talking about the boat.

'Sailing's a lot of hard work, isn't it?' Dad had never taken them sailing. He'd been born in London, so the sea wasn't in his blood as it was with many of the islanders, and they'd never owned a boat like some of her friends. She'd gone sailing with the Guides once, but hadn't particularly taken to it. She probably wouldn't have agreed to go today had it not been a chance to get close to Pip.

Pip looked out to sea but didn't reply. Alice wondered if he'd heard her, or if it was a silly question. Presumably sailors sailed because they enjoyed all that effort. Perhaps he was ignoring her because he thought she was stupid. Why on earth couldn't she say something clever like Jenny would, impressing him with a calculation about the frequency of waves or some other interesting fact?

He had clearly lost interest in the account of her day. Perhaps it was better she stayed quiet for a while.

She stared down at the water. It was a deep blue today. Sometimes the sea looked almost metallic, as though the waves had been hammered out and painted. If it wasn't for them constantly shifting and re-forming, you'd think it was a relief painting.

The low rays of the sun glanced off the water. The air was still warm; her face glowed from where the sun had seared it earlier. If this was a romantic film, the boat would be steering itself and Pip would be beside her, holding her close with his arm as she leant her head on his shoulder. There'd be swelling music in the background. He'd be looking at her adoringly while she snuggled into him, secure in the warmth of his love.

But of course this wasn't a film. The boat wouldn't steer itself. It was a big responsibility for Pip; he had to give the trip his full attention. And he was probably thinking about the planes too. Still, he'd invited her on board. Sort of. She just had to wait for him to make the first move.

They skirted round Portelet, the little boat hugging the coastline, and as they approached Ouaisné, Pip pointed out the caves at La Cotte. She peered across at the gloomy recesses gouged into the cliff.

'Dad was telling me about the archaeologists investigating those. They've been doing it for years,' he said.

'Yes, I think I saw some of them a couple of years ago. Do you know what they found?'

'Stone Age stuff, I think. Tools . . . a few bones. Rumour has it that Ice Age cavemen used to herd mammoths over the cliff to kill them for their meat. Must have been some banquet!' He laughed.

Alice laughed too. She loved the way dimples appeared in Pip's cheeks when he chuckled.

Then they were streaming across St Brelade's Bay, the sail full in the wind. She glanced at her watch. They'd been on the boat a while now and Pip hadn't tried to make any kind of move. Could she be more encouraging? Perhaps she ought to stage some sort of drama – like falling into the water, to see if he would rescue her. But the thought of sitting shivering in her soaking clothes with Pip silent and resentful at having to go back early dissuaded her.

By seven, they'd rounded the headland and had the Corbière lighthouse in their sights.

As she stared at the chalky-white tower rising up from a reef of wave-whipped rocks that extended way beyond it, another lighthouse slipped into her mind. Years ago, when she was about ten and Jenny eight, Dad had taken them over to St Catherine's Breakwater, in the north-east of the island. Mum must have been expecting William at the time, as she remembered Dad telling her to get some rest while they were out. They'd run along the narrow stone strip that jutted out to sea and climbed down the steps to the lighthouse at the end. Jenny had pestered Dad with questions about the height of the tower and how far the light could be seen, a budding mathematician even then, but Alice had only one question: 'What's it *for*?'

Dad's voice came back to her through the years. 'It acts as a guide and warning,' he'd said, in his precise scientist's tone. 'It keeps sailors away from danger and leads them safely home when they return.'

'So lighthouses help people?'

'Yes, you could put it that way,' he'd said.

Alice smiled at the memory. 'I love lighthouses. They're such beacons of hope,' she told Pip. She hoped that didn't sound too highfalutin.

Pip nodded. 'We don't need to go out that far, though,' he said. 'We'll sail her through the Fisherman's Passage. It's a great shortcut. I just need to make sure we avoid the Kaines over there. Many a ship has been wrecked on them.'

He navigated the passage skilfully, well away from the treacherous rocks, and soon they were out into St Ouen's Bay, where the light still sparkled on the water.

'It's quite shallow here,' he said. 'Must be about under the flight path. We'll go head to wind. I'll drop the anchor, then we'll take down the sails.' The boat slowed as he threw the huge metal hook overboard. 'Can you give me a hand with the gaff, Alice?' He was lowering the top part of the mast ready to stow it in the boat. She helped take the weight.

After the flurry of activity, the boat was suddenly still, the waves lapping against the hull. A mellow warmth wrapped itself round her. Pip slumped on the thwart opposite, then looked across in the direction of the airport. 'I would imagine they've had time to refuel by now, assuming that's what they were doing. Should be taking off soon.' He stood up suddenly and delved under the foredeck. 'I'll see if I can pick anything up on the wireless.' He returned with a small set, which he placed carefully on one of the seats, then knelt in front of it, turning his ear towards the machine while twiddling the dial. There was a scribble of static. He tried again. 'No luck. Must be too far out to get a signal.' He wound up the leads and returned the set to the hold before resuming his seat opposite Alice. 'Thought I might tune into the BBC, see if I can hear the latest.'

'Perhaps you can find out when you're back.'

'Yes, I'll try then.'

Alice was hoping he might talk to her about the hospital again, or ask her something else about herself, or even suggest another outing, but he continued to be more interested in the planes. Eventually, when there was still no sound from the airport, he turned back to her.

'Do you think Jenny will get into Cambridge?'

Not Jenny again. Alice pleated the material of her slacks, where it was a little loose over the knee. 'Dad seems to think so. She's really clever.'

Pip's eyes were intense as they locked on to hers. 'But it's not guaranteed.'

'No, of course not.' Did he look relieved?

'Has she said anything to you?'

'About what?'

He looked out to sea. 'About how keen she is to go. Whether she'll miss anyone . . .'

He didn't turn back, so she couldn't see his face. Her heart started to thrum. Was this why he'd agreed to her coming on the trip? So he could find out more about Jenny?

But before she had a chance to answer, there was a sudden roar behind them. Pip twisted round. 'There they are!'

Alice followed his gaze and saw the planes flying in the same straight line as earlier, over the cliff and out to sea. The noise was as deafening as before, but she wasn't frightened this time. In fact, her thoughts were more occupied with what might be going on between Jenny and Pip than any anxiety about the planes. She couldn't say too much to Pip – she didn't want to come across as jealous – but she'd try to get the truth out of Jenny that evening.

Pip was counting again. 'Fifteen . . . sixteen . . . That's odd. There's only sixteen planes this time. Two can't have taken off.'

'Are you sure you counted them properly?'

'Of course I did!' He sounded irritated.

Oh no, she was annoying him now.

'See how low they're flying.' He pointed to the last of the departing aircraft, perilously close to the waves, making a laboured chugging sound. 'They must be weighed down with bombs and fuel.'

'S'pose so.'

He watched as the planes banked round to the south. 'I wonder where they're going. They're headed towards France, not England. Must be on a raid. If they've stopped here to refuel, they'll be going on a long trip. Perhaps they're going to bomb Germany. Let's hope they cause havoc.'

'Yes indeed.' Alice tried to catch his excitement but could only think of the possible injuries or fatalities. Shrapnel could do terrible things. Even if the Germans were the enemy, they were still people.

She wondered how long Pip wanted to stay anchored. It was getting colder now. She rubbed her hands up and down her arms, hoping he would lend her his jacket, but he was still looking out to sea, where purple clouds bruised the horizon. Another tendril of unease wound through her.

'I guess the last two were too heavy to take off. I hope it's nothing more sinister.' He leant over the side of the boat to pull up the anchor. 'Let's turn back. We'll make it home a lot quicker, as the wind'll be behind us and the tide has started to flood now.'

She wondered if he'd grown tired of her company. This outing hadn't gone anything like the way she'd hoped, and time was running out. But she decided that, like her, he was probably just getting cold and wanted his supper.

'Let me know if you find out anything later,' she said.
'Will do.'

She helped him raise the sail again, and they turned for home.

She felt a bit shaky cycling back up from the harbour, and her stomach growled with hunger. When she came in, everyone was clustered round the wireless. Mum got up and absent-mindedly handed her a plate of dried-up stew that had been perching on a pan of water on the stove for goodness knows how long, then sat back down, frowning. Alice grabbed some cutlery then drew up a chair at the table.

The voice boomed out of the set. Italy had just declared war on the Allies.

'Bloody Eyeties,' Dad said. He rarely swore. 'Mussolini's only joined the war because he thinks the Jerries are going to win.'

Alice's skin prickled. *Could* the Germans win the war? What would happen to Jersey? To them? To her and Pip, she wanted to say. But of course there was no her and Pip.

'I'll never shop at Rossi's again,' said Mum.

'Don't be daft, Annette,' replied Dad. 'Paolo Rossi hates the Jerries. It's just that madman Mussolini. There are lots of sensible Italians who think like we do.'

'What will happen to the Channel Islands?' Jenny asked.

Dad patted her hand. 'We'll be fine, love. The islands have been dependencies of the Crown for nearly a thousand years. There are two-thousand-odd British troops here. The Jerries left us alone in the last war and they will now.' Some of the colour returned to Jenny's face.

They went upstairs soon after. Once she'd put on her night-dress, Jenny knelt beside the bed and pulled out a low wooden trolley containing a small box. It was a ritual they'd performed since childhood, when Dad had made the storage items to contain their midnight feasts. When they were young, they'd often written little letters, leaving them in the box for the other to find. Alice had a sudden memory of her name scrawled on an envelope in Jenny's childish handwriting, and the excitement of delving inside to find a page of drawings – often of the lighthouses they loved – or tiny messages. They'd been so close then, telling each other everything, sharing their hoard of snacks long after Mum had thought they were asleep, whispering in the dark . . . How had they grown apart? As a little girl she'd never imagined a time when they wouldn't be friends. But a distance had opened up between them over the years, even though the food ritual remained.

'Only apples left, Alice.'

'That's fine.'

Jenny passed her an apple, then closed the box and pushed back the trolley.

As they lay munching in their narrow twin beds in the shadowy bedroom, Jenny finally asked her about her sailing trip.

'Did you have a good time?'

Alice couldn't see her sister's face in the dark, so it was hard to know what she was thinking.

'Yes, thanks. Pip was anxious to see the planes. I suppose he was glad of some company on the boat.'

'Yes, I expect so.' Jenny bit down hard on her apple.

'Would you rather have gone instead?'

'Alice, it's fine. I don't have a claim on Pip.'

'But you do like him?'

Silence, apart from the munching. What was Jenny thinking?

'Yes . . . I do like him.'

'And he likes you. I could tell.' The darkness sharpened around them.

'Yes . . . I know. I think he wants something more than friendship, though.'

'And you don't? What's the problem?'

Jenny threw off the bedclothes and sat up. 'You *know* what the problem is, Alice!'

'What, Dad?'

'No, not Dad – except indirectly.'

'What d'you mean?'

A swift sigh. 'Cambridge.'

'Oh. But that's not until next year.'

'But how can I get close to Pip if I might be leaving him?' Jenny nibbled the flesh round the core of her apple.

'Well, if it's serious, he'll wait for you.' Alice tried to hold back the emotion from her voice. She finished her own apple in a series of rapid bites, reached out for Jenny's core, and took them both over to the bin.

'But it takes three years to do a degree. I can't ask him to wait that long.'

Alice got back into bed but stayed sitting up so she could see Jenny more easily.

'There are the holidays, surely. And he could visit.' She felt a sharp stab of jealousy at the thought of Jenny and Pip together. Jenny obviously wasn't aware of Alice's feelings for him, and she certainly wasn't going to admit to them now.

'Perhaps. But there's also the little matter of the war.'

26

'Dad thinks we're safe here.'

'Jersey might be safe, but it could be another story in Cambridge.'

'You might not even get in.' Alice regretted her words as soon as they were out. She didn't mean to be nasty, but it was hard to deal with her feelings.

'I know.' Jenny thumped the counterpane. 'Everything's going round and round in my head.'

'Try not to think too far into the future. Just enjoy the moment.' An image of Pip on the boat flashed into Alice's head: his bright eyes and ruddy cheeks. 'You're lucky to have someone who's interested in you. Especially someone like Pip.' She snapped off the memory and promised herself that from now on, she would stop thinking of him. It was Jenny he wanted.

'I don't know. Maybe.'

'All the more reason to see how it develops. You're not leading him on. He knows about Cambridge.'

'Yes, I suppose you're right.'

Alice reached across to Jenny's bed and her hand connected with her sister's. But the gesture felt empty; there was none of the old closeness.

'What's that thing in Latin that means just have a good time and don't worry about the future?'

'*Carpe diem?*'

'Yes, *carpe diem.*' Alice wriggled down the bed again. 'Night.'

'Night,' said Jenny.

But it was a while before Alice drifted off. And when she did, her bed tilted and lurched on the waves as German planes circled.

3

The next day, Alice was just about to go off duty when Mrs Le Maistre called out in her imperious voice, 'Nurse! My flowers need some attention.' She suppressed a grimace. Trust Mrs Le Maistre to delay her. She picked up the vase of purple irises from the bedside locker and carried it into the sluice room. Normally she wouldn't mind staying to help a patient – she'd gladly spend hours with Mrs Perchard, whose husband had died in the last war, listening to her reminiscing about him while she rubbed her back or her heels, or spooned junket into her mouth in an attempt to nourish her shrunken frame. People like Mrs Perchard deserved her time, but Mrs Le Maistre, who treated her like a servant, did not.

'Want a hand?' Rebekah stood in the doorway. The sun slanting through the small window lit up the smooth whiteness of her cap and apron.

'Oh, would you mind? Mrs LM is being demanding as usual.'

'Of course not. Your shift finished half an hour ago. I can take over now. I'll rearrange madam's flowers then await her next orders.'

'You're an angel. I'm desperate to get out of here and breathe some fresh air.'

Rebekah nodded. 'It is muggy today. Should be cooler outside.'

Alice pushed a strand of hair under her cap; her dress was sticking to her damp back and her apron was creased. She had a sudden urge to run down to the sea, plunge into the cool water and let the surf rinse the grime from her body. Never mind, she'd be home soon, then she could get out of her sticky uniform. She wiped her palms down her skirt. 'By the way, Mum was asking how you are. And Tom. Have you heard anything more from him?'

Rebekah turned away and moved the flowers around the vase. 'Not a word. It's been ages now. Things must be hotting up over the Channel.' Alice couldn't see her face, but she could hear the forced flippancy in her voice.

'It seems that way. Did you see the planes go over yesterday?'

'I certainly heard them. Thought they were Germans at first.'

'So did I! Terrifying. Do you know what type Tom's flying?'

Rebekah shrugged. 'Spitfires, I think.' When she glanced back, her face was pale.

Alice squeezed her friend's arm. 'I'm sure you'll hear soon.'

Rebekah smiled, a little tightly.

Alice took a deep breath. 'Rebekah. When you first met Tom, how did you know you were in love?' Five years ago, as an eighteen-year-old, Rebekah had visited Jersey on holiday, met Thomas Liron, and never left. Alice had always thought of theirs as a true love story.

'Ooh. What a question.' Rebekah leant against the sink. 'I suppose it just felt right. Natural. Like we were always meant to be together.' She laughed. 'Is that corny?'

'Not at all. It's helpful.'

Rebekah shot her a glance. 'Do we deduce Miss Robinson has met a young man?'

Alice fanned her face with her hand. 'Sadly not. I just thought I'd ask. In case I ever did meet someone.'

'Of course you will. And when you do, remember what Aunt Rebekah told you.'

She laughed. 'Thanks.' She gave Rebekah a quick hug. 'Stay strong. I'll see you tomorrow.'

She left the sluice room and walked back down the ward.

⊥

At his father's accountancy office, Pip stuffed a pile of papers into a folder and stood up to drop them into the filing cabinet. His neck was tense from sitting slumped over the desk all morning, and he massaged it with his fingers.

'Can you take these to the post for me?' Dad asked. His father was an elderly figure these days, but still actively working. He was training Pip up to take over the business when he retired. Not that that was imminent; Mr Marett had also been given the role of Jersey jurat two years ago and was busier than ever.

'Of course.' Pip took the envelopes from his father and escaped from the office. It would be a relief to get some fresh air and exercise his stiff limbs, even for a brief while.

There was only a tiny window in their cramped office, and it didn't get the sun until the end of the day, so Pip was surprised to realise how bright and hot it was outside. He loosened his tie – Dad wouldn't approve, but he would make sure it was back in place by the time he returned. As he sauntered down to the post office, preferring to prolong his journey rather than using the nearby box, he looked wistfully over in the direction of the harbour. Even though he couldn't see her, he knew *Bynie May* would be there, bobbing up and down on the water, awaiting their next adventure together.

It had been fun sailing round to St Ouen's with Alice. Dad had found out later that two of the planes had indeed failed to take off, Pip's suspicion that they were weighed down with bombs and fuel proving correct. He tried to recapture the feeling of freedom and excitement he'd felt watching the Whitleys fly over. Envy too, if he was honest. His frustration was mounting each day, knowing the Germans were advancing through France, getting ever closer to Jersey. When he'd heard about the daring rescue of British soldiers from near the Belgian border, he'd been desperate to sail over to Dunkirk and help. It was hard to control his anger at Dad for not letting him enlist. He could have been in the RAF or the navy by now, engaged in active combat, rather than stuck in an airless office, performing perfunctory clerical tasks. That was the trouble with an older father. His parents had waited years for him to come along, only for Mum to die giving birth to him. No wonder Dad was overprotective.

Pip wasn't at all sure he wanted to be an accountant as his father intended. He was reasonable at arithmetic and had a fairly logical brain, but other people's finances bored him rigid. Where was the excitement in that?

When he'd been at school, an English teacher had read them Herbert Asquith's 'The Volunteer'. Pip could still remember the first few lines:

> Here lies a clerk who half his life had spent
> Toiling at ledgers in a city grey,
> Thinking that so his days would drift away
> With no lance broken in life's tournament.

He knew exactly how the clerk felt. Was he too destined to live and die in a dull job while life's adventures passed him by? Other young men his age were learning to fly Spitfires, or doing army training, or being taught lifeboat drill. The only lessons he learnt were how to work an adding machine or correctly address envelopes.

He reached the post office and dropped the letters into the box built into the outside wall. No excuse to dawdle any longer. So, ignoring the beseeching calls of the seagulls, and the even stronger lure of the waves, he resisted the temptation to visit the harbour and plodded back to the office.

Unusually, Dad failed to remark on his longer-than-necessary absence. He was leaning back in his chair with his eyes closed. A few beads of sweat gleamed on his forehead.

Pip felt a twinge of anxiety. 'Everything all right?' he asked.

Dad opened his eyes. 'Unfortunately not.'

Pip sat down and turned his chair to face him. 'Bad news?'

'I've just had a call from the lieutenant governor. Churchill's withdrawing the troops.'

'What?' Pip's heart started to thud. 'I thought you said he would protect us.'

Dad sighed. 'I believed he would. I think he still wants to, but the War Cabinet has voted. Apparently they just can't afford to keep the military here. And the islands aren't considered to be of strategic value.'

Pip's mouth was almost too dry to speak. He swallowed. 'What will happen?'

'The soldiers will be evacuated and we'll have to hand in all our firearms. There'll be an official announcement tomorrow.'

'So we'll be sitting ducks?'

Dad shrugged. 'Effectively. We might be able to get the children out.'

A vision of Jenny's little brother William swam into Pip's head. He always looked so baffled and confused by life. How on earth would he react to being sent away? His stomach twisted with fear for Jenny and Alice too.

Dad stumbled to his feet. 'I'll go over to the bailiff's office now. See what more I can find out.' His face was grey, his forehead more furrowed than ever; he looked years older than he had that morning.

Pip stood up too. He had to get over to the Robinsons as soon as possible. The sooner they were aware of the situation, the longer they had to make some key decisions.

As he sat at the table in the Robinsons' cluttered kitchen, a cup of tea in front of him, Pip realised how much he missed his lessons with his old schoolteacher. Mr Robinson had worked him hard, but Pip knew he wouldn't have been so successful without his relentless discipline and insistence that he answer a question again and again until he got it right. And there'd been the added bonus of Jenny, slowly wiping plates at the sink, or sitting reading a book in the corner, or hovering shyly in the doorway, a shadowy but welcome presence in the room. Since Pip had left school, he and Jenny had met outside the house. Their snatched hours at the beach or cycling out to St Catherine's and pushing their bikes through the cool woods were precious ones. He knew he was falling for her. But first Cambridge loomed, and now war was coming ever closer. Who knew what the future held?

Mr Robinson's face turned as grey as Dad's had earlier.

'I can't believe Churchill's abandoned us.'

'Dad said it was the War Cabinet's decision.'

Mr Robinson shrugged. 'Same difference.'

Mrs Robinson placed a plate of scones in front of Pip. 'What about the children?' she asked. There was a catch in her voice.

Pip smiled his thanks, picked up a scone and took a bite. 'Dad says they might be able to travel to England. It should be safer for them in the countryside.'

Mrs Robinson pulled out a chair and slumped into it. Pip had a feeling her legs were too weak to stand. 'I can't send William.' Her mouth started to quiver.

'We've got to think what's best for him,' said Mr Robinson, reaching across the table to take her hands.

'I know what's best for him. Staying here. We understand him. He'd be terrified with strangers. It could completely unravel him.'

Pip felt awkward intruding on this private moment. He wondered where Jenny was. At the beach possibly. And Alice would be at the hospital. He pushed the rest of the scone into his mouth and tried to swallow down the dry lumps as quickly as possible. It wasn't like Mrs R not to offer him butter or jam, and the scone was hard work without them. He downed the rest of his tea to ease down the remaining crumbs and stood up.

'I just wanted to tell you the news as soon as I could.'

Mr Robinson stood up too. 'Thanks, lad. That was good of you.'

In his old schoolteacher's eyes, Pip would always be a

teenage boy in grey trousers and pullover. He wasn't sure how Mr Robinson might react to him and Jenny having a relationship. He tried to keep his voice casual. 'Do you know where Jenny is?'

Mrs Robinson seemed to look at him strangely, but he might have imagined it. 'Down at the beach, I expect. Relaxing now her exams are over.'

Pip nodded. 'It's a lovely afternoon.' He kept his tone mild, but underneath he was worried for Jenny. There'd be no more blissful hours on the beach if the Germans arrived on their shores.

Mr Robinson gazed out of the window, as if registering for the last time the flower beds that glowed in a buttery light. 'It certainly is,' he said.

Pip said his goodbyes.

⚓

Jenny unfurled the towel she'd brought and spread it over a flat rock. Despite the cloudless day and the shimmering heat, the beach was deserted. It was a relief to be on her own. She tugged off her clothes – she'd already put on her costume earlier – and threw the discarded garments into an untidy pile before sitting down on the towel.

At last she could permit herself to look out to the bay and enjoy the fluid movement of the water with its constantly shifting colours. She watched the waves, idly wondering, not for the first time, why the seventh was thought to be the biggest. Was it the action of the moon, as conventional wisdom had it, or was it just the wind? And why seven? Surely that was significant. Seven was such a perfect number. She counted the waves as each one reared up far out to sea then charged inland until it thrashed itself out on the shore. Some waves were indeed bigger than others, and some sent their white froth further up the beach, but she couldn't discern a regular pattern. It was strange. Perhaps she'd find the answer – to that and so many other questions that crowded her brain – once she got to Cambridge.

The heat was still intense, scorching her face and limbs until she couldn't bear it any longer. She stood up and ran down to the sea.

There was the usual shock of cold, even in midsummer, then she pushed off the bottom, plunged into an incoming wave and swam towards the horizon. Here was the cleanness she longed for, the icy water energising her limbs and rinsing the fog of anxiety from her brain. At last she felt free.

The adrenalin rush of her last exam seemed a long time ago now, even though it had only been four days. She'd come in from school, dumped her bag by the door, then gone upstairs to change out of her uniform for the last time. Of course, there was still the long wait for results, then she'd need to start cramming for her Cambridge exam, but even Dad had agreed she deserved a few weeks' break. Now that she'd finally left school, the summer was her own. It would have been bliss except for her growing anxieties about the war. The Allies were doing badly. There'd nearly been a bloodbath at Dunkirk, and they'd heard on the wireless yesterday that Paris had surrendered to the Germans. It was a nightmare, albeit still a distant one.

Was it naïve of her to assume that Jersey would always be safe? Even though she planned to leave the island, she still loved it dearly. She and Alice had made sandcastles on this beach as children, had held hands and jumped the waves. They'd even played on the steps of a lighthouse when Dad had once taken them over to St Catherine's Breakwater. He'd taken a photograph of them with his Brownie camera, had it printed and framed, and presented them each with a copy for Christmas. On the back he'd scrawled: *The Lighthouse Sisters, St Catherine's 1930.* Jenny smiled to herself at the memory. They both still had their pictures. She'd probably take hers to Cambridge, if she got in.

As soon as she'd put some distance between herself and the seashore, she flipped over and sculled gently with her arms, allowing the soft waves to lap her skin and the weak current to carry her backwards and forwards. It fascinated her how the action of sunlight on water created a tortoiseshell pattern on her bare legs. She knew the sea well, had done since she'd been a child, and it was in a gentle mood today. She tipped her head back: no sign of a cloud, no storm brewing to threaten her. All was calm.

She squinted up at the bright sky. Thank goodness all that school stuff was now behind her. Once she started at Cambridge – assuming she got in – she'd just be one of a number of students. Not the school prodigy, trying to fulfil everyone's expectations, especially her own. She wondered what Cambridge would be like. She'd miss the sea, that was for sure. The fens didn't sound a patch on the beach at St Helier.

She'd miss her family too, although perhaps it would be good for her and Alice to have some time apart. They'd been so close as children. She wasn't really sure what had come between them, but recently they always seemed to be falling out. It was annoying when Alice barged into the bedroom when Jenny was trying to study, or woke her up at the crack of dawn when she was on early shifts. If Jenny went to Cambridge, she might have a room of her own. She couldn't wait to be independent. And maybe she and Alice could regain their closeness when she returned in the holidays. They loved each other really. Underneath, they were still the lighthouse sisters of their childhood.

She turned onto her front and swam slowly back through the syrupy water. There was still plenty of time before dinner. At least another hour of sunbathing and a chance to dry off before she needed to get dressed again.

But as she stood up in the shallows, the undertow sucking at her feet and the shingle piercing her soles, she glimpsed Pip walking along the dunes, shielding his eyes against the sun. She waved and ran up the beach. She felt happier when she was with Pip. She'd miss him terribly too if she went to England. She'd always thought of Alice as her best friend, but lately it had been Pip she'd confided in if she was worried about an exam, or irritated by her sister.

Pip smiled as she approached. 'Hello. Your parents said I might find you here.'

Jenny reached for the towel, but Pip grabbed it first and wrapped it round her, then rubbed his hands up and down her back.

'That's nice. I'm warmer now.' The water droplets on her skin were already evaporating. She took off the towel and placed it widthways so they could sit side by side. Pip put his arm round her and she nestled her head on his shoulder. But his muscles felt rigid against her neck. She wriggled free and turned to face him. 'Are you all right?'

He picked up a stone and threw it towards the sea. 'Not really. That's why I went over to see your parents.'

'Oh?'

Pip told her about Churchill's plans to remove the army, his voice laced with anger.

At once the sun's heat made Jenny queasy. 'What does that mean for us?'

He relayed her parents' reaction and the debate about William.

'I think they're right. Will wouldn't cope away from us all. He's better staying at home.'

'Yes.' Pip's fingers scrabbled for another stone.

Jenny glanced at his profile: the taut jawline, the sunburnt skin stretched across his cheekbones. He still looked more like a sailor than an accountant. 'And what do you think about this, Pip?'

'I'm furious that the troops are going.' He hurled the stone towards the sea. It fell short. 'And even more angry that I'm not going with them.'

Disappointment snagged in Jenny's chest. She knew all too well that Pip would join up straight away if his father allowed him. He'd go marching off without a backward glance. And although part of her wanted him to be allowed to do his bit for the war, another part was relieved he'd be staying safely on the island. She dug her toes into the sand. Sometimes she struggled with her feelings towards Pip. She loved him as a friend, but she knew he wanted more. She just didn't feel able to cross that line yet. He'd always been more of a brother to her. It was probably unfair of her to want him to remain on Jersey when she was contemplating going to England. In some ways it would have been easier if he had fallen for Alice instead. But there was nothing Jenny could do. She couldn't commit to anything more when life was so uncertain.

'Just promise me you won't do anything dangerous.'

'If I run away to enlist, I'll let you know first.'

'Don't even joke about it.' Jenny stood up. The sun was clouding over now and she didn't fancy another swim. Pip was clearly distracted too. She pulled her clothes on over her still-damp costume and took his outstretched hand.

They trudged back towards the town, each lost in their own thoughts. They were halfway along La Route du Fort when a large truck packed with British soldiers drew up at the Hill Street junction.

'Blimey,' said Pip. 'They must be leaving already.' His tone was surprised, but Jenny caught a look of envy on his face as he stared at the men in their khaki uniforms and steel helmets, surrounded by large kitbags. Poor Pip, another reminder that he was stuck on Jersey while other boys his age were off fighting. Jenny had never met any of the British soldiers – although she and Alice had once been to an army band concert at Howard Davis Park – but she'd assumed they'd always be over at Fort Regent, ready to protect them from enemy attacks. There'd been British troops on Jersey for hundreds of years.

Yet now they were abandoning them. Her chest tightened with dread. Soon Jersey would be defenceless. And each day the Germans were coming closer.

She clutched at Pip's hand more tightly as they walked on.

4

On Sunday morning, Pip slept in late. As he finally came to, he was aware of the bells ringing out from the parish church. They sounded forlorn to his ear. He saw again the lorry full of British soldiers he and Jenny had encountered, obviously en route to the harbour. Perhaps even the bells were reacting to the fear and worry everyone was feeling, issuing a plaintive warning that soon the islands would be on their own, defence-less against Hitler.

Pip loved Jersey; he'd lived on the island all his life. He loved the rugged cliffs, the sweeping bays, the sun-dappled woods. But most of all he loved the sea in all its moods: turquoise and tranquil, grey and sullen, navy and threatening. Sailing was in his blood; the only time he felt really alive was on the water. In another life he'd have been a fisherman like old Jack, braving the elements day after day, alone in the buffeting wind, the *Bynie May* dancing on the waves, the salty air filling his nostrils as he pitted his wits against the strength of the ocean. If only Dad had let him enlist, he'd have joined the navy and fought for the island he loved with every ounce of his being. He was a Marett, after all. The Maretts had been on Jersey for hundreds of years. They were part of its history.

He sat up and looked out of the window for a bit, watching the seagulls wheel and swoop, before reluctantly turning away.

Time to get up and endure one of Dad's attempts at a jolly family lunch, then he could escape to the yacht club and try to keep himself busy. It would be good to see what others there were thinking too.

Dad was in the dining room when Pip came down, reading the newspaper and surrounded by breakfast detritus, even though it was nearly twelve.

'Morning.' Pip grabbed a cold piece of toast from the rack and smeared it with marmalade.

'Good morning, Pip. You're up late.'

'Yes, sorry.' The toast was soggy in his mouth. 'I'll just make a cup of tea, then I'll help you clear away.'

'Make me one too, son.'

'Righto.'

He went into the kitchen and lit the ring under the kettle. The visit to the Robinsons the other day had unsettled him. Mrs Robinson treated him almost like a son, always shoving food under his nose and refilling his teacup. It was nice, though – even if the scones hadn't been up to her normal standard. Pip still fantasised about what it would have been like to have a mother. Would she too be trying to feed him up, tutting with annoyance when he left a trail of breadcrumbs on the kitchen table, or forgot to put the lid back on the jam? Would she have been proud of him when he passed his Highers? Would she have sometimes taken his side when Dad was too firm?

Dad rarely spoke about Mum. There was one photo of her on the mantelpiece. She was sitting on a sand dune, shielding her eyes and laughing into the camera. Her brown hair was tousled; she looked impossibly young. Would there have been other children, had it not been for Pip's traumatic birth? If he'd had several siblings, perhaps she and Dad would have been prepared to let him enlist. Or perhaps Mum would have persuaded Dad to relent.

He opened the larder door and discovered a plate containing two lamb chops sitting in a pool of blood.

'Shall I get started on lunch, Dad?'

'Oh, yes, please. I'll join you in a minute.'

Pip rummaged in the vegetable rack for some potatoes and set to work.

They'd barely started to eat when the telephone rang. Dad threw his napkin on the table and went into the hall. Pip strained to listen to the conversation. He couldn't distinguish the words, but Dad's tone was shocked and indignant. He returned a few minutes later.

'That was Major General Harrison. He's received a telegram from the Admiralty. Apparently there are still men stranded on the French mainland, at Saint-Malo. They want us to send over some boats to rescue them. Bloody cheek really. Churchill isn't prepared to defend our islands, but he'll happily call on us to rescue his troops when they're in trouble.' He picked up his knife and fork.

Pip thought instantly of Dunkirk again. The rescue had played on his mind ever since he'd heard about it two weeks ago, imagining himself on *Bynie May* sailing out to help the helpless troops and returning a hero. That would have impressed Jenny – although he had no idea what Dad's reaction would have been, assuming he'd allowed him to go in the first place.

'Will you contact the yacht club?' he asked Dad.

'Not immediately. I need to find out how much capacity is required. We can use the lifeboat, of course, and there are a lot of freight craft in the harbour waiting to carry potatoes. We can press those into service.'

'So no smaller boats?'

Dad's look was sharp. 'Not at the moment, no, and certainly not the *Bynie May* under any circumstances.'

Pip stabbed at his lamb chop. 'Of course not, Dad,' he said.

When he got down to the yacht club that afternoon, the place was buzzing. Clearly the news was out. Mr Le Masurier, the commodore, was standing at the back of the room, surrounded by eager members. Pip joined the crowd, fascinated to hear what he had to say.

'The *Duchess* hasn't been fitted out for the season,' an older man with a lugubrious face was saying. 'It's this bloody war. Put paid to all my plans.'

'The *Lady Jane* is fitted,' said someone else. 'But her owner left for England last week. Do you think he'd mind if we borrowed her?'

The commodore shook his head. 'Shouldn't be necessary,' he said. 'Let's work out which boats are seaworthy and whose owners are present. I'll be taking *Klang II*, of course.'

'The *St Clement* is ready to go,' shouted a sun-weathered man in a navy jumper. 'And Fred here will act as crew.' His neighbour nodded eagerly.

'I'll take *Teazer*,' said a burly man with a bird's nest of a beard. 'I've a couple of crew and I'll let young Bob come along too.'

Pip looked across at Robert Falle, pink with pleasure. Bob

was only sixteen, three years younger than him. How come he was allowed to go when Pip was forced to stay behind?

The skipper of the ketch *Clutha*, Mr Langlois, offered his services as well.

'There's a destroyer setting off from Portsmouth as I speak,' continued the commodore. He glanced down at a sheet of paper in his hand. 'HMS *Wild Swan*, under the command of Lieutenant Commander Younghusband. She's going to call in here and we'll set off alongside her tonight.'

'What about the smaller craft?' shouted someone.

'There'll be another flotilla leaving tomorrow. Easier to handle in daylight. Let the big ships risk the night conditions.'

There was a murmur of disappointment, but the commodore was right. I'd rather take *Bynie May* out in the daytime, Pip thought to himself. He bit his lip. *Bynie May* wasn't going anywhere. Dad's instructions. Once again he had to miss out. He slipped out of the door and strolled down to look over the harbour wall. Might as well watch the preparations. He had nothing else to do.

Someone was already aboard a fishing boat, mopping the deck. Pip smiled in recognition as the stooped figure straightened up and arched his back.

'Jack!'

The old fisherman swivelled in his direction. 'Hello, Pip, lad. Thought you might be here.' His wide smile added another slew of lines to his already wizened face.

'Couldn't resist it. Are you going across to Saint-Malo?'

Jack dipped his mop into the grey bucket on deck and twisted it to squeeze out the excess water. 'Yes. I'll be off first light tomorrow. Want to come along?'

Pip hesitated. 'Dad said I wasn't to take the *Bynie May*.'

'I quite agree. You're a good sailor, but you'll be safer as crew on this trip. There are no navigation marks, remember. Best for old sea dogs like me to do the steering.'

Pip looked down. Jack was still calmly mopping the deck. Pip had never known him show a shred of fear or panic. He knew every inch of the waters round here, and never took risks with the sea. He'd steered Pip out of many a potential danger over the years. Perhaps even Dad would let him sail across with Jack.

'I'll go and ask him,' he called down.

'Right you are, lad. Be here at four a.m. sharp if you want to come.'

'Aye aye,' shouted Pip, and sped off.

It took him a long time to convince Dad. He'd poured him a glass of his favourite Scotch after supper, but it didn't prevent him from raising objection after objection. In the end, Pip had resorted to a low punch. 'Dad, I know you couldn't keep Mum safe, but that was a long time ago now. You can't put chains on me forever. I agreed not to enlist, I've promised not to take the *Bynie May* to Saint-Malo, but you have to let me go across with Jack. You know I'll be safe with him.'

Dad swirled the last drops of whisky around his glass then emptied it in a gulp. His face looked white in the harsh glare of the overhead lamp. 'All right, you win.' He stood up to go to bed. 'But you'd better come back safely. No risks, mind.'

Pip stood up too and put a hand on his father's shoulder. 'I'll come back, Dad. I promise,' he said. As he followed him up the stairs, he realised his own legs were trembling.

* * *

He was up at three, pulling on the thick trousers and the two jumpers he'd already draped over his chair the night before. Although it was mid June, it would still be cold in the Channel, and this early in the morning the air could be surprisingly fresh.

He couldn't face breakfast, so he gulped down two cups of tea in the still-dark kitchen and made up several rounds of sandwiches for later. Who knew how long the trip would end up being? And they might have hungry passengers too. As an afterthought, he grabbed the rest of the loaf and a hunk of cheese and shoved them into his knapsack. Dad wouldn't mind; he could always pop to the baker's later. It was strange that Dad hadn't come down to wave him off. Best not to wake him. Pip grabbed his sou'wester and slipped out of the house.

He arrived to a frenzy of activity in the growing light: provisions being stowed, sails hoisted, rigging checked. Jack was sitting in the rear of his boat, deep in thought.

'Jack!' Pip called.

The old fisherman looked up and waved. 'Come on board, lad.'

As Pip approached, he glanced across at the *Desiree-Jacqueline*, moored alongside. A young chap stood on deck, winding a rope around his forearm in a neat figure of eight. He grinned at Pip and Pip smiled back. It was good to see someone of a similar age. Most of the other sailors looked elderly. Probably all the men in their twenties and thirties were away fighting. He suppressed a surge of guilt. At least he was doing something to help now – and even with Dad's permission.

'It won't be an easy journey,' Jack told him once he'd climbed on board. 'I reckon it'll be about four hours before high water by the time we set off. We'll head due south, then sail east-about the Minkies.' Les Minquiers, known as 'the Minkies', were a series of islets and rocks about nine miles south of the island. They were beautiful and tranquil in calm weather but could prove treacherous in a storm. Many ships had been wrecked there in years gone by. 'Should be a fair enough trip out. We can go through the Cocq Passage. That'll save about three miles. Might be a bit rough on the way back, though.'

Pip had checked the forecast this morning. It looked as though it would be stormy later. And the boat would be weighed down by passengers, another complication. He wondered how many they'd be able to take.

They set off soon after daybreak as a low sun was turning the sky orange and creating a glittery amber path on the water. The air grew a little warmer. Jack followed the *Desiree* as they navigated their way through the choppy waters around the Minkies and deeper into the bay of Saint-Malo. On the way, he filled Pip in on the mission from the briefing the skippers had been given earlier.

'We're to head right into the harbour and get as many chaps on board as we can. I don't know what state they'll be in. We'll ferry them across to one of the big ships anchored further out and then go back for more. For as long as it takes.'

'It's wonderful to do something to help at last.'

Jack gave him a warning look. 'It's not a game, lad.'

Pip swallowed. 'Of course not. I just meant I'm glad to be actively involved in the war effort.'

But Jack was looking grimly ahead. 'The demolition squad was taken across yesterday on HMS *Wild Swan*. As soon as we've got the troops out, the plan is to blow up the fuel tanks and the lock gates on the inner harbour. Deprive the Jerries of ammunition supplies and stop them from launching attacks on Atlantic convoys.'

Pip felt a surge of excitement. 'Sounds dangerous.'

Another sharp glance. 'If they're caught, the engineers will be shot on sight. We'll be in firing range too. There's no guarantee how this will end. The Germans are advancing rapidly on the port.'

'Dad thinks it's a bloody cheek of Churchill asking us to do this when he's pulled his troops out of our islands.'

Jack's mouth twitched. 'It *is* a bloody cheek. But it's not Churchill we'll be rescuing. It's those poor stranded buggers. They're the ones we're doing this for.'

The sound of a motorboat charging towards them drowned out any further talk. Pip looked across as it rocketed past in a rush of foam, causing Jack's boat to lurch from side to side. He could just make out soldiers on board, standing forlornly, weighed down with equipment. Even from a distance, he could see the shame mixed with relief on their faces. Poor sods. Such an ignominious retreat. But at least they'd been rescued.

The sun was high in the sky by the time Jack navigated his way skilfully into the harbour. Despite his skipper's warnings, Pip had felt exhilarated during the trip. Everywhere he looked were little ships: fishing boats like Jack's, ketches, sloops, yachts, all with sails full in the wind as they sailed out in convoy. He tried to capture the sight on the screen of his memory. This could be the high point of his war. Provided they got back safely.

* * *

They picked up their first passengers, a group of squaddies from the Yorkshire Light Infantry, and were soon ferrying them back to the *Duchess of Normandy*. Pip handed round his sandwiches and the soldiers chipped in some bars of chocolate they told him the NAAFI had distributed before they left. The men were hollow-eyed and grey with exhaustion and anxiety. They'd taken off their thick army coats and knapsacks by now and piled them neatly on the deck. Some of the soldiers were chatting quietly; others sat in silence, their eyes closed, their faces uplifted to the sun.

'What was it like, over in France?' Pip asked his neighbour, a chap who looked to be in his early twenties.

The man turned to him. 'Hell,' he said briefly.

Pip didn't know which emotion he felt most: envy of the soldier, who'd at least seen some action, or relief that he'd been spared the very evident horror.

By half past two they were back in Saint-Malo harbour, having discharged their passengers. The weather had changed now, the skies leaden, the waves faster and more furious, the deck lashed with salty spray. Up above, seagulls were being tossed around like paper.

'We'll stay on for the engineers,' Jack shouted. 'The *Wild Swan* has buggered off back and left the bastards stranded. We'll wait until they set off the explosives and then take them on board.' He braced himself against the tilt of the boat as an extra-large wave hit them broadside.

'Righto.' Pip couldn't say any more. His heart was suddenly thrumming, the inside of his mouth bone dry. No risks, he'd promised Dad. It was a good job he couldn't see him now. The storm was about to break in more ways than one.

'Heard the news?' another skipper yelled across to Jack above the shrieking of the wind.

'What's that?' His words were snatched and borne away by the gale.

'The Jerries are only nine miles away. Won't be long now.'

Jack muttered a word Pip had never heard before, even though he could guess its meaning.

Pip's ribcage tightened. What if the Jerries got there before the engineers could blow up the gates? What if flying debris from the explosions tore into the boat? What if they sank? Jack was a good sailor, but he couldn't work miracles. *Oh Dad, I'm sorry*, Pip said inside his head. And then: *I'm sorry, Jenny* too. He looked at Jack's white knuckles on the tiller and realised that even the calm sailor didn't fancy their chances. His heartbeat accelerated further.

But before he had time for another thought, a deafening explosion tore through the air, followed by a searing blast of heat as a huge white cloud mushroomed out of the dock area. His ears roared and his skin felt as though it would melt.

Jack shoved him onto the deck. 'Stay down,' he shouted. Pip had never seen him look so alarmed. He could hear people screaming and shouting all around. The air was thick with acrid smoke and the smell of burning oil.

Pip did as he was told, his face pressed to the wet boards on the bottom of the frantically lurching boat as he braced himself to be burnt alive.

5

Rebekah came into the sluice room and dumped a pile of used bed sheets in the laundry bin as Alice was filling up some sterile water bottles. They both jumped as a noise like far-off thunder boomed through the open window.

'What was that?' Rebekah asked.

'I've no idea. Sounded a long way off. Saint-Malo direction.'

'Hope it's not the Jerries already.' A thread of anxiety was wrapped around her voice.

Alice put an arm round her friend. 'Maybe you should leave Jersey?' She didn't actually want her to. How would she manage without Rebekah? But it would probably be safer for her in England. Hitler's hatred of the Jews was terrifying, and the reports they'd heard of Jews being attacked in Germany had been deeply disturbing.

Rebekah shrugged. 'What's the point? Jersey's my home now and I don't know what I'd do without my work at the hospital.' Her parents had been furious with her for marrying a Gentile, but the Jersey islanders had taken the young nurse to their hearts. This really was her home. At least her family was safely in England.

'Don't worry,' Alice said. 'We'll look after you. We won't let the Germans get anywhere near you.'

Rebekah gave her a wan smile. 'Thank you,' she said.

'Nurse Robinson!' Sister's voice was sharp. 'Where are those sterile bottles? I sent you off for them ten minutes ago.'

'Coming, Sister.' Alice raised her eyebrows at Rebekah and returned to the ward.

When she left the hospital later that afternoon, Alice was tempted to go down to the harbour, but she was worried she might bump into Pip. She wasn't sure how she'd behave around him now, having had her suspicions about him and Jenny confirmed. She felt inexplicably as though he must have seen through her somehow, and that he'd pity her. Jenny didn't even seem to like him the way she did. But that didn't change anything. Pip was interested in her sister and not her, and she would have to accept that. Besides, the weather had changed. It was wet and squally. Not a pleasant day for sailing.

As she let herself into the kitchen back home, she realised she'd walked in on an argument.

'Besides, I can't leave you all now,' Jenny was saying.

'But you were going to leave us next year to start at Cambridge, so what's the difference?' Dad's face wore its stern look.

'Nearly a whole year with my family. That's the difference.'

Alice sat down at the table and helped herself to a cup of tea. 'Where are you going?'

'Nowhere!' said Jenny. Her face was red and her fingers gripped her teacup.

Dad sighed. 'None of us wants you to go, Jenny, but you have to think of your future.'

'I *am* thinking of my future.'

Dad picked up a copy of the *Jersey Evening Post* from the table and riffled through it. 'Here.' He smoothed down the page. Alice glanced across. It was a notice inviting people to board evacuation boats for England. 'You can't mess around, Jenny. The first boat leaves on Wednesday. It'll probably be a filthy old cargo ship, but it doesn't matter. If it gets you safely to England, you can stay with Charles and Cynthia for as long as you need.' Charles and Cynthia were Dad's cousins.

Jenny stared into the middle distance. 'I don't know . . .'

Alice couldn't resist giving her a sly glance. 'I would imagine there's quite a bit to keep you on the island these days.'

Jenny's face reddened even further. 'I'm still intending to go to England at some point.'

'Jenny, you need to go *now*,' said Dad. Alice could hear the desperation in his voice.

'Why? I'll be stuck over there for months. The Cambridge exam isn't until November. And even if I get in, term won't start until the following October. What on earth can I do for all that time?'

'It doesn't matter what you'll do. The most important thing is you'll be *safe*.'

Alice took a sip of tea. 'If it's that dangerous over here, shouldn't we all be evacuating? I'm more English than Jenny, after all.' Alice had been born in London. Her parents had visited her paternal grandparents when her mother was eight months pregnant, and Mum had gone into labour early. Alice had been born at St Bartholomew's Hospital. Dad had had to return to Jersey for the start of the school term and Mum had stayed on until she and Alice were fit enough to manage the boat journey back. Jenny and William had both been born at Jersey General.

'The rest of us aren't planning to go to university in England. We can stay on the island for as long as the war lasts. Even if we're trapped here, it doesn't matter. But if Jenny doesn't go soon, she might not get away, then all her hard work would be for nothing.' Dad let out a low breath.

The shrill ring of the phone interrupted the conversation. Jenny jumped to her feet and went into the hall.

She returned several minutes later looking anxious. 'That was Mr Marett. Pip's gone missing.'

'Missing?' Alice's legs felt suddenly hollow.

'Yes.' Jenny drew out a chair, sat down at the table, then ran her hands through her hair. 'Apparently he went out to Saint-Malo to rescue some British troops with a fleet of other boats from the yacht club. The boat he was on hasn't returned.'

'Idiot boy,' said Dad. 'I always thought he was too impetuous for his own good.'

'Dad, it sounds like he was attempting to *help* people,' said Jenny. 'At least he was trying to do something positive and not just dashing off to England when the going got tough.'

Dad ignored her. 'Let's pray he turns up safely. Poor old Mr Marett can't take another loss.'

Jenny didn't answer. She just twisted a few strands of hair round her fingers, her face white with fear.

Alice thought of Pip as she'd last seen him: suntanned, happy, his eyes vivid with excitement. An image sidled into her mind of him flailing helplessly in a storm-tossed sea, his wet hair plastered to his head, his screams for help whipped away by the fierce wind. The waves engulfing him as he slipped under the water . . . Her heart hammered in horror.

Jenny stood up suddenly, knocking her chair over.

Dad raised his eyebrows at her.

'Okay, you win, Dad,' she said. 'I'll go to England.'

Dad's expression went from shock to relief to delight in a split second. 'Good girl,' he said. 'You won't regret it.'

With nothing more they could do but wait for news of Pip, Alice and Jenny eventually went up to bed, even though Alice doubted if either of them would sleep.

'What made you change your mind?' she asked Jenny as they lay subdued and tense in the darkness.

Silence.

'Jen?'

Jenny's voice sounded thick. 'It was Pip.'

'I thought it was Pip you wanted to stay for.'

A sigh gusted through the darkness. 'I know. But he promised me he would always tell me if he was going to do something dangerous. How could he just disappear like that without letting me know his plans? I had no idea what he was up to.'

'I wouldn't imagine he had much time. You know Pip. He does things on the spur of the moment.'

'Yes. Impetuous, Dad called him.'

Alice remembered him rushing over to see if anyone wanted to sail round to watch the planes. He had certainly acted impetuously then. 'I expect he got the call and set off without thinking.'

'But he could have phoned me, or left a message.'

'Perhaps.' Alice looked at the ghost of Jenny's suitcase in the darkness. She'd packed as soon as they'd finished supper. Jenny could be impetuous too. 'So that's why you're going.'

Another sigh. 'Pip's always wanted to enlist. He'd have joined up at the beginning of the war if his father had let him. I've a suspicion he's secretly enrolled in the navy. If so, I might not see him again for months.'

Alice struggled up the bed. 'But won't he think you don't care if you leave? You're lucky to have a boy like Pip. Doesn't he mean anything to you?' She could have said more, but she stopped herself. She didn't want Jenny to think she was jealous.

Jenny sat up too. 'Of course I care, but if he has enlisted, I might just as well go over to England. He'll be more likely to end up there. And perhaps I need to consider my future too.'

Alice could almost feel Jenny's determination coming at her across the gap between their beds. 'Well, I hope you'll be happy with your decision.' She shut her eyes against the image of her sister on a boat headed for England, the distance between them increasing. At least while they were still together on Jersey, they could rekindle their childhood closeness, but how would their relationship work if they were far apart?

And what if neither of them ever saw Pip again?

6

The queues were six or eight people deep on the quayside. Everywhere Jenny looked there were families. Fathers in suits and homburg hats, mothers in thick winter coats over summer dresses, children bundled up in warm clothes to save space in their suitcases. She felt a sudden pang for her own parents and siblings. She'd told them not to come down to the quayside with her. She couldn't bear public farewells, and she needed to get used to being on her own.

She'd tried to be brave when she'd said goodbye that morning over one of Mother's special breakfasts. William had even allowed her to kiss him, but she saw the bewilderment in his eyes and wondered how he would cope with the disruption to his safe little world. She wondered if Alice would miss her too. Things had been so strained between them lately. Perhaps she'd just enjoy having a bedroom to herself. And her mother would have one less mouth to feed, although Jenny knew she'd worry. When she'd gone to leave, Mum had hugged her tightly as though to draw her back into the body that had once held her. Dad had turned his face away, but when he looked back, his eyes were red. It had been his idea for her to go, but she knew he'd struggle without her.

She pulled back her shoulders. She'd just have to do her very best to get into Cambridge and make them all proud.

She'd never met Charles and Cynthia, although Dad had apparently seen quite a lot of Charles when they were growing up. They lived in London; she had the address in Mum's old handbag – her handbag now. It turned out Dad had written to them earlier and they'd offered to put her up for as long as it took. Kind of them really. She just hoped she wouldn't get under their feet. Apparently they were quite rich; she hoped their house would be big enough that she could lose herself. Evacuees were only permitted to take one suitcase, and she'd prioritised her books, although she had to take a few out at the last minute as they were only allowed twenty-five pounds in weight. She planned to spend the next six months cramming in as much maths knowledge as she could. It was the best way to prepare, and besides, it would keep her mind off missing everyone.

She tried hard not to think about Pip. What if Alice was right? It would be awful if he came back from Saint-Malo, found out she'd gone to England and thought she didn't care. She still couldn't think of him as anything but a friend, despite knowing he wanted more, but she never wanted to hurt him. She'd assumed he'd joined up, that he'd put his desire to be involved in the war before their friendship. But what if he was in trouble? Desperate? Hurt? Was it fair to run away and leave him? On the way to the quayside that morning she'd passed a poster that read: *Don't be yellow, stay at home*. Was she being yellow: running away from the island – and Pip – in a cowardly fashion? A dribble of sweat ran down her back as she tried to focus on Cambridge.

The crowd inched forward as another ship approached the harbour. Dad was right. It was a 'dirty British coaster' arriving with a plume of tarry smoke billowing from its funnels. Feathery wisps broke off and shimmered in the midday heat.

The woman in front of her turned round. 'I don't think we'll be travelling in luxury,' she said wryly.

Jenny grimaced. She'd earlier heard someone say that women and children would be packed into the hold while the men went on deck. Her stomach felt uneasy at the thought of being trapped below in the churning seas. Goodness knows how long it would take to get to Weymouth. And then there'd be the long train journey into London. Mum had slid a packet of sandwiches and an apple into the pockets of her serge coat earlier. Jenny intended to make them last. Good job the anxiety that gnawed at her stomach had banished all hunger.

'Such a hard decision,' the woman continued. A little boy who was sitting beside her on a battered brown suitcase wiped his eyes with the back of his hand.

Jenny nodded. 'Is your son all right?' she asked. The lad was about William's age.

The woman passed him a hanky. 'Don't use your hand, love.' She turned back to Jenny. 'We had to leave his new puppy behind. He's more upset about being separated from Buddy than from his friends.'

Jenny had a sudden memory of William cuddling his pet rabbit, burying his face in the animal's soft fur, talking to it gently as Binkie snuggled into his arms.

'Poor thing,' she said. 'Is anyone looking after the puppy for you?'

The woman threw her a warning glance, then lowered her voice. 'We didn't have time to find him a home. We had to set him loose. At best he'll turn feral. At worst . . .' She shrugged.

Jenny was appalled. Would the islanders end up eating animals? There was enough food at the moment, but what if the Germans invaded? At least if she left the island she'd be one less drain on Jersey's supplies. But what about the rest of her family? How would they cope without food? Apprehension inched up her spine.

'D'you hear that?' The woman's husband had turned away from the group he'd been deep in conversation with and was speaking to his wife, including Jenny in his comments.

'What, love?' The woman passed him a tin mug of tea she'd poured from her Thermos. She'd offered Jenny some earlier, but Jenny had shaken her head, not wanting to deprive the family.

'Thanks.' The man took a sip, then set the mug on the ground. 'A chap up ahead said Russia and Turkey have joined the war and are smashing back the Jerries.'

'Really?' The woman's forehead furrowed. 'Then what are we running away for? We don't want to go all the way to England only to find the war's over.'

'Yeah.' The man mopped his forehead with a handkerchief. 'And that a load of scavengers have looted our house.'

'I knew we should have bolted the front door and gone out through the back.'

'Don't be silly, love. If people have a mind to get in, they'll just kick the door down. I told you, if we leave things open, folk are more likely to think we're still around.' He tapped his nose. 'Psychology, you see.' He winked at Jenny.

Jenny wasn't sure about this theory, but the news that the war might soon be over did disturb her. What if she was leaving unnecessarily? What if she could have stayed and enjoyed one more Jersey summer? Grown close to Alice again before she left for Cambridge? Spent more time with Pip – if he returned? But she could already hear Dad's argument. 'We couldn't take the risk, Jenny. At least this way you'll be where you need to be eventually. And the months will fly by.'

But the next rumour to travel up the line was even worse. 'Bloke at the end says the last evacuation ship was torpedoed by the Germans,' the man told her.

Fear began to stir in the pit of her belly. 'Do you know that for sure?'

He shrugged, then turned back to listen out for his next titbit.

Jenny was aware of the sweat smell coming off her body, whether from wearing too many clothes in the summer heat or from the terror that coursed through her she didn't know. Yet in a few minutes' time, when the ship docked, she needed to make a decision once and for all. What on earth should she do: risk a trip to England and the possibility of being torpedoed or stuck there unnecessarily for months, or return home to her family, in which case she might be trapped for the duration of the war?

But as her slippery fingers tried to get a grip on the suitcase handle, she thought she heard someone calling her name. She turned round. A bright head bobbed swiftly through the crowd. As it came closer, and she recognised the familiar figure, unexpected joy surged through her. 'Pip!'

He enveloped her in his arms and lifted her off her feet. 'It's all right. I made it.'

Suddenly she could no more step onto the ship than jump into the water. Pip hadn't enlisted or been lost at sea. He was safe. All she wanted to do now was to return to her family and spend time with her dearest friend again. 'Let's go home,' she said.

Pip grabbed her case, slung an arm round her shoulders and steered her back through the crowd.

'I'm sorry I didn't let you know beforehand.'

Jenny frowned at him as they walked along. She wasn't going to make this too easy. 'You promised you would tell me if you were about to do something daft.'

Pip frowned too. 'Something daring and selfless, you mean?'

'But you could have phoned.' In spite of her intention, she was starting to feel a grudging admiration.

'I really am sorry. It all happened so quickly. By the time I'd managed to persuade Dad, it was too late to phone, then I was off at first light . . .'

Jenny firmed her lips. 'I was terrified.'

'So terrified you decided to set off to England?'

She explained her suspicion that he might have enlisted.

'I'd never do that without discussing it with you first. You're far too precious to me.'

She squeezed his arm. 'I'm sorry. I was furious with you for risking your life like that, and Dad was determined I should go. I thought I could wait for you there while I prepared for Cambridge.'

'I know. But I'm back now. You can prepare for Cambridge here. And we can spend more time together.'

Jenny smiled at him. It was a relief not to be facing a long journey across the Channel and the prospect of staying with strangers, even if they were Dad's cousins. She'd be back with Pip, as well as her own family and the island she loved.

They'd face whatever the future had in store for them together. Cambridge was still there, shimmering in the distance, but it could wait a few more months.

'Tell me what happened,' she said, permitting herself a weak smile.

His eyes became vacant as though he'd stopped noticing the busy quayside and the cluster of houses in the distance and had turned his gaze inwards, revisiting yesterday's horrors. He started to tell her the story.

It turned out that once they'd got away from the harbour – and recovered from the heat that had threatened to engulf them – Jack's boat had developed engine trouble. In spite of his every effort, he hadn't managed to get it started, so they'd had to wait until another boat could return to tow them. It had taken them over twenty hours to struggle back to the yacht club in a Force 5 wind. To make things worse, the navigation buoys had all been removed, so there was nothing to guide them back in the dark.

Exhausted, Pip had crawled into bed as soon as he'd got home, intending to phone Jenny in the morning. But by the time he'd finally woken up and contacted the Robinsons, he'd discovered she was about to board the evacuation boat for England. Mr Robinson had tried to dissuade him, knowing his appearance would unsettle his daughter, but he'd ignored his old teacher's pleas and sprinted down to the harbour. Just in time, as it turned out.

'And you're sure you were beginning to change your mind anyway?' he said for the third time.

Jenny reached up to kiss his cheek. 'Sure,' she said. And at once the world felt right again.

* * *

When they arrived home, walking into the kitchen just as Mum was serving tea, everyone seemed to freeze. Then William ran over and wrapped his arms round Jenny's waist, burying his face in her stomach, and her breath caught as she smoothed his hair with her hand. He didn't even flinch. Mum hugged her too, reaching her arms awkwardly round William.

Only Dad remained seated, frowning down at his newspaper.

'Dad?' said Jenny.

He looked from her to Pip, a defeated expression on his face. 'You'd better know what you're doing.'

'I'd decided to come back anyway. I can't leave you all right now,' she said, but nobody seemed to be listening to her. Dad was still staring at Pip.

Pip returned his gaze. 'We do,' he said.

But Dad's hands were shaking as he returned to his paper.

At Dad's insistence, Jenny wrote to Charles and Cynthia, apologising for changing her mind and disrupting their plans, even though she privately thought they might be grateful not to have to put up with her. When she came downstairs with the letter and announced she was off to the post office, Mum asked her to take William along too.

'He could do with the exercise,' she said, 'and I'd like a few minutes to myself.' She dabbed at her forehead with a tea towel.

'Come on, William.' Jenny held out her hand, even though she knew he wouldn't take it.

William ignored her.

'Will . . .' She leant over his shoulder as he sat at the table and twisted his face round to meet hers. 'How would you like to get some sweets? I've some pennies in my purse.'

He shot up.

They walked down the road with William doing his usual strange things. Sometimes he walked along the kerb with his hands outstretched, sometimes he took elongated strides to avoid pavement cracks. Once he even walked sideways. Jenny was used to his behaviour, as were several familiar people she greeted on the way, but the few strangers they passed stared in surprise, often looking back over their shoulders to scrutinise him further. She ignored them. She'd long since stopped being worried about what people thought. Mum and Alice were the same, but she knew Dad still found it difficult being out with him. Such a shame they didn't have the father–son bond she saw in other families. Pip, for example, was very close to his dad, even though Jenny knew he resented Mr Marett's strictness at times. Perhaps his father was harder on him because he was the sole parent.

As they turned into the high street, she saw long queues of people all down the pavement.

'What now?' she muttered to herself. She'd been relieved that she hadn't left the island, but the place was still in turmoil. No one knew if or when an attack might come. Everyone seemed to be on edge.

William didn't reply, but moved closer towards her, looking at the crowds nervously.

'It's all right, Will. We'll just skirt round them.' She stepped out into the road and he followed.

As they walked past the straggly line of people, Jenny spotted one of the pupils from her old school.

'Louisa!'

A girl with a cloud of frizzy auburn hair turned round. 'Hello, Jenny!'

'Do you know what's going on?'

Louisa grimaced. 'We're queuing for money.'

'But why so many people all at once?'

'Most of us have registered to be evacuated, so we need to draw out our savings, though we're only allowed to take out twenty pounds each.'

Jenny half turned as a large man with a florid complexion barged past her. He muttered an apology and she nodded. She could feel the waves of anxiety coming off William.

She'd have liked to speak to Louisa further. She'd been one of the few girls at school she'd got on with. They hadn't been particular friends, but Louisa had always been pleasant to her, and Jenny had sensed she wasn't the sort to gossip about her behind her back as some of the other girls used to, always making snide remarks when Jenny did well in a test or had her work praised in class. But William was clearly agitated, and she didn't want to make him wait any longer. 'Well, good luck,' she said to Louisa, and led her brother on down the road.

They turned from the bright heat of the high street into the cool gloom of the post office.

William looked round the shop disdainfully. 'No sweets!'

'No, we'll go to the sweet shop in a minute, Will. I just need to buy some stamps first.' There was a long queue here too, and Jenny hoped William wouldn't play up.

Mrs Bracy, the elderly postmistress, huffed and puffed behind the counter, issuing stamps, cashing postal orders and counting out money. She was a large woman, wearing a voluminous tea dress with a vivid floral pattern that made her look even bigger. Her bulging stomach strained against the material whenever she reached up to the pigeonholes to retrieve a form for a customer.

William was watching her, fascinated.

When they finally got to the head of the queue, and Jenny had purchased her stamps, he remained at the counter, still staring at Mrs Bracy.

'Are you all right, dear? Is there anything else you need?' The words were addressed to Jenny, but the postmistress kept darting little glances at William out of the corner of her eye.

'Are you going to have a baby?' William asked her.

All the conversation in the room stopped like a radio being switched off.

Jenny felt the blush surging up her neck and filling her face with heat.

'*William!*' She looked at Mrs Bracy, who was standing stock still, an awkward half-smile on her lips. 'I'm so sorry, Mrs Bracy.' She turned back to William. 'That was a very rude thing to say. Please apologise right now.'

'I'm sorry you are fat, Mrs Bracy,' he said.

There was a collective intake of breath from the people in the queue, who seemed to have taken on the role of a Greek chorus.

Jenny's face was fiery now. A line of sweat ran down her cheek.

'I really am most sorry, Mrs Bracy. I can't think what's come over him.' She ought to make William apologise again, but she didn't dare risk it in case he came out with something even more unfortunate. He was always a liability when he was stressed. Better to make their excuses and leave.

William had taken the stamps from the counter and was licking them and placing them on the envelope in perfect alignment, seemingly unaware of the embarrassment he'd caused.

'Please move aside,' said Mrs Bracy, a tight smile on her face. 'I have other customers to serve.'

'Of course.' Jenny tried to convey as much contrition as she could with her still-red face. She grabbed William's arm, ignoring his protestations, and frogmarched him out of the shop, trying to avoid looking at anyone in the queue.

'Are we going to buy my sweets now?' he asked.

'Yes, we are,' she replied. Had William been an average nine-year-old, she'd have made him forgo his sweets as a punishment, but he had no idea he'd done anything wrong, and refusing to let him visit the sweet shop would just unleash a tantrum. She could certainly do without any more humiliation. She wished Alice had taken him. She'd have handled him so much better, and probably Mrs Bracy too – she was used to difficult patients. Jenny sometimes wondered if she herself just made him worse. She knew what to do in theory, but in practice he just made her over-anxious, which William picked up on, starting to behave badly as a result. A vicious cycle really.

They purchased his quarter of mint toffees from a sweet shop that was mercifully free of queues, and set off home. As they made their way back along the high street, William now walking quietly beside her, too busy chewing to utter another word, Jenny wondered again if she'd done the right thing staying on Jersey. She'd been acutely aware of the atmosphere of restrained panic in the town, the sense of chaos bubbling just beneath the surface.

She just hoped she wouldn't regret her decision.

7

'And you're sure you don't mind staying here with William?' asked Mum for the third time as she adjusted her hat in the hall mirror.

'Of course not,' said Alice. 'It's much better that you and Dad go on your own. William would only be bored, and besides, my feet are killing me.' After a day spent pounding up and down corridors in tightly laced shoes, her toes were scorched with friction. She rubbed at them, trying to induce some relief through the thick wool of her stockings.

Mum made a sympathetic face. 'Plenty of bread in the crock, but go easy on the butter and jam,' she said.

'Righto.'

Dad appeared in the doorway. 'Have you seen the shoe polish, Annette?'

'Why now?' said Mum, delving inside the cupboard. 'You've had all day to clean your shoes. You're going to make us late. Can't you just apply some spit and forget the polish?'

'If a job's worth doing . . .' said Dad. He looked strangely diminished, standing in his socks with the hems of his trousers sagging round his feet.

Mum located the polish and passed it to him.

'Brush?'

She raised her eyes to the ceiling, took out an old black-bristled brush and passed that over too.

Dad knelt down and started rubbing the polish into his shoes. 'Well, at least we can go up to the school with Jenny now. That's some consolation.'

'Mmm,' said Mum, applying a sheen of lipstick and then blotting her mouth with a tissue. She turned round. 'Too much?' she asked.

Dad was preoccupied with his shoes, so Alice answered. 'You look lovely, Mum. Jenny will be proud of you.'

'I rather think it's us being proud of Jenny,' said Dad, breathing on his shoes and wiping them with the back of his suit sleeve for a final polish.

'James!' said Mum. 'Honestly, you might have shiny shoes, but now you have polish on your suit.'

'It's fine,' said Dad, clamping his arm to his side. 'I'll hide the marks like this.'

Mum tutted, then returned the polish and brush to the cupboard. 'Go and call for Jenny, will you, Alice? I can't think what's keeping her.'

Alice went to the bottom of the stairs, but there was no need to shout up. Jenny, dressed in her school uniform, freshly washed and pressed by Mum, her chestnut-coloured hair swept back and clipped, had just closed their bedroom door and was coming down.

'You look nice,' Alice said. 'Ready to be the school star?'

Jenny grimaced. 'I don't want to stand out.'

'Of course you'll stand out. This is your evening.'

'I just want to get it over with as soon as possible.'

Alice nodded. 'I'm sure it will be fine.' She forced out the words. 'You've made Mum and Dad so proud.'

'What? By not going to England?'

'Well, not that obviously, but you had your reasons.'

Jenny chewed at her bottom lip. 'Yes, I did,' she said.

As soon as Mum, Dad and Jenny had gone, Alice switched on the wireless. William, who was doing his homework at the kitchen table, immediately clapped his hands over his ears.

'Too loud, Will?' asked Alice.

He nodded.

She turned it down a fraction. 'Better?'

He shrugged and picked up his pencil.

Alice went over to the bread crock, drew out a ragged loaf and tracked down the breadknife. William was clever, there was no doubt about it. Like Jenny, who was sure to be show-ered with prizes that evening, he always got top marks in class. He'd inherited Dad's brains – he might even follow Jenny to Cambridge one day, assuming she ever went. But he never brought friends home and he never went outside to play football with the other lads on their street. She and Jenny were used to his funny ways, although she knew Mum worried about him. It was the right decision not to send him to England. He'd have been confused and bewildered. A new family would probably have no idea how to treat him. Much better he stayed home under their protection and took his chances with the rest of them.

Since Jenny had returned with Pip the other evening, things were frosty between her and Dad. Alice had caught Dad pinching the bridge of his nose, or massaging his forehead – sure signs of worry – on more than one occasion. Jenny pretended not to notice, but Alice knew she felt bad at letting Dad down. Hopefully tonight's school prizegiving would make up for it.

Alice applied a scraping of butter to two slices of bread, piled them on a plate, and put them in front of William, who picked one up and crammed it into his mouth without taking his eyes off his exercise book. Alice knew better than to expect any thanks.

She buttered a piece for herself and drew her chair up close to the radio. There was a variety show from Canada coming on soon. Even if she couldn't turn up the volume, she could still enjoy the music.

Two years ago, it had been *her* school prizegiving, and it'd been Jenny who'd babysat William. Alice couldn't remember Mum and Dad making much effort to dress up, but maybe she'd got that wrong. She did remember sitting on a slippery bench with the rest of her year, watching as one after the other of her friends went up to collect their prizes. She knew she wasn't in line for maths or English awards, but she'd nurtured a secret hope she might win the science cup. Her heart raced when the prize was announced, then plummeted when it was awarded to Suzanne de Grunchy. She forced her lips into a smile as a delighted Suzanne mounted the steps to the stage and took the cup from Miss Dickie, the severe headmistress. It was passed along the line once Suzanne had reclaimed her place on the bench. Alice held it for a second, trying to imagine receiving it on the stage while Mum and Dad clapped proudly in the audience. She'd been so lost in the daydream that she started when Joan Norman, who'd been sitting next to her and digging her elbow into her side for most of the evening, suddenly gave her an even sharper prod than usual.

'Alice! It's you!'

Alice looked up. 'Alice Robinson. Is she here?' Miss Dickie was peering myopically into the audience.

Alice thrust the cup at Joan and got to her feet. She'd been sitting on the bench for so long that her left leg had gone numb. She tried to walk without a limp up to the stage, but her leg was doing strange things, dragging along behind her as though she was a wounded soldier. A faint titter drifted from the audience.

She managed to climb the steps and approach Miss Dickie. 'Well done, dear,' the headmistress said, taking her hand in a vice-like grasp while handing her a large certificate with the other. Alice stumbled down the steps on the other side of the stage and lurched back to her seat, conscious that her face was a vivid red.

'Let's see,' said Joan. Alice finally looked at the certificate. *Alice Robinson*, it read, *For Kindness*.

'*Kindness!*' Dad exploded as they walked home.

Alice saw Mum shoot him a warning glance. 'You did very well, dear,' she said. 'And it's true. You *are* kind.'

Alice briefly felt a warm glow, which cooled as soon as she saw Dad's expression.

She kept the certificate in her room, but nobody ever referred to it again.

Jenny, Mum and Dad were back by nine. The prizegiving had been brought forward because of the blackout. Alice had already pulled down the blinds.

'So,' she said to Jenny as the three of them came in, in a waft of humid night air. 'What did you get?'

Jenny laughed and slapped a clutch of certificates and a huge volume down on the kitchen table, making William jump.

Alice went over and looked at the book's cover. '*The Complete Works of William Shakespeare*,' she said. 'Nice. The top scholar prize, I assume?'

Jenny nodded. 'Honestly, I know there's a war on, but you'd have thought they could have given me something maths-related.'

Alice grinned and struck a pose. 'Once more unto the breach, dear friends . . .'

'Enough.' Jenny grabbed the book and shoved it in Dad's bookcase, beside a copy of Euler's *Elements of Algebra*. 'Glad that's over with, anyway. Now to get on with the rest of my life.'

Alice wasn't sure, but she thought she saw Dad raise an eyebrow at Mum.

The following night, their evening meal was a jumpy affair. For a start, Dad wasn't there, so it was just the four of them at the table. When Alice asked Mum where he was, she was evasive, just saying he was 'on important business' and nodding in Jenny's direction. Alice couldn't imagine what that might be, but Jenny seemed oblivious, stirring her tea while explaining some theorem or other to William.

Then, just as they sat down to eat, there was an almighty roaring sound followed by several terrifying whistles and explosions. William rammed his hands over his ears and Alice put an arm round him and drew him close.

'What's happening?' asked Jenny, looking up in alarm.

'It must really be the Jerries this time,' said Mum. 'Maybe they think we still have defences for them to destroy. I wonder if Churchill's told them he's left us in the lurch.' She gnawed at a bit of skin beside her nail and then started gathering up plates.

'Pip said we'd be sitting ducks if the Germans attack,' muttered Jenny, her eyes wide with shock. 'He was right.'

Alice got up and went over to the window, squinting up at the still bright sky, then flinched as another explosion ripped through the air.

Mum snatched the rest of the plates from the table and thrust them underneath it, before gathering up the cutlery and throwing that in to join them.

'What on earth are you doing?' asked Jenny.

'I'm not taking any risks. If the planes come over our way, we'll be safer under the table than anywhere.'

Alice shrugged. 'Come on, William. It'll be like having a picnic.' She drew him under the table with her, and Jenny joined them. It was awkward all squashed into the small space, and hard to eat without knocking into someone. Any time Alice bobbed up to change position, she scraped her head on the table's rough underbelly until her scalp felt raw and her hair became tangled in wild wisps. They sat there for the remainder of the meal, trying to force down liver, onions and mash, until the sounds died down and they emerged shakily, clutching their now empty plates.

But just as Mum switched on the wireless to see if there was any news, another shrill sound invaded the room. She put her hand to her chest, then her shoulders slumped and she exhaled quickly. 'Thank God – it's only the phone,' she said. She darted into the hall, wiping her hands down her overall. There was a short silence, then, 'Alice! It's the hospital.'

Alice took the receiver from her, listened for a few seconds, then dashed upstairs.

'What is it?' shouted Mum.

Alice's voice floated down. 'Casualties! They want all the staff in.'

'I hope there aren't too many,' said Jenny.

Mum didn't reply, just gnawed at her finger again.

Alice emerged, hastily pinning on her cap. 'I'm off, don't know when I'll be back.'

Only Jenny said goodbye; Mum seemed lost in a world of her own.

As Alice approached the hospital, still trying to pin her cuffs in place, two ambulances drew up outside the main door. Then the gravel crunched behind her, and she stood aside to let another ambulance pass, its headlamp sweeping over the ground in a semicircle as it swung round.

A shadowy figure emerged from the first ambulance and unbolted its rear doors. Another figure joined it and helped draw out a stretcher bearing a humped shape. The tail lamp of the ambulance cast a red glow over the inert body, and Alice shivered. Then the other ambulances began to discharge their occupants, and stretcher after stretcher was borne into the entrance of the hospital.

She hurried past the gloomy cavalcade of injured, possibly dying people. The corridor was bustling with medical staff: doctors with grave faces, pairs of nurses talking rapidly to each other, and porters pushing wheelchairs that clanked and squeaked in protest at being hurried along. She flattened herself against the wall as an orderly approached with a gurney, glancing automatically at the patient as the trolley rattled past.

But as she registered the white face and blood-matted hair, she realised it didn't belong to a stranger as she'd imagined. The features were all too familiar. Her ears roared and her heart plummeted as she slumped to the ground in shock.

'Dad,' she whispered.

'Are you all right?' The concerned face of a porter loomed in front of her. He held out a hand. Alice grasped it and got shakily to her feet. 'Thanks,' she said. She barely recognised her own faint voice.

'Looks like your legs gave way there. Had a long shift?'

Alice nodded. 'I was off duty, but I've been summoned back in to help with the emergency.' Her brain was haywire, but remarkably, the words still came out.

The man blew out his cheeks. 'Bloody Germans,' he said.

'What happened?' asked Alice, surges of panic still rocking her body.

'Raid on the harbour. Buggers dropping bombs everywhere.'

What on earth had Dad been doing at the harbour? 'I need to go,' she said, and hurried down the corridor in the direction Dad had been taken, as fast as her straw-like legs would allow, conscious of the porter staring at her.

8

Alice had been told to report to men's surgical, but she had to find out about Dad first. As she made her way deeper into the hospital, she saw Rebekah coming towards her.

Rebekah's warm smile of greeting turned to concern when she saw the expression on Alice's face.

'Are you all right? You look as though you've seen a ghost.'

Alice told her what had happened.

Rebekah hugged her. 'Listen, you go onto the ward, otherwise you'll get into trouble. I've just been sent on my break, but frankly, the thought of tepid tea and a stale bun doesn't entice me. I'll see what I can find out about your father.'

'Oh, would you?' Good old Rebekah. If there was a hospital award for kindness, she'd have got it every time.

'Do you want me to contact your mother as well?'

'Yes, please. But best tell her not to come in. She won't be allowed to see him at this time of night. I'll call her as soon as I have some news.' Poor Mum. She'd be worried sick but it was better she stayed at home for now.

'Of course.' Rebekah smiled at her then turned and walked back down the corridor.

* * *

When Alice arrived on the ward, it was a frenzy of activity. All the lights were on, despite the late hour, and the long-stay patients were all sitting up in bed, agog to see what was happening.

Alice scanned the room, trying to find Dad, but there was no sign of him.

The ward sister grabbed her arm. 'Don't just stand there, Nurse. You're here to help, not gawp.'

Alice started.

'Bring me the hypodermic tray, and the adrenalin.'

Ward discipline took over, and she rushed off to locate the items Sister required. After that, she became an automaton: dressing and treating wounds, helping men off stretchers and into beds, heaping blankets on motionless bodies, checking pulses, filling hot-water bottles. But underneath, she was horrified. Innocent people had been machine-gunned down going about their daily work. Apparently John Adams, the air raid warden, had been shot on his own doorstep. Others had been mangled by bomb splinters or wounded by shrapnel. The war had come to Jersey in the most appalling way.

It was a good job Rebekah had offered to find out about Dad, as Sister was obviously in no mood to allow Alice time off. Yet all the while her mind was whirring. Where on earth was he? When he'd been wheeled into the hospital, he'd been unconscious but breathing, his face waxy, with an ominous blue shadow around his lips, but still definitely alive. It had been such a shock to see her normally strong and confident father looking so frail. She wondered again if she ought to call Mum now, but decided she still wanted some more specific information.

Jenny and William would probably have gone to bed by now. Jenny was used to Alice's erratic hours as she alternated between day and night duty. She wouldn't have worried at her absence, and William was oblivious to her comings and goings. But Alice had a sudden vision of Mum sitting at the kitchen table nursing a cold cup of tea, her face full of foreboding. She had seemed to know where Dad was, but presumably hadn't imagined he'd be in so much danger. Poor Mum. Poor all of them.

She was checking a patient's temperature when Rebekah came down the ward. She picked up the man's chart from the end of the bed and held it up, pretending to show it to Alice.

'He's in theatre. They're removing a piece of embedded shrapnel.'

Alice saw again the blood-soaked bandage wrapped round Dad's head. She screwed her eyes tight shut.

'It's a good sign that he's in surgery,' said Rebekah. 'They must think they can patch him up.'

Alice opened her eyes. Of course. If they hadn't thought he had a chance, they'd have just given him morphine and let him slip away. She hoped his body was strong enough to cope. He'd looked so frail lying on the trolley.

Rebckah gave her a quick hug. 'Must dash, but let me know how things are when you can.'

Alice clung to her, inhaling the coal-tar soap smell of Rebekah's hair. They hadn't had proper shampoo for months. 'Thanks for everything. I'm really grateful. I'll go and update Mum.'

As Rebekah sped off, Alice went to track down Sister to ask permission to use the ward telephone.

* * *

Towards midnight, a patient was brought back from theatre. As Alice rushed forward to help move him onto a bed, she realised it was Dad. His head was swathed in a fresh bandage and his face and neck were dark purple where he'd been coated in gentian violet, already hardening to a sheen on his skin. Alice had never seen him without a shirt on before. Even on the beach he refused to strip down to a singlet as some men did, his only concession being to roll up his shirtsleeves and take off his tie. Now she was conscious of the hollowness of his bare chest covered in wispy white hairs, his bony shoulders, the indents of his ribcage, his pale, clammy skin. Without his clothes, he was just a vulnerable old man.

She took his hand. 'It's all right,' she said. 'I'm here.'

Sister appeared by her side. 'We'll do all we can for him,' she said. Her attitude to Alice had softened as soon as she knew her father had been injured. 'They've removed the pieces of shrapnel from his head; it's just a case of supporting his recovery as best we can now.' She put two fingers on Dad's thin wrist and looked down at the watch pinned to her front. Despite the clatter and clanging on the ward, the air around the bed was silent and heavy. 'His pulse is weak,' she said eventually. 'You sit with him while I set up a saline drip. That should help.' She disappeared in search of apparatus.

Alice took Dad's hand and stroked the crêpey skin with the back of her thumb, smoothing and flattening it gently again and again. 'Come on, Dad,' she whispered. 'You've got to pull through.'

* * *

When Alice was sent home around six, as the relief shift came onto the ward, Dad was stable. The drip had helped. All they could do was wait to see if his body was able to recover. She was keen to stay, but Sister insisted.

'Grab a few hours' sleep,' she said. 'Otherwise you'll be no use to anyone.'

'I'm fine,' Alice protested. 'If I'm officially off duty now, can't I just stay with him?'

Sister's voice was kind, but her expression was firm. 'You are here in a professional capacity, Nurse Robinson,' she said. 'I am giving you an order and I expect you to follow it.'

Alice glanced back at Dad's face. Purple-lidded eyes were closed in sleep, the folds beside his nose drooping, the mouth slack. Shallow breaths whispered in and out. He'd probably sleep for a while.

'Yes, Sister,' she murmured, and set off down the ward.

When she emerged from the hospital entrance into the already warm air, the sky was streaked with mauve and yellow, a pale sun rising above golden clouds. It would be another hot day. She unpinned her cap from her aching head, not caring if she broke protocol, and steeled herself to talk to her family.

As she walked down the path and glanced at the downstairs window, she realised Mum was still up, just as she'd imagined. She'd peeled back a corner of the blackout and was sitting with her elbows on the sill, her chin drooping onto her hands. Her eyes were shut. Alice slid her key into the lock as quietly as she could, turned it slowly and nudged open the front door. Even so, by the time she'd tiptoed down the hall and into the living room, Mum had snapped awake and was looking at her through red-rimmed eyes, her face the colour of the bleached bandages Alice had been winding earlier.

She knelt beside her and told her that Dad was as well as could be expected. She didn't want to give her any false hope. Sister had warned her that the next few hours would be critical.

Mum let out a strangled sob. 'I knew he shouldn't have gone down to the harbour.'

Alice put her arm around Mum's shoulders. They felt as bony and thin as Dad's. How had her parents aged so suddenly? 'What was he doing there?'

Mum drew a shuddering breath. 'Looking for Pip.'

'Pip?'

She nodded. 'Dad is sure there's something going on between Jenny and Pip. He went down to the yacht club to see if Pip was there. He didn't want to have it out with him in front of his father.'

'Have what out with him?'

Mum sighed. 'He thinks Pip will turn Jenny's head and that Jenny will give up on Cambridge. He just wanted to make it clear that Jenny has a brilliant future. He doesn't want Pip to jeopardise it.'

Alice stood up. Of course Dad would have tried to speak to Pip, even if he had got it wrong about their relationship. Suddenly she felt furious with Jenny. Why on earth hadn't she gone to England as Dad had asked her? Why did she have to change her mind and put them all in danger? Stupid, careless Jenny, only thinking of herself and not the conse-quences of her actions. And what about Pip? Had he been caught up in the bomb attack too? Surely she would have heard by now if he had.

She went into the kitchen to make a cup of tea for them both, trying to keep her hands still enough to complete the familiar actions without spilling anything.

Mum went over to the hospital with Alice later that morning. Neither was allowed onto the ward, but the sister, who was more understanding than Alice had expected, reassured them that he'd had a reasonable night. Mum would be allowed to see him during afternoon visiting hours. She looked calmer when she left.

Alice was back on the women's ward now, and her day vanished in the usual round of blanket baths, gastric feeds, diabetic specimens and wound dressings. But as soon as her shift was over, she dashed back to men's surgical. Hopefully Mum had been able to visit by now. Jenny couldn't accompany her, as she had to supervise William after school. They'd decided not to bring Will. It would be too upsetting for him to see his father like that, and they couldn't predict how he would behave in front of the other patients. He rarely had tantrums these days, but the appalling screaming fits he'd had growing up were too vivid a memory. None of them wanted to risk one of those again.

The only good news was that Jenny had phoned the Maretts the previous day and discovered Pip was safe. He hadn't even been near the harbour.

As Alice approached Dad's bed, she was struck anew by how old and frail he looked. But at least he was awake now. She pulled up a chair and took his hand again. It seemed strange to have such contact with him. She hadn't held his hand since she'd been a small child – and then it had normally been him grabbing hers to stop her crossing the road too soon or forcing her to walk when she'd wanted to run. She looked down at his slim fingers and neatly trimmed nails. There was a permanent bump on the side of his middle finger where he pressed too hard with a pen, but otherwise they were white and smooth: the hands of an academic, not a manual worker. Mum's hands were red and calloused, often with a burn mark on her wrist from where she'd snatched a pie or a casserole too quickly from the oven and scorched herself. There was a faint criss-cross of lines on her index finger, scars of careless chopping, and lately her nails had been bitten and the skin around them frayed. Mum always did things too quickly – Alice was the same – rushing at tasks to get them finished. Neither Dad nor Jenny ever seemed to hurry. The busyness was all in their brains rather than their hands.

'Alice?'

She looked across at Dad. His voice was faint, but he spoke clearly enough.

She placed her hand over his. 'I'm here.'

He struggled to sit up, then his head flopped back against the pillow.

'Don't move. I'll come to you.' Alice pulled her chair further up the bed, then leant close to Dad's mouth.

'Jenny,' he whispered.

She sat back down. 'Jenny's not here, Dad. She'll come in tomorrow.'

She reached out to smooth Dad's wispy hair where it protruded from the bandages wrapped round his head, noting

86

with relief that there was no fresh blood on the dressing. He was still very pale, though, his complexion almost grey in the evening light.

'Kind girl.'

She darted a look at Dad's face, but he wasn't being ironic.

'Kind but not clever.' She regretted the words as soon as they were out, but they came from deep down inside of her; she hadn't consciously framed them.

Dad's mouth twisted. 'I'm sorry.'

'You've nothing to be sorry for, Dad.' Was he apologising for going down to the harbour? Being in the wrong place at the wrong time? 'You did what you thought was right,' she added.

But he was shaking his head slowly from side to side, wincing at the action.

'It's all right, Dad. You don't need to talk.'

Yet something was obviously troubling him. Perhaps this was about more than the trip to the harbour.

'Jenny's like me.'

'Yes.' Alice smoothed Dad's blanket with her other hand. She found it hard to meet his eyes. 'She's a chip off the old block all right.' How often had she heard that phrase at home? Usually from Dad's own mouth.

'Understand her better.'

Alice looked up. 'You understand Jenny because she's more like you?'

Dad nodded imperceptibly. 'But love you both so much.' His voice was getting weaker now. Alice had to strain to hear it.

'I know you love us.'

'Both the same.' His head lolled and his eyes closed.

Alice slipped her hand down to his wrist, her thumb reaching automatically for his pulse. Faint but still discernible.

She continued to watch his face as his features relaxed into sleep. So that was what he was trying to tell her. He understood Jenny better – they were clearly cut from the same cloth, with their sharp minds and clever ideas – but he didn't *love* her better. He just found her easier to comprehend. Perhaps he really did value Alice's kindness. And perhaps he really did love them both the same.

'Thanks, Dad,' she whispered, leaning forward to kiss his papery cheek.

And as she set off home, she realised that despite the terrible fear and worry, something had lightened inside her at his words.

As soon as she walked in, Mum pulled out a chair for her at the table. She'd even laid her a place. 'Come on, eat up. I managed to get a chicken from Vitel's on my way back from seeing your father.' She carved a slice and deposited it on Alice's plate. Jenny and William already had their food, although Alice noticed Jenny's was untouched.

'How was Dad this evening?' asked Jenny. Her lank hair was pushed back behind her ears, making her face look thinner.

Alice picked up her knife. 'Frail,' she said. 'It was a bad injury.' Apparently he'd been quite a while in theatre, and Sister had warned her it was still touch-and-go.

Mum stopped carving and clutched at the table to steady herself. 'Did he talk to you?'

'A little.' Alice put some chicken into her mouth and tried to chew it.

'He said he wanted to speak to you about something.'

'What was that?' asked Jenny.

'Oh, nothing much.' Alice forced herself to swallow. William was doing his usual thing, pushing his meat away from his vegetables until everything was separate on the plate. Mum watched him absent-mindedly.

'I'm desperate to see him, but I know I'll have to wait until tomorrow,' Jenny said. 'I wonder why he wanted to see Pip. Apparently the bomb exploded before he could find him.'

Alice exchanged glances with Mum. They were probably both thinking the same. Dad must have misread the signs between Jenny and Pip. He'd risked his life to remonstrate with him about a romance that didn't even exist.

Dad remained stable for the next couple of days. They all visited on a rota basis, except for William, who seemed to spend more and more time with Binkie, endlessly stroking his fur and whispering into his ears. Jenny was subdued when she came back but didn't mention anything Dad had said to her. Alice had thought a lot about her own conversation with him. For years she'd assumed Jenny was his favourite and she herself very much second best. But as he'd said, it was just that he understood Jenny better. And maybe being in hospital had helped him to appreciate Alice differently too. He'd be able to see the nurses coming and going from his bed in the corner of the ward, giving him an understanding of the challenges she faced every day. Whatever it was, she was grateful for what he'd told her. He could so easily have died at the harbour, as so many others had done, and she'd always have been under the impression he'd never valued her. She had his words to treasure, whatever happened now.

9

The next morning Pip was still dozing in bed, despite knowing he really should be getting ready for work, when the piercing ring of the telephone stunned him into full consciousness. He stumbled downstairs to answer it, then realised Dad had got there first. As he tiptoed into the kitchen, he heard Dad say, 'My God, no,' and his heart plummeted.

Jenny had called him as soon as she'd found out her father was in hospital. She'd been anxious about Pip too – he could well have been caught up in the bomb attack. Thank goodness he'd decided not to go down to the yacht club that evening. He'd dashed round to comfort her and reassure her he was all right. She'd met him at the end of the lane and stood mute with shock while he hugged her, trying to inspire her with an optimism he didn't feel. And now it seemed his premonition had been right. Mr Robinson must have died in the night. Why else would they have been called so early in the morning?

He hovered by the door, trying to control his anxiety and waiting for Dad to hand over the receiver, or at least fill him in on the contents of the call, but Dad kept talking. And nothing he said made sense.

'An ultimatum?'

Why would Jenny's dad offer an ultimatum?

'All right. I'll be round then. Thank you. A sad day for us all, sir.'

Who was his father calling 'sir'?

After a few more baffling exchanges, Dad put the phone down. He pushed past Pip into the kitchen and started opening and closing cupboards. 'Where's the cooking brandy?'

'Dad – what's happened?'

He located the brandy, poured a large slug into a glass and emptied it in one gulp. Then he slumped into a chair and put his head in his hands.

Pip sat down opposite him. 'Is it Mr Robinson?'

Dad looked at him through heavy eyes.

'No – why on earth would Mr Robinson be phoning me?'

'I meant is the call *about* Mr Robinson. He's in hospital, remember, after the bomb attack.'

Dad dismissed Pip's question with a wave of his hand. 'That was the bailiff. The Germans have delivered an ultimatum. We're to surrender immediately. There'll be a session of the Royal Court later this morning, but it's really not up for discussion.' He let out his breath in a low sigh. 'The Channel Islands will soon be occupied by the enemy.'

Pip had a sudden vision of the Union Jack that had flown over Fort Regent for as long as he could remember being torn down and replaced with a German flag, or worse still, a swastika. His chest felt hollow.

'What does that mean in practice, Dad?'

'I don't know. I'll have a clearer idea when I've seen the document, but it's a terrible blow for us all.'

Pip nodded mutely.

Dad sighed and stood up. 'I'll go and get ready. Will you open up the office?'

'Yes, of course.' Pip followed his father up the stairs to change out of his pyjamas. But he had no intention of opening up the office just yet. As soon as he could, he'd cycle over to Jenny's.

Half an hour later, Pip was propping his bicycle against the wall of the Robinsons' house, ready to ring the bell, when Jenny emerged from the front door, a basket over her arm.

'Pip!' She put the basket on the ground and kissed him quickly on the cheek.

Pip put his hands on her shoulders, trying to show by his expression that it wasn't a social call. 'I'm afraid I've some terrible news.' Better to come straight out with it; he really needed to get to the office as soon as possible. If Dad got there before him, he'd be in trouble. But he had to warn Jenny immediately.

She blanched, and Pip realised she must have jumped to the wrong conclusion.

'It's all right. It's nothing to do with your dad.'

Her face sagged with relief. 'Thank goodness. Let's walk down the lane.' Despite Mr Robinson's absence, she still seemed unwilling for the rest of the family to see them together.

As soon as he told her about the ultimatum, she stopped in her tracks. 'Perhaps I should have gone to England after all, as he wanted.'

Pip sighed. 'You've got to stop torturing yourself about this, Jen.'

'But I do torture myself. Dad was so upset when I came back. He thought I only changed my mind because of you.

He assumed we were romantically involved and went down to the harbour to have it out with you. That's why he was caught up in the bomb attack.' Her eyes were glassy. 'I'll never forgive myself if he doesn't make it.'

Pip winced. 'Try not to think like that. He's going to pull through, although he'll be devastated to know we're to be occupied by the Germans. I know he's an Englishman, but your father loves Jersey as much as the rest of us.' Jenny had told him the story of her dad meeting her Jersey-born mother when he'd accepted a temporary teaching post on the island. He'd fallen in love with her, the teaching job had become permanent, and he'd spent the rest of his career in the maths department of the grammar school, continuing to tutor pupils in retirement.

Jenny nodded. 'I can't believe we won't be putting up any resistance.'

'What can we do? The army have left us, most men my age are away fighting . . .' He felt another prickle of frustration at his father's refusal to let him enlist. At least he'd helped rescue those men from Saint-Malo. 'There just aren't enough of us to defend Jersey in any organised way, although perhaps we can make the Germans' life here more difficult.' He kicked at the dirt with his foot.

Jenny shivered. 'I wonder what they'll be like. There've been such disturbing reports from the mainland. Beatings, rapes . . .' Her voice quavered and tailed off.

'Over my dead body.'

'Not literally, I hope.'

'Don't even joke about it.' Pip drew his shoe along the ground again.

'If a German comes to our house, I'll spit in his tea!'

'That's my girl. Spit in his tea, not at his face. Much more subtle. And that way there'll be no reprisals.'

Jenny smiled weakly. 'I'd better get on with my errands.' She picked up the basket. 'Let me know if you hear anything more.'

Pip delivered one last stab at the dirt. 'I will.' He pulled her towards him and enveloped her in a hug. She smelt of honeysuckle and strawberries. He'd have loved to stay longer, be able to press his mouth against hers and breathe in her sweetness; it took a big effort to break away. It was only when he bent down to brush the dried mud off his shoe that he noticed he'd traced a V for victory sign in the dust.

The next day, Jenny stood with Pip amongst the crowds in Royal Square, watching as a large white cross was painted on the pink granite paving. Despite the awfulness of the event, her mind was focused on Dad; she was still so worried about him. The news of Jersey's capitulation would be another blow to his already fragile health.

She was dimly aware of bossy Captain Benest in his pork-pie hat ordering people around. 'You must stand back,' he bellowed. 'The States is in session and the bailiff will be coming out any minute.' The crowd retreated grudgingly, people muttering to each other or raising their eyes in shared resignation. Jenny looked at Pip. His jaw was clenched, his mouth a hard line.

A pigeon flew overhead and deposited something white directly on top of Captain Benest's hat. He took it off and shook it rapidly before storming off towards his office.

Faint laughter rippled through the crowd, and Jenny had the feeling they would seize on the slightest thing to ward off the fear and horror.

But the levity soon evaporated, replaced by the chill of despair. She looked around her: everywhere were women with anxious faces, men looking stern, children – picking up on the gloomy atmosphere – fretful or frightened. Her heart ached for them all.

Eventually a door in the States building opened, and the bailiff emerged, his face rigid with tension. He made a short speech explaining that he'd had no choice but to surrender the island to the Germans, and that they were now under enemy rule. Every property must display a white flag to indicate there was to be no resistance.

'White flag? Where on earth am I to find a white flag?' asked Mum when Jenny returned home with the news.

'I don't know. A bed sheet maybe? It looked like other people were hanging old sheets out of the window. I'm sure not all of them had flags.'

'Why should I waste good bed sheets on those bloody Germans?' Mum said.

'You'll risk getting into trouble if you don't. I'm sure you can take it back in as soon as we've surrendered.'

'I've got a better idea.' Mum rushed out of the kitchen and dashed upstairs.

Jenny listened to the sound of her opening and shutting drawers in her bedroom.

Eventually she returned, something white bundled under her arm. 'Run to the shed and fetch a cane, would you, Jenny?'

Jenny went out into the garden, wondering with a pang whether Dad would be back in time to pick raspberries and runner beans this year. An image of him back in March hammering in canes at an angle to create a criss-cross cage for the plants flashed into her mind. She took a sharp breath and entered the dusty gloom of the shed. Thankfully there were plenty of spare sticks lined up in the corner.

'Here you are, Mum.'

Mum grabbed the cane from her and spread out the item of clothing she'd retrieved earlier on the dining room table. Jenny looked at the soft white garment gathered at the waist and the bottom of each leg, and realised it was a pair of long johns that had belonged to her grandmother. For some reason Mum had kept them even though Granny was long since dead.

She watched in amazement as Mum knotted the bottom of one of the legs and thrust the cane down it. Then she went upstairs again. Jenny heard a rattling sound at her parents' bedroom window. She dashed out of the front door and squinted up at the top storey of the house.

Mum was leaning out of the window, attaching the voluminous pair of bloomers to the catch as the legs fluttered in the wind. Jenny had to suppress a laugh. On this most disastrous of days for the whole of the Channel Islands, Mum was signalling her capitulation to the Germans with an item of Victorian underwear.

That evening, Jenny strode tensely over to the hospital to visit Dad. At first she tried to ignore the flutters of white from each window, outraged to see how quickly the islanders had surrendered. But when she looked more closely at the signs of submission, she realised they weren't flags at all. An ancient vest, yellow-crusted from sweat and hoisted onto a broom handle, hung from the ironmonger's. Elsewhere she saw old nappies, threadbare pillowcases, grimy tea towels and ripped sheets. Gestures of defiance from every window. Tears swelled in her eyes. Good old Jersey.

But as she entered the hospital and the usual smell of disinfectant washed over her, her stomach started to churn. How on earth could Alice stand working in this place? Admittedly the corridors were gleaming and the medical staff cheerful-looking, but essentially the place was full of death and disease. She had to acknowledge a grudging respect for her sister, pounding the wards all day long and having all that contact with sick people. Jenny could never have been a nurse. She much preferred the smell of old maths books.

As she approached Dad's bed, around which the curtains had been drawn, a grim-faced sister intercepted her. 'Miss Robinson?'

Jenny nodded, her throat suddenly too tight to speak.

'I'm afraid your father's become a little worse in the last hour.' She put her hand on Jenny's arm.

The room tilted. 'How much worse? What are you saying?'

The nurse turned away from her. When she looked back, her eyes were full of sympathy. 'We think he may have had a myocardial infarction. It's quite common in an older patient with a major injury.'

'What's that?' Jenny couldn't even pronounce the words. Where on earth was Alice? 'My sister . . .' Her chest tightened, her breath coming in short, shallow bursts.

Again the squeeze of her arm. 'A myocardial infarction is

a heart attack. I believe Nurse Robinson is on duty. Would you like me to send someone to fetch her?'

'Is my father conscious?'

'He's been in a lot of pain. We've given him some morphine, so he's rather sleepy. But you can still speak to him.'

Jenny had a sudden vision of her and Alice sitting either side of Dad's bed, each holding one of his hands, as if they were sharing him between them. She'd sensed the other day that Alice had had some sort of deep conversation with him when she'd visited. She'd never told Jenny what was said, but she had looked as if she'd been savouring a secret ever since. It was only right that Jenny had some time alone with him too. But Mum ought to be here.

'Would someone be able to contact my mother?' she asked.

'Of course. I'll do it myself. Why don't you go and sit with your father?'

Jenny thanked the sister, pushed aside the curtain and drew out a chair. Her legs were so weak she doubted if she'd be able to stand anyway.

Dad's eyes were closed, his head still bandaged from the bomb wound. He looked like a marble statue.

'Dad?'

His eyelids flickered, but he didn't move.

She reached out for his fingers and squeezed them, trying to coax a response, but the hand remained lifeless.

'Dad. Please say something to me.'

The eyelids slowly lifted, revealing Dad's dull brown eyes. 'Jenny.' His voice was scarcely more than a breath.

'You've had a heart attack, but you're going to be fine. You just need to rest. The doctors here are wonderful.' Alice had often told her that and she hoped it was true. 'The nurses too. All you have to do is sleep, and in a few days you'll be as right as rain. You've got to help me with my Cambridge exam, remember? You never did explain Dirichlet's theorem to me.'

Dad's mouth twitched, but he remained silent. Then his head sagged against the pillow, his features motionless.

'Dad?' Jenny could hear the panic in her own voice. 'Dad!' She pressed his hand hard. 'Dad!'

The sister appeared at her elbow. She placed two fingers on the inside of Dad's wrist, then frowned. She leant forward, turning her ear towards Dad's mouth. Then she gently prised open his eyelids, took a small torch from her pocket and shone it into his eyes. Nothing.

Jenny dry-retched into her hands.

'I'll just fetch a doctor, dear. Would you like me to get your sister now?'

Jenny nodded mutely. It was obvious what the doctor would say. It had been obvious from the moment Dad had slumped back in the bed. And all she'd done was to prattle on about Cambridge when she should have told him how much she adored him, idolised him even. Ever since she could remember, he'd been her hero. How could she bear it? How could Mum bear it, not getting there in time? And how would she explain to Alice why she hadn't summoned her earlier?

10

Pip didn't think Jenny would ever stop crying. He'd answered the door to her frantic pounding earlier and ushered her into the kitchen. Luckily Dad was still over at the bailiff's. She'd run all the way from home and her breath was ragged, her face streaked with tears. Pip sat her down at the table and made her a cup of tea, offering to add a dash of Dad's medicinal brandy, but Jenny had shaken her head when he held up the bottle. She didn't even touch the tea either.

'Whatever are we going to do, Pip?' Her eyes were wet, the lashes drawn down into spikes.

Pip reached out to take her hand. An image flashed into his mind of her dad holding Mrs Robinson's hands that time when he'd come to tell them the troops were leaving. He saw the red-checked oilcloth on the table, a jam jar of flowers, and remembered the faint smell of baking. Was it mothers that made homes feel so welcoming and attractive? The kitchen back home was chilly and bare. Neither he nor Dad had ever attempted to make it homely.

'I'm here for you, Jen. I can come over whenever you want and help with things. Keep an eye on William.'

Jenny took a shaky breath. 'William looks so lost.'

'I know. He will be. But I grew up without a mother. He'll survive.'

'Finding out about the Germans and then losing Dad . . . it's all too much.' She wiped her cheeks with the pad of her thumb.

'It's a terrible time. But your father wouldn't want you to give up.'

Jenny's answer was lost in juddering sobs. Pip felt his own eyes brimming in sympathy. What on earth could he say to comfort her? He felt awkward and out of his depth. He'd been a baby when Mum had died so had never known anything else but him and Dad on their own. But Jenny had been so close to her father; to lose him now was devastating. She clearly blamed herself for his death. Pip felt a sharp stab of guilt too, remembering how he'd stopped Jenny from getting on the boat. But all of this was really down to the bloody Germans. None of it would have happened without the war.

'Jenny. You have to be strong.' He had no idea whether it was the right thing to say – he just had to follow his instincts. 'You need to support your mother and help take care of William. Alice will be out most of the time, so you'll be the one at home looking after everything.'

'I know. But it's all my fault. Why on earth didn't I explain to Dad how things really are between us? Then he might never have tried to find you at the harbour.'

'But you weren't to know that's what he'd do.' Pip tried to put his arms round her, but she wriggled out of his embrace.

When she spoke again, her voice was thick with grief and despair. 'Alice was working at the hospital when Dad died. She's furious with me for not getting someone to track her down earlier so she could be with him at the end. And poor Mum was on her way but didn't arrive in time.' She wiped her cheeks again. 'I just thought Dad would always be there for us. And I wanted to make him proud.' She put her head in her hands and gave way to another tidal wave of grief, sobbing and sobbing until Pip could hardly bear it.

He got up and walked round the table to crouch down in front of her, stroking her hair while she cried. Poor, poor Jenny. Poor all of them. However were they going to manage?

He insisted on walking her back home, and she appeared relieved, even allowing him to hold her hand. She was no longer crying, but her eyes were red and puffy and her shoulders hunched. He tried to speak to her a couple of times, but she didn't answer. Her expression had turned inwards, as if she was so focused on her grief that she couldn't even register his words.

The roads were quiet now, the flags and garments people had strung up earlier fluttering limply in the gloom. Pip imagined the families inside the houses they passed, huddled anxiously around their wireless sets waiting for news, or hastily wrapping their most treasured possessions in brown paper or old curtains, ready to hide them in the attic or bury them in the garden. There were so many rumours about what the Germans would do. How they would plunder and steal, rape even . . . Scenes filled his head: his father being interrogated by Nazis, Jenny screaming as a horde of soldiers advanced on her, William taken captive . . . He shut his eyes against the imagined horrors and tried to focus on the present.

Jenny seemed a little calmer. She hadn't withdrawn her hand. It felt cold, despite the mildness of the evening, and he wrapped his fingers even more tightly around hers, trying to pass on some warmth and strength. He was glad she'd turned to him, despite her guilt about her father's death. All he could do was try to be the best friend he could.

By the time they got to the Robinsons', the garden was almost in darkness. As they walked across the damp lawn, Pip remembered the day he'd rushed over to tell them about the Whitley bombers. He'd always envied Jenny her brother and sister, her devoted parents. And now they were ripped apart, just as he and Dad had been all those years ago.

He swallowed as Jenny showed him in through the back door, trying to think what he might say.

Mrs Robinson was sitting at the kitchen table, her head in her hands. William was beside her cuddling his rabbit and looking bewildered. It was hard for Pip to imagine he'd never see Mr Robinson there again, reading the local paper or doing the crossword with Jenny. During their tutoring sessions, the red-checked cloth had been strewn with maths books. Mr Robinson's voice would be full of patience as he explained a theorem or corrected Pip's algebra. He had a way of ordering the numbers and symbols that swirled round Pip's head so that they made sense. The air would be infused with pipe smoke and the old-wool smell of Mr Robinson's jacket. If Pip got a sum wrong, Mr Robinson would make him rub it out and do it again until it was right. 'No half-measures, lad,' he'd say, his ink-stained finger pointing at the offending error. And Pip would attempt the calculation again until he was satisfied.

Sometimes he'd been invited to stay on for supper, and he'd listen in awe as Jenny and her father talked. Mr Robinson didn't need to correct Jenny as he did Pip, or explain a process at length. When Jenny spoke, he'd sit with his head slightly tilted, a half-smile on his lips, and Pip could tell how proud he was of her. Jenny adored him too. She was lost without him.

He sat down next to Mrs Robinson as Jenny made tea. 'I'm so sorry,' he said.

Mrs Robinson lifted her head and looked at him through red-rimmed eyes. Pip thought he saw a flicker of anger along with the grief, and his face flared with heat. Was she blaming him for her husband's death? Should he say something or keep silent? Any apology would sound lame, and he might have imagined her bitterness because he felt so guilty. Perhaps it was better to focus on what he could do to help. He stood up to collect the teacups from Jenny and placed one in front of Mrs Robinson. She nodded. He gave the other to William, who picked up his spoon and started whirling it around the cup, sloshing some of the liquid onto the cloth.

'Stop it, William!' Mrs Robinson said. She plunged her fingers into her hair, ramming her palms against the sides of her head.

'Come on, Will,' said Pip. 'Let's take Binkie outside and find him some food.'

Will stood up, still cuddling Binkie, and followed him out.

Pip persuaded him to put the rabbit back in its cage, then they tore up clumps of damp grass and pushed them through the chicken wire. The rabbit snatched at them with its white teeth, then munched in a steady rhythm as Will went to pick some more. It was good he had agreed to taking Binkie outside, and he seemed content to leave him in his cage. At least Pip could keep William occupied and give Jenny and her mother a little peace. Perhaps that was the way he could help.

By the time they returned to the kitchen, the two women were deep in conversation.

'Shall I take William up to bed?' Pip asked.

'That would be kind,' said Jenny.

Pip took the boy up to his bedroom and folded his clothes neatly as Will put on his pyjamas.

'My dad does that,' Will said. 'He reads me *Wind in the Willows* too.'

Pip looked at the pale-green book on William's bedside table. The cover showed Ratty and Mole in a boat, in front of a full yellow moon. His own father had read it to him when he was little as well. He picked it up, noting with a pang the brown leather bookmark marking the last place Mr Robinson must have read from.

'Chapter Six,' he said. 'Mr Toad.' Then he read the next twenty pages, trying to imitate all the voices as Mr Robinson might have done, until Will fell asleep.

The next morning, Jenny stumbled downstairs after a sleepless night. Every time she'd closed her eyes, she'd seen Dad's pale face and haunted eyes, and heard his exhausted sigh, as his head sank back against the pillows, whispering at her through the darkness.

Pip had been a comfort yesterday, reassuring her again and again that her father had known how much she loved him, that she could still make him proud. She'd believed him at the time, but as soon as she and Alice had gone up to bed, and she'd felt the despair and resentment radiating from her sister's rigid back as she turned away from her to face the wall, the guilt had sidled in. How on earth would they ever regain their former closeness?

She poured some water into the kettle in the gloomy kitchen

and took out the tea caddy. Mum hadn't yet emerged, although she probably wouldn't have slept much either. At least Jenny could make breakfast for everyone. She reached inside the bread crock, but it was empty, only a few crumbs nestling in the bottom. They were down to their last bottle of milk too. She doubted if anyone would have much appetite, but they still needed food. The Germans would probably ransack the shops; if she didn't lay in supplies now, it might soon be too late.

She grabbed the basket from the hall table, trying not to look at Dad's jacket still hanging on the coat stand, or his brown shoes on the rack, and picked up her purse. If she hurried, she could pop into town and be back by the time the others were up. It would be a relief to do something physical after the long night spent tossing and turning. Anything to keep herself busy and drive out the thoughts crashing through her brain.

As she hurried down King Street in the early-morning light, the shops seemed to tilt forward as though to crush her under their weight, and it seemed that faceless eyes were watching her. Although it was barely seven o'clock, there should have been some signs of activity. Instead the streets were silent, not even a stray cat sloping along the side of a building, or a bird searching for crumbs. St Helier was holding its breath, waiting for the enemy to strike.

She pushed open the door of the bakery, triggering the sound of the shop bell and half registering the odour of newly baked bread. Mr Le Brun emerged from the back, wiping floury hands on his white apron.

'Good morning, Miss Robinson. I was so sorry to hear about your dear father.'

Jenny nodded briskly, determined not to cry. The news had travelled fast. 'I'll have a couple of baguettes, please,' she said, trying to keep her eyes on the neat rows of loaves on the shelf behind the baker. Dad had loved visiting the bakery. There was something about the symmetry of the stacked bread that had appealed to him. She knew that if she allowed herself to glance at the owner's brown eyes, which would be staring at her, full of sympathy, she'd be lost.

'Of course.' Mr Le Brun went to collect the long French sticks that Jenny had requested from the back of the shop. As he did so, the bell rang again and she heard the sound of the door opening. She kept her gaze on the shelf. It was best she faced as few people as possible this morning. Even though everyone meant well, she couldn't cope with too much sympathy. But as the shopkeeper approached to drop the loaves into her basket, he froze, his eyes wide with shock, all the colour leaching from his face.

Jenny turned slowly. Two tall men in grey-green uniforms were standing in the entrance, blocking the light. Each held a tin helmet under his arm and had a rifle hanging over his other shoulder. Medals glinted on their chests. The air in the shop sharpened. Jenny felt her chest tightening, squeezing the air out of her body. She took a shallow breath, trying not to make a sound.

'Goot morning,' said one. He bowed his head to Jenny, then included Mr Le Brun in a wide smile. His hair was short and blond, his parting slightly sunburnt, his nose peppered with freckles.

Jenny moved aside, clutching her basket tightly to stop her hands from shaking, while the baker rushed back behind the counter, his forehead beading with sweat.

'Please, continue,' the soldier said. 'We have come to buy bread, but we can wait.'

Jenny turned her back on the pair and handed over some coins. Little electrical pulses of fear and anger were shooting through her. So this was what the enemy looked like. These were the men whose kinsmen had killed her father. Part of her wanted to whip round, spit in their faces and shout 'Murderers!' but she knew it wouldn't do any good. And how would it help the rest of her family if she was arrested? Better to suppress these powerful feelings and maintain her dignity. That was what Dad would have advised.

The baker took the money, then nodded at her grimly. 'Please remember me to your mother.'

'Thank you.' Jenny hesitated, uncertain how to manoeuvre round the soldiers in the small shop area. Thankfully one stepped out of her way, while the other held the door open for her. He bowed his head again as she muttered her thanks.

She rushed back home as fast as she could on shaky legs, her mind filled with images of tin hats and rifles, her heart bursting with hatred for anyone who shared a nationality with her father's killers.

Two weeks later, Jenny, Mum, William and Pip were in Hill Street, standing amongst the sullen, fearful crowds as hundreds of Germans marched down the road behind a full military band blaring out bombastic music. Alice wasn't with them. She'd insisted on going back to work, despite the ward sister offering her compassionate leave. She said she needed to throw herself into her job in order to keep herself occupied. Jenny understood – and even envied – her decision. All she could do was support Mum and William while trying to ignore the silent reproach of Dad's empty chair.

As the soldiers advanced, a man in front of her abruptly turned his back on them, his expression defiant. Further down the line, a woman was shouting abuse. Jenny clenched her fists. What if the Germans singled them out for punishment?

She glanced up at Pip's face as the troops strutted past. His expression was impassive, but she knew he'd be churned up inside.

'I can't believe it's come to this,' she said. It was a terrifying show of force: so many men, all marching in perfect alignment, their eyes staring straight ahead, their rifles all held against their shoulders at the same angle. For a second she wondered if the soldiers she'd met in the shop were there. But if they were, she'd never have recognised them; it was impossible to tell one from another. They were packed into identical blocks: twelve men across, nine men deep – one hundred and eight moving parts in huge human machines rolling relentlessly down the road.

Pip didn't reply, but Jenny felt him clenching his fist as he stood beside her, his rigid knuckles pressing into her leg.

Some of the soldiers would be Pip's own age. It must be desperately frustrating to watch other young men fighting for their country while he wasn't allowed to join up. She didn't blame Mr Marett – Pip was all he had – but the resentment was coming off Pip in waves. Poor Pip, stuck in a collar and shirt when he longed to be in uniform.

The soldiers she'd met in the shop hadn't been menacing. In fact afterwards, once she was seated at the kitchen table nursing a cup of tea and telling Mum about her encounter, she had acknowledged how polite they'd been. But now, seeing the enemy en masse, she was only conscious of its power. And in spite of his obvious fury, she was grateful to have Pip's solid figure next to her.

She was vaguely aware of a disturbance in the crowd around them. Some people were turning round, and an elderly lady in front of them tutted loudly, her cheeks flushed with indignation.

'William!' hissed Mum. 'Stop that now.'

Jenny peered past Pip and caught sight of William marching on the spot in time with the soldiers. Why couldn't he just stand still and watch like other boys his age? Why did he always seem to draw attention to himself? Her stomach swooped as he shot his bony wrist out of his cuff, the watch Dad had bought him for his last birthday glinting in the sunlight, and extended his right arm towards the soldiers. Mum clamped her hand over his mouth before he could utter a word, and Jenny lunged towards him. 'No, Will!' People were openly staring now.

'It's all right, Jen.' Pip pulled her back. 'I'll deal with it.' He reached into his pocket, scooped a small object into his palm and offered it to William. William lowered his arm immediately, far more interested in unwrapping the object and putting it into his mouth than mimicking the soldiers. Jenny's body sagged in relief. Pip had saved the family from the ignominy of William giving a Hitler salute to the soldiers by successfully bribing him with a toffee.

Her heart rate settled as William continued to chew, showing no signs of repeating his action, and the crowd turned its attention back to the Germans. She flashed Pip a quick smile and he squeezed her fingers, but his face was still grim. Jenny's heart went out to him. Poor Pip, powerless to defend the island he loved. And poor Jersey, she thought. Whatever will become of us?

11

Alice found it a comfort being in the operating theatre at night. The darkness outside the windows was reassuring, a contrast to the bright lights in the room; as if everyone else was in bed and she and the theatre staff were the only ones awake, intent on their vital work. The atmosphere of calm intensity, the focused movements of the surgeon and the quick smile behind the mask when she passed him the right equipment all helped to take her mind off her grief. And doing her best for some other poorly patient helped assuage a little of her guilt for not having been able to rescue Dad. As well as her still-hot anger at Jenny.

She hadn't set out to be a theatre nurse, but with so many hospital workers having left in the evacuations, it was a case of all hands to the pump for the staff that were left. Mostly she was still on the women's ward, but increasingly she'd been drafted in to assist in the theatre. And increasingly she found herself valuing the responsibility.

It was Sir Andrew Beaumont operating today, a bear of a man with surprisingly nimble fingers. He manoeuvred his bulk around the patient with dexterity, his movements as deft and neat as a much smaller person's. He was generally good-humoured and would spend most of the operation humming. The current favourite was 'Land of Hope and Glory'.

'Swab, please, Nurse,' he said. '*Tum tum tum-tum tee tuum tuum . . .*'

Alice handed him the item, wondering bizarrely if she ought to join in the tune. She felt quite light-headed at the thought. It was a humid night and the operating theatre was stuffy. The ward had been so busy that she hadn't had time to eat earlier either. She took a shallow breath and willed herself to stay upright.

Luckily no one was looking at her: all eyes in the room were concentrated on the illuminated area of the patient that was the centre of everyone's existence for the duration of surgery.

'There you go, Fritz,' said Sir Andrew as he held up a red fleshy object with a pair of small forceps then deposited it on the tray Alice held out.

Normally Alice wouldn't have dared speak during surgery, but today she couldn't help herself. 'Fritz?'

'Yes,' replied Sir Andrew, reaching for a clamp. 'German chap. Admitted earlier with tummy pain and a high fever. Tender on palpation. Got him in here just in time.'

'But a German?'

He looked at her steadily. 'Yes, Nurse. A German. But also a human being in pain. My job is to make people well. Whatever their nationality.'

Alice swallowed down a rush of bile and said no more. But inwardly she was thinking of Dad. She was furious with Jenny, but Dad would still have been alive if the Germans hadn't bombed the harbour. This man might not have been involved, but he was still the enemy. Dad's face with its grey pallor hovered in front of her, and she saw again his blue lips and

113

the blood-streaked bandage around his head. Outside in the darkness, an owl screeched.

It was even hotter in the room now and the fumes of ether combined with the humidity made her feel queasy. That and the knowledge they were treating a German soldier.

At last Sir Andrew stitched up the wound and left Alice to tidy up. 'Good job, Nurse,' he said, peeling off his scrubs in the corner. There was the sound of running water and more humming.

Alice gently dabbed iodine over the patient's stomach – it was a neat job, caught just before the appendix perforated. There shouldn't be any complications. She glanced up at the man's face as she peeled back the sterile drape that had covered his body during the operation. Sometimes she was so intent on the procedure, the passing of instruments and the focus on one tiny portion of human anatomy, that she forgot there was a whole person underneath. But now she wanted to see what this German looked like. She wanted to look at the kind of man who could have murdered her father. Yet all she saw was a boy with a pale face and fair hair. He didn't look evil. He looked vulnerable and defenceless. She wondered what his name was. She picked up the notes that Sir Andrew had scribbled on earlier. *Stefan Holz.*

Stefan. That meant Stephen, didn't it? Etienne in French. Sir Andrew was right. He was still a human being. He doubtless had a mother and father somewhere, perhaps a sweetheart. Maybe even a wife and children, although he looked too young to be married. She took a deep breath and went to check the monitor readings.

* * *

Half an hour later, she was in the nurses' toilets, standing at the washbasin, when Rebekah emerged from the other cubicle.

Rebekah returned her smile in the mirror. 'Busy night?' She picked up the dwindling bar of soap and lathered her hands. If new stocks didn't arrive soon, they'd all end up with impetigo.

Alice nodded. 'I've just come out of theatre. Appendectomy with Sir Andrew.'

Rebekah started humming, and Alice laughed. 'We got "Land of Hope and Glory" today.'

'Really?' Rebekah raised an eyebrow. 'I'm surprised he's so pro English when Churchill's lot have landed us in it.'

'I doubt he was thinking about the significance of the tune. Probably just automatic.' Alice wiped a sheen of sweat from her forehead and pushed a stray strand of limp hair under her cap.

'How are things at home?' Rebekah's tone became softer.

'Oh, you know. Mum barely speaks, Jenny looks tortured all the time and William's retreated even more into himself. Apart from that, we're fine.'

Rebekah gave her a wry grin. 'I'm sorry.'

'We're all suffering. How's Tom?'

'I don't know really. There's some big offensive on. He can't say much – and it's even harder for us to communicate now that Jersey's occupied – but I sense he's worried.' Recently, the wireless had been full of news of British pilots fighting the Luftwaffe, and the skies over Jersey had been filled with German planes. Poor Rebekah. She must be eaten up with anxiety. And it wasn't as if she had any family around to comfort her. Alice was her closest friend at the hospital.

The door swung open and another nurse came in. She nodded at Alice but brushed past Rebekah to go into a cubicle without apologising or even acknowledging her presence. Alice raised an eyebrow at Rebekah. Rebekah shrugged.

'Why don't you come back to ours when you've finished your shift?' Alice said loudly. 'Mum can manage one extra at breakfast, I'm sure. And you could always use Jenny's bed if you'd like a few hours' shut-eye afterwards.'

'Won't Jenny mind?'

'She'll probably be out with Pip all day. And even if she isn't, I'm sure she'll be fine about it.' Jenny had got on well with Rebekah on her occasional visits to their house. Alice was confident she'd be happy to lend her her bed.

'All right then. Thanks.'

The toilet flushed and the other nurse emerged. This time she scowled at both Alice and Rebekah as she washed her hands, then flounced out of the room.

'What a cat!' said Alice when she had gone. 'I did a stint on maternity with her a few months ago. She wasn't particularly friendly then, but she was downright unpleasant just now.'

Rebekah grimaced. 'It's not just the Germans. Not every islander is so welcoming of someone like me settling here.'

Alice gaped at her in the mirror. 'I will never understand such small-mindedness. It's a disgrace. And from a nurse, whose job is to care for people, whoever they are.'

'She's a good nurse. I suppose it's not her fault she's been brainwashed by the general feeling against us.' Rebekah's forehead creased with worry.

Alice linked her arm as she pushed open the door. 'Just ignore her,' she said. 'I'm your friend and nothing is ever going to change that.'

* * *

116

As they strolled along Rouge Bouillon later, the street bathed in pink dawn light, Alice thought about how much this war had broken and reshaped allegiances. If she'd come across a young blond lad in the past, she'd have smiled at him and said hello; now he was the enemy, in spite of what Sir Andrew said. And there'd been Jews on the island for hundreds of years, but suddenly people like Rebekah were being shunned. War was a strange beast – it created artificial divisions between people, hatred and cruel bigotry, yet they all shared a common humanity.

Shopkeepers were pulling up shutters, sweeping pavements and turning *Closed* signs to *Open* all along the road. Maybe it was Alice's imagination, but the familiar routines seemed tainted with weariness. Store owners no longer shouted to each other across the street, enquiring how each other's businesses were faring or passing on the day's weather forecast; instead they exchanged grim smiles, looking nervously up and down the road for German soldiers. This is what occupation feels like, she thought. It's sucked the colour out of us, turned us into a monochrome community, a wary people. Sometimes a passer-by would dart a curious glance at Rebekah, and Alice wondered if her friend had any regrets about staying on the island, but she didn't want to bring up a painful subject.

The two of them chatted idly as they walked. Sometimes Alice wished Rebekah had been her sister. She felt she understood her better, and there wasn't that prickle of tension and distance between them that had developed with Jenny – in fact more of a yawning chasm since Dad's death. But perhaps it was always like that between sisters. Of course blood was thicker than water, but really she had more in common with Rebekah than she did with Jenny.

117

A couple of German officers in smartly pressed uniforms and gleaming jackboots, standing outside the Savoy hotel, nodded politely to them as they walked by.

'I have to say,' said Rebekah, once they were out of earshot, 'the Germans have been pretty civilised so far. Thank God they're Wehrmacht and not Nazis.'

'So far,' Alice agreed. 'But it's early days. And I don't like all these restrictions. Pip's furious he's not allowed to take his boat out.'

Rebekah smiled. 'Poor Pip. No cars either. But at least we can still cycle.'

'And walk,' said Alice, looking down at her own tired legs.

'Oh yes,' said Rebekah, 'there's always Shanks's pony.'

They traipsed up the front garden towards the house. Already the flower beds looked neglected: hollyhocks drooping and weeds sprouting amongst the sweet peas. Whatever would Dad have thought of their lack of care? As Alice led Rebekah through the side gate, she glanced across at the runner beans and raspberry canes. At least those were healthier. You couldn't eat flowers, but they needed to keep the vegetables and fruit going. She picked a raspberry and handed it to Rebekah.

Rebekah's eyes closed in pleasure as she ate it. 'Delicious.'

Alice gave her a fleeting smile. 'Dad would have been pleased with the crop.'

Rebekah's own smile was sympathetic. 'He's still providing for you all.'

Alice nodded, suddenly too choked to speak.

* * *

Breakfast was a quieter affair these days. There'd been less food around of late, but even if there'd been plenty, Mum rarely made the effort to cook. She'd placed a cabbage loaf and a bowl of dripping on the kitchen table. William was cutting his home-made sandwich into tiny squares and popping them in his mouth. Jenny was poring over the crossword and Mum was staring blankly at a cup of tea.

They greeted Rebekah warmly, and Mum gestured to her to sit down on Dad's old chair. Alice had a slight pang as she watched her friend sitting in her father's place, but dismissed it quickly. It was nice to have five of them in the kitchen again, and Rebekah would cheer them all up.

Rebekah chatted easily to William, and Alice noticed her brother's normally impassive face become animated. Rebekah had grown up with a little brother too and seemed to know how to engage William in conversation without making him anxious.

By the time Alice had brewed some more tea and poured them each a cup, Rebekah was studying the crossword with Jenny. Jenny had carried on Dad's habit of doing a daily puzzle. Perhaps it helped her to connect with him, or maybe she just enjoyed crosswords – or possibly both. They all had their own rituals, their own way of remembering. Of trying to cope. Alice watched their heads close together, one chestnut, one dark, and noticed their easy conversation and shared purpose, and something twisted low in her stomach.

When she was ten, she'd had a friend called Fleur. Fleur was pretty and funny and clever. She'd shared a desk with Alice at school and had made her laugh with her impersonations of teachers and the quirky drawings she did in her rough book. When Alice was with Fleur, she felt witty and lively too. So different from the dull, stupid girl she seemed to be at home. One day Mum asked her if she'd like to invite Fleur back to tea. The two of them had walked home from school arm in arm, Alice regaling her friend with the silly things Dad did – not on purpose, of course; Dad wasn't deliberately funny, but his head was in the clouds so much that he sometimes went to work in his slippers, or wearing odd shoes, and once he put a pile of exercise books in the larder. Fleur had laughed and laughed, and the closer they got to home, the more excited Alice became at the extraordinary family she was going to introduce Fleur to, and how much she'd grow in her friend's estimation as a result.

But as soon as they'd walked into the kitchen, everything changed. Mum was flustered and short-tempered. Dad was lost in a book and barely looked up as they came in. Then over tea he tried to compensate for his earlier neglect by barking questions at Fleur about what her father did. Fleur, who wasn't normally shy, became awkward and tongue-tied. In the end, Jenny came to the rescue, inviting Fleur up to her bedroom – they had a room each before William came along. When Alice tried to join them, Mum had insisted she help her wash up. By the time she finally got upstairs, Jenny and Fleur were sitting on the bed doing each other's hair.

After she'd returned from walking Fleur back home, Mum had rounded on her in surprise. 'Alice, honestly. Why did you invite Fleur back and then ignore her all evening? Poor Jenny had to occupy her instead. Really, you need to treat your friends better, otherwise you won't have any.' Alice had bolted upstairs and flung herself on the floor, staring up at the ceiling as hot tears misted her eyes.

120

The next day at school, Fleur joined the French-skipping girls in the playground, and gradually she spent less and less time playing with Alice. One time Alice caught sight of her laughing and chatting with Jenny in the corridor, and she flushed with resentment – it was so unfair when Jenny wasn't even in Fleur's year. It took her a long time to resign herself to Fleur never being the close friend she'd hoped for.

They ate a subdued breakfast, then Jenny disappeared off to see Pip, as Alice had expected, telling Rebekah to nap on her bed for as long as she wanted.

Alice lay on her own bed, listening to Rebekah's quiet, even breaths. She was fairly sure her friend had dropped off to sleep quite quickly, but hard as she tried, she herself couldn't relax. Restless thoughts whirled round her head: how much she missed Dad, and how they were all going to cope without him; how Mum would manage; how William would deal with everything; even what would happen to Jenny now she was trapped on the island. The thought of Jenny sent a bolt of anger through her. If she'd gone to England as planned, Dad might never have been injured, and Jenny wouldn't have spent his last moments with him. It would have been so much easier if Alice didn't have to see her sister every day. So many things to fret about. She tried to banish them from her mind. All she could do was be the best nurse she could. Dad had been proud of her eventually; she'd make him prouder still.

But then there was Rebekah. It was obvious from their conversation earlier that her friend was concerned about her own fate. Alice had read about the way Jews were being treated in Europe: their shops looted, businesses destroyed, curfews imposed. And often worse ... Nothing seemed to have happened on Jersey as yet, and the few Jerry officers she'd encountered had been civilised enough, but they were still Germans. And Germans didn't like Jews.

12

Jenny crouched in the bottom of the *Bynie May*, which was moored in the harbour, trying to ignore the bilge water seeping into her skirt as Pip fiddled with the wireless controls. Although he glanced at her from time to time, she could tell he wasn't really registering her: all his concentration was focused on the scribble of sound that poured out of the set. Finally a voice emerged from the chaos. Pip gave her a thumbs-up sign and put his ear closer to the machine. Jenny crept towards him and pressed her head against his, straining to hear the clipped male voice describing a dogfight between Spitfires and Junkers.

'There now, oh, one . . . two . . . three . . . four . . . five . . . six . . . about ten German machines dive-bombing the British convoy, which is just out to sea in the Channel . . .'

Jenny looked towards England, imagining the battle going on in the skies above the coast, the planes looping and diving through the blue air, chiffon wreaths of smoke trailing behind them. She'd heard the Junkers crossing earlier, on her way down to the harbour. They'd sounded ferocious as they stormed across the Channel, intent on annihilating the poor Spitfires. She thought of Charles and Cynthia. Would the Germans bomb London? She'd probably have been in more danger if she'd evacuated. She imagined Jersey would no longer be a target now it was occupied. Once again her heart heaved for Dad: German planes could do terrible things.

'All right?' Pip asked. He put his arm round her, and the boat rocked slightly from his movement.

Jenny laid her head against his shoulder. The announcer carried on.

'There's a terrific mix-up now over the Channel. It's impossible to tell which are our machines and which are the Germans' . . .'

Jenny caught the excitement in his voice. Why did men find war so exhilarating? As if it was some deadly global football match. Pip was just as bad. Always trying to listen in to the radio, sighing with frustration when he heard what other boys his age were doing, constantly analysing how the war was going. He didn't want to talk about anything else. Jenny tried to join in, but all she could think was how much she hated the Germans for taking her father's life.

'I'm not sure if it's safe to keep the wireless here for much longer,' Pip said. 'The boat's in full view in the harbour and the Germans could easily requisition her. I'd be devastated to lose her, but if I lost the wireless, all our links with the outside world would be cut.'

'You're not supposed to be listening to the BBC news anyway. We've been told only to tune in to German stations.'

Pip laughed drily. 'Well, that's not going to happen,' he said. 'I don't even speak German.' His eyes narrowed. 'But I probably do need to find somewhere safer to stow the set.'

Jenny looked down at the black machine with its array of wires and dials. It was complicated, but it wasn't big. 'I don't know. Under your bed?'

He shook his head. 'Too easy to find.'

'Up the chimney?'

'Same.' He switched the set off and removed his arm from Jenny's shoulder. 'We need to think of a really clever place, somewhere the Germans would never look.'

'All right. I'll try to come up with something.'

Pip slid the wireless back into the hold.

They walked back through the darkening streets just before curfew. The islanders had to be indoors by eleven o'clock now, even though that was really only ten. The Germans had insisted all the clocks be put forward an hour, in line with German time. Another imposition. They both looked up as a couple of Junkers with their distinctive shapes flew over, making for the airport.

'They must be stationed here,' said Pip. 'I can't believe we're hosting those murderers.'

'Let's hope the Spitfires gave as good as they got,' said Jenny. 'The commentator certainly seemed to think so.'

'Yes, indeed. Those British pilots are pretty gutsy. This could be over by Christmas, you know.'

Jenny smiled at him hopefully in the gathering gloom.

Two weeks later, they tuned in from the *Bynie May* again to hear Churchill's speech from the House of Commons. Jenny watched Pip's face as he listened to the British prime minister's words.

'Never in the field of human conflict was so much owed by so many to so few,' the elderly premier growled.

'Rebekah's husband is a fighter pilot,' Jenny said. 'She hasn't heard from him in weeks.'

Pip's face was grave. 'Lots of lads went down.'

'But there were more Germans taken out.'

'Yes, amazing really. No wonder Churchill's so smug about it all.'

Jenny nodded. 'I just hope Tom survived. Poor Rebekah.'

Pip turned to her, his expression fierce. 'What if that was me over there, flying Spitfires. How would you feel?'

'Well, I'd be worried, of course. But I never think of you in a plane. Always a boat.'

'Yes, you're probably right. I'd be in a British warship, like the ones we heard bombarding the coast of France the other day.' Pip's face was wistful now.

Jenny covered his hand with her own. 'I know it's hard. I know you don't want to be here. And I should have been in England by now. But let's make the best of things.'

'You're right.' He leant forward to kiss her, and she pulled back.

'What's the matter?'

'I'm sorry, Pip. You know how I feel.' She just couldn't seem to make the transition from friend to lover. It felt all wrong. She didn't mind Pip holding her hand, or even kissing her cheek, but anything more felt too intimate. She couldn't offer him that kind of relationship.

A muscle flickered in his jaw. 'It's all right,' he said. 'I'm sorry if I rushed things. We should be getting back anyway.' He held out a hand, and Jenny stumbled to her feet.

He insisted on walking her home as usual, but for once he didn't make any plans for the next time they met. Jenny sensed he was still worrying about her reaction earlier, as well as mulling over a hiding place for the wireless. And she was still too pierced with grief and guilt to mind.

* * *

When Alice asked her that night how things were going with Pip, Jenny answered: 'I honestly don't know. He's my best friend and I love us spending time together, but I'm not sure that's enough for him.'

'You know he's in love with you?' Alice's voice was tight.

Jenny flushed in the darkness. 'Yes, I think I do. I just can't feel the same way. I love him like a brother, that's all.'

'Like William?'

'Er, not William. Perhaps an older brother.' She certainly didn't have those feelings of anxiety with Pip that she had with William, who was always so unpredictable. She thought again of that day when the Germans had marched in and Pip stopped Will saluting them. He always seemed to do the right thing, and he'd been more caring than ever since Dad had died.

'Are you sure you're not just stringing him along?'

'I don't mean to. Maybe we will have something more one day. I can't imagine being with anyone other than Pip. I don't want to hurt him. And he knows how I feel.'

'You're lucky to have him, you know. Some girls would give their eye teeth to have someone like Pip yearning after them.' Alice sounded wistful now.

'I know.' Jenny felt a stab of guilt. Alice was right. Perhaps she didn't value Pip as she should. He wouldn't stay loyal for ever; one day he might find someone who could love him back. She suspected Alice might have treated Pip differently if she'd been in her shoes. Perhaps she even had feelings for him. She certainly seemed to want to talk about him a lot, and she'd been so keen to go sailing with him that day. Poor Alice. No wonder she'd been prickly. And then there was her still-simmering resentment that it had been Jenny, not her, who'd been with Dad at the end. So much had come between them lately. She decided to move onto safer ground. 'How are things at the hospital?'

Alice sighed. 'Every time I see an injured patient, it takes me back to Dad.'

'It must be very hard for you.'

'It is. I just try to keep busy.'

'Yes. It's better to be worn out physically than mentally. I haven't enough to occupy myself with now Cambridge is out of the picture.' At least Alice had a focus, even if the hospital brought back bad memories. Jenny just seemed to be marking time now.

'I think Mum could do with some help, Jen.'

She recalled Mum's blank face, her listless movements, her frequent moments of indecision. She was completely lost. 'Yes, you're right. Perhaps I could do more around the house and take over the food shopping. Even the cooking.'

'We're not that desperate!'

Jenny smiled. It had been months since Alice had teased her. 'Keep an eye on William, then.'

'That's better. He's really struggling without Dad.'

'Thanks. You've helped.'

Alice fell asleep soon after, but Jenny lay awake, her stomach churning. Alice was right. Keeping busy would fill her days, and provide some support for Mum too. And maybe she could come up with a hiding place for Pip's wireless, if ever it was needed. There were some practical things she could do. But none of them was enough to push back the creeping dread of how the occupation would develop and what the Germans might do to them. She couldn't get away from the horror of

128

how much more they might lose and the fear that Pip might get fed up with waiting for her and run away to enlist.

She thumped her pillow, wishing she could pummel her fears as easily. But she was still the same girl who had fought and clawed her way to being the best mathematician she could. Maybe there was another way to make Dad proud of her. She was tired of waiting for things to happen. It was time she took some initiative herself. Her clever brain whirled in the darkness as she planned how she could fight back.

Part Two

June–December 1942

13

Jenny sat at the kitchen table, grating potatoes to make potato flour. Pip had helped her dig up Dad's precious flower beds back in February, and they'd planted the seed potatoes then, on a blustery day with an ever-changing sky and the smell of salt in the air.

It was nearly two whole years since Dad had been killed. And Jersey had been occupied by the Germans for twenty-three months.

Jenny glanced up at Mum as she stood at the kitchen sink, gazing out of the window. Her shoulder blades jutted out sharply and her old blue jumper no longer clung to her curves but hung loosely. Her dark hair was lank and matted. She seemed to have lost all sense of purpose since Dad had died and Jersey had been occupied. It had been a double loss, really – the man she'd adored for nearly a quarter of a century and the island she'd loved all her life.

'Come and sit down, Mum. I'll make you a cup of tea.'

Her mother emerged from her reverie. Jenny saw her wipe her face with the back of her hand. 'No, dear. I'm fine. I need to get dinner on. Alice will be home soon.'

'Well, I'll make you a cup of tea anyway. You can drink it while you work.'

'Thank you.' Mum slid open the kitchen drawer and drew out a knife.

Jenny had been down to the market that morning, as there'd been a rumour of fish for sale. The market had been crowded – everyone with the same aim in mind – yet the counters were empty. How on earth could they live on an island yet not be able to buy fish? As usual, the Germans had taken all the supplies. She waited patiently in the queue, just in case a new catch came in, but when she got to the front, there were still no crates piled with plump black bream, or nets bulging with mussels, or even a bucket of writhing eels.

'Wait a minute,' Mrs Roundel, the fishmonger, said as Jenny turned away. She delved under the counter, drew out a couple of mackerel, wrapped them in newspaper and popped them into Jenny's shopping bag, waving away her thanks. 'I was in your dad's class at the grammar school for two years. Never forgot his lessons. He was a wonderful teacher. I won't see his widow and her family starve.'

Jenny's eyes had misted up, but she forced out a smile of gratitude and hurried off before anyone else could see. The smell of mackerel followed her all the way home and was now tainting the whole kitchen, but at least there was food for tea.

Mum slapped the fish onto a plate, their scales iridescent in the evening sun, and started gutting them deftly. 'Well done, Jenny. I'll use some of that potato flour to make a sauce. We'll have mackerel pie for tea, and I can boil up the bones, head and tail for stock later.'

Jenny forced a smile. She tried so hard to support Mum and keep them all fed. Dad's death was still a terrible void in their lives – a searing wound that would never heal. They'd had no option but to keep going, strengthening the bonds between those of them that were left, getting through each day, each month; journeying further into the desperate existence to which the occupation had condemned them. Life was dismal and limited, but it was still life; Jenny would do all she could to sustain it.

She handed Mum her cup of tea and started peeling carrots. Their leaves and skin could go in the fish stock later, although she put a couple of peelings by for William's rabbit. Sweet little Binkie. William doted on him so.

It was only when she paused in her chopping that she registered a knock on the back door. She wiped her hands down her apron and pulled back the bolt. Since Dad had died, they'd taken to locking the house, something they'd never done before. There were also reports of food being stolen from larders – another reason to take precautions.

'Pip!' She smiled and drew him in. 'I wasn't expecting you.'

'Clearly. I was knocking for ages.'

'Sorry.' She gave him a peck on the cheek, conscious of Mum's presence. Although Mum was always civil to Pip, there was still a reserve about her behaviour towards him. They all knew why. Sometimes Jenny felt that she and Pip would spend the rest of their lives trying to atone for the guilt of Dad's death.

Pip was carrying his wireless set. They'd long since brought it up from the boat, but usually he kept it at home in his bedroom. He tuned in to it most evenings. Sometimes, if Mr Marett was out, Jenny joined him. Together they'd rejoiced over the RAF victories against the Luftwaffe back in 1940; charted the German failures in Russia the following summer;

and listened in shock on a freezing December night to the news of the Japanese attack on Pearl Harbor. Pip would be lost without his wireless.

He put the set down on the kitchen table, his nose wrinkling at the smell of boiling fish.

'Why have you brought that all the way over here?' Jenny asked.

He grimaced. 'The Germans have ordered all wirelesses to be handed in, as we feared. Supposedly it's for military reasons – whatever those are – but I bet they've found out that people are still listening to the BBC. I'm supposed to take this over to the parish hall later.'

'And will you?' Jenny sensed Mum's back stiffening.

'Of course.' Pip winked at her. 'I just thought I'd pop in here on the way.'

Jenny glanced at her mother. 'Shall Pip and I pick you some gooseberries for later?' she asked. 'I'll only get the soft ones; they'll be nice and sweet.'

'All right,' said Mum. 'We could mash them up with some top-of-the-milk – and maybe a grain or two of sugar if necessary. Are you staying for dinner, Pip?'

Pip wrinkled his nose again. 'No, thank you. I said I'd eat with Dad.'

Mum shrugged and turned away.

Jenny nodded towards the cutlery drawer. 'Grab a couple of knives, will you, Pip?'

He looked a bit confused, but thankfully did as she asked.

While Pip was rattling cutlery, searching for knives, Jenny checked that Mum was still busy with the mackerel, then rushed to the bookshelf, picking up the huge volume of

Shakespeare she'd been given for prizegiving and shoving it under her arm. 'Come on.' She darted through the back door and stood waiting for Pip in the garden.

Pip found the knives and followed her out. 'What was all that about? And why have you brought the Shakespeare? Surely you don't want us to act out *Romeo and Juliet*?'

'Don't be daft.' Jenny pulled him towards the shed. This wasn't about romance, it was about resistance. 'You'll see.'

She opened the door and went in. Every time she entered the shed, she was struck anew by its smell – kind of warm and earthy, but in a pleasant way. Even after two years, it was a smell that instantly summoned up Dad, coming into the kitchen after an evening spent taking geranium cuttings or pricking out seedlings. He'd usually be wearing an old pullover with holes in, and his fingernails would be filthy, causing Mum to tut and pass him a nailbrush. But Dad wouldn't care. He'd carry on whistling, smiling at Jenny as he scrubbed his hands. Jenny blinked away the image. She mustn't think about Dad now. There wasn't time. Would he condone what she was about to do? 'Clever girl,' she imagined him saying. He'd approve of her using her brain to outwit the Germans, even if it was a small gesture. Although he'd be less happy about the risks involved.

She put the heavy volume down with a relieved thump on Dad's bench and took one of the knives from Pip. Then she opened the book and started gouging out a large hole in the pages.

'What the . . .?' Pip's forehead contracted.

Jenny kept stabbing, balling up the ruined pages of printed words and tossing them into an empty flowerpot. After a while, she stopped and dabbed her forehead with the back of her hand. 'The knife isn't sharp enough. I know . . .' She scanned the tools on the shelf Dad had built years ago, pushing aside the trowels and hand forks and picking up a penknife. 'This should work better.'

'Tell me what you're trying to do and I'll help,' said Pip.

'Isn't it obvious?'

'Not to me.'

She put down the penknife. 'I'm making a hole for your wireless set. If we can find a way of concealing it in the book, we've a much better chance of preventing the Germans from finding it.' She'd hatched the plan way back when Pip had first expressed concern about the set but had decided to wait until the need arose.

'How do you know I've no intention of handing it in?'

Jenny snorted. 'I know you.'

Pip grinned and picked up the knife. Before too long, a neat wireless-shaped hole had appeared in the book.

'You pop in and get the set,' said Jenny. 'You could say goodbye to Mum at the same time. Then come back here and we'll fix it in. I can smuggle the book back after Mum's gone to bed.'

Pip disappeared back into the house, returning a few minutes later with the wireless. Together they slotted it into the book. It was a perfect fit.

And if Mum wondered later why it took them nearly an hour to pick a handful of gooseberries, she didn't comment.

In fact Pip had no intention of eating with his father that night. He had another invitation for the evening, one that even Jenny didn't know about.

As he made his way back to the town from the Robinsons', he smiled to himself at Jenny's clever plan for hiding the wireless. Most people would have urged him to hand it in, but Jenny's brain was more than a match for the Germans. Since her father had died, she'd hated the occupying forces more than ever. This plan to thwart them was as much for Mr Robinson as it was for Pip.

Something had shifted over the last two years. After Jenny's dad had been killed, it was as if his ghost forever hovered between them, reminding them that he'd only died because of their relationship. Pip had tried to bury his feelings for her and think of her only as a friend as she'd urged him to do, but he couldn't deny how he felt. Sometimes he convinced himself that he might be able to get through to her, that she felt something more than friendship for him too, but the guilt of her father's death had put even more of a barrier between them, and he'd given up trying to kiss her again after that moment in the boat, although he'd been tempted many times.

Lately, it had felt more as if they were comrades than sweethearts, united in their determination to protect the island they loved. In fact, defending Jersey was the subject of his meeting that evening. He just had to find out more before he involved Jenny.

He made his way down Cattle Street until he reached the Caesarea. Someone was coming out, releasing a surge of voices and the sound of clinking glasses, which snapped off again as the pub door shut. It wasn't Pip's normal drinking hole. To be honest, he'd rather sip cider with Jenny up on Mount Bingham or share a tot of rum with Jack on the *Bynie*

May than sit in a stuffy bar all evening. Although even that was preferable to those awkward hours pretending to like Scotch as he and Dad sat in uncompanionable silence in their shadowy lounge.

As he entered the pub, he was greeted by a warm fug. The thick air was tainted with a beery odour, and thin plumes of smoke curled upwards from a number of lit cigarettes. The place was packed: full of workers having a swift pint with colleagues before they made their way home, or hardened drinkers buoying themselves up with alcohol before the curfew. There were a few German soldiers too – greenfly, as the islanders now called them – standing self-consciously in groups and given a wide berth by the locals. In the last two years, more and more Germans had come to the island, no longer just the stiffly polite officers but also rougher rank-and-file soldiers. Lately there'd been increasing reports of petty thefts and violence. The tentative relief the islanders had felt at their respectful treatment by the occupying forces had been replaced by wariness and suspicion.

As usual, guilt sliced through Pip at the sight of the young men in uniform. He locked eyes with one chap, a stocky youth with a thatch of blond hair. Was it Pip's imagination, or did the German sneer at him before he looked away? Pip put his hand in his pocket and made his way through the gloom towards the back of the pub.

A figure waved at him and he lifted a hand in return. Robert Durand had filled out a bit since they'd left school. The strands of dark hair that flopped over his forehead were too long to identify him as a soldier, and Pip felt a tinge of relief to greet another man of military age who hadn't enlisted.

'Pip.' Robert stood up, his hand outstretched.

'Robert.' It seemed strange to shake hands with someone who a couple of years ago he'd have slapped on the back or jostled in the lunch queue.

'Hope you like beer.' Robert gestured at the full glass on the table. Pip noted that Robert's own was already half empty.

'Thank you. Am I late?' he asked, sitting down and reaching for his drink.

'Not at all. I just wanted to make sure I got here first to grab the corner seat. I don't want anyone to hear us.'

Pip's attention sharpened at Robert's air of secrecy. They hadn't been particular friends at school. Robert had been more academic than Pip, always in the library or having earnest discussions in the common room. Pip had preferred the rugby pitch or the running track. So he'd been curious when Robert had phoned him out of the blue and asked to meet up.

They chatted for a few minutes about their lives since school. Pip suspected that Robert's job in an insurance office was as boring as his own work for Dad, although he tried to make it sound important, talking – rather pompously, Pip thought – about *liability* and *loss adjustment*.

Then he took a packet of Gauloises from his blazer pocket and offered one to Pip.

Pip shook his head. There was enough smoke in the room already, and he preferred to fill his lungs with sea air rather than tar.

'Do you mind if I do?' asked Robert.

'Of course not.' Cigarettes were hard to come by these days. Pip wondered where Robert had managed to procure his. He decided not to ask.

141

Robert lit up and took a drag, blowing the smoke out in a lazy spiral. Pip wondered if he was playing for time. He took a sip of beer and waited.

Robert looked round the room to check no one was listening, then leant forward. The acrid smell of the Gauloises came with him. 'What do you know about communism?' he asked.

Pip was taken aback. 'Nothing really.' A dim memory stirred of studying the Russian Revolution at school, and something about Karl Marx, but other than that, his mind was a blank.

Robert tapped his cigarette on the edge of a glass ashtray on the table, triggering a snowfall of grey powder. 'A group of us want to take the JDM in another direction.' Pip knew that Robert had been involved in the Jersey Democratic Movement for a while. At one stage he'd even considered joining them. He was all for a fairer society, and the island's government certainly needed to be hauled into the twentieth century. But that was the problem. Dad was part of that government, and for his own son to oppose him would bring huge public embarrassment. Pip couldn't do that to him. But he'd heard another rumour, that the JDM were trying to undermine the Germans. And that certainly did spark his interest.

'We've decided to re-form the Jersey Communist Party. We'll have to go underground with it, of course, but it's the only way to oppose those bloody fascists.' Robert's eyes glittered as he launched into a lengthy explanation, using words like *proletariat* and *bourgeoisie*.

When he finally stopped to draw breath, Pip leant forward. 'And where do I come in?'

'Will you join us?' Robert's voice was low and urgent.

'I'll need to give it some thought. It's awkward with Dad.'

Robert nodded. 'Your father need never know.'

'That may be true. But I'd like to find out more.' Pip's instinct told him to stall for time.

'Of course.' Robert took a swig of beer, then stared down at the table. He seemed to be weighing something up. Finally he said, 'Did you take Spanish for Highers?'

Pip laughed. 'No, languages weren't my strength. But Jenny did.'

'Jenny Robinson?'

'Yes.'

Robert's gaze was intense. 'Would she be able to translate some leaflets for us?'

'I'd imagine so. She's good at everything.'

'Excellent.'

'What's it for?' Pip didn't want to get Jenny into anything too dangerous, but he was intrigued as to what Robert was up to.

'We want to get something out to the Spanish slaves.'

'I see.' Since the end of last year, the Germans had been shipping Spanish men to Jersey, Republicans who'd fled to France after the civil war, and pressing them into service building tunnels and fortifications on the island. 'What would the leaflets be about?'

Robert sighed as though the answer was obvious. 'We've got a team of people listening to the BBC news and creating transcripts. We need someone to translate them into Spanish so the Republicans can read them. We've got a Gestetner machine at JCP headquarters, and we're going to smuggle leaflets into the camps with the delousing teams.'

Pip's skin prickled. 'I could help with that,' he said. 'I've managed to keep my wireless and I listen to the news most evenings.' He couldn't resist telling Robert about Jenny's clever hiding place. It was a risk, but he trusted him with anything anti-German.

'That's great,' said Robert. 'Welcome on board.'

Pip grabbed his glass and some of the beer sloshed over the top. He took a long slurp, uncertain afterwards whether his light-headedness was from the sudden surge of alcohol or the excitement. 'I'll ask Jenny about the Spanish as well. And I'll let you know about the other stuff.'

'Please do.' Robert raised his glass too. He glanced around the room quickly. 'To the party,' he said.

Pip mimed his gesture silently, but inside his head he was drinking to an opportunity to finally take action and get one over on the Germans. Some of the exhilaration he'd had at Saint-Malo bubbled up again. It was dangerous – he'd seen what had happened to some of those taken in for questioning – but worth the risk. And he knew Jenny felt as strongly as he did about resisting in whatever way they could. Working on the project with her might bring them even closer together too. His body fizzed with anticipation all the way home.

14

When Alice came in from her shift one warm June evening, Mum greeted her at the door looking even more anxious than usual.

'Are you all right?' Alice unpinned her hat, hung her cape over a chair and walked over to the sink to splash water on her face. She needed to cool herself down after the hot walk home.

'It's William.'

'William?' She turned round sharply. 'What's the matter?'

'I don't know.' Mum's face was drawn and haggard in the mellow light that slanted through the window. 'He's complaining of a sore throat, and his voice is hoarse.'

'Pharyngitis, probably. I'll have a look at him. Where is he?' Pharyngitis was painful but not life-threatening. William must have got run down. Despite Mum making sure he had as much food as she could spare, usually by going without herself, he was still looking a lot peakier than at the start of the war. They all were.

'He's in his bedroom.'

Alice ran up the stairs and into William's room. He was lying on his bed, visibly shivering despite being huddled under the covers, and his breathing was ragged.

'Will?'

He looked at her and whimpered.

Alice knelt down by the bedside. 'Let's have a look at your throat, dear. Open wide.'

He opened his mouth a fraction, but it was impossible to see inside. She felt his neck gently and the whimpering increased.

'I'm just going to pop down for a torch, Will. I'll be back in a minute.'

William didn't even answer, just looked at her through glassy eyes.

She sped downstairs and into the kitchen. Mum was chopping vegetables at the kitchen table.

'How is he?'

Alice bit the inside of her cheek. 'I don't know. I'm not sure that it is pharyngitis. Can you hand me the torch? I'll have a quick look at his throat.'

Mum took the torch off the windowsill. 'I'll come up with you.'

They both returned to William's room and Mum held his head still while Alice shone the light into his open mouth, pressing down on his tongue with her finger. It was as she feared. His throat and tonsils were covered with a grey substance. As he breathed out, she caught a whiff of sickly sweetness. 'All right, Will.' She removed her finger and the torch. 'All done.'

'What do you think it is?' Mum's voice was tinged with apprehension.

'Can you get him a warm drink?' Alice tried to signal with her eyes that she couldn't speak in front of him.

Mum seemed to understand and went back downstairs.

Above the sound of William's jagged breaths, Alice heard

Mum filling the kettle. She stroked his hair, smoothing it back from his forehead with slow movements. An image of Dad's bandage-covered head flashed into her mind and she sent up a silent prayer. Mum couldn't cope with any more losses. None of them could.

After Mum had returned with the drink and William had taken a few sips, wincing with the pain of swallowing, he lay back on the pillow. They both waited. The model de Havilland Dragon that Dad had helped him build and hang from the ceiling with fishing line tilted and swayed in the warm air. William had insisted on following the instructions to the letter. Dad had got impatient with him, convinced he knew a quicker way to build the plane. Then Will had had a tantrum and Dad had given in. They'd never built another model together.

Eventually Will's eyelids drooped, and they tiptoed back downstairs.

Mum automatically reached for the kettle again. 'So, what do you think it is?'

'There's been an outbreak of diphtheria at the hospital,' Alice said, trying to keep her voice level and not panic Mum too much. 'I think William has some of the symptoms.'

'Oh God, that's serious, isn't it?'

'It can be. We need to get some antitoxin in him quickly.' What Alice didn't tell Mum was that they'd treated so many diphtheria patients that the antitoxin stocks were running low. 'I'll phone Dr Morgan.' She knew he'd come if he could. He had been their family doctor all her life; he'd delivered Jenny and William and seen them all through measles, whooping cough, chickenpox and mumps. He'd been one of the first to visit after Dad had died. He was a good man.

Dr Morgan arrived within the hour. Alice took him upstairs, woke up William, who immediately started moaning again, and held his head carefully while the doctor examined him.

'Your diagnosis is correct, young lady,' the doctor said. 'I think the best thing would be for me to take him across to the General now. You can come with me in the car.'

'We're running low on antitoxin at the hospital,' said Alice. There was a hollow sensation in her legs, making it difficult for her to keep her balance.

The doctor nodded gravely. 'It's the same story everywhere. Bloody German troops brought the disease in, and now it's spread to the islanders. But at least we can monitor William in hospital.'

Alice wanted to say she could monitor him from home, but she knew Dr Morgan was right. The nurses could put him on a drip to save him having to drink. Normally she'd be nervous about how he'd cope in hospital, but he was so weak and ill she knew he wouldn't be any trouble. She'd be able to visit him around her shifts, but neither Mum nor Jenny would be allowed in. The hospital was closed to visitors because of the epidemic.

She rushed around collecting his pyjamas and wash things. At the last minute she popped in a couple of puzzle books. Goodness knows when he'd be able to sit up and do them, but it might keep him occupied when he recovered. If he recovered.

Dr Morgan carried him downstairs in a blanket and Alice helped lift him into the back of the car. Mum stood outside the house in the syrupy darkness, mute with anxiety. Alice's heart ached for her. She had to do all she could to help William get well.

* * *

148

William was taken to the emergency department, and Dr Morgan stood to one side as he was examined. Alice waited nervously at the end of the bed. After talking to the duty doctor in a low voice, too quietly for Alice to make out any words, Dr Morgan approached her.

'It's as you feared, my dear: diphtheria. He'll have to be in isolation.'

Alice nodded. Poor Will. But there was worse to come.

'The doctor confirmed there is no antitoxin left on the ward. All they can do is make William comfortable and hope for the best.' He put his hand on Alice's arm. 'Are you all right? You've gone very pale. Come and sit down.'

He led her to a seat, and she slumped onto it, relieved to no longer have to stand up. He passed her a glass of water. 'Drink this.'

She took the glass with shaking fingers and gulped down a few drops. She was dimly aware of all the activity going on around her: nurses replenishing the trestle tables in the middle of the ward with sterile dressings, rubber tubing, antiseptic and adhesive tape; more patients being brought in; curtains being drawn.

'Whatever am I going to do?' she whispered. Her gut twisted in a strange spasm.

'Alice.' Dr Morgan crouched down beside her, his kind grey eyes level with hers. 'It's not your fault William became ill and it's not your job to make him better.'

She took a shuddering breath. 'But Dad died on my watch.'

'No, he didn't.' The doctor's voice was firm. 'He died because the Germans bombed the harbour. You did all you could to make his last days comfortable. He died knowing how much you all loved him.'

He was right. She thought back to her last conversation with Dad. She still felt doubled up with grief at times, but knowing he had loved her, really loved her, brought some comfort at least. She'd never told Mum or Jenny about the conversation. It was something precious she kept close, returning to it whenever she felt low.

But William was only eleven. He had his whole life ahead of him. She couldn't let him die.

'You're looking a bit better now,' Dr Morgan said. 'I have to go back to my surgery, but I'll call in from time to time to see how William is doing.' He hesitated, looked intently at Alice, then whipped out his prescription pad and a pen. 'Look, this is a long shot, but I'll write you out a prescription for DAT.'

'But you said the hospital had run out.'

'I said there was none on the ward.' He gave her that intent look again. 'But I dare say the Germans will have some.'

'The *Germans*?'

He nodded. 'As I said, it's a long shot, but you could take the prescription over to their pharmacy and see if they'll give you the medication.' He scrawled something on the pad, tore off the sheet and handed it to her. 'Good luck, my dear.'

'Thank you,' Alice whispered, a faint hope fluttering in her chest.

She watched Dr Morgan's reassuring figure disappear down the ward, then transferred her gaze to William. He'd fallen asleep again, and his breathing seemed a little easier. She stumbled to her feet and made her way along the corridor. If the Germans had stores of antitoxin, as Dr Morgan thought, she would do all she could to get some for William. The doctor had given her a lifeline. She had to make it work.

The German medical team had been at the General for over a year now. They'd taken over the whole of the first floor of the hospital. There'd been a mad scramble at the time to reorganise the facilities, but they'd all got used to it eventually. The Germans had also taken over the main operating room, leaving the locals with only the small maternity theatre. The male geriatrics had even had to be rehoused in the Gloucester Hotel. Yet somehow or other the Jersey medical staff still managed to admit, treat and discharge patients. And the fact that most of them recovered was down to their sheer hard work and skill.

Alice hadn't visited the first floor since the Germans had arrived. She just took the lift or the stairs to the second each morning. If she passed a German doctor in the corridor, she kept her eyes averted and muttered a good morning or good afternoon in response to their greeting. But other than that, she had as little to do with them as possible. Now, as she hurried through the doors, she could see that it was completely changed from when she'd worked there in men's surgical. Everything looked new. They must have had equipment brought over from Germany, she thought, remembering the rickety beds in her own ward that had to be levelled with folded-up bits of newspaper, the thinning blankets and lumpy pillows.

The pharmacy had a wide window through which she could see neatly stacked shelves of medicine, each clearly labelled.

She placed her hands on the wooden counter to steady herself, her legs weak with fear.

Eventually a severe-looking man in uniform appeared. '*Bitte?*'

Alice didn't know a word of German. She drew the prescription out of her pocket and gave it to the pharmacist.

The man shrugged. 'This is in English.'

'Yes, it was given to me by Dr Morgan. We've run out of antitoxin on our wards.'

'But I am a chemist for the German doctors. We do not treat English patients.' His words were heavily accented, but their meaning was clear enough.

Alice's heart thrummed. 'I know. But my little brother is very ill with diphtheria. I'm worried he'll die without it. Dr Morgan was hoping you'd be kind enough to help.'

The chemist shrugged again. 'That is regrettable. But I am afraid I can only supply drugs for German patients.'

Alice felt tears prickle the back of her eyes. 'I'm begging you,' she whispered.

The pharmacist handed back the prescription. 'It is not allowed. I am sorry. I hope your brother recovers.' His tone was mild, but Alice could see from his face that he was not going to change his mind. She put the paper back in her pocket, trying not to cry in front of him, then stumbled back down the corridor.

What on earth was she going to do? The only other option was to send to France for the medication Will needed. But that would take ages, and it could well arrive too late – assuming the French even had any. For one mad moment she considered asking Rebekah to help steal some from the Germans. Perhaps

Rebekah could lure the chemist out of the pharmacy on some pretext, then Alice could vault over the counter and scan the shelves until she found the antitoxin. But what if they were caught? She'd be no use to Will in a German prison.

She needed to clear her head before she went back to Will, so she took the lift to the ground floor and walked out of the hospital. As soon as she was away from the entrance, she slumped against the wall and put her face in her hands. Dr Morgan had been right: it was German bombs that had killed Dad, not her lack of care, but she had to do all she could for William. An image sidled into her mind of the kitchen table with another place empty – just her, Mum and Jenny in a desolate group; then she saw Binkie sitting forlornly in his cage and imagined the de Havilland Dragon hanging motionless in Will's silent bedroom. Pierced with grief, she bent over, trying to sob quietly, when all she really wanted to do was howl.

'*Was ist los?*'

She opened her eyes and stood up, frantically scrabbling in her pocket for a handkerchief. A tall German doctor stood in front of her, looking concerned.

She shook her head. 'Nothing.' She certainly wasn't going to tell this man about William, despite his kind eyes. She took a quick look at his name badge: *Dr Holz*. It rang a faint bell.

'Please tell me,' he said. 'I may be able to help.' His English was good and his tone kind. A few locks of blond hair had escaped his cap.

Suddenly she was back in the operating theatre – before the Germans had taken it over – helping Sir Andrew Beaumont with an appendectomy. The patient was a young German soldier with blue eyes and fair hair. She even remembered his name. Stefan Holz. Could this be the same man? She had no idea how common the name was in Germany.

The right thing to do was to walk away. To get back to William and talk to the ward sister about how they could help him. But her legs refused to move. And all at once she was telling Dr Holz about her brother's illness.

'Would you like me to get you some antisera?' His smile revealed straight white teeth and light curves around his mouth.

'Really? You could do that?' The tight ball of anxiety in her stomach loosened a little.

'Sure. I also have a patient with diphtheria. I will ask for a bigger dosage than I require. Please. Wait here.' He hurried off.

Alice's mind whirled. A minute ago she'd been in despair; now it seemed William would get the treatment he needed. She just hoped it would be in time.

The doctor had been so gentle. There was no haughtiness, no abrasive orders, just concern for someone in trouble. Sir Andrew had told her that the desire to heal transcended war and national boundaries. Perhaps this man felt the same way.

She wiped a film of sweat from her forehead with the back of her hand and pushed a damp tendril of hair back under her cap. Then she leant her head against the wall and closed her eyes, acutely aware of the thudding of her heart.

Fifteen minutes later, Dr Holz was back with a small package. 'Here you are.'

'Thank you so much. This will make all the difference to William. It could even save his life.' She tried to stretch her lips into a smile.

He bowed his head. 'Let me know how he progresses.'

'I will.' She smoothed the surface of the package, weighing up whether to tell him about the appendectomy she'd assisted at. She decided to risk it. 'Two years ago I was in the operating theatre helping one of our doctors perform an operation on a young man. I think his name was Stefan Holz.'

Surprise rippled across his features. 'That was me! So you were the theatre nurse?'

'I was.'

'Then I'm even more glad to have helped you today. You and your surgeon probably saved my life.'

Alice looked at the ground. She didn't know what to say.

'Now go and save your brother,' said Stefan Holz.

'I will. Thank you.' She made her way back to the second floor with lighter steps, feeling his presence keenly behind her as she went.

15

Jenny wasn't sure how she felt about Alice's explanation. 'You got the antitoxin from a *German*?'

'A German doctor, yes. It was either that or let Will take his chance against diphtheria. Lots of patients die from it without treatment.'

Jenny glanced at Alice's pale, pinched face as she stood in the kitchen, still in her cape and shoes. Her eyes were blood-shot and her skin was blotchy. Perhaps she'd been a bit harsh. It was a huge relief that William was now getting the treatment he needed; she was just concerned whether this doctor could be trusted. 'And are you confident this medicine will work?' She didn't like to ask Alice how she could be sure it was the genuine article and not some bogus remedy that he'd palmed off on her.

Alice frowned. 'There are no guarantees. But he has a much better chance with a DAT than without.'

Jenny nodded. Maybe she was overreacting. There was still a risk that the doctor's motives were questionable, but the alternative, William dying from diphtheria, was unthinkable. She lit the ring under the kettle, then returned to her seat at the kitchen table. Before Alice came in, she'd been trying to make some bramble tea. The berries were still tight green bullets on the bushes, but the leaves were edible. She'd picked some in the lane earlier and had been cutting them up to go in the teapot. They hadn't tasted real tea for months, although Alice had told her there were still some supplies in the hospital, kept under lock and key. When people went in to give blood, they were given a cup of tea afterwards and a voucher for chocolate. Some of Jenny's friends had become donors just for the rewards. It was tempting, although Jenny felt she should only give blood for the right reasons, not the ever-present craving for long-denied food. A question of principles really. Like accepting medicine from German doctors.

She stood up again to pick up the kettle, which was now shrieking on the stove, and poured hot water into the teapot. She swilled it around, tipped it into the sink, then added the bramble leaves and more water. A sweet smell oozed through the kitchen, before it was extinguished by the tea cosy.

'Shall I get the cups?' Alice's voice sounded weary.

'No, you sit down. I'll do it.'

She slumped onto a chair, still with her cape on, and massaged the space between her eyes. 'Thanks.'

Jenny reached into the cupboard and put the cups on the table. They'd stopped using milk in their tea ages ago. It was too scarce and expensive. The Germans took such a huge share of supplies these days. If Mum managed to get some, she always gave it to William. In other circumstances Jenny would have been glad he'd at least have access to good food in hospital, but with diphtheria he probably couldn't even eat.

She gave the teapot a stir and poured some of the hot liquid into Alice's cup before passing it to her. Alice blew on the surface, took a sip and grimaced.

'That bad?' Jenny poured a cup for herself.

Alice shrugged. 'It might have been more palatable with a grain or two of sugar.'

'Sorry. Run out.'

She nodded. 'Where's Mum?'

'Gone for a walk. Said she was too knotted up to stay in the house any longer.' Jenny sipped her own tea. At least it was hot. And her anxiety about Will had dulled the usual hunger. 'Tell me about this German doctor. What made him give you this medicine?'

'Nothing to tell. He did a kind thing when he saw how upset I was.'

'Will he get into trouble for it?'

'I wouldn't imagine so, even though they're not strictly allowed to give us their medicine. In fact . . .' Alice stopped and looked out of the window. Jenny noticed the faintest of blushes creep up her face.

'Go on.'

'Nothing.'

She was about to press further when the back door handle rattled and Mum came in from her walk. Her hair was wild and her face white with worry. The exercise didn't seem to have given her any comfort.

Jenny stood up to make more tea as Alice told Mum about Will's medication.

'Thank God,' said Mum, drawing out a chair and sagging onto it. 'So you think he has a chance?'

Alice cupped her hands round Mum's. 'Better than a chance,' she said.

Jenny smiled at the look of relief on Mum's face. But she

hadn't forgotten Alice's expression earlier. There was more to her interaction with this German doctor than she was letting on.

When Pip came round that evening, Jenny told him about Alice gaining favours from the German doctor in the form of the diphtheria antitoxin. She'd taken the volume of Shakespeare into the shed as usual, sandwiching it between two maths textbooks in case anyone saw her.

Pip eased the wireless set out of its hiding place and placed it on Dad's old workbench. 'I don't know why you're being hard on her, Jen. She did what she had to.'

Jenny gnawed on a fingernail. 'I know. I'm sure I'd have done the same in her position. Anything to save William. It's just that I hate Germans so much.'

'We both do.' He reached up to remove a flowerpot from a shelf and drew out the circle of wood that fitted neatly into the base, revealing a false bottom in which nestled the headphones. He put them on, attached them to the wireless and started to inch the tiny dial backwards and forwards.

Jenny opened her bag and drew out a notebook and two pencils. She knew better than to talk when Pip was trying to tune in to the BBC news. It was such a delicate operation, and if she made any noise, he would shush her before returning to his task with a frown. She looked round the shed. She loved how she still felt Dad's presence so strongly here. He seemed to have faded from the house now. Mum had eventually cut up his pyjamas for dusters, although his clothes remained. She'd packed them up in a suitcase one drizzly afternoon, and Jenny and Alice had helped her lever it into the loft – where it was to remain until William was big enough to inherit the garments. Jenny had kept his books, but otherwise it felt as if all traces of him had disappeared. She'd been surprised how few items she actually associated with her father. There were a few pairs of horn-rimmed glasses, a polished wooden box of fountain pens, which he used for marking and filling in the crossword puzzle, and the brown glass bottle of aspirin he kept by his side of the bed. Poor Dad always suffered from headaches. All the other household things belonged to the rest of the family.

But the shed had been his domain, and its earthy smell evoked him more strongly than anything else. Here she could still picture him taking chrysanthemum cuttings, dipping each stem into the little tub of rooting powder, then transferring it carefully to a new pot of soil; splitting dahlia tubers with his penknife, then wrapping them up in old newspaper to be stored for the winter; pricking out lettuce seedlings in the spring. The childhood ghosts of her and Alice hovered there too. Jenny sitting on an upturned flowerpot listening to Dad talking about Fermat's last theorem or some such, and Alice calmly pushing radish or carrot seeds into earth-filled trays. They'd been different even then. But there'd been such a strong bond between them. *The lighthouse sisters*. How she missed that closeness. She hadn't felt it in years. She really missed the sister she'd known then.

Sometimes Jenny wished she could be practical like Alice. It was hard to switch off the thoughts that crashed around her brain all day long and focus on something physical. She even envied Alice's job. Nursing gave her a structure, a purpose – and wore her out so she could sleep soundly at night. Jenny's days were haphazard: sometimes spending hours queuing for food, other times helping Mum with the cooking, or doing the housework. But none of it felt very fulfilling. And none of it stopped the incessant thoughts about Dad, or Pip, or Cambridge. And now, of course, there was William to worry about as well. Damn those bloody Germans. They'd wrecked everything. She was bitterly resentful that she hadn't found a more active way to retaliate, although her work with Pip was helping a little. She'd been pleased and flattered when he'd asked her to translate the leaflets into Spanish. But now she'd got a taste for resistance work, she wanted more. She'd do anything to thwart the enemy.

'Got it.' Pip had stopped twiddling and was listening now, a satisfied smile on his face. 'Are you ready?'

Jenny tore a page from her notebook and handed it to him, together with one of the pencils. As he started writing furiously, she leant over his shoulder and read his notes. *Further heavy bombing of industrial sites in Germany*, he'd written. She thought for a bit, then scribbled: *Más bombardeos intensos de zonas industrials en Alemania*.

She looked at his next sentence: *Japanese forces invade Attu and Kiska*. That was easier: *Las fuerzas japonesas invaden Attu y Kiska*.

Pip glanced across and grinned, then made a thumbs-up sign. Something fluttered in Jenny's chest. Thank goodness she'd been well taught by Señorita Pérez at school.

They stayed in the shed for another half an hour, Pip writing and Jenny translating. By the time they emerged, it was dark outside, the garden shadowy and a pale crescent moon hanging in a navy sky. She could hear Binkie moving around on his straw bedding and realised with a pang that he wouldn't have been fed for a while. She grabbed a handful of damp grass and thrust it through the wires of his cage. Binkie started munching, his little teeth chips of white in the gloom.

Pip put his arm round Jenny's shoulders and his lips grazed her hair. 'Thanks for your help. More good news to pass on.'

'Yes,' said Jenny. 'Perhaps things are on the turn.'

'Let's hope so.'

She still felt guilty that she couldn't think of him as anything more than a friend, but it was a relief that he was channelling his energy into their work. There were bigger battles to fight now.

'I'll put the book back.' She gestured to the Shakespeare.

'All right. I need to get these notes down to HQ straight away. Do you want to come with me?'

She shook her head. 'I ought to stay home. Just in case there's news of William.'

'Of course,' said Pip. 'I'll be off then.' He kissed her on the cheek. 'Same time tomorrow?'

'Yes, please.'

He went to set off, then turned back. 'Stay strong,' he said. 'I'm sure William will recover.'

'I hope so.'

She watched as he skirted round the side of the house and headed out into the lane. He'd been elated by the news on the wireless. Jenny loved it when he was buoyed up by activity, his eyes shining, his voice crackling with energy. It was infectious too. She felt exhilarated by the evening's work. She loved how they performed as a team, Pip listening and writing, her translating. He'd go over to the cottage now that served as

JCP headquarters, type the notes up as a leaflet, then run off copies on the Gestetner. It was someone else's job to distribute the leaflets to the Spanish workers. She imagined how for every piece of positive news of the Allies beating back the Germans, word would spread round the dormitory, each man starting the next day with a little more hope in his heart to keep him going, despite the brutal conditions of their work. Pip would never know the danger of active combat, but he was certainly doing his bit for the war effort now. They both were. And somehow they were doing it for Dad too.

16

As Alice arrived for her shift the next morning, Stefan Holz was outside the entrance, smoking. When he saw her, he took one last drag on his cigarette, threw it down and ground it in with his heel.

'Good morning.' A shy·smile lit up his face. It was almost as if he was waiting for her.

Alice stiffened. She didn't want anyone to see her fraternising with a German, even if he was a doctor, but he'd been so kind yesterday. She couldn't ignore him.

She forced a smile and a greeting in return.

'How is your brother?'

'I'm just going in to find out,' she replied. 'We didn't hear anything overnight, so we're hoping that it'll be positive news.'

'DAT is a good medicine. I am sure it will make him feel better.' His English was excellent, with only a trace of an accent.

'Thank you for getting it for me. I didn't know what else to do.'

That smile again. 'I was glad to help. I have a younger brother at home. Dietrich. He's twelve.' His eyes had a faraway look now.

'Just a little bit older than William,' Alice exclaimed. 'You must miss him.' Then she stopped herself. What was she doing, sympathising with a German?

'I do. Very much.'

She nodded. She was about to make her excuses and rush on in to see Will when Stefan asked, 'What time do you have lunch?'

'Um . . . about half past twelve.'

'Good. I could try to meet you here then? You can let me know how William is.'

She hesitated, reluctant and unsure. But anything less than agreement would look ungrateful, and he really didn't seem like the others. She hoped her instincts were right and that he was a good person, not someone waiting to take advantage of her. 'Of course. Thank you.' She turned to go inside. When she glanced back several seconds later, Stefan Holz was still looking at her.

The sister was at her desk as Alice rushed up to the isolation ward.

'Nurse Robinson.' She beamed at Alice.

Hopefully that was a good sign. 'How is William today, Sister?' Alice asked.

The cheerfulness persisted. 'He's had a good night. Such a quiet little lamb.'

It became easier to breathe. Since yesterday, her lungs had felt so restricted. 'Thank you. So you think the antitoxin is working?' She'd told the staff yesterday that the Germans had donated the medicine but had made it clear the gesture was a one off. Sister had given her a searching look but hadn't questioned her further. Alice wasn't sure what conclusion she'd come to but at least she seemed focused on William's recovery now.

'Well, the doctor hasn't done his rounds yet, but William is certainly no worse. And his temperature is down.'

'That is good news. May I see him?'

Sister hesitated. 'You're not supposed to. And he was asleep last time I checked on him. Maybe you could just look through the window.'

'Of course. Thank you.' It was better than nothing, and there was no point disturbing him.

Alice made her way to William's room and peered through the small porthole window. He was still asleep, his dark hair tousled on the pillow, his mouth slack. But even from a distance, she could see he was a better colour. What a mercy Dr Holz had given her the antitoxin. She never thought she'd be grateful to a German but now a warmth towards him surged up in her.

'I'll pop back at lunchtime,' she said to Sister.

Sister nodded. 'Very well. We should have some more news by then.'

Alice dashed back to William at the end of her morning shift and Sister told her the doctor had confirmed clear signs of improvement. 'We are still very cautious at this stage,' she said, 'but the antitoxin definitely seems to be working.'

'Thank you, Sister.' Alice was almost dizzy with relief.

She glanced at her watch as she left the ward: 12.30. All morning, in between the usual duties, she'd been wrestling in her mind whether she should meet Dr Holz. She concluded he deserved to know about William's progress. He'd taken a risk to help her, after all, and seemed genuinely concerned about his welfare.

She was panting slightly as she neared the entrance, and suddenly conscious of her flushed, shiny face, and the wisps of hair that had escaped her cap. She darted into the ladies' room to repair the damage as best she could. They'd long since run out of face powder on the island, although nurses were strictly forbidden to wear it anyway, but at least she could blot some of the moisture from her nose and cheeks, and tidy her hair.

Stefan Holz was already waiting outside. Again the shy smile. He didn't have the swagger other Germans did; in fact he looked almost apologetic as he greeted her. Was he unsure himself about their meeting?

But when she told him about William, he beamed. 'I'm so pleased to hear that. I think he will continue to improve now.'

'I hope so. Thank you again, Dr Holz.'

'Please call me Stefan.' He ran a palm down his jacket. 'And I never asked *your* name.'

Alice hesitated. Telling him her Christian name felt like another level of intimacy, but she couldn't let herself be rude. 'Alice,' she replied quietly.

The door burst open and a gaggle of probationers emerged. They stopped talking when they saw Alice and Stefan together, and she was aware of curious glances, then their voices rose again as they strode off towards the seafront.

Stefan gave her a regretful look. 'I'm sorry if I am causing you embarrassment.'

Alice half turned to hide the flush that had travelled up her face at the nurses' reaction. 'That's all right,' she murmured, even though it wasn't really.

The doctor bent down to retrieve a small basket that had been on the ground on the other side of him. Alice hadn't noticed it before. 'I wonder if you would do me the honour of having lunch with me?' he asked.

She smoothed down her uniform. If she wasn't careful, people would start calling her a Jerrybag. But there was something rather touching about the fact that he'd packed up a picnic, even if the sky did look a bit overcast. And once again she told herself she shouldn't be ungrateful to the man who might have saved her brother's life.

There was a large baguette protruding from the basket, and its yeasty smell reminded her how hungry she was. She hadn't had a fresh baguette in months. Even the local cabbage loaves were quite hard to come by these days.

'Thank you.' She hoped he didn't want to eat by the seafront. She couldn't bear to face those nurses again or submit herself to the disapproval of the crowds on the esplanade. Instead, though, he led her round the side of the hospital and into the small garden, where mercifully they were the only occupants.

They sat on a bench next to a flower bed crammed with lush delphinium spires, roses and peonies. A light breeze rustled the leaves of an overhanging sycamore, and the air smelt damp from an earlier downpour. Alongside the bread, he'd brought a pat of creamy butter wrapped in greaseproof paper, a slab of ripe Camembert and a bottle of ginger beer. There were tomatoes and some crisp red apples too. A feast. And certainly food she hadn't seen for a long time. It was clear the Germans were well fed at the islanders' expense.

Alice glanced across at his profile. He had a strong chin and a long, straight nose, with lightly tanned skin and dark eyelashes. She thought back to the young man on the operating table. Time had chiselled his features, firming their soft contours and tightening his jawline, but his smile was gentle, his expression diffident.

At first, she was worried that someone would come into the garden, or look out of the window and see them. A couple of times she glanced up sharply, thinking she'd heard voices, but nobody appeared, and after a bit she started to relax. Stefan asked her about her family, her job, her friends, and in return he told her about his life back home in Germany, where he'd first decided to become a doctor. He'd been drafted into the 15th Medical Battalion in 1939, already wary of fighting a war whose cause he'd never believed in.

'My father was in the last war,' he told her. 'He saw the terrible suffering at first hand and has been a pacifist ever since. It nearly killed him when I had to enlist. But it is of some comfort that I spend most of my time at the hospital. All I want to do is make people well. I hate violence of any kind.' He looked grim.

Alice nodded. To her shame, she realised she'd never thought about how some Germans might feel. They were just the enemy, her father's killers: one murderous mass, not individuals with their own beliefs. Stefan had a family who cared about him – and clearly a father with principles. He'd mentioned a brother earlier.

'Do you have any other brothers and sisters?' she asked him.

'Yes. A sister, Elsa.'

She pictured him sitting with his family round the dining room table, his siblings hanging on his every word, his mother lovingly serving up dumplings or whatever they ate in Germany, his father tormented with memories and full of anxiety for his elder son.

'Do you miss your family?'

'Of course.'

She felt her cheeks glowing. Perhaps it was a silly question.

But Stefan didn't look annoyed. Instead he looked sad. 'I miss them a lot,' he added. 'Elsa's friends want her to join the BDM, but she isn't keen.'

'The BDM?'

'The Bund Deutscher Mädel,' said Stefan. He searched for a translation. 'It is the girls' wing of the Nazi Party youth movement. I worry she might be forced to belong against her will.'

'I see.' Again, Alice had assumed that nearly all Germans supported Hitler, but it was clear that Stefan's family were against everything he stood for. In some ways they were victims just as much as the Channel Islanders – forced to tolerate a regime they were fundamentally opposed to. He'd had no choice about joining up. And if he had, I'd never have met him, she thought.

Half an hour passed before she knew it. He gave her a regretful smile as they walked back together to the hospital entrance.

'May I see you again?' he asked tentatively, taking out a packet of cigarettes.

Alice couldn't answer. She'd really enjoyed his company. She could talk so easily to him. It also felt good to have someone asking her about herself, and interested in her answers. She hadn't had that for so long. But nothing changed the fact that they were at war; her father had been killed by Stefan's comrades, and she didn't want to be seen consorting with the enemy.

'Maybe,' she finally said.

He nodded. 'Just another lunch, perhaps? I could bring a picnic again.'

Alice's stomach had relished the feeling of being sated, the bread and cheese warming her body, but she certainly wasn't going to be bribed. And was it fair to the other islanders, who lived on such meagre amounts of food, to be gorging herself on abundant supplies? Especially those donated by the enemy.

She decided to be honest. 'I don't know.'

He bowed his head as if he understood. 'Please think about it,' he said. 'My offer is always there.'

Alice smiled her thanks and disappeared into the hospital, leaving Stefan to his cigarette and his thoughts.

When Alice visited William at the end of her shift, Sister assured her he'd continued to recover, even managing a little soup for lunch. He was awake when she peered through the window to his room, responding to her wave with a wan smile. As she glimpsed his improved colour and more alert expression, she thought of Dr Holz again. She owed him so much. But just how far could her gratitude extend?

She walked back along Rouge Bouillon, skirting round groups of German soldiers. Not one of them moved out of her way, and often she had to step into the road – even, once, into a puddle, which soaked her shoes and stockings – in order to avoid them. The hard eyes and raucous laughter followed her down the street. So different to Stefan's amiable smile and shy manner. She wondered what Rebekah would think of him. Her friend had been living more and more on edge over the last two years, and although she was often the first to see the good in people, she was all too aware what some Germans could do.

Back in October, she'd had to register as Jewish, and there was now a large red 'J' stamped on her identity card. There'd been reports of other Jews on the island deported to unknown destinations, and she lived in constant fear of a knock on the door. Alice was always anxious for her safety, another reason to be cautious with Stefan.

As she turned into Midvale Road, she became aware of a strange noise behind her. It didn't sound human, but neither did it have the military precision of machinery, or marching men. She looked over her shoulder and saw a ragged line of people – she supposed they were men; it was hard to tell as they were so thin and frail. They were shuffling slowly on bandaged feet. Their clothes were little more than threadbare sacks. Her heart squeezed with anger and sadness. When she'd been at school, the art teacher had shown them a picture of *The Last Judgement* by Jan van Eyck, and there was something about these men that reminded her of the tortured, emaciated figures in the painting. They must have been the foreign slaves she'd heard about. She couldn't imagine islanders looking that haggard, despite the current food shortages.

As they came closer, an appalling smell of sour sweat and excrement accompanied them. Horror coiled in her guts. She flattened herself against a shop to let them by, trying not to show her revulsion. Instead, she glanced down at their feet. Most wore shoes of scuffed and faded leather. One man looked as though his feet were shod in tar and gravel. She looked up and saw their shaved heads, their sallow faces and skeletal bodies as they stared at her with haunted eyes.

She walked home appalled.

* * *

She told Jenny about her encounter as they lay in their respective beds later that evening. They'd raided their secret box for apples and were eating them while they talked.

'They'll be the Organisation Todt workers, poor things. Pip told me they've been sent across by the Nazis to help fortify the island. Hitler's orders, apparently. They're mostly foreign prisoners – subhuman, according to the Führer.' She said the last word mockingly.

'It's *in*human. They must keep them half starved.'

'Yes, and work them to death. In fact they don't care if they do die – there are always more to take their place.' Jenny's mouth twisted. 'And I think Todt means "dead" in German. So appropriate.'

Alice thought how hard they strove in the hospital to preserve life, and shook her head in disgust at this brutality. 'You seem to know a lot about them.'

'Pip fills me in,' said Jenny quickly. Alice wondered if she knew more than she was letting on, but didn't dare press her – she would only clam up.

She changed the subject. 'I had lunch with Dr Holz today, the man who got William's medicine for me.'

'Why? Since when do you fraternise with the enemy? You'll get labelled, you know that.' Jenny's eyes were fierce in the darkness.

Alice's chest prickled with anxiety. Perhaps it hadn't been a wise decision to tell Jenny about the lunch. 'Of course I know. But he went out of his way to help. Will might not have survived without him.'

'Then just say thank you, or give him a bottle of Dad's old blackberry wine or something. Nothing more.' Jenny prised out a bruised part of her apple with her teeth and spat it into her hand.

Fraternise. But it hadn't felt like that at lunchtime, sitting in the garden, the hot sun on their faces, roses and peonies imbuing the air with their fragrance. Alice munched on her own apple, imagining it was the one she'd eaten with Stefan. 'But he's not like most Germans. He didn't want to join up and he doesn't believe in the war. He's a doctor, not a soldier.'

Jenny snorted. 'Very admirable. He might have cured William, but it was his comrades that killed Dad.' She hurled her apple core towards the bin. It missed.

'I know.' To her own ears, Alice's voice sounded thin. 'But if Stefan had been at the harbour that day, he'd have tried to save him, I'm sure of it.'

Silence. Animosity came at her in waves from the other bed. Eventually Jenny said, 'Are you attracted to him?'

Alice felt heat spread across her cheeks and was grateful for the cover of darkness. 'Of course not! Just grateful.'

'Then leave it at that.' Jenny turned onto her other side to end the conversation, and very soon was breathing deeply.

Alice got out of bed to put her apple core in the bin, along with the one Jenny had thrown onto the floor, then lay on her back in the darkness, stung by her sister's words. It was clear Jenny thought she was on the way to being a Jerrybag. How dare she label her when all Alice had done was spend her lunch hour talking to a good man who'd done an act of kindness? Had Jenny forgotten that it had been her own recklessness in deciding to stay on the island that had caused Dad to be at the harbour in the first place?

She stopped herself – that was unfair, it was the war that

was to blame. But she had found it hard to watch Jenny and Pip together, witnessing Pip's wasted feelings for her sister. They would have been a well-matched couple; she didn't know why Jenny couldn't see it. She'd long since realised it had been stupid of her to think that she could have something with Pip. He'd been Jenny's all along, whether she wanted him or not. But what Alice was now feeling in Stefan's company was something entirely new, and different . . . How could he be the enemy?

17

Alice was still at the hospital, and Mum was out queuing for food when Jenny heard the sound of tyres on their drive. She peered out of the lounge window and saw Dr Morgan's car pulling up. He got out, scooped William up from the back seat and carried him into the house. Jenny opened the front door to show him in. She was relieved to see that Will's face had lost the pallor of the early days of his illness and his eyes were a lot brighter. Even the fact that he was squirming in the doctor's arms and refusing to allow Jenny to prise his puzzle books from his grasp was a good sign.

'Thank you very much, Doctor,' she said. 'May I trouble you to take William up to his room?'

'No,' said William. 'I want to stay down here with you.'

Jenny shrugged and pointed to Dad's old armchair by the fire in the lounge.

The doctor placed William in the chair and they made him comfortable. He was immediately engrossed in a crossword.

'Lad had a lucky escape,' said Dr Morgan as he followed Jenny back into the kitchen. 'Thank goodness we managed to get hold of the antitoxin.'

'I understand it was a German doctor who gave Alice the medicine.' Jenny was conscious of the stiffness in her voice. Alice had told her she'd confided in Dr Morgan about William's rescuer.

'Indeed. Stefan Holz is a good man. A skilled practitioner and a compassionate human being.'

'So unusual for a Kraut,' Jenny couldn't resist adding.

Dr Morgan gave her a sharp look. 'He had nothing to gain by becoming involved, you know. He could have got into trouble for procuring the antitoxin. But he saw how upset your sister was and did his best to help.'

Jenny nodded. The doctor was right. She really shouldn't be so prickly. 'We're grateful to him,' she said. 'And also to you, of course, for acting so quickly.' She picked up the kettle. 'Will you stay for a cup of tea – not that it's the genuine article, I'm afraid.'

Dr Morgan glanced down at his fob watch. 'Thank you, Jenny, but I need to get back to the surgery.'

She saw him out, assuring him once again of their gratitude. By the time she'd returned to William, he'd fallen asleep, so she tiptoed back to the kitchen, took a bowl of beetroots from the larder and started to prepare them for supper. She didn't know what food Mum would bring home – if any – but at least beetroots were still plentiful. Even if they did give you terrible wind.

She'd just opened the rabbit hutch and deposited the beetroot peelings in front of an eager Binkie when Mum arrived back. Sometimes Jenny would catch sight of her mother when she didn't realise she was being observed, and register how grim and sad she looked. New lines had appeared on her face in the last couple of years, none of them from laughter. And she looked more shrunken than ever in her patched winter coat.

'William's home.' Jenny took the half-empty shopping bag

from her. 'Dr Morgan brought him back this afternoon. He's in the lounge.'

A rare smile appeared on Mum's face. 'Thank God. I'll pop in and see him.'

'He was asleep when I last looked,' said Jenny. 'But do check again if you want.'

While her mother went next door, she picked up the shopping bag and inspected its contents: a small block of butter wrapped in greaseproof paper, a bunch of carrots and a tin of sardines. She opened the tin using the key on the side, scooped the fish out of the oily liquid, and divided it four ways. Not that there was much to go round. A good knob of butter would make the carrots more palatable, but she didn't dare use any of Mum's precious ration. It would have to last a whole week.

By the time Mum returned to the kitchen, supper was well under way.

'Thanks, dear,' she said, glancing round the room. The beetroots were already in a pan of water on the stove, and the meat was evenly distributed between four plates. She dropped a kiss on Jenny's head. 'And to think you were never my practical daughter. Dad would be proud of you.' She sat down at the table.

Jenny suppressed the obvious reply. 'How was William?' she asked instead, scrubbing her hands under the tap to get rid of the beetroot stains. She didn't want to look like Lady Macbeth.

'Awake and asking for some food.'

'Excellent. I'll just get the carrots on, then I'll take him in a glass of milk.' They'd been saving some from their allowance for his return, in the hope of building him up, although it looked as though hospital food had already done a good job. Dr Morgan had panted under the strain of lifting him into the house.

But before she could reach for a knife, there was a sudden rap on the front door. Mum's frightened eyes met hers. They weren't expecting visitors, and Alice would never knock. The neighbours all used the back entrance. Jenny got shakily to her feet, stumbled down the hall and opened the door a fraction. The gap was filled with a flash of grey-green wool that could only belong to a German soldier. Her mind fizzed with fear.

'Good evening.' The voice was quiet, diffident even, not the harsh tones she had expected.

She pulled the door a fraction wider, revealing a tall, slim figure with – it had to be said – a gentle face and shy eyes. He thrust a basket of food at her. Jenny peered inside and saw a hunk of ham, a handful of Jersey Royals, a cucumber, some boiled sweets and four ripe peaches. She hadn't seen some of these items for a long time.

'Forgive me for the interruption,' said the man. 'My name is Dr Holz and I have brought these for William. I came also to enquire after his health.'

Jenny's heartbeat slowed a little at the kind words, but she was still on her guard. The Germans always had some ulterior motive.

'Would you mind if I came in?'

She hesitated. What if he suddenly insisted on searching the house and found the wireless? Perhaps the food was just a cover to put them off their guard.

He must have seen her indecision, as he lowered the basket

onto the doorstep and held up his palms towards her as if in surrender. 'I can see this is difficult for you,' he said. 'I will leave the food for William. I do hope he continues to get well. And please tell Alice I called.'

Jenny felt a frisson of indignation that he'd called her sister by her Christian name, ignoring hospital protocols. And such an overfamiliar gesture, coming from a German. But then she realised this was the man who'd got hold of the medicine for William and possibly saved his life. She swallowed. 'Please come in,' she asked.

He smiled his acceptance and followed her down the hall.

At the sight of her daughter leading a German soldier into her kitchen, Mum leapt to her feet, the chair skittering from under her, her hand to her chest.

'It's all right, Mum. This is Dr Holz. The man who helped William,' Jenny said. She kept her eyes on her mother's face to avoid her gaze shifting to the bookshelf, although the temptation to do so was immense. Even if he was a good German, he'd still be honour-bound to turn them in if he came across the wireless.

Mum nodded, mute with shock.

Jenny righted the chair and sat her mother down. 'Alice told us about Dr Holz, remember?'

Mum nodded again, her face still white.

'And he's brought us some food for William.' Jenny deposited the basket she'd retrieved from the doorstep on the kitchen table. She noticed Mum taking a quick peek inside.

'May I see William?' the doctor asked. He had a sweep of blond hair across his forehead, and intelligent blue eyes.

'Of course. Follow me.' It was probably safer to take him

into the lounge rather than risk him lingering in the kitchen. In any case, the beetroots were boiling furiously on the stove, imbuing the room with their earthy smell and steaming up the windows.

It was obvious from his reaction that William had seen Dr Holz before. Perhaps he'd visited him in the hospital too. The doctor examined William's throat, felt his glands and listened to his chest before smiling at Jenny. 'I think he will make a full recovery.'

'Thank you,' said Jenny. 'And thank you for getting the antitoxin for him.'

Dr Holz nodded, patted Will's shoulder and turned to go. To Jenny's surprise, William thanked him too. That was so unlike him. It took a lot for him to trust people.

She showed the doctor out and returned to find Mum eagerly slicing the cucumber. 'What a kind gesture,' she said.

Jenny sat down and chewed her thumbnail. Was everyone in her family enthralled by this German? 'William seems a lot better.'

Mum smiled her agreement, her cheeks flushed. She looked more relaxed than she had in months.

Jenny had just finished setting the table when Alice arrived home half an hour later. By now each plate was piled high with fish, meat and vegetables, the items carefully separated on William's; still the only way he was prepared to eat. Mum had added a few slices of ham to the sardines, having wrapped the rest in muslin and placed it in the larder. Jenny had taken William's carefully arranged dinner to him on a tray and was pleased to see him digging into it straight away.

Alice's eyes widened at the abundance of food. She grabbed a slice of cucumber from her plate and started nibbling it, reminding Jenny, bizarrely, of Binkie. 'Goodness. Did Mum get extra coupons?'

Jenny shook her head. 'We've had a benefactor.'

'Who?' Alice peeled off her cape and hung it on the hook by the door.

'Your new friend.'

'Dr Holz?' Alice quickly turned her back and made a great show of taking off her shoes and rubbing each foot in turn. But Jenny had already noticed the pink stain creeping up her neck.

'Yes, your Dr Holz.'

'He's not *my* Dr Holz. Anyway, what was he doing round here?'

'Checking on William and bringing some food for him.'

'How kind of him. I'd better check on William too. Is he upstairs?'

'No, in the lounge.'

Alice hurried out of the kitchen.

Jenny raised an eyebrow at Mum, who shook her head. 'I hate Germans as much as anyone,' she said, lifting her knife and fork, 'but you have to admit this one seems different.'

Jenny picked up her own cutlery in silence.

Later that evening, she and Pip sat side by side in the shed as usual, Pip transcribing the BBC news as it poured out of the wireless, and Jenny translating it. It had remained warm, the wooden walls retaining the heat of the day. The window framed a yellow and mauve sunset, its colours bleeding into the still-bright sky. As Pip switched off the wireless and started to pack it up, Jenny massaged her forehead.

He glanced at her. 'All right?'

'Mmm.'

'Still fretting about that German?'

She forced herself to respond. 'Alice is falling for him, I know it.'

Pip wedged the wireless into the Shakespeare, ready for it to be returned to the house. They'd decided to continue hiding the set from the rest of the Robinsons. Mum and Alice thought they just went into the shed for a bit of privacy, and William wouldn't have given their activities a single thought. Jenny always made sure she took the Shakespeare back after the others had gone to bed. The wireless was safe there: none of the family had any interest in old plays, and she was confident it would never be opened and its vital contents discovered. If the Germans came knocking, the others could deny any knowledge of the set in all innocence.

Pip took the sheaf of translations from her and tucked it under his jumper, ready to transport to headquarters later. 'Don't be too hard on Alice. It's not as though she's a Jerrybag.'

'Give it time,' Jenny muttered. Why on earth couldn't Alice fall for an islander? Not that there were many left her own age. A few years ago, she'd suspected her sister might have had a bit of a crush on Pip but had backed off when it became clear he was interested in Jenny. She felt a split second's pity for her. It couldn't have been easy. But that was still no excuse to let herself get involved with a German.

'Why don't you talk to her?' said Pip. He gave her a quick

kiss on the cheek. 'Got to go. I need to get these papers down to HQ.'

'Maybe,' Jenny replied, and trudged back to the house as Pip slipped eagerly through the side gate, excited to be off on his latest mission.

As she and Alice were getting ready for bed, Jenny said, 'Dr Holz is very handsome, isn't he?'

Alice shrugged, then pulled her nightdress over her head.

'Dr Morgan spoke highly of him.'

'Did he?' asked Alice. She grabbed a hairbrush and started dragging it through her hair.

'He was very good with William. And William doesn't usually respond so well to outsiders, especially a German.'

'Indeed.'

Jenny climbed into bed. 'Will you see him again?'

'I don't suppose so. Unless I bump into him at the hospital.'

'Or he bumps into you?'

Alice just nodded and turned on her side, leaving Jenny with her own thoughts in the darkness.

18

It was another fourteen-hour shift. Sometimes, when spasms of pain shot through her back and the skin on her fingers split from endless hand-washing, when she shook with the effort of pinning a smile on her face before submitting to yet another querulous demand, or failed to remove the stench of geriatric urine from her uniform – they hadn't had a single bar of soap in months – Alice was tempted to march into Matron's office and hand in her notice. But then she'd recall Dad's obvious pride in her when he'd been in the hospital, or she'd be given a posy of flowers by an appreciative relative or hear a whispered *thank you* from a patient whose bedside she'd attended for most of the night, and she'd remember why she'd taken up nursing in the first place, and why, deep down, she still loved her job in spite of the relentless work and the inhuman hours.

She'd already smiled a weary goodbye to Jeanne on reception, and was about to begin the long walk home when someone pushed past her, running towards the two German ambulances that were parked up to the side of the entrance. The vehicles were there every time she came into the hospital: dark grey half-cars, half-wagons, the back imprinted with the familiar red cross of international medical aid, and the front with the German iron cross, like a sinister parody of the former emblem.

Suddenly the air was filled with the sound of pounding feet. A stream of German doctors and nurses poured out of the hospital and into the ambulances, which left in an urgent clanging of bells.

Alice dashed back in. 'What's happened?' she asked Jeanne.

'A rock fall at St Lawrence. The Germans have been blasting out some tunnels over there. Apparently some of the workers have been injured.'

'Do they want any help?'

Jeanne shrugged. 'I'm sure they can look after their own.'

'But the workers aren't German.' Alice saw again the dishevelled line of labourers shuffling along Midvale Road like a parade of weary ghosts. Jenny had told her that the Organisation Todt workers were Russian, Polish, Spanish. Not German. She hesitated. All she wanted to do was get home and eat whatever meagre meal Jenny and Mum had managed to scrape together, before collapsing into bed. And they were short-staffed as ever on wards full of Jersey people who needed nursing, even though her shift had finished and others were now on duty. But then again, this was her own time and her decision as to who she helped. She turned back to Jeanne, who was banging an upright sheaf of papers on her desk to neaten them. 'Are we sending any of our own ambulances?'

'The German command has asked for some assistance from those of our medical staff who are free to attend,' she said. 'A couple of nurses have already gone, but we can't spare any more.'

'I'm off duty,' Alice replied. 'Where should I go?'

Jeanne jerked her head. 'There's a British ambulance standing by next to East Wing.'

Alice nodded. East Wing was over the other side of the hospital. Typical of the Germans to take over the nearest spaces with their vehicles, forcing the island emergency transport much further out. She sped out of the entrance and along the path to the far side of the building.

The driver was just about to close the door when Alice arrived, panting. 'One more?' he asked.

Alice gasped her assent and climbed in. It was a relief to be able to flop onto a seat and acknowledge the bleak smiles of her fellow rescuers. There were a couple of Irish nurses she recognised from the wards, and one of the medical doctors. Clearly no one else could be spared, or was inclined to help.

The ambulance rumbled along through the darkening streets, following the curve of St Aubin's Bay and affording them occasional views of dark blue sea, its white breakers surging near the shoreline. Their rhythm soothed her. The beaches were shut off now, coils of barbed wire blocking their entrance, and rumours of mines planted in the sand. Since the Germans had arrived, the island had been heavily fortified. Hitler apparently thought Jersey needed to be robustly defended. And the Allies had left the occupiers to it.

The doctor had his head back against the padded seat of the ambulance, his face a mask of exhaustion, and the two nurses were talking in low voices. Though they darted friendly glances at Alice from time to time, they made no effort to involve her in their conversation.

Alice continued to look out of the window. The road had taken them further inland now, and she could no longer glimpse the sea. Flat fields lay to her right, some filled with lettuces and carrots, some dotted with cattle. Farmers were probably better fed than many of the islanders, although even they were finding it hard now. Every newborn animal had to be logged and reported to the Germans, who had first claim to it, along with the crops. Occasionally she'd heard of a farmer deliberately concealing a newly slaughtered pig or sheep and distributing parts of its hastily butchered carcass around the neighbourhood, but none had ever come their way. The only meat they'd had lately was the ham Stefan had brought across, and her mouth watered with the memory of its savoury succulence. *Stefan.* She hadn't seen him for a few weeks; they worked in separate parts of the hospital and their paths hadn't crossed. He hadn't tried to intercept her for another lunch, despite his offer, and she sensed a similar concern from him not to overstep the mark and get either of them in trouble.

The ambulance lurched to the right and the doctor jolted awake. He sighed, caught Alice's eye and smiled ruefully. 'Occupational hazard, falling asleep everywhere.' He had a thin face and bright, intelligent eyes, despite having only just woken up. He held out a hand. 'Raphe Gallichan.'

'Alice Robinson.' She shook his hand. It was warm and firm. 'I've just done a six till eight. I was dying to get back home to my bed.' She'd spent an hour earlier holding up a saline drip for a dehydrated patient, as they'd run out of stands. Her arms still ached from the effort.

Dr Gallichan rummaged in his pocket. 'It was good of you to come. You didn't have to.' He produced a bar of chocolate and offered Alice a piece.

She took it and popped it into her mouth, shutting her eyes briefly at the blissful rush of sugar.

The doctor laughed. 'You obviously haven't had chocolate for a while.' He leant forward to offer some to the other nurses, who shook their heads. Alice felt a tinge of guilt that she'd accepted the chocolate, but it'd been his decision, and besides, it might give her a bit more energy for the night ahead. Medicinal really.

The ambulance ground its way uphill, the road narrowing to a lane flanked by trees. Alice caught glimpses of foxgloves, valerian and woundwort on the banks, a blur of red and purple. The light inside the vehicle dimmed whenever they passed under overhanging branches, and the mood became more sombre. Alice wondered what they would find at the site. She snapped off the image of mangled bodies, men screaming in pain, perhaps even severed limbs, and took a deep breath.

'Nervous?' The doctor looked at her sympathetically.

'A little. But I'm sure my training will kick in. And the German medics will have been there for a while, assessing the situation.'

He nodded. 'They've got much more up-to-date kit too.'

'I know.' Alice thought back to the gleaming equipment she'd spotted in the German part of the hospital.

The ambulance was really labouring now as the road climbed more steeply. Alice saw a huge wall to her left and reddish-grey rock to the right. She hoped the driver was good at steering; it would be easy to scrape the sides. At least there was little danger of encountering an oncoming vehicle. There were very few cars on the roads these days, the Germans having commandeered most of them.

They finally drew up outside a cave-like structure, seemingly built into the side of a hill. Alice could see the two German ambulances alongside and a smattering of medical staff on the scene. She glanced at the doctor, took a deep breath and climbed out, closely followed by the others.

Her first impression was that everything was grey. Grey bodies stretched out on the ground; grey dust hazing the air; picks and shovels coated in ash. The only colour in the mono-chrome scene was the doctors' uniforms. A cluster of medics stood around the body of an OT officer, his red swastika still visible on his brown sleeve; a couple of men were taking it in turns to do chest compressions on him, and three nurses were attending to various wounds. Alice winced as she saw blood soaking through a bandaged laceration. It was on the tip of her tongue to offer to apply a tourniquet, but she knew better than to interfere. Germans didn't like islanders taking charge. She needed to wait for their instructions.

She glanced round the area. All the injured were being attended to. She walked towards the cave entrance, and as she did so, she heard a faint sound. Was someone still trapped in there? She hesitated. Was it wise to go in without permission? But if there were wounded men in there, there might be something she could do to help. Deciding to take the risk, she drew her torch out of her pocket, switched it on and quickened her pace.

The early reaches of the cave had been gouged out, creating a passageway that led further in. Primitive wooden struts held the walls and ceiling in place, and several long metal poles lay on the bumpy floor. It was dank and cold inside, her footsteps echoing and a musty smell permeating the air. The walls were brown and clammy. She rubbed her suddenly goosebumped arms. The sound came again. It was definitely human. The further she walked towards it, the darker the cave became, and she was conscious there could be another rock fall at any moment. Blood pounded in her head and the ground felt liquid under her feet. At last she turned a corner and her torch lit up a ragged figure sprawled on the ground, his lower leg oddly angled. He was moaning in pain; that must have been the sound she had heard. His thin body was shivering with shock and his arms and legs were covered in burns.

Alice went up to him and squatted down. 'Hello?' she said. The word sounded weak and lame in the echoey cavern.

Another moan. Two dark, frightened eyes met hers.

'Where are you hurt?'

The man didn't answer, but his deep growl said it all. Perhaps he didn't understand English. There was no way she could attend to him by herself, and he certainly couldn't be moved.

'I'll get some help,' she said. Did she sound reassuring? Even if he couldn't understand her, her tone might comfort him. But when she went to get up, the man became more agitated, gesticulating towards the back of the cave and making strange sounds.

'Are there others?' she asked.

He caught the gist of her words and nodded rapidly.

Alice made her way further down the tunnel, past abandoned drilling equipment, crates piled high with stones, and a single discarded shoe, its sole riddled with holes. After a few hundred yards, the ceiling supports gave out and her path was partially blocked by a huge pile of rock. Weakened cries travelled towards her through the thin air, and she felt another surge of anxiety.

She approached the rocks, her heart in her mouth. In the centre, the pile reached up to the ceiling, but there was a section at the side that was lower. She took a deep breath and picked her way over the fallen debris, ignoring sharp edges that tore her stockings and stabbed at her legs. She stumbled several times as the stones tilted and shifted under her feet and once she gouged her palm as she put out a hand to steady herself. But when she eventually made it through, the scene in front of her drove all awareness of pain from her mind. Three men with blackened hands and faces lay sprawled on the ground. One had a head injury, his hair dark with blood, another was writhing in agony, a third was clearly unconscious, maybe even dead. Now there was even more need for medical support.

'I'll fetch a doctor,' she told them, trying to convey as much sympathy as possible with her expression.

One man muttered something in reply. She couldn't understand him, nor he her, but at least he knew someone had discovered them and that rescue was at hand. She climbed back over the pile as quickly as she could and sped off down the tunnel.

The injured man was where she'd left him, shaking even harder now. She mimed to him that she'd return with reinforcements and he smiled at her weakly.

She threaded her way through the supine figures outside until she saw Dr Gallichan. He was helping a wounded soldier into the ambulance, assisted by one of the Irish nurses. Alice dashed up to him. 'Can you help?' she said. 'Some of the slave workers are trapped in the cave. There's a head injury and a possible broken leg. Another man seems unconscious.'

The doctor checked with the nurse that she could manage

on her own, then picked up his medical bag and went to join Alice. 'All right. Lead on.'

'We'll need to get some help. There are too many for us to manage on our own.'

He nodded and charged off to speak to one of the German medics. He obviously spoke fluent German. But the man shook his head and muttered something in reply. Dr Gallichan threw him an angry glance and strode off. Alice watched as he approached doctor after doctor, seemingly with the same response each time.

He was scowling by the time he returned to her. 'Seems slave workers don't count.'

'Well, we'll just have to do what we can by ourselves,' said Alice. At least they could attend to the first man.

The injured labourer hadn't moved. He was very pale, his hair matted, dark strands clinging to his forehead. Dr Gallichan squatted down and felt the man's leg, reassuring him whenever he moaned in pain.

'It's definitely broken. Looks like a fractured tibia. I'm going to have to realign it, then we'll get him stretchered out.' He clicked open his bag. 'I'll give him a shot of morphine first.' He took out an ampoule of liquid and a syringe, drew up the morphine and injected the man in the thigh.

The man cried out and Alice murmured soothingly to him.

'Shouldn't take long to work, but it's still going to hurt like hell.' Dr Gallichan delved into the bag again and handed Alice a rubber pad. 'Get him to clamp down on this when I manipulate the limb.'

Alice took the pad. She pointed to the man's leg, then mimed putting the pad in her mouth and biting on it.

The man nodded, grim-faced.

They waited a few minutes, then Dr Gallichan took hold of the man's leg, signalled to Alice to insert the rubber pad, and pulled steadily.

The labourer's eyes bulged, the veins on his forehead standing out like cords and he bit down hard on the pad.

'It's all right. You're going to be all right,' Alice said.

'Damn.'

'Is there a problem?'

'Can't get the bugger to go back. I'll try again. Ready?'

Alice took a deep breath and turned back to the man. She didn't need to mime this time. It was obvious what was in store. She wiped a film of sweat from his forehead with her handkerchief and tried to smile encouragingly. Out of the corner of her eye she became aware of another figure joining Dr Gallichan, but she didn't turn round. It was important to stay focused on her patient.

The newcomer was obviously a medic. He helped Dr Gallichan support the man's leg while together they manoeuvred it into position.

After a few stomach-churning moments, they sat back, exhausted.

'Thanks,' said Dr Gallichan to the other doctor. 'You came along just in time. It was a tricky procedure but I think we've got there now.'

'I was glad to help.'

Alice whirled round. 'Stefan!'

'Hello, Alice.'

Dr Gallichan looked from one to the other but didn't comment.

'Are there others in the cave?' Stefan asked.

Alice jerked her head down the passageway. 'Several.' She outlined the possible injuries again.

'All right. I will leave you to tend to this patient and I will try to get some help.'

Dr Gallichan scowled. 'I don't fancy your chances. I tried to enlist some of your colleagues earlier, but they refused.'

'I'm sorry,' said Stefan. 'I will do my best.'

Dr Gallichan nodded. 'Alice, can you stay with the patient? I'll go back for some splints and a stretcher.'

'Of course,' said Alice. She felt a little flustered at having seen Stefan, but she knew where her priorities lay. She turned back to the injured man and gently removed the rubber pad. His head lolled back and he closed his eyes. His forehead was beaded with sweat again, and she dabbed at it with her hanky. The leg looked much straighter; the doctors had done a good job.

Before long, Dr Gallichan returned with the ambulance driver, who carried a stretcher. They worked together to fit the splints, then lifted the man onto the canvas.

'I'll carry him back to the ambulance with Hedley here.' The doctor turned to the ambulance driver, who nodded his assent. 'Can you stay within earshot of the others?'

'Of course,' said Alice again.

The men departed and she was left listening to the ever-fainter groans of the wounded men, and nearer at hand, the steady dripping sound from the cave walls.

She tried not to think about Stefan, or acknowledge the way her senses had heightened when she'd realised it was him. But now was not the time to think about her feelings; she was here to do a job. She had to remain professional.

Eventually Stefan returned with Dr Gallichan and a scowling OT overseer. The latter, tall with stony eyes, motioned to the two islanders to stay where they were before striding off into the cave. Stefan followed him, throwing Alice an anxious glance as he did so.

'You know that German doctor?' asked Dr Gallichan.

Alice pushed a strand of hair out of her eyes. 'He managed to get me some antitoxin when my brother had diphtheria and our stocks had run out.'

'That was good of him.' It was hard to interpret the doctor's expression.

'It was. I trust him.'

Dr Gallichan glanced down at the watch pinned to his uniform.

'Should we go and investigate?' asked Alice.

He shrugged. 'We've been told to stay here. Let's see what the Germans decide to do. We can't disobey their orders.'

'How is the labourer?'

'Resting in the ambulance. The driver helped me strap the splints on. He's reasonably comfortable. The morphine will stay in his system for a while.'

They both suddenly jumped as several shots rang out from deep inside the cave. Nausea travelled up Alice's throat.

'Oh my God.' Dr Gallichan's face had turned as white as his coat.

'What was that?' Alice whispered.

They didn't have to wait long. Soon the German officer emerged from the cave, accompanied by a haunted-looking Stefan.

'We will not be needing your help in here,' the officer told them. 'The slave workers have been put out of their suffering.

There are plenty more where they came from. I will send some more labourers over tomorrow to remove the bodies. In the meantime, I would be grateful if you would help me to attend to our own injured.'

Alice didn't dare look at Stefan, although she could sense Dr Gallichan swallowing rapidly beside her.

They spent the rest of the night mechanically patching up the wounded and seeing them into the ambulances. But as they drove back to the hospital in silence through the pitch-dark lanes, all Alice could see was the injured man, little more than a skeleton wrapped in skin, and all she could hear were the strangled cries of his desperate comrades.

19

Pip cycled through the early-morning streets of St Helier, squinting against the bright August sun and trying to avoid eye contact with any German soldiers. There seemed to be more greenfly than ever around these days. Dad had told him there was about one German to every two islanders now. He could well believe it. Eleven thousand at the last count. He swerved round a clot of Wehrmacht soldiers smoking on the corner of Clare Street and Savile Street, his eyes fixed on the black handlebars of his bike.

The ride was hard going. The bike's inner tube had punctured a while ago; no one had any mending kits, and it was impossible to buy new. So he'd cut a length of hosepipe and filled it with sand from the beach as a makeshift tube. It worked well enough, although it made for a bumpy ride – he had to push down really hard going uphill – but it was important he went as fast as he could.

He and Jenny had worked until late last night in Mr Robinson's old shed, transcribing and translating the latest BBC news, the results of which were pinned inside the lining of his jacket. He'd often cycled over to drop papers off at Stan Hamon's cottage, which served as Jersey Communist Party headquarters, and he'd never been stopped and searched. But he lived in constant fear of it happening.

He made it safely along Savile Street, turned off into Gloucester Street and headed south. As he cycled towards the opera house, he saw a couple of girls he recognised, dressed to the nines in furs and high heels, their hair elaborately coiffed, each with her arm linked with that of a smug-faced German officer. *Jerrybags.* He waited until he'd passed them, then spat at the road. It was appalling how many local girls had thrown in their lot with the Germans and were now openly consorting with the enemy, enjoying lavish meals and expensive clothes at the islanders' expense. They were scum.

The air was warmer now. Normally he'd have taken off his jacket and folded it into his saddlebag but he didn't dare risk being parted from the papers. Safer to keep it on and try to ignore the sweat running down his armpits. He could remove it on the way back and try to cool down then.

An old man cycled towards him. His face was creased with effort, but he still managed to raise his hat to Pip, who acknowledged him in return.

Squeezing the brakes, Pip turned into Sand Street, dismounted in front of one of the cottages and pushed his bike through the little wooden door that led to the rear gardens. He propped his bike against the wall, ensured there was no one around, then tapped on the back door.

The little house was in the old style, made of granite and covered in ivy. The duplicator was kept in the loft, accessed by a ladder from the upstairs landing. When Robert had first referred rather grandly to 'JCP headquarters', Pip had imagined some imposing building staffed by loyal party workers, but the reality was very different.

There was no answer to his knock. Damn. Where on earth

could Stan be? If he was up in the loft, he might not have heard him. He tried again, and waited several minutes, but there was still no response. Stepping back from the cottage, he looked up at the pink-curtained window, but could see nothing.

Stan had never been out when he'd visited previously. Pip usually went round before work. It was safer that way. If there was no answer soon, he'd have to go. It was quarter to nine now, and he'd get into trouble with Dad if he delayed much longer.

When there was still no response, he pushed his bike back to the road and cycled off to the office, rigid with frustration. He'd have to keep the papers on him all day and try again this evening. Damn, damn, damn.

'Nice of you to join me,' said Dad as Pip hurriedly sat down at his desk. He ran a hand over his hair. His armpits were still unpleasantly damp, rivulets of sweat slid down his back and the papers felt red hot through his jacket lining and shirt, but at least he'd made it safely into work.

'Sorry, Dad. I bumped into a friend.' It was becoming harder and harder to keep his two lives separate. Although working for Dad was more of a half-life really: reading, sorting, stacking, filing. He felt like an automaton in the office. It was at night that he did his real work: sitting in the shed beside Jenny in the light of a flickering oil lamp, twiddling the wireless dials until the outside world burst in. Transcribing the BBC reports was no less time-consuming, repetitive and exhausting than his work in the office, but those evenings still fizzed with energy and excitement. At least they were doing something to help the Allies now, and Robert had suggested there would soon be other communications that he needed to get through to the labourers. Pip knew that food and clothes were being left for the slaves at agreed drop-off points, and there was talk of sending them coded messages about where they could find refuge as they moved from one safe house to another to avoid capture. Jenny would be brilliant at coding, with her sharp maths brain. She'd asked him to notify Robert of her willingness to volunteer next time he saw him.

'Bloody idiots,' said Dad.

Pip looked up. 'Pardon?'

Dad was brandishing a piece of paper, one of those confidential memos that were wired over to him with increasing regularity from the bailiff's office. He peered at Pip over his glasses. 'Apparently the Germans have taken all their personnel off the Guernsey lighthouses.'

'Why?'

'Some idiot commandos captured Les Casquets last week.'

'Blimey!'

'Pip, I've asked you not to use that expression.'

'Sorry, Dad. But how did they do it?'

Dad pushed his glasses back up his nose. 'They drove a torpedo boat out late at night, anchored it near the lighthouse, rowed up to the shore, stormed the tower, captured seven Germans and took them across to England.'

Pip had a sudden vision of Jersey's La Corbière lighthouse when he'd sailed past it with Alice that day over two years ago. It had been one of his last trips on the *Bynie May* before the Germans had arrived. He hadn't been near the boat in months, although thankfully the Germans hadn't requisitioned her. He imagined sailing up to La Corbière with Jenny and emulating the commandos' daring raid. But there were too many fortifications along the cliffs now. The OT workers had been building them for months. And the place was crawling with Germans anyway. They wouldn't be able to get near it.

'So why have they taken the personnel off?'

'Seems it took them a week to discover the guards were gone. They must reckon it's too dangerous to man the light-houses now. I wonder whether they'll follow suit in Jersey.'

Pip unscrewed a fountain pen and drew up some ink from the bottle on his desk. 'I suppose we'll find out soon enough.'

Dad gave him a sharp glance. 'I don't want you planning anything stupid,' he said.

'Of course not, Dad. I haven't put a foot wrong since Saint-Malo, have I?'

'Mmm.' Dad returned to his memo.

The morning passed in the usual paperwork tedium. Pip was just about to ask Dad if he could go for lunch, and had already retrieved the copy of *For Whom the Bell Tolls* that he'd borrowed from the library and intended to read down by the seafront, when there was a loud knocking on the outer door of the office.

He went to open it and saw a smudge of field grey through the glass. His heart started to thrum. This obviously wasn't a customer.

He opened the door to a thickset German soldier emitting a pungent mixture of boot polish, gun oil and eau de cologne.

'Phillip Marett?'

'Yes.' Pip tried to let his breath out slowly. The papers burnt against his chest.

'May I enter?'

He widened the door, and the soldier strode in.

Dad stumbled to his feet. '*Guten Tag.*'

'*Guten Tag*,' replied the soldier.

Blood roared in Pip's head. What if the Germans had come across the wireless? Perhaps someone had tipped them off and they'd searched the Robinsons' house. He'd been a fool to endanger them. An image of Jenny being escorted down the lane by German soldiers filled his mind. He'd have to confess and swear she was innocent. What might they do to her in custody? He snapped off the thought that she might even be dead already. It was too horrific to contemplate.

'How may we help you?' asked Dad.

The German resumed his clipped English. 'We are recruiting workers from non-essential occupations.' His gaze seemed to hover over Pip's library book, still on the desk where he'd left it. 'We require young men to assist in the work of the Third Reich on the island.'

Pip's knees almost buckled in relief. So this wasn't about the wireless, or even the translations. Unless the soldier was toying with them, intending to come back and accuse him later. His heart was pounding so hard he thought it could be seen through his shirt.

'No!' Dad's face was bright red. 'Civilians are forbidden from carrying out military duties on behalf of an occupying force.'

Good old Dad. He knew his law. The Germans must be trying their luck. Nevertheless, Pip was still in danger.

The German gave an oily smile. 'Very good, Mr Marett. But we are not requisitioning men for military work; Phillip will be engaged in civilian activities.'

'Such as?' Pip could see Dad trying to stand as rigid as possible.

'Such as strengthening walls, quarrying stones, turfing soil.'

'Helping you fortify the island, you mean.'

Pip shot him a warning glance. Dad couldn't afford to antagonise the soldier, or his own life would be in peril. Besides, if Pip cooperated with the enemy, they were less likely to suspect him of being involved with the Resistance. But he couldn't let Dad know that.

'Nonsense, we are offering valuable employment to islanders, for which we will pay a good wage.'

'But Pip *has* valuable employment.'

The German sighed theatrically. 'We do not consider accountancy to be an essential occupation. Mr Marett, you will need to work alone in future. We have need of your son.'

'This contravenes the Hague Convention,' said Dad. 'I will be consulting with the bailiff of the island.'

The soldier shrugged. 'By all means, Mr Marett, but my orders are to demand that Phillip reports to the Feldkommandant's office at eight o'clock sharp next Tuesday, the first of September.'

The knot in Pip's stomach loosened a little. There was still a bit of time for Dad to look into this. He went to protest again, but Pip stopped him. 'It's all right, Dad.'

The officer clicked his heels and departed. Pip shut the door behind him.

When he returned, Dad was already dialling the bailiff. 'They won't get away with this,' he said. 'We'll check our facts first, then I'll report to the bloody Feldkommandant myself and remonstrate with him. There's no way any son of mine will be working for the Germans.'

Pip slumped in his chair. He could have been deported, shot even, for possessing a wireless — or worse still, Jenny could have been. The transcripts of the BBC news he had on him would have implicated her as well. He'd take them over to Stan's as soon as he could later on. And with a bit of luck, the Germans would remain unsuspecting of what he was really up to.

20

Pip stood up to rub his back and take a break from the hard work. Building walls was much more difficult than he'd imagined. And he hated working for the Germans, even if it had put them off the scent. Dad had tried his best to get him exempted from civilian duties, but even the bailiff had conceded that Pip would do better to cooperate, and eventually Dad had backed down. Secretly Pip was relieved that his apparent compliance would act as a smokescreen for his more illicit activities. And in spite of himself, he appreciated being in the fresh air again, although even that was beginning to pall now that the summer's heat had dissipated and the days were getting shorter.

There'd been a frost that morning and he'd been glad of his gloves as he'd picked up the hard stones from the ground and wedged them between the others already in place in the next layer. He'd spent the morning on one stretch of the wall, choosing the best rocks to fit the A-shaped structure as he'd been taught, using the wooden spirit level he'd been given to check everything was aligned and stable. He might be working for the enemy, but the wall would be in place for future generations of islanders once they regained their freedom. It was repetitive work, but at least it gave him time to think, and it meant he didn't have to put up with Dad's incessant demands and the endless stream of paperwork in the office. It was hard on Dad, though. He really missed having Pip around, and the work was almost too much for him now, especially with all his extra jurat duties.

Pip looked up at the sound of a whistle. He glanced at his watch. Five o'clock. Another day done. The nights were drawing in now it was September, and it was impossible to build walls in the dark. Thank goodness for autumn. He trudged over to the makeshift shed that served as a storeroom and deposited his pickaxe and shovel inside. Then he picked up his rucksack, slung it over one shoulder and began the long walk home.

There were other lads from the island working with him, although they were too spread out to be able to chat, and the foreman kept them busy. Ed and Tom weren't too bad, but all they wanted to talk about was what they'd got up to with their girlfriends the night before, and Pip didn't feel he had much to contribute. But he had taken a dislike to the fourth lad, Peter Dewe, a small, surly chap who largely ignored the others but seemed very keen to talk to the Germans. Pip didn't trust him. And he had a suspicion the feeling was mutual.

Luckily Peter lived in the opposite direction, so he didn't have to walk home with him, and Ed and Tom had gone on ahead. As Pip made his way back to the main road that led to St Helier, he mulled over the problem of Dad. He could have offered to work for him in the evenings, but he needed any energy he had left to listen to the wireless with Jenny and distribute the Allied news. An image of Jenny's intent expression as she'd sat next to him in the Robinsons' shed last night came into his mind. She seemed to come alive when she was translating the news into Spanish. And she'd taken on more responsibilities lately with the coding work. As Pip had expected, Robert had been delighted to have her on board, and Jenny relished another opportunity to get back at the Germans.

Pip stopped walking. *Jenny*. Of course. Even though she was busier now, she could still spare Dad a few hours a week at the office. It would give her something more to get her teeth into and Dad would be glad of the help.

His pace quickened as he resolved to broach it with them both that evening.

⚓

Alice drew a tray of acorns out of the oven. She'd read in a magazine that if you roasted them until they were just turning brown, then let them cool, you could make a kind of coffee by pounding them with a rolling pin then pouring boiling water over the small shards. It was a time-consuming job and sometimes she wondered if it was worth it for the bitter brown liquid produced, but it was better than nothing. She tried not to dwell on the steaming cups of rich French coffee they'd had before the war. Like a lot of things – bananas, icing sugar, silk stockings, perfume – that luxury was a distant memory.

She'd made a bit of a mess in the kitchen. Some acorn fragments had spilled onto the floor and there was a pile of discarded cups and stalks on the table. Her fingers were sore and her thumbnails black from easing the acorns out of their scaly husks. She wondered if Binkie would like the remains, but they were probably too tough to chew. She swept them off the table and into the bin.

Mum and Jenny had walked into town with William to

queue for sausages – currently the only meat he would eat – while Alice had a rare few hours at home. She was on early shifts this week, which meant she'd been able to leave work in the middle of the afternoon.

As usual, she hadn't slept well. She couldn't forget what she'd witnessed at St Lawrence. She'd lain awake much of the night trying to blot out the sound of the gunshots and suppress the vision of men writhing in agony. Talking to Jenny about it had helped a little, although she'd spared Mum and William the details. Jenny had been horrified at her account, her ever-present hatred of the Germans fuelled even further. She'd confessed in return that she and Pip had become involved in a scheme to help some of the OT workers but had refused to elaborate. 'It's best you don't know too much,' she'd said. 'That way you can genuinely claim ignorance if the Germans come calling.' Alice felt a surge of anger. Why was her sister being so secretive? It was typical of her to play at being spies, or whatever she and Pip were up to, and endanger them all.

It had been a relief to be able to change into an old skirt and blouse and potter about the house after she returned from the hospital, concentrating on mundane tasks in order to tame the still-vivid trauma and ward off the weariness.

She looked up at the sound of an engine. Hardly anyone drove a car these days – those islanders who'd possessed one had had it requisitioned by now. It must be a German driver. Her pulse accelerated at the sound of a door shutting and clipped footsteps coming up the drive. Was this the interrogation Jenny had hinted at? What on earth had she got involved in? By the time the knock on the door came, Alice had convinced herself she was about to be arrested.

But when she lifted the latch, she discovered Stefan standing there. As soon as he saw her face, he apologised for frightening her.

'It's fine,' said Alice. 'I didn't realise it was you.'

He smiled diffidently. 'Is it all right if I come in?'

Alice peered over his shoulder. There didn't appear to be anyone else around; it was all quiet in the lane.

She widened the door. 'Of course.'

Stefan followed her down the hall and into the kitchen. Her nerves felt taut, her senses heightened. It was a risk to allow him in, but she couldn't suppress the bubble of excitement at his nearness.

'Would you like some coffee?' she asked, pointing to the acorns, her mouth suddenly dry.

'From *acorns*?'

She explained the process, trying to sound matter-of-fact.

'I think we still have some real coffee in the doctors' mess,' said Stefan. 'I'll bring you some next time I come.'

'Thank you.' *Next time* sounded promising, but Alice just as quickly pushed down the feeling.

'Do you want to sit down?' she asked. She picked up some of William's school books that had been piled on Dad's old chair and put them on the table. It felt awkward both of them standing in the kitchen with acorn debris everywhere. She half wished Stefan had accepted her offer of coffee. At least she could have occupied herself then, heating up the water and fetching cups, saucers and spoons.

'No. I have come to ask if you would like to come out for a drive,' said Stefan, somewhat shyly. 'I have the loan of the unit's car for the day. I was sent out to a German officer with a suspected heart attack over at St Mary, but it turned out to be indigestion instead. I do not need to return the car until tonight.' His expression was half expectant, half apologetic.

Alice was torn too. She could think of nothing more wonderful than sitting close to Stefan, talking, getting to know him better. What had Jenny said all those months ago? *Carpe diem*: seize the day. But it was still a risk. Finally she stuttered, 'Yes, I suppose I'm free.'

He smiled with apparent relief.

She took a piece of paper and a pen from Mum's drawer and scribbled a note to the others to say she'd gone for a walk. 'I'll just pop up to change,' she told him. This was the first time he'd seen her out of uniform, and she was embarrassed to be found in her old clothes.

'Of course.' Stefan wandered over to the window and looked out into the garden. Alice hoped no one would be able to see him from there.

She dashed upstairs and opened her wardrobe. None of them had had new clothes for months. Even William, who was shooting up, had to make do with Mum's attempts to let down his trousers and extend the waistband. Everything they wore was patched and darned these days. Alice seized her old navy dress. It was a bit loose now, but at least it was reasonably smart. She put it on, pulled a comb through her hair, then borrowed a squirt of Jenny's perfume, although there was barely any left. That would have to do. She didn't want to take too long in case the others came back early.

She ran back downstairs to find Stefan still by the window. 'You look lovely,' he said, turning towards her.

'Thank you.' She grabbed her cardigan and a headscarf

from the hall stand and showed him out of the back door and through the garden. It was less obvious to go out this way. Perhaps she'd been hasty accepting his invitation with such alacrity. Was it sensible to be on her own with him when no one knew where she was? But all her instincts told her he was safe – even Mum and Jenny had warmed to him. And Rebekah had said his reputation at the hospital was faultless.

He showed her into the passenger seat, nudged the door shut, then went round to the driver's side. He backed the car efficiently down the drive and out into the lane.

'I thought we could go over to the cliffs at Noirmont. I have heard the view is good from there.'

'Yes, it is, it used to be one of my favourite places – although I haven't been for a while.' It would be nice to sit overlooking the sea with Stefan, feeling the salty breeze on her face and listening to the whisper of the waves.

'How are you after the other night?' he asked.

She pushed a strand of hair off her forehead. 'I'm still having nightmares.'

He reached across for her hand. 'I also,' he said, and then went silent.

She couldn't remember when she'd last had a peaceful night's sleep. She no longer saw Dad's haggard face every time she closed her eyes, although she had for a long while. In truth, it was only this latest horror that blotted out the former. This is what it's like to live through a war, she thought: one terrible image replacing another.

But it was comforting to feel the warmth of Stefan's hand on hers, its golden hairs illuminated by the soft light in the car, his fingers long and slim. She leant her head against the car seat. Was this just a soothing gesture or a precursor to something else? What did he have planned for the evening? She told herself to stop worrying. Stefan was an honourable man; she'd seen it time and time again: the way he'd helped with William's medication, the food he'd brought them, his concern for the workers at St Lawrence. If he'd wanted to molest her, he could have done so at the house, or even in the hospital gardens. She glanced at his profile again and found reassurance.

As he pulled out into Queen's Road, she surreptitiously tugged her headscarf round her face and slid down in the seat. Stefan shot her a glance. 'I don't want to make things difficult for you,' she said.

She imagined the busybodies whispering about that Robinson girl, the nursing one, being a Jerrybag. And what if someone told Mum they'd seen her with a German? No one would understand that Stefan was a good man and a caring doctor. He was the enemy and that was that.

'It's a little awkward,' she told him.

He took his hand away to turn the wheel as he swung the car round onto the esplanade. 'I understand we are at war,' he said. He completed the manoeuvre, then, to her relief, took her hand in his again. 'But I hope we can be friends.'

Her chest tightened. Friends. Her mind travelled back to that evening with Pip when they'd sailed round to the airport. She'd misread the signs then, thought he was interested in her when he was actually after Jenny. Her hand tingled from the light pressure of Stefan's fingers. Pip had never squeezed her hand or made overtures to her. Any sign of interest had been in her imagination. And Stefan had deliberately sought her out for this trip, whereas Pip had only invited her onto the *Bynie May* that day because Jenny had had to revise for her exam. She looked out of the window at the turquoise sea with its white-capped waves and felt calmer. There was no denying the connection she felt to Stefan. It was similar to her feelings for Pip, but deeper, stronger. A mature emotion rather than a young girl's crush.

Half an hour later, they'd skirted round St Aubin's Bay and were driving along the Route de Noirmont. Alice felt safer now they were away from St Helier and out in the open country. She'd taken off her headscarf and had started to relax, talking to Stefan about some of her cases on the wards. He was much more confident in doctor mode, asking questions about some of her older patients and giving advice on geriatric care. And his hand had more or less stayed put all that time.

But as they rounded the bend just past Noirmont Manor, he brought the car to an abrupt halt. The road to the headland was blocked. Beyond the barriers Alice caught sight of men mixing concrete and others carting stones in wheelbarrows. Perhaps the Germans were building more fortifications. She held her breath to stop herself voicing her anger. Hitler was ruining their island with walls and bunkers.

'*Verdammt*,' muttered Stefan.

For one crazy second Alice thought he might be able to persuade some of his comrades to let them through. But then she realised how daft the idea was. Even assuming he could sweet-talk the workers into allowing him to bring a local girl on site, it was no way to spend a romantic evening. Assuming that was what he had in mind.

'It's all right,' she told him. 'We can go out to Portelet Common instead. If you turn the car round, I'll direct you.'

He did as she suggested, and soon they'd retraced their route, driving past the beach and the Smugglers Inn towards the next headland. He parked the car and they made their way on foot to the cliffs. It was late afternoon now, the cooling air carrying the earthy undertones of autumn and the heathland glowing with purple heather. Creamy pearlwort and star-shaped squills bordered the path.

'What's that?' Stefan stopped at a sound in the distance like two pebbles being knocked together.

'That'll be a stonechat. There are loads on the common.'

'Stone . . . chat. So its name resembles its sound?' His expression was earnest.

Alice laughed. 'I suppose it does.'

'And how did you know that?'

A memory filtered through: Jenny in a pink summer dress with a deep frill and a wide satin sash, inspecting holm oak leaves to check for symmetry; Dad, his thin legs protruding from a pair of flannel shorts, scouring the horizon with his binoculars, and that same rock-rattling sound coming to them through the warm air. When Alice had asked what it was, he had put his arm round her and allowed her to look through his binoculars at the red-breasted bird perched on a gorse bush, explaining carefully how it differed from a robin.

'My father taught me,' she said.

Stefan grinned. 'My father loves nature too.'

Alice hadn't thought much about Stefan's homeland. She wondered what it was like. She couldn't imagine anything lovelier than Jersey, but perhaps he felt the same way about his own country. 'Do you have this kind of scenery in Germany?'

'Oh yes, and hills and mountains and deep dark forests.'

'It sounds beautiful.'

'It is.'

'You must miss it . . . and your family.' For a second she wondered if he had a sweetheart back home.

A dark film of sadness passed across his eyes. 'I do,' he said. Then his face relaxed. 'But now I have some delightful company here. And that is helping me not to miss home so much. Also to try to forget why I'm here.'

'Of course.' She tried to sound casual. 'And is there anyone special you've left behind?'

He paused. 'Not really. No one like you, anyway. I never met anyone at home who is so beautiful inside and out.'

Alice smiled. That sounded promising. She gestured towards the path to prevent him from seeing the blush she felt creeping up her neck. 'Shall we continue?'

'Yes, please. You lead the way.'

The closer they got to the sea, the stronger the headwind became, ruffling Stefan's hair and tugging at the hem of Alice's dress. She pulled her cardigan tightly round her, relieved that the stiff breeze had cooled her face.

'Are you cold?'

'A bit.'

Stefan curved his arm around her, narrowing the distance between them. They walked on, Alice's whole body alive to this new intimacy, his hip nudging hers, his hand a firm warmth on her upper arm, their footsteps in tune. Even through her cardigan, her skin felt electric from his touch.

At last they came to the end of the headland, in full view of the gold-splashed sea. Alice loved sunsets: they made her feel calm and replete, as if all was well with the world, nature in harmony. Only the distant sound of machinery drifting across from Noirmont reminded her there was still a war going on.

'Shall we sit?' asked Stefan. He took off his jacket and spread it over the springy grass, already darkening under the falling autumn light.

'You're sure *you* won't be cold?' Alice sat down next to him.

He put his arm around her again, and in return she rubbed her hand up and down his shirtsleeve to warm him. He laughed. 'Always the nurse.'

Alice smiled back. She looked out towards Noirmont, where the lighthouse beam pulsed steadily across the bay. Most lighthouses had been switched off since the occupation, but sometimes they were reignited for enemy manoeuvres. She wondered what the Germans were up to. It was easier to see from this headland the wall they'd built near the watchtower, the dull concrete blocks a backdrop to its monochrome solidity. She counted the flashes every twelve seconds. Jenny would have been proud of her precision.

In spite of the soothing light and the stillness around them, she felt another spark of anger at what the enemy was doing to Jersey: corrupting its beautiful coastline with its ugly fortifications. This was their island. How dare the invaders brutalise it like this?

In her mind, it was easier to cast their occupiers as 'the enemy'. If she called them Germans in her head, that would have to include Stefan, and she couldn't bear to see him in that light. The hands that were now stroking her arm were made to heal and soothe, not maim and destroy. He was a doctor far, far more than he was a soldier.

The faintest trace of cologne drifted towards her. He was close now, lightly tilting her face.

'Would it be all right if I kissed you?'

Alice smiled her assent. She knew her voice would give her away if she spoke; it would be too eager.

He moved his lips against hers. At first she tensed, uncertain what to do with her mouth, but his kiss was so lovely and the smell of his skin so heady that the world slowed and time fell away. She wasn't lonely or tired or angry or ignored. She just was. She closed her eyes and felt at peace for the first time in months.

Afterwards, she wasn't sure who'd broken off first, but it didn't matter. This was not a game of who was keener than the other. It was mutual and natural.

'That was wonderful,' he said softly.

She closed her eyes again, tilting her chin herself this time, confident he would kiss her once more.

And when he did, she felt the same sense of completeness as before, as though Stefan was filling a void she hadn't realised existed. Perhaps it had been there all her life.

He drew her down beside him, cushioning her head with his arm, and they kissed again and again, each kiss longer and deeper.

Finally Stefan drew away and propped himself up on his elbow. 'Alice, I don't want to take advantage of you. I could kiss you all night, but I am not going to do anything you don't want me to do. Just tell me to stop if I go too far.'

Alice nodded. She knew her face was flushed and her eyes glazed. Greedy for more, she arched her body towards him, closing her eyes again at the movements of his hands and the quickening beat of her own blood. Twilight wrapped itself around them.

But the tiny part of her brain she managed to hold on to told her it was getting late, that she needed to return home or Mum would be worried, and that losing her virginity to a German soldier on a cold clifftop was probably not a good idea.

'Stefan . . .'

'Yes?'

'My body wants you to go on, but my mind thinks you should stop.'

He laughed and felt in his jacket pocket for a cigarette. 'Would you like one?'

She shook her head.

His lighter flared and she tried to gauge his mood from his expression.

'Thank you.' Her mouth framed the words.

He kissed her on the forehead, then helped her back to her feet. They returned to the car, their steps in rhythm, their fingers entwined.

21

'You were right,' she said to Rebekah, the next time they were together alone in the sluice room.

Rebekah dropped a load of soiled bandages in the bin, then turned to the sink to wash her hands. 'Well, much as I'd like to think I'm always right about everything, can you specify the particular matter you had in mind?'

Alice laughed. Since last night, she'd felt freer, more confident, as though a burden had been lifted. 'Right about being in love. It does feel natural. As though it was always meant to be.'

Rebekah blotted the skin between each of her fingers with a towel. 'I assume you're talking about a certain German doctor.'

'Yes. Stefan.' Alice told her friend about their evening on Portelet Common.

Rebekah folded the towel in half, then folded it again until it was a small square. 'Oh Alice, be very careful, won't you?'

The bubble of happiness threatened to burst. 'Please don't lecture me. I just can't think of him as the enemy.'

'I know. Dr Holz appears to be a good man and a good doctor too. I haven't heard a bad word said about him in the hospital. But he's a German. They're not to be trusted, however civil they may seem. You're still playing with fire.'

Alice's throat tightened. She'd met a man for whom she

felt something she never had before, and he seemed to want her too, but he was off limits because of a stupid war neither of them wanted any part of. But she understood where Rebekah's antipathy came from. Tom was out there fighting for the British. And rumours of Jews being badly treated in Europe were almost too disturbing to comprehend. Since Rebekah had registered as Jewish, Alice knew she lived in a constant state of fear.

'I'm sorry. It can't be easy for you to hear I've fallen for a German. I just don't know what to do.'

Rebekah smiled, albeit thinly. 'I know what it's like to love someone from a different country. It should never have worked between me and Tom, but it does.' She picked up a tray of water bottles. 'I have to go or Sister will get cross. But promise me you'll be cautious, Alice.'

Alice pushed the door open with her elbow so Rebekah could keep both hands on the tray. 'I promise,' she said.

The rest of the day was too busy to allow her much time to think, although whenever Sister sent her on an errand, or when she nipped to the dining room for her lunch break, she scanned the corridors for Stefan. But he didn't appear. She could still recall the warmth of his hands, the scent of his cologne, and her face reddened at the memory. Should she have let him go further? It was wartime after all. Who knew whether either of them would be alive tomorrow? But some deeper instinct had told her to hold back, and Rebekah's advice had confirmed it. If Stefan was the one, he would wait for her. Everything could wait until this ghastly war was over.

Jenny enjoyed working for Mr Marett. Pip had always made the job out to be tedious, and to some extent the filing and envelope-addressing was dull, but Mr Marett was teaching her some of the basic elements of accountancy, probably sensing she had much more of an interest in figures than Pip. They got on well too: he was an old-fashioned man in many ways – another source of frustration for his son – but Jenny rather liked his old-school charm and courtesy. He reminded her a little of Dad. And it was nice to get closer to Pip's father and gain more of a sense of his childhood.

Mr Marett was at a client's when the phone rang. Jenny went over to his desk and picked up the receiver. It was the bailiff.

'Coutanche here. I need to speak to Marett urgently.'

'Sorry, sir, I'm afraid he's out.'

'Damn. It's this business about the deportations. Need to discuss it. Get him to ring back as soon as he returns, will you?'

'Of course,' replied Jenny.

She replaced the receiver, her skin prickling with anxiety.

When Mr Marett returned, she gave him the bailiff's message. He picked up the phone straight away. She tried not to listen to the conversation, but all the time her heart was hammering. Deportations? What deportations? And the phrases she was hearing were even more alarming. 'British parents? . . . All right . . . And he's adamant? Yes, good not to involve the constables. Can you send a boy round with the list and I'll give it some thought? Thank you.'

She looked up as he replaced the telephone in the cradle and his eyes met hers. She didn't even pretend to be busy; his expression worried her too much.

'Is everything all right?' she asked.

Mr Marett pinched a fold of skin above his nose. 'A year ago, Winston Churchill imprisoned some Germans working in Iran.' His voice was laced with worry. 'In retaliation, Hitler ordered that ten Channel Islanders should be deported to Poland for every German hostage.'

'I see.' Jenny couldn't remember hearing anything about that.

'For some reason, the deportation order was never carried out. But now it appears Hitler has reissued it. Colonel Knackfuss has requested that all British citizens on the island, and children with at least one British parent, are to be deported to Germany.'

She felt a rush of blood to her face and the room tilted. 'Does that mean me, Alice and William?' she whispered.

Mr Marett took the top off his pen and placed it on the desk. It rolled along the polished surface and dropped with a clatter to the floor. 'Your father was born in England, wasn't he?' he murmured.

She nodded.

'How old is your brother?'

'William is twelve.' She heard the catch in her own voice.

'He's too young. He won't be deported without an accompanying parent. And your mother is an islander, isn't she?'

She nodded again. 'But Alice and I might be summoned?'

Mr Marett leant down to retrieve the pen lid, then sat staring at it as if he couldn't remember where it came from. 'There is a danger, yes. We'll have to wait until the list arrives. Try not to worry, my dear.'

Jenny blinked back tears at the paternal note in his voice.

No one could ever replace Dad, but it was comforting to have another father figure in her life. One she shared with Pip. Things were still tricky between the two of them. She just couldn't seem to cope with any intimacy. She was fine when they were listening to the wireless or cycling out to St Catherine's, but whenever he tried to kiss her on the mouth, or even put his arms round her, she just wanted to back off, despite his obvious frustration. What was wrong with her? Why couldn't she give him what he wanted? She was lucky he was still prepared to be friends.

She tried to do a bit of filing, but her hands were shaking too much to be effective. And Mr Marett seemed to have been reading the same sheet of paper for ages.

At last there was a sound at the door, and a young lad appeared, holding out an envelope. His face was pink and he was breathing heavily. Jenny noticed his bicycle propped up outside. Mr Marett took the envelope, rummaged in his pocket for a coin and handed it to the boy, who took it and sped off.

Jenny watched as he opened the envelope. He quickly scanned the list, then stopped and looked up at her.

A chill moved through her. 'Are our names there?'

'I'm afraid so, my dear.'

'May I see?'

'Well, it's supposed to be confidential, so you must keep this to yourself.'

'Of course.' She went over to his desk and he angled the pages so she could look. The names were listed alphabetically, and 'Alice Robinson' and 'Jenny Robinson' were neatly typed halfway down the Rs. She clenched her fists to stop her hands from shaking. There were a few other names she knew, but she didn't let on she recognised them. But just as she was about to reposition the sheets, her eye drifted to the top of the page and she saw the name Rebekah Liron. Alice's friend. Poor girl. She was Jewish too. Everyone knew that Jews were especially vulnerable. Confidential or not, she had to tell Alice.

She straightened the pages and returned to her own desk, her legs suddenly straw-like.

'Don't worry, my dear,' said Mr Marett. 'I'll see what I can do. I may be able to plead special dispensation, as accountancy is a reserved occupation.'

'But didn't you try making that case for Pip? The Germans didn't listen then, did they?' Her heart pounded at her chest.

Mr Marett blanched. 'They didn't,' he said. 'But they don't need you to build walls. They might be more lenient because you're a girl, and they owe me one because of Pip. I can but try.'

'Thank you,' said Jenny. 'And I would imagine nursing is definitely a reserved occupation.'

'Nursing?'

'My sister Alice is a nurse.'

'Of course. I expect the hospital will try to gain exemption for her.'

Jenny longed to ask Mr Marett if he could fight for Alice too, but she had to be content with his assurance that he would try to get her own name removed from the list. And perhaps the hospital would indeed save Alice. It was their best hope. She massaged her forehead with her fingers.

'Why don't you go home, my dear? You've had quite a shock.'

Jenny nodded. She really did feel weary, and she doubted she'd be any more use in the office. She picked up her bag and coat. 'Thank you,' she said. 'Goodnight.'

'Goodnight, Jenny. And don't worry. You can leave all this with me.'

The next day, Alice was rebandaging a patient's head after his dressing had slipped when she looked up and saw Stefan signalling to her from the doorway. Something surged low in her body. Luckily her task was nearly finished. She tucked the end of the bandage neatly into the wad of crêpe and fastened it with a safety pin.

'All finished, Mr Cabot. That should hold for a good while now.'

Mr Cabot smiled his thanks and Alice strode up the ward. She knew from experience that if she looked confident about her business, Sister was less likely to challenge her. The worst thing she could do was to appear furtive.

She reached the door safely. Stefan was still there, looking anxious.

Alice wasn't sure how to greet him, but something about his expression triggered a lurch of anxiety.

'What is it?'

He looked round, but the corridor was empty. 'Walk with me, Alice. I have something to tell you.'

She wondered if he'd found out about the deportations. When Jenny had filled her in last night after they were in bed, Alice had been shocked and then panicky about what to do next. Jenny told her she'd avoided saying anything earlier so as not to worry Mum or William, but it was obvious that she herself was equally terrified. Alice couldn't bear to contemplate being sent to Germany. How ironic to be deported to Stefan's homeland while he was stationed in hers. She'd been going over options for the best course of action in her head all morning, trying to pluck up courage to go to Matron's office to find out where she stood. Another thought snagged at her too. She'd been born in England, not Jersey like Jenny and William. Would that make her additionally vulnerable?

She and Stefan walked down the corridor together. Alice's face grew warm as she thought back to the other night, when they'd walked hand in hand. But this was a very different Stefan. His body was rigid, and worry lines played around his mouth.

An orderly came towards them pushing a trolley, and they both stood aside to let him pass. If he was surprised to see a Jersey nurse with a German soldier, he didn't show it. Stefan waited until he'd gone, then turned to face Alice.

'Your father was British, was he not?'

Alice nodded. She'd told him about Dad coming across from the mainland on holiday and meeting Mum. 'And I was born in London.'

His frown deepened at that. A couple of nurses approached. Again they stood aside. Alice kept her eyes on the ground.

'Is there somewhere more private we can go?' Stefan asked when the pair had passed.

She gestured to a door further down the corridor. 'There's a stock room along there. With a bit of luck no one will need to come in.'

Stefan reached the room in several strides and held the door open for Alice. It smelt of surgical spirit and clean towels.

There were shelves all around the walls piled with sheets and pillowcases. No medicine, though. All drugs were kept in the locked cabinets on the wards.

It was hard to be in such a confined space with Stefan without touching him, when the scent of his cologne was so arousing. She searched his now familiar face for golden skin and ruddy cheeks, but he looked much paler than he had at Portelet Common.

'Alice, I heard something this morning that is making me uneasy.'

The tight knot of anxiety she'd felt since yesterday loosened a little with his obvious concern. 'I think I might know what it is. The deportations?'

'How did you find out?'

'Jenny warned me. She heard about them from her employer, who works for the bailiff. He thinks he can get her an exemption. I was hoping the hospital might persuade your field commandant to take me off the list too.'

She froze as footsteps approached, convinced someone would come into the stock room and discover them. They waited in silence until the sound grew louder then died away. Alice put her hand against the wall to steady herself.

'I was going to suggest that also,' said Stefan. 'And it might be better coming from me.'

Hope rose in her like a breath. 'Would you?'

'Of course. I will go to Colonel Knackfuss and explain you are needed here as a nurse.'

'Thank you,' whispered Alice. She wanted to hug him in relief, but there was something else she had to ask first, and it was another test of her trust in him. 'I have a Jewish friend called Rebekah,' she said. 'A fellow nurse. According to Jenny, she is also on the deportation list.'

Stefan frowned. 'That is not so good. British citizens should be quite well treated in Germany. I will try to get you off the list, of course, but even if you were to go, you would have nothing to fear. But it is a very different case for the Jews.' The muscles in his face tightened. 'I have heard terrible rumours.'

Alice felt a stab of fear. 'Then we need to save her.'

Stefan reached out for her hand. 'I can try to save you both.'

And then he kissed her, cupping her face with his hands, and she felt safe again.

22

Dad was on jurat business all evening, so Pip had the house to himself. He phoned Jenny early that morning and asked her to bring Alice round. As a result, by eight o'clock that evening, the three of them were sitting in the living room.

Pip was wary about Alice's relationship with Stefan. His previous encounters with German soldiers had been harsh ones: the man who had come to the office that day, requisitioning him for civilian duties; the stern overseer of his wall-building work at Grouville; and the German that existed only in his mind – the menacing Nazi who searched the Robinsons' home and had Jenny shot for possessing a wireless. That was the one who kept him awake at night, even though the hiding place was a safe one and no German apart from Dr Holz had visited the house in all this time.

In the early days of the war, the first occupiers had been civil – charming, even – keen to make a good impression and treat the islanders well. But things were different now. Back in March, a boy a few years above him at school, François Scornet, had been shot for trying to escape to England, and in May, Maurice Gould from the St Helier herbalist's and young Peter Hassall from Byron Lane were both sent to Germany for attempting to leave the island in a small boat. It had even occurred to him that Stefan might be a spy sent to trick Alice into finding out what he and Jenny were up to – even though they'd been careful not to tell her anything – but Jenny had assured him he was trustworthy. She still hated most Germans, but Holz's care and generosity to William had convinced her of his good intentions. And by all accounts, Alice was smitten with him.

'Dad is pretty confident he can get Jenny removed from the deportation list.' Pip looked across at Jenny, who smiled warmly as she sat next to Alice on the brown leather sofa. He cleared his throat. 'But I'm afraid we agreed that he wouldn't seek exemption for you, Alice. It might be pushing his luck and could turn out to be counterproductive.'

Alice tucked a strand of hair behind her ear. 'It's all right. Stefan has spoken to Colonel Knackfuss and he's considering my case.'

'That's good,' said Pip, relieved. Although once again he hoped Stefan was genuine.

'So that leaves Rebekah,' said Alice quietly. 'Stefan has told us that Jews will doubtless be treated more harshly than Gentiles.'

Pip nodded. He'd never met Rebekah, but Jenny had often mentioned what good friends she and Alice were. Jenny liked her too, and Pip trusted her judgement. Stefan's conjecture about the treatment of Jews didn't surprise him. They'd all heard about Kristallnacht, when, a few years ago in Germany, Jewish businesses, shops and synagogues had been smashed. Even on Jersey, Jews were now forbidden from entering shops between three and four o'clock in the afternoon, and couldn't go to public buildings or theatres at all. And it was only because she was a nurse that Rebekah was exempt from the curfew. If she were deported, who knew what awaited her in Germany.

Alice leant forward. 'Stefan and I have come up with a plan to save Rebekah.'

'What's that?' asked Pip.

She shook her head. 'We can't tell you. The less you know, the better, but we'll need your help to smuggle her to a safe house.'

'I think I can arrange that,' said Pip. Robert Durand had contacts. There was bound to be somewhere. He stood up and poured himself a glass of whisky from the decanter on the sideboard. He still hated the stuff, but felt a sudden need for alcohol. Hopefully Dad wouldn't notice.

'Rebekah will leave the hospital while the deportations are taking place,' continued Alice. 'Most people will be down by the harbour, waving goodbye to their friends and relatives, so it should be possible for her to get away without anyone noticing. Please suggest a place she can meet you. You will need your bicycle, and perhaps Jenny would lend hers to Rebekah. You can take over from there.'

'Of course,' said Pip.

They discussed the finer details of the rendezvous, then Alice got up to go.

'I think our plan could work,' she said, massaging her forehead. 'But it's going to be incredibly difficult to pull off.'

As Pip showed the sisters out, he realised that no amount of whisky could numb his rising anxiety at the prospect of Alice's request.

⚓

'I really admire what you're doing,' Jenny told Alice that night after they'd gone to bed. 'But you and Stefan are putting yourselves in a lot of danger.'

'We are.' Alice twisted a strand of her hair as she lay propped against a pillow. 'There are worries going round and round my mind. But letting her be deported is just not an option. Who knows what they might do to her? Besides, I'm a nurse. I do everything I can to help people survive, not leave them to their fate.' She glanced across at Jenny. 'Anyway, talking of risks, what about you and Pip?'

'What about me and Pip?'

'I know you're up to something. Have been for months. Always off in Dad's shed with your Shakespeare book. I don't imagine for one second you're play-reading in there. It's got something to do with the Resistance, hasn't it?'

Jenny smoothed down the covers. 'Maybe. But it's best you don't know.'

'Fair enough. But it's obvious you're involved in some sort of secret activity. Why shouldn't I do something too?'

'But you're doing your bit at the hospital.'

'I know. But I need to protect Rebekah. She's been good to me, always helping me out on the wards. The patients love her; she always goes the extra mile for them. How could I look Tom in the face if I didn't try to save her?' A tic pulled at the corner of Alice's eye and she rubbed at it. 'Just promise me you'll keep her safe if anything happens to me.'

'Of course. You know I'd do anything to save someone from the Germans. I hate them so much.' Jenny leant over to punch her pillow into shape, then laid it flat, ready to lie down. 'But if you get caught, I'll never forgive you.'

23

Alice donned her surgical mask and grimaced at herself in the cloakroom mirror. She hated wearing a mask: breathing in her own stale air and not being able to smile at the patients she wanted to reassure. On the other hand, it solved the dilemma about lipstick. They weren't allowed make-up on the wards, although in the past some of the more brazen girls had risked it. Most people had run out of cosmetics by now anyway, but several times she'd noticed a fellow nurse with unusually stained lips and wondered if she'd daubed them with beetroot juice, the current substitute. Apparently it worked well, but Alice wasn't inclined to try it.

She tucked a few stray hairs under her cap, pulled on a pair of surgical gloves and made her way down the corridor. But instead of going straight onto the main ward as usual, she turned right towards a wooden door with a small porthole window cut into it. She peered through the glass, then knocked softly.

'Come in,' said a shaky voice.

Alice entered the room. 'Good morning, dear.'

The patient was sitting up in bed in a pink crocheted bed jacket, looking pale. Even the act of greeting Alice caused her to cough.

'Did you have a good night?' Alice drew a small test tube out of her apron pocket and removed its rubber bung.

'Not too bad, Nurse, although I still have this wretched cough keeping me awake.'

Alice made sympathetic noises, but inside she acknowledged that that was exactly what was needed.

'All right. Let's test that cough, shall we? I need you to take a deep breath and hold it for five seconds.'

The patient inhaled raggedly, watching Alice's face as she counted.

'. . . two, three, four, five. Good. Now breathe out.'

She exhaled, and Alice heard a rattling sound.

'Now take another deep breath, cough hard and don't swallow.'

The woman followed Alice's instructions, then clamped her hand to her chest and slumped back on the pillows.

'I'm sorry – one more thing. Do you have any sputum in your mouth?'

The woman nodded.

'Then please spit it into here.' Alice held the test tube under the patient's mouth as she hawked up some phlegm, then spat it out, until a few globules nestled in the bottom. She rammed in the bung and stowed the tube safely.

'There we are. All done. Thank you. Someone will be in with your breakfast soon.'

The woman wheezed her thanks and Alice replaced the test tube in her apron then left the room. She'd have liked to bring the patient a cup of tea herself, but time was of the essence. She needed to find Stefan.

She whipped off her surgical mask and gloves and made her way to the stock room.

As soon as she stepped inside, someone grabbed her.

'Stefan!'

He put his arms round her and drew her towards him. 'Good news. Colonel Knackfuss has agreed. You're off the deportation list!' Relief rippled across his features.

She hugged him back, enjoying his reassuring warmth. 'Thank God. How did you convince him?'

'He was reluctant at first, probably suspicious that I was pleading for an islander. But I impressed on him how you had volunteered to help the injured after the explosion . . . and how you helped save my life when I had that appendectomy. I convinced him we needed to keep such a skilled nurse. Why send all that expertise and care to the internment camps? I even implied that you could be transferred to our part of the hospital . . .'

'Well, I'm not sure I'd be prepared to do that, but thank you.' She felt weak with relief; she hadn't realised until that moment how much strain she'd been under. But although she longed to kiss him, there was something she had to do first. She delved into her pocket and drew out the test tube. 'I got the sputum. Here it is. Should be a good sample.'

Stefan held the test tube up to the dim light of the stock room and nodded. 'Well done, Alice.'

'Do you think it will work?'

'I will do my best. Thank goodness for my fellow country-men's hatred of disease.' His blue eyes darkened. 'But we're taking a huge risk.'

Alice gnawed at her bottom lip. 'Are you sure you're prepared to do this?' She knew she was asking a lot of him. Their love was so new, so fragile. Did she have any right to put it to the test like this? And what if they were caught? She could hardly bear to think what the consequences might be.

His grip on her shoulder tightened. 'I know we've only been

together a short time, Alice, but I've never felt this way about anyone before. I would give up my life for you.'

Her body flooded with warmth as she reached up to him. Their kiss aroused the same strong feelings as before. She saw again the flaming sunset, heard the call of a stonechat and felt the softness of Stefan's arm under her head. And at once she knew she wasn't prepared to wait. No one knew what the future would bring. If their plan failed, she might never see him again. He'd told her he loved her. She'd never forgive herself if she didn't show how much she loved him back. 'Can you borrow the car this evening?' she asked.

'I can try. Why?'

'Then take me back to Portelet Common.'

Her breath caught as she saw the longing in his eyes. And she knew she'd made the right decision.

Alice hurried round to Rebekah's house after her shift. Rebekah led her disconsolately into her bedroom. Several drawers had been pulled open, revealing neatly stacked, if frayed, underwear and a number of folded jumpers. A couple of dresses and blouses were strewn on the bed. There was little trace of Tom in the room. He hadn't been home since he went to England to enlist, three years ago now. Sometimes Alice forgot that Rebekah was a married woman; she seemed more like a fellow spinster these days.

'Do you want a hand?' she asked her.

Rebekah shrugged. 'I'm only allowed to take a small bag. What on earth should I bring?' She picked up a photo from the table beside her bed. The picture must have been taken on their wedding day: Rebekah, small and dark, swathed in

237

white satin, and Tom in uniform, smiling into the camera. 'I wonder if I should take this out of its frame so it's easier to hide. I can't bear to be parted from it.'

'Why don't you sit down, Rebekah?' Alice asked. 'I've something to tell you.'

Rebekah gave her a puzzled look, but moved aside the garments on the cream candlewick counterpane and perched on the bed.

'I think we've found a way to prevent you being deported.'

'How?' Rebekah's expression was a mixture of hope and disbelief.

'All deportees have to pass a fitness test before they can be shipped out.'

She nodded. 'The Germans are keen to get rid of us, but they won't risk it if we're not healthy,' she said bitterly.

'Well, that's it. You won't be taking that test. You've given a positive result for tuberculosis.'

'What? But I haven't . . .'

'It's all right. It's a ruse.' Alice explained about the sputum sample. 'Stefan is arranging it with the authorities now. You won't be sailing to Germany tomorrow. You need to go into quarantine at the General.'

'But what if the medical staff find out I don't really have TB?'

'You won't be staying long enough,' replied Alice. 'There's a plan in place to move you somewhere safer.'

'How?'

'Stefan will smuggle you out of the hospital while everyone's down at the harbour seeing off the deportees. Then Pip will take you to a safe house. You can hide there until the war is over.'

Rebekah swallowed. 'It's all so much to take in. How will Tom be able to contact me? What if he comes back and thinks I'm dead? And my family will be worried sick.'

Alice joined her on the bed and put her arm round her, aware of Rebekah's rapid heartbeat, her small frame rigid with shock. 'We'll sort all that out further down the line, but try to trust us for now. It's your best chance of surviving the war, and of being reunited with Tom and your family.'

Rebekah swallowed again and turned away. 'Please don't think I'm not grateful,' she said, her voice muffled. 'It was such a shock finding out I was going to be deported. I knew we were all vulnerable, of course, but I convinced myself that my job would keep me safe, so I just kept my head down and worked as hard as I could. I'd give anything to stay on the island, but what if Stefan is unsuccessful? Or someone sees me leaving the hospital and follows me? Or the safe house is ransacked? I could be shot if the Germans found out I'd deceived them.'

Alice squeezed her arm. 'There's always a risk. But the risk of where the Germans will send you is far greater. You've heard the reports, and Stefan has confirmed that Jewish people are being badly treated at the camps. If you stay on Jersey, you're more likely to survive. I'd never forgive myself if I didn't try everything to save you. You've been such a good friend to me, Rebekah. And to my whole family.' She thought of William's face lighting up whenever he saw her, and Mum and Jenny adored her. And then there were all the patients who loved her too.

She hugged her tightly. 'Be strong,' she urged.

Rebekah gave her a watery smile.

24

Pip stood at the junction of Lempriere Street and Devonshire Lane, waiting for Rebekah to arrive. A sharp breeze rustled the browning leaves and dislodged acorns from an old oak that stood on the corner. Every so often one would fall with a plop to the ground, making him jump. He'd stowed Jenny's bike in the woods and covered it with fallen branches for camouflage. He had his own bike with him. If anyone came past, he'd pretend to tinker with the chain, muttering to himself, and hope no one would offer to help.

Pip finally felt he trusted Stefan, and thought of him as an ally now; in some ways he preferred him to Robert Durand, who was all talk and flash idealism but didn't seem to care much about people. Stefan was much more humane and prepared to act on his principles. Clever, too. He'd successfully got Alice off the deportations list, and had managed to convince the German medical officer that Rebekah had TB. So far, so good. The risk now was to ensure she emerged safely from the hospital without anyone realising she hadn't gone into isolation as medical rules dictated. Once she was admitted, it would be harder to help her escape without someone noticing. She'd taken her nurse's uniform with her, and the plan was for her to wear it out of the hospital. Hiding in plain sight, it was called, the theory being that people didn't question what they usually saw – their brains just pronounced it normal. Luckily, everyone was so busy now at the General that he doubted anyone would give her a second glance. And of course, most of the population was making its way down to the harbour to wave goodbye to the poor sods who were being deported.

He'd managed to get her a safe house for the first couple of nights. Robert had come good and found an old barn over near La Rocque. They'd decided not to involve Jenny and Alice in today's rescue mission. Alice had played her part getting the sputum, and Jenny was needed at Dad's. Besides, if something went wrong, it was better not to risk all four of them.

It had been difficult to get away from his wall-building duties, but he'd managed to send word to Ed, one of his co-workers, that he'd got a bad bout of flu. He'd probably be made to work twice as hard to make up for lost time, but as long as no one spotted him, he could get Rebekah over to the barn and make sure she was okay before he returned to work later in the week.

Another gust of wind ruffled his hair, and he smoothed it down. It would be quite rough in the Channel. Poor bastards. It was bad enough being deported, let alone encountering a gale on the way out. He imagined the storm-tossed boats with their bilious passengers, some crying, others throwing their guts up over the sides. What a nightmare.

At long last, Rebekah appeared. He'd imagined she'd look relieved, if wary, but one glance at her white face and fear started to spread through his veins.

'Are you all right?'

She shook her head. She appeared to have been crying. 'I got away safely,' she said. 'But there's been a problem with Alice.'

'Alice?'

She ran her hands through her hair, dislodging her cap. 'Apparently Colonel Knackfuss wasn't happy that they were one nurse down in the deportation, with me having contracted tuberculosis. It seems that a certain quota of medical staff is needed to accompany the passengers.' She made an apologetic face. 'So he demanded that another nurse be sent in my place.' She took a shuddering breath. 'He consulted the list and reinstated Alice.'

'My God.' Pip's stomach lurched.

'She's making her way to the harbour now.'

What on earth was he going to tell Jenny? 'That's appalling. Was she allowed to say goodbye to her family?'

'I'm afraid not. I'm so sorry, Pip. There was nothing Stefan could do this time. I feel terribly guilty. It was only because she was determined to save me that this happened. And now she's on her way to Germany and Stefan is distraught. Her poor, poor family.' The tears ran unchecked down her face.

'Well, it's good that you're safe,' he said lamely, although his heart still pounded against his chest wall.

Rebekah shot him a guilty look. 'Stefan thinks Alice will be well treated in Germany,' she said. 'And maybe the war will not last so long.'

'I hope he's right,' said Pip.

'I can't thank you enough for helping me, but I feel so awful about Alice. I warned her to be wary about trusting Stefan. I was worried she was too blindly in love to use her judgement. But it seems she was right: he was true to his word in helping me, and it's poor Alice who has paid the price.'

'Well, let's concentrate on getting you to safety.' He helped Rebekah onto the saddle of his bike, trying to remain positive. But deep down, he was devastated to hear what had happened. He couldn't imagine how the rest of the Robinsons would cope. They'd already lost so much. He'd cycle over there as soon as he could. But first he had to get Rebekah to the safe house, even though his heart was no longer in the mission. All he could think of was Alice on her way to the boat that would take her to Germany. And how the terrible news would affect Jenny.

'Hold on tight to me,' he said, climbing on in front of her and standing on the pedals. 'It'll be hard going, but we don't have to go far.'

He gritted his teeth and pressed down, and they wobbled off, Rebekah's arms round his waist and Pip pushing with all his strength. Luckily she was small and slim, but it still required a lot of effort. The anxiety about Alice and the fear that they'd all be discovered and arrested filled his mind as he pedalled. He was worried too that someone would have discovered Jenny's bike – all transport was so hard to come by these days, and there were often bicycle thefts. When they reached the woods, Rebekah kept watch while Pip rushed towards the trees. He hoped he'd remembered where he'd left it. It wasn't in the first place he looked, and his heart was starting to hammer again. He was too exhausted to take her pillion the whole way to the barn. He had to find it.

After ten minutes of increasingly frantic searching, he

unearthed the bike buried in some undergrowth. He'd obviously hidden it well. He took out his tool kit and lowered the saddle for Rebekah, then they cycled sadly off to La Rocque together.

⚓

Alice stood on the quayside, numb with shock. It had always been a risk trying to save Rebekah, and she was still glad that that part had gone well. But she'd never dreamt she'd be summoned instead. Colonel Knackfuss had personally intercepted her as she was leaving the hospital. He wouldn't even let her go home to say goodbye to her family or fetch her belongings. 'No time,' he'd shouted, his eyes seething. 'Go! Now!' And Alice had fled, charging down to the harbour, her breath ragged, snot and tears clogging her throat, her heart screaming for Stefan.

She scanned the crowd frantically, but there was no sign of him. Surely he'd try to get away and say goodbye? What if someone had found out about the sputum? Was he even now being interrogated? Her pulse accelerated with each terrible thought. Thank goodness they'd had that last night together. She allowed herself to remember the electric heat of his touch, the quickening of their breath, the melting of skin into skin. Those memories might be all she had now.

The crowd shuffled forward as the passenger boats arrived in a surge of spray. Alice looked around for anyone she knew. There were a couple of girls from the year below her at school, presumably of English parentage like herself, and a lad she knew vaguely from the youth club she used to attend.

The elderly woman in front of her, with a missing front tooth and foul breath, turned round and peered at the ground

244

beside her. 'Don't you have any belongings?' she asked. Alice realised how she must stand out. Everyone else was clutching bags or suitcases, packed, no doubt, with warm clothing.

She explained about the last-minute decision to add her to the list.

'Here.' The old woman took off her bulky serge coat and drew a blue knitted jumper up over her head, exposing several other layers of clothing. 'Have this. I can do without it.'

'Are you sure?'

'Yes, love. You'll catch your death otherwise.'

'Thank you.' Alice took off her cape and put the jumper on over her uniform. When she replaced the cape, she struggled to do it up, but at least she was warmer. Her heart swelled at this stranger's generosity.

There was a nudge at her elbow. A little girl appeared and handed her some black socks. 'From my mum,' she said.

'Please thank her for me,' said Alice, rolling the socks into a ball.

The child ran off.

More and more garments were passed forward: a Fair Isle cardigan, a pair of woolly stockings, some greying underwear, and even a small rucksack. Alice piled the items into the rucksack, smiling her thanks to the rest of the queue. How selfless people were, handing over items they must have needed for themselves. It wasn't as though they'd been allowed to take much. However much of a disaster it was being deported at the last minute, at least she was with other islanders, and kind ones at that.

Gradually she found out more from her fellow passengers. Some soldiers had told them they were to cross to France, then go by train to Germany. One theory was that they might be headed for the south of the country. Despite Stefan's assurances, she knew it would certainly not be a holiday. But she was probably better able to cope with a tough regime than most. She was used to early mornings and long days from her time as a nurse. And she certainly wasn't a stranger to hard work – she'd endured many a fourteen- or sixteen-hour shift since the beginning of the war. Nor was she unfamiliar with meagre rations and grinding hunger.

He still hadn't arrived, and it was almost too late now. She hoped to God he was all right. And he'd be worried sick about her too. 'Just keep us both alive,' she prayed.

Loud booming sounds travelled across the water. The Germans must be defending their occupation of France against the Allies. She hoped they wouldn't be caught up in the attack on the journey to Saint-Malo. The war felt horribly close.

The boats were docked now and the crowd thronged forward, but German soldiers with red faces and veins bulging in their foreheads held people back. Alice thought of Stefan's gentle doctor's hands – lover's hands now – and recoiled from the guards. Some of them started to search the deportees, confiscating cameras, photographs, jewellery and excess cash; Alice was worried they'd find her nurse's watch, but it remained safe under her cape.

As they waited to board the boats, she caught sight of a familiar face in the crowd. Dear Mrs Perchard, one of her ex-patients. Alice had nursed her back to health and she was now living with her daughter in one of the little cottages down by the harbour. The poor woman, it must be her daughter being deported. She wondered why.

'Mrs Perchard!' she shouted above the noise of the crowd and the soldiers. She waved frantically. 'Mrs Perchard!'

The woman's milky blue eyes scanned the passengers in the queue, but she clearly hadn't seen her.

'Mrs Perchard!' Alice thought she'd have a damaged larynx if she screamed any louder. The crowd surged forward as the Germans motioned to people to start boarding. She tried to stand her ground but was swept along by the tide of people. She couldn't risk leaving the queue or she'd lose her place, so she swivelled round, stood on tiptoe and waved frantically. 'Mrs Perchard!'

Suddenly Mrs Perchard spotted her. 'Nurse Robinson!'

Alice had once mentioned to the elderly lady where she lived. She just hoped she'd remember. 'Can you get word to my family?' she shouted. 'Tell them I love them. That I'll be back as soon as I can.' She was suddenly too choked to continue.

Mrs Perchard smiled and nodded sadly. Her words were borne away by the wind, but Alice hoped she'd heard her and that she would contact Mum and the others. It was all she could do. She daren't leave a message for Stefan.

There was no time for anything else. The men were herding them onto the boats, which were little more than cleaned-up coal vessels with rust-caked sides. Alice stumbled up the gangway and rushed to the far gunwale, the one that faced shore, suddenly conscious that she wouldn't see the familiar coastline for a long time. She took out her hanky and blotted her cheeks. She was still shaking from the horror of the last few hours.

'Are you all right?' A dark-haired woman about her own age looked at her sympathetically.

Alice sniffed and nodded. 'I've just had a shock.'

'I'm sorry to hear that. Is there anything I can do?'

She had such kind eyes that Alice found herself telling her about the morning's ordeal.

'How terrible to be deported without notice.' The woman looked devastated for her. She held out her hand. 'I'm Clara Steiner.'

'Alice Robinson.' It seemed odd to be performing an act of such civility on the filthy deck as sailors bustled around them preparing to weigh anchor. Like most of the deportees, the woman was dressed in old clothes, chosen for practicality rather than style, yet she wore them with an elegance that made her stand out. She had a strange name too. Steiner wasn't a Jersey surname, although there'd been a Clara at Alice's school. Nothing like this slim, dark woman, though. 'You're not an islander then?' Alice asked. In normal circumstances the question might have appeared over familiar, but there was something about the intimacy created by being jostled together as more people joined them, and the process of confiding her story, that emboldened her.

Clara grimaced. 'I'm from England originally,' she said. 'My husband was Jersey born and bred. But he was also Jewish. He had his identity card stamped with a J early on. Stupidly, we thought that would be it. He wasn't a threat to anyone, working in his parents' jewellery shop. We imagined he'd be safe if he kept his head down. But then the edicts started.'

Alice looked at her sympathetically. Rebekah had suffered from the succession of German orders too: the identity cards, the curfews, the restricted shopping. Thank God they'd rescued her in time.

Clara pinched the top of her nose. 'First we had to put up a sign on the shop saying that it was Jewish-owned. Then we were prohibited from owning a business altogether. The shop has been taken over by "pure" islanders now.' Her tone was bitter.

'I'm so sorry.' But there was worse to come.

Clara took a juddering breath. 'Samuel was arrested back in April and taken to France.' She fiddled with the handles of her carpet bag. 'I don't know where he went from there.'

'How awful. You must be out of your mind with worry.'

She nodded mutely, and Alice put a hand on her arm.

'Were your parents-in-law taken too?'

'Thank God no. They got out before the war, leaving Samuel in charge of the business. It's my only consolation, that they at least are safe in England.' Clara's voice was heavy with sadness. 'It's the not knowing where my husband is that's hardest. I've spent six months trying to find out where he was taken, but there's been no word from him. And now I'm being deported too. How on earth will I ever track him down?'

Alice moved her hand to Clara's shoulder and squeezed it. She knew that she herself would miss Stefan desperately, but they'd only been together for a few weeks. She couldn't imagine how Clara must feel, being separated from her husband. And it was so cruel that she was also being sent away.

They fell silent as the boat chugged out of the harbour. People were still standing on the quayside, waving and chanting. A cry of 'One, two, three, four . . . who the hell are we for?' went up from the crowd.

All around her, Alice's fellow deportees yelled back: 'Churchill . . . England . . . Jersey!'

The defiant rendition of 'There'll Always Be an England'

continued to drift across the sea long after the crowd had become a blurred mass.

Someone announced that the boats were the same ones that had been used to transport the slave workers. Alice saw again the tortured, emaciated figures of the OT gang. She imagined them clutching the sides of the boat, rigid with terror as to what lay ahead. And now she was standing where they had, equally fearful for the future. Her body tensed with fear. In saving Rebekah, had she signed her own death warrant? Her heart heaved for Clara, and her husband too. For all of them really. And in front of her the boat pitched and lurched in the increasingly strong wind.

⬧

Jenny was in the garden cleaning windows with newspaper soaked in vinegar when she heard the whirr of a bicycle and caught sight of Pip speeding up the drive. The brakes screeched as he came to a halt and propped the bike up against the front wall of the house.

'I'm in the back garden, Pip,' she called. But at the sight of his expression, her body turned icy.

When he told her about Alice, the ground rushed towards her.

'It's all right. I've got you.' Pip was kneeling beside her, his arm under her shoulders. She couldn't speak. 'I'll get you some water,' he said.

'Mum?'

'Do you want me to tell her?'

Jenny nodded, gagging on the astringent odour of the vinegar. She turned aside and vomited her lunch onto the grass.

* * *

Later, after Pip had spoken to Mum, he escorted Jenny into the kitchen, where she slumped, still dizzy, onto a chair.

An urgent thought penetrated the fog of horror. 'What about Rebekah?'

'She's fine. Safely installed in Farmer Picot's barn. He's supplied her with food, and there's plenty of straw, so she should be warm for the night. And there's an outside wash-house she can use.'

'That's good. I'll try to cycle over there tomorrow.'

'Only if you're up to it.'

'I'll see.' She curled her fingers over the edge of the table; she felt she had to hang on or she'd fall.

'I'm sorry, but I'll have to get back. I'm supposed to have flu,' Pip said, looking at her anxiously. 'I can't risk being seen out.'

'Of course. I'll be all right now.' Her head was throbbing. She still felt cold, but the dizziness was receding.

'I'll give you a ring this evening.'

'Thanks.'

He kissed the top of her head, said goodbye to Mum, who was standing hunch-shouldered by the window, and left.

Once he had gone, Mum started to clean the kitchen furiously. They'd long since run out of Oxydol, and didn't even have a sliver of carbolic, but she added a teaspoon of baking soda to some hot water and scoured the inside of the oven with that. Jenny sat at the table and watched Mum's elbow frantically pumping up and down in time with a lock of hair that had escaped its clip and was pounding her forehead. She knew better than to talk when Mum was in this kind of mood. She glanced at Alice's empty chair and her breath caught in her chest.

Her sister must be close to the French coast by now. When Dad had tried to persuade Jenny to go to England, she'd imagined she'd be the one abroad while Alice stayed home to carry on nursing and keep Mum and William company. It was a mercy their father had never known how things would turn out.

She felt a panic as she imagined getting into bed without Alice to chat to. They'd long since buried the hatchet over Dad's death, although deep down she still felt guilty, and she knew instinctively that Alice would always blame her. Things had grown frosty again lately over Alice's relationship with Stefan. Perhaps Jenny had been too hard on her, allowing her hatred of Germans to blind her to her sister's feelings. She wished she'd had time to tell her how much she loved her, how terribly she'd miss her. A few days ago she'd come across some of the letters they'd written to each other as children, when they'd been the lighthouse sisters, and she realised with a pang how far they'd grown apart since those days.

The sound of frenzied cleaning drew her back. 'The kitchen will be sparkling soon, Mum.'

Mum stopped and rubbed her back. 'It needed a good going-over.' Her eyes were bloodshot and ringed with purple shadows. Poor Mum. Would there ever be an end to all the worry? 'I can't stop thinking of poor Alice on her own, crossing through Europe.'

'She's not on her own, Mum. There are plenty of islanders with her. She'll soon make friends.'

'But most of them will be in families.'

'I expect she'll be in demand once they know she's a nurse.'

'Yes. And Alice is so practical. Takes after me,' said Mum.

And I take after Dad, thought Jenny. The cream limestone colleges of Cambridge loomed in front of her. Mostly her ambition was to the back of her mind, a faint desire, but now it blazed vividly again, fuelled by a surge of anger. Bloody Germans and the bloody war. How dare they take away everything she held dear? 'Mum, the war has to end at some point,' she said. 'We have to win. And then Alice will come back. And I will go to Cambridge. It will all be fine. Just you see.'

'I hope to God you're right,' said Mum.

Jenny tried to smile reassuringly at her, but inside her resolve hardened. She'd redouble her efforts to help with the Resistance work. Pip had spoken about further aid needed for the labourers, and the possibility of getting coded messages to them about safe houses. She'd volunteer for everything she could. And try her utmost to convince herself that she'd see Alice again.

25

Alice lay in the chasm-like hold of the ship, her body pitched backwards and forwards by the rough sea, trying to fight the swell of sickness. They'd been sent below deck as soon as they were out in open water and the other deportees were packed in around her, many of the men having to lie between the rafters. Every time the boat lurched one way, she was thrown towards Clara on her right; every time it lurched back, Clara rolled towards her and she was shoved into an elderly lady on the other side. After a while, they gave up apologising. The icy water from the bottom of the ship seeped into her cape, and the air was rancid with the stale breath and farts of the other passengers. There was always a baby or a young child crying, and often several. She hadn't expected a glamorous crossing, but this was beyond her worst nightmares. She shut her eyes and tried to block out the stench and sounds, taking her mind to Portelet Common with Stefan's body pressed into hers and the clean, warm smell of him as they lay on the soft grass with the watchtower gleaming in the distance.

The boat see-sawed its way across the Saint-Malo basin until eventually word got round that they'd reached the lock gates. She told Clara about the engineers blowing them up two years ago when Pip had sailed out to rescue the British soldiers. They must have been mended by now. Pip had found

254

the whole experience exhilarating, although by all accounts he'd been in awful danger, but he'd gone home to his own bed and his own life. Goodness knows when Alice or Clara would see home again – they could be away for years. And Clara might never be reunited with her husband. Alice breathed in the scent of her own sweat and fear and tried to take her mind back to Stefan once again.

Eventually the ship docked, and they were herded onto the quayside. When everyone had stumbled out, clutching their scant belongings, they were lined up and marched off to the station. A number of scowling soldiers holding rifles or fixed bayonets, and dressed in grey uniforms and black jackboots, pushed them onto the train. Alice was jolted towards a window seat and Clara managed to get a place opposite. She stuffed her backpack into the overhead rack and offered to do the same with Clara's belongings. Then she slumped down, her body tense with fear, as she watched the soldiers still shouting and waving their arms around on the platform.

'Look.' Clara wiped the dirty window with her palm. Alice did likewise and noticed a number of French women approaching the carriages, carrying bread and sausages. One of them motioned to her to lower the window, which Alice did, receiving the food gratefully. How brave of them to defy the soldiers, she thought as she shared the food with Clara and the other occupants of the carriage.

After a while, the train rumbled off. By now the seats were full. A large man with a continuous cough was pressed up against her. Clara's head was tipped back and her eyes closed. Perhaps, like Alice, she was trying to shut everything out and focus on her inner world.

Alice continued to look out of the window as the train rattled east towards Paris. If she gazed at the view, the world opened up – even if it was a dismal world unfolding before her. Every town they passed through seemed to have been bombed. Flattened houses, scarred fields and damaged buildings flashed by. Occupation was hard, but at least Jersey had largely remained intact: the Germans weren't going to attack their own soldiers. France, though, had had it bad. Maybe England was the same.

By the third day, they'd used up nearly all their rations. People had long since stopped talking to each other. Instead they conserved energy by sleeping or staring into space. Travelling was exhausting, and who knew what lay ahead.

When the train crossed the border into Germany, she reminded herself that this was Stefan's place of birth – she imagined him running through the green fields, jumping over brooks, climbing trees. The daydream sustained her through a blur of landscapes and stations.

They stopped near Cologne, where the twin spires of the cathedral towered over the bomb-damaged landscape. Alice was appalled to see an open railway truck crammed with men, women and children. They had no shelter from the cold and the driving rain, which streamed down their hair and saturated their ragged clothing. Her heart ached at the haunting sight. She pulled down her window and threw the last of her bread and sausage across to them. There was a nudge at her elbow, and the large man gave her a half-empty packet of cigarettes, which she tossed across too. A thin woman with wet hair so tightly plastered to her head that she looked like a seal smiled faintly at her, and their eyes locked.

'Jews,' muttered Alice's neighbour.

Alice winced, immediately conscious of Clara. She thought of Rebekah too. If she'd saved her friend from this miserable fate, she'd done a good thing. But Clara's husband had had no such reprieve. The poor man.

There'd been many rumours on the train as to their final destination. Some thought it would be Dorsten on the Dortmund Canal; others thought Essen, where they had to stay all night while Allied bombs whistled overhead and the air was filled with the crash and crack of falling masonry. They were terrified the Allies would attack the train, not realising it was full of Channel Islanders, and most of them spent a sleepless night before they finally departed.

By the time they arrived in Biberach, where they discovered their camp lay, Alice's back ached and her mind was filled with foreboding. She set off with Clara and the other prisoners up the steep and winding path from the station, longing for the glistening sea and golden bays of Jersey. But all she saw were hills and trees and dull dirt paths. The long trek elongated the line of prisoners: she and Clara were with the younger, fitter members at the front, then came men lugging heavy suitcases, followed by women struggling with babies and young children, and finally the elderly and infirm, who fell further and further behind, only to be rounded up and shouted at by bad-tempered German guards.

The light was fading and a mean autumn wind numbing their hands and ears by the time they arrived at the camp. First they had to hand in any jewellery. Alice reluctantly surrendered her watch. It had seen her through all her years at the General. Another link with Jersey gone. She felt strangely diminished without it. No longer capable Nurse Robinson, but just a young, frightened girl again.

'I'd give anything to keep my wedding ring,' Clara murmured. 'When Samuel placed it on my finger five years ago, I swore I'd never remove it.'

A guard approached her, and she shrank back, her face filled with alarm. 'Put it in your pocket,' he whispered in English. 'I'll let you through.'

Clara shut her eyes in relief. 'Thank you.' She passed by without being searched.

Alice hoped they'd be allowed to go straight to their dormitories to unpack, but the Germans had other ideas. Stern-faced guards with whistles herded them over to a parade ground, where they stood in the freezing gloom for a roll call. As the searchlights swept over them, Alice saw faces etched with exhaustion, trepidation and misery. What on earth was in store for them all?

'I don't know how much more of this I can stand,' she whispered to Clara. 'Surely they'll give us some food soon.' Her gaze followed the barbed wire that encircled the camp, draped at intervals with what appeared to be washing: pale garments that flapped like trapped birds in the gloom. Low buildings lay in the distance. Perhaps those were the dormitories. She couldn't smell any food cooking.

Clara nodded, white-lipped. 'I just want to climb into bed and sleep for ever.'

They were eventually released, row by row, and directed towards an officer with a typed list of names in his hands. Alice could hear him barking questions at each prisoner, his Adam's apple straining against the stiff collar of his tightly buttoned uniform.

Most people were directed to the man's right, where the dormitories lay. But some of them were sent to a shadowy area on the left where it was too dark to make anything out.

Clara was ahead of her in the queue.

'*Name?*'

'Clara Steiner.' Clara's back was rigid, her fingers straining on the handle of her bag.

The officer consulted his list. '*Jüdin?*'

'My husband is Jewish, yes,' answered Clara in a low voice. 'But I am a Gentile.'

He looked her up and down, his eyes glittering in the darkness. '*Jüdin,*' he pronounced, and shot his arm out towards the left.

Clara looked back at Alice, her mouth trembling.

Alice tried to smile encouragingly. 'I'll see you later,' she whispered.

Clara nodded and trudged off in the direction the officer had pointed. Alice took her place at the front of the queue.

'*Name?*' The man's voice was sharp in the cold air.

'Alice Robinson.'

He looked down at his list, his stubby finger tracking the names. His eyes lingered on her face, his expression inscrutable.

Alice didn't dare breathe.

Again the arm shot out, this time in the other direction. '*Rechts.*'

She picked up her backpack and headed towards her designated barrack room, relieved to at least be housed in a brick building, but dismayed to be separated from Clara. Where had the guard sent her friend?

* * *

Later, as she sat in the bleak refectory, eating the watery stew and gristly meat they were eventually served, Alice scanned the other inmates for Clara, but couldn't see her anywhere. Perhaps her barracks had a separate dining room. She felt an unknown dread creeping through her and hoped Clara was all right.

She tried not to think of Mum, Jenny and William sitting down to vegetable broth or potato peel pie, or of the picnic she'd shared with Stefan in the hospital gardens. She was here now and she had to make the best of things. Although she couldn't suppress another stab of anxiety for Clara.

The next morning revealed surroundings that had been hidden in the darkness of the night before. The area where Clara had been sent was much more run-down than Alice's own barracks, which were spartan enough. The Germans had obviously put those with Jewish connections in a separate part of the camp. Alice was desperate to visit her friend but was told in no uncertain terms that that wouldn't be allowed. She'd just have to hope she came across her soon.

The camp was situated on a river, high above sea level, on a huge plateau with views across to the Bavarian Alps. Through the barbed wire that surrounded it, Alice could see wide, gently rolling hills, dark-green forests, and fields where shire horses pulled farm ploughs. It would have been beautiful but for the biting cold that saw her breath become clouds in the freezing air and made her toes and fingers shriek with pain. It would be lovely here in summer, she thought to herself, then stopped, horrified. If they were still here in summer, it would mean the war was still going on. And there was a long and arduous winter to face before that. This might be Stefan's birth country, and he might have assured her that prisoners would be well treated, but the thought of being separated from him for so long was almost unbearable.

And she still hadn't found Clara.

Jenny and Mum sat in the small lounge, needles and thread in hand, sewing up seams. Earlier, Mum had cut down the middle of their old bed sheets and turned them over so that the less worn bits were now in the centre: 'sides to middle' it was called. There hadn't been new linen in the shops for years, so this was the only way of making the sheets last longer. William in particular, with his ever-growing feet and restless limbs, seemed to tear at the thin fabric with his toenails during his sleep, even though they made him cut them regularly. Jenny wondered how long the repairs would last and what they would do when William ruined another sheet. The thought that they could give him Alice's brought her little comfort.

They'd drawn their chairs closer to the window to catch the dwindling light. Jenny glanced at Mum's face, lit by the low sun seeping through the lace curtains. Even more lines had appeared recently, and her skin sagged in a way it hadn't before the war. Her hair was threaded through with silver now, and she wore an expression of almost permanent anxiety. Poor Mum. She'd suffered so much.

But her hands were still nimbler than Jenny's as she stretched the fabric between the thumb and forefinger of her left hand, while making tiny, even stitches with her right.

Mum had tried to teach Jenny to sew when she was younger, but Jenny had much preferred doing crossword puzzles with Dad, her brain intoxicated with the challenge of fathoming out the clues. Sewing was mind-numbingly boring, and she clearly lacked Mum's finesse. Alice had been much better at those practical tasks.

Alice. As usual, Jenny's thoughts turned to her sister. She must be at the camp by now. She hoped the conditions were as tolerable as Stefan had suggested. It would be unbearable to think of Alice in terrible squalor.

As if to echo her thoughts, Mum asked, 'What do you think Alice is doing now?'

Jenny reached for the scissors and snipped the end of a thread. 'I don't know. I just hope she's all right.'

'So do I.' Mum handed Jenny the cotton reel. 'I'm glad Rebekah's safe, of course, but Alice has paid such a high price to save her friend.'

'I know. None of us anticipated that getting one nurse off would mean they requisitioned another. We just didn't think things through carefully enough.'

'If that Stefan really loves her, as you seem to think he does, why didn't he try harder to save her?'

'He tried as hard as he could. As soon as he heard about Alice, he rushed to the Feldkommandant and attempted to persuade him.' Colonel Knackfuss had been furious, and it had taken all Stefan's skill to calm him down. He'd been worried that if he persisted in begging for Alice to be let off, the Germans might uncover the plan to save Rebekah, and then they would all have been in danger. Poor Stefan. How was he to know their plan would go so wrong?

Mum sighed and jabbed at the sheet with her needle. 'Ouch.'

'Oh Mum, your finger's bleeding.' A red smudge appeared on the sheet.

'Damn,' she said, dropping the sewing and running into the kitchen to put her finger under the tap.

'I'll get a bandage,' said Jenny. 'I think Alice's first-aid box is still there.' She put down her own sewing and followed Mum into the kitchen, rummaging in one of the cupboards. 'Yes, here it is.' She opened the metal box and drew out a strip of gauze, which she wound clumsily round Mum's finger, trying to ignore the fact that Alice would have done it so much better. Would she be using her nursing skills at the camp? A faint stain appeared on the bandage, but didn't spread.

'Thanks, dear. I think that's stopped it.' Mum went to fetch the sheet, and scrubbed at the bloodied patch. 'And I've got the stain out too. No harm done.'

They returned to the sitting room. Mum sewed on in silence for a while. Jenny glanced at the dressing surreptitiously from time to time, but it stayed in place with no further bleeding.

Eventually Mum put down the finished sheet. 'I'll need to get supper on soon,' she said, but she didn't move.

'Mum, are you all right?'

She was gazing through the window, but Jenny could tell she wasn't looking at the view. 'I've always worried about Alice,' she said. 'She was never brainy like you.'

'Yes, but she was – is – practical,' replied Jenny. 'Much more useful these days.'

'I tried to compensate,' said Mum, drawing her hand across her eyes.

'Compensate for what?' Jenny could hear the sharpness in her own voice.

'For the fact that your father always favoured you.'

Jenny put down her own sewing. 'I suppose he did,' she

said. 'We thought alike. We understood each other. But I always thought Alice was *your* favourite, so it balanced out. And all of us favour William!'

Mum smiled wryly. 'Did you know that Alice liked Pip?'

Jenny paused. She thought back to that bright summer's day in 1940. All of them in the garden. She and Dad buried in a maths book as usual, William feeding Binkie, Mum dead-heading snapdragons. Then Pip arriving on his bike and suggesting they sail round to St Ouen's to watch for planes. Alice had accepted his invitation eagerly. 'I think I probably did deep down,' she acknowledged. 'But she never said anything. Did she confide in you?'

'Not in so many words, but I could tell.' Mum stood up to pull down the blackout, then walked stiffly out of the room.

Jenny followed her into the kitchen and watched her open the larder door, then stare vacantly at the scant contents.

'I'll start peeling vegetables,' she said, reaching past Mum for a limp cabbage and a couple of tiny turnips. She put them on the kitchen table and drew a couple of small knives from the cutlery drawer. 'Come and help me.'

Mum picked up one of the knives, then sat down wearily and started hacking at the cabbage. 'I just wonder whether this was some sort of test.'

Jenny joined her and began to peel one of the turnips. 'What do you mean?'

'Well, perhaps she thought she'd lost your father, then she lost Pip, so she wanted to test whether Stefan really loved her.'

'But it wasn't her decision to go!'

'It was her decision to save Rebekah. Being caught and deported – or worse – was always a risk.'

Jenny finished peeling the turnip and started cutting it into pieces. 'I don't know,' she said. 'I think you're making too much of this. It was just a horrible accident of fate.'

Mum was silent for a moment. 'I hope she didn't let things go too far with him,' she said quietly.

'Let's not worry about that now,' said Jenny.

Mum firmed her lips, then pulled a saucepan down from the rack, filled it with water and placed it on the stove.

Jenny gathered up the chopped vegetables and added them to the pan. 'Vegetable stew again,' she said.

Mum smiled thinly. 'Let's be grateful we at least have something to eat.' She took three knives and forks out of the drawer and laid them on the table.

There used to be five of us at this table, and now we're down to three, thought Jenny, staring at the empty places. She squeezed Mum's arm. Poor Mum. She was so tired and defeated. Jenny certainly didn't want to cause her any more pain, but she couldn't just sit back and do nothing. She was still actively looking for ways to help the Resistance, and she'd do everything in her power to help protect Rebekah. Stefan and Alice had risked their lives for her. Jenny would face whatever danger came her way.

26

With each day that passed, it became colder up at Grouville. Pip's breath was a white fog in the freezing air and the tips of his ears and nose were numb, despite the physical effort of picking up the stones and wedging them in place. He'd left his gloves behind too, and his raw fingers tingled from the cold and the sharp edges of the stones. He wondered how Rebekah was faring in this weather over at the barn. He and Jenny had visited her each day: she had plenty of warm clothes and blankets, thanks to the Robinsons' generosity, but the hours must hang heavy. At least he had something to occupy himself. He'd see if Jenny had any more books she could lend her when they cycled over that evening.

He was still working with Peter, Tom and Ed. They'd formed a functional friendship after days of labouring together, although he still thought Peter was on the sly side, forever watching him under that long fringe of his, or trying to get pally with the overseer. Mind you, the overseer had left them on their own a lot more recently. It was clear they were all hard workers – the wall was taking shape quickly – and despite them having been novices, the results were strong and neat. He still didn't like taking orders from Germans, but he told himself again that he was building the wall for the island, and Jersey deserved his best work.

He paused to look out across the bay. A seagull wheeled below him, searching for fish, soaring and plunging in the currents of air. And lower still, the waves surged in a boiling mass of white spume as they rushed up the sand. All around the island the sea was pounding at beaches and rocks, advancing and receding with the tides, oblivious to the war raging at its fringes. The *Bynie May* remained anchored at the yacht club, mercifully not yet requisitioned by the Germans and waiting for him as soon as he was free to sail her again.

Even though he saw this view each day, it still took Pip's breath away: the sweep of yellow sand, the lacy surf, the stern grey walls of Mont Orgueil Castle – or Gorey Castle, as the locals called it – in the distance.

Jersey had been under German control for twenty-six months now, and the island had become increasingly pockmarked by their fortifications and bunkers, but it was still beautiful, still the island he loved. And thanks to his dedication to wall-building, his resistance activities continued to go unnoticed.

Unusually for him, he had woken up early. He'd had time for an extra cup of tea that morning – or the bilge water that answered for tea these days – and it was now making his bladder uncomfortably full. Normally he waited until lunchtime to relieve himself in the makeshift latrine at the back of the storehouse, but it was only eleven and he couldn't hang on any longer. He checked the overseer was still absent, walked round to the back of the building, unbuttoned his fly and unleashed a stream of urine. Afterwards he decided to visit the storehouse to see if there were any gloves lying around. It would certainly make it easier to pick up the stones if he could borrow a pair. He pulled open the wooden door and went inside.

The storehouse was little more than a shack, hastily erected from old timber. The floor became damp in the rain, and the cold air penetrated every crack, but at least it was a shelter of sorts. A few implements were propped up against the wooden sides: two hoes, a rake and a couple of spades. There were some dusty sacks of cement and sand, and a box full of trowels at the far end. An intricate spider's web spanned two of the ceiling struts. Pip checked the shelves for gloves, but couldn't find any. What he did find, though, was a small wicker basket pushed into a corner. After peering through the window to check there was still no one around, he investigated the basket and found a hunk of cheese and a few small brioches. He seized one of the rolls and shoved it deep inside his pocket. Hopefully no one would miss it, and he could take it over to Rebekah later.

He resumed his place at the wall, picked up a large rock in his gloveless hand and continued his work.

He and Jenny cycled over to Farmer Picot's barn that evening. No one had stopped him to question him about the missing brioche and he hadn't seen anyone visit the storehouse all day. It seemed he'd got away with it. He'd never consider stealing from an islander – they were all struggling to find enough to eat, and it would be quite wrong to deprive one of his fellow countrymen – but he reckoned theft of German food was fair game. They'd requisitioned enough from Jersey folk. He was only taking what was rightfully theirs anyway.

They found Rebekah sitting on a hay bale, reading a battered copy of *Cards on the Table* by Agatha Christie. She looked up at the sound of voices. Jenny dashed over to give her a hug and Pip drew the brioche out of his rucksack. They'd found a few windfall apples on the way and had brought those along too.

'A feast!' exclaimed Rebekah, grabbing the roll and biting into it. 'Mmm. Still fresh. Thank you.'

Jenny smiled. 'I hope we're finding you enough to eat.'

'Of course you are. Food is hardly plentiful at the moment. I'm so grateful to you. Farmer Picot brings me milk each morning – and cheese when he can spare it. I have more than enough. Really.' She took another mouthful of brioche. 'I'm sorry,' she said. 'I've forgotten my manners. Would you like some?'

Pip shook his head.

'What, and spoil my appetite for the delicious vegetable broth awaiting me at home?' said Jenny.

Rebekah laughed. 'If you insist.' Then the vitality leached from her face. 'Have you picked up any signs that people are looking for me?'

'No,' said Pip. 'So far, so good.'

She took a juddering breath. 'I can't believe we've got away with it. I keep expecting German soldiers to burst in at any moment.'

Jenny put an arm round her. 'It was all so chaotic on the day of the deportations. If the hospital staff suspect anything, they must be keeping shtum, and the Germans seem satisfied they've still got their nurse.' She gnawed at a loose bit of skin beside her fingernail.

'Have you heard from Alice yet?' Rebekah's expression was a mixture of relief, concern and guilt.

'Nothing so far,' replied Jenny. 'I guess mail takes a long time to arrive, if they even allow them to write. Or maybe it won't get through at all.'

'I'm so worried about her,' said Rebekah. 'It's only September and it's already getting cold here. Goodness knows what it must be like in Germany. How will she manage through the winter months?'

'I expect there are heaters at the camp,' said Pip. 'They're probably a lot better equipped than we are here.' The Germans had cut their fuel allowance again recently. It was going to be a tough winter for them all. He wasn't worried for himself: all those weeks outside had toughened him up, and as a sailor he was already fairly hardy, but Dad had been looking frail recently, his skin papery and dark shadows under his eyes. The occupation had taken its toll on him: he seemed to have aged a lot in the last two years, and he worried about Pip working for the Germans. Thank God for Jenny. It was obvious Dad had grown fond of her since she'd started helping him at the office. She was much more suited to accountancy than he was. And she could keep an eye on him too.

They spent another hour with Rebekah. Pip had produced an old pack of cards and they played a few games of rummy, using the hay bale as a table, until the light in the barn started to grow dim.

'You two need to go if you're to get back before dark,' said Rebekah. 'Thanks for keeping me company. I've enjoyed it.'

'Are you sure you're all right?' asked Jenny, starting to collect up the cards.

'Of course. All mod cons here.' Rebekah waved a hand around her corner of the barn. She'd made it almost homely, rigging up a makeshift rail for the few clothes she'd brought with her, and arranging her books and a now lit torch on another bale that served as a bedside table. She slept on a blanket spread over a pile of straw, with another blanket and more straw on top. They had no idea how long it would have to serve as home, but it would certainly do for the time being.

Rebekah seemed calmer after Jenny's assurances that no one was looking for her. Pip had a feeling Stefan had done something to change the records too – the Germans were normally so efficient, it was hard to believe they weren't suspicious, but he hadn't heard anything to give him concern. It seemed she was safe for now.

They said their goodbyes, and Jenny and Pip set off back through the darkening lanes.

After a day spent familiarising themselves with the camp and its routines, which seemed to involve endless roll calls, the new inmates were given a little free time after the meagre meal that served as supper. At last Alice could search for Clara. Checking that no one was following her, she hurried down to the Jewish area, determined to find her new friend. Her heart thumped as she walked across the damp grass towards the cluster of shabby huts huddling together in the gloom. It was strangely silent; just the faint sound of wind riffling through the row of dark linden trees at the rear. She'd expected to hear human voices by now, the rattle of cutlery or even the sound of Germans giving orders. What on earth were the inmates doing? Ice inched up her spine. Was she about to come across a scene of carnage?

But before she could investigate further, three German

271

guards stepped out of the shadows, their expressions menacing in the darkening air. One rasped out a few words, which Alice couldn't understand, although the meaning was clear enough. They weren't going to let her go any further.

'Please,' she said, trying to make her voice sound as confident as possible. 'May I just see my friend? She was taken here last night.'

A second soldier spoke in English. 'It is forbidden for you to be here.'

'I haven't seen anyone from these huts all day. Are they all right?' Whenever she could during the day, she'd looked over towards the buildings Clara had been shown to but hadn't once glimpsed a sign of activity.

The soldier made a dismissive gesture with his hand. 'Go back to your own area.'

There was nothing else she could do. Reluctantly she turned back towards the main camp. How she wished Stefan was with her to remonstrate with the guards in his own language, or Jenny to come up with a clever plan. But she mustn't think of them now. She was on her own and she had to survive as best she could.

She spent the night worrying about Clara. She wasn't there at breakfast the next morning either, adding to Alice's fear. Where on earth was she? Did the guards last night know more than they'd let on? Were they in fact guarding a murder scene?

Alice could barely eat any breakfast, not that the watery porridge provided any temptation. But as she was leaving the refectory, a bedraggled line of prisoners arrived, and she glimpsed Clara amongst them. Thank God. Even from a distance she could see how pale her friend looked, and how subdued and wary her fellow Jews were, but at least they were alive.

She sidled past Clara as she waited in line, conscious of a guard staring at her. 'Meet me outside the latrines when you've finished,' she whispered.

Clara nodded.

Alice waited anxiously behind the grey concrete building that served as a toilet block until Clara appeared.

She embraced her friend with relief. 'I was so worried about you.'

Clara smiled thinly. 'Thank you, Alice. The Germans are making things as difficult as they can for us.'

'What happened?'

She pushed back a limp strand of hair. 'As you saw, everyone who is Jewish, or married to a Jew, was sent to the huts. We sleep on straw bedding and there is one basin between thirty people. Last night we were given orders that we had to stay put until the morning. But it seems someone relented and we're now allowed to come to the refectory.'

'You poor thing. Our accommodation isn't good, but at least we have proper beds.'

Clara shook her head. 'It's bearable,' she said. 'And somehow, experiencing these conditions makes me feel closer to Samuel. Things are doubtless much worse where he is. I couldn't bear to be sleeping in comfort when he's suffering so much.'

Alice smiled at her sadly. Poor Samuel. At least Stefan was safe on Jersey. And Rebekah had been spared the fate other Jews seemed to be suffering. She'd been so relieved to find Clara again. She'd felt an instant bond with her on the boat and she sensed they could help each other through the bleak days at Biberach, even if they wouldn't see as much of each other as she'd hoped. She embraced her friend again before making her way back to her own dormitory, ready for the day's chores.

Time passed slowly. During the day, it was possible to keep busy. There were three roll calls to attend, one before breakfast, one at eleven and one just before dinner. The guards seemed to spend so long over the process that at first Alice thought they weren't very good at counting – or maybe it was just that they enjoyed watching the prisoners shivering on the chilly parade ground. On one occasion they were furious that an internee had apparently gone missing. They counted and recounted everyone three times before someone remembered that the woman they were trying to track down had in fact been buried that morning.

Clara confirmed later that the deceased was from her hut. The weeks of deprivation had taken more of a toll on those in Clara's dormitory than elsewhere, and several of the women had fallen ill – or worse. Each day Clara appeared a little thinner, her face more pinched, her hair more lank. It was hard to associate her with the elegant woman Alice had first met on the Jersey quayside. But even more chilling was Clara's suspicion that the authorities didn't care about Jewish deaths.

'I can't believe the Germans miss them by mistake,' Clara said one bitter, windy day as they walked back from a roll call. 'They're far too precise in other ways. Look at how deftly we undesirables were picked out of the queue and sent to those squalid huts. They know exactly what they're doing.

Jews and spouses of Jews don't count. In more ways than one. It's obvious.'

Alice had to agree.

They were allowed to visit each other's barracks during the day. Sometimes Alice and Clara would play cards with a couple of other Jersey women. On other occasions they would go for walks in the still-luscious green forests, or along the meandering river, with the Bavarian Alps towering blue and rugged in the distance. As long as Clara returned to her sleeping quarters each evening, she and her fellow inmates were allowed relative freedom in the daytime. In some ways the camp was idyllic: the beautiful scenery, the pure mountain air. But then there were the overcrowded rooms, the dingy wooden beds, the endless shouting of the guards, the meagre food. A hellish place in a heavenly setting.

It was at night that Alice felt most homesick. She missed Stefan desperately, of course, and Jenny, Mum and William too, but she was surprised how much she longed for Jersey. Biberach was hundreds of miles from the sea. After lights-out, in an attempt to blot out the sighs and mutterings of her fellow inmates, she traced Jersey's coastline in her mind, viewing in her memory the sparkling bays, the craggy cliffs, the golden beaches. But her most vivid recollections coalesced around the lighthouses. At times she was back at St Catherine's Breakwater with Jenny and Dad, running down the steps to the tower, Jenny full of questions about measurements and frequency, Alice imagining frightened sailors on a storm-tossed sea, grateful for the guiding light. In her mind they were the lighthouse sisters once more, begging Dad to tell them a story about lamplighters, or how terrible shipwrecks had been avoided; writing little messages to each other to post in the box under the bed, along with their trademark drawings. Then she was on the boat with Pip, sailing towards the chalky-white tower at La Corbière, admiring its imposing presence as it stared implacably out over the Atlantic. But always her daydream ended with the watchtower at Noirmont, as she and Stefan glimpsed its gleam across the bay. There was something about its solidity that reminded her of him. And like him it would always be there, waiting for her.

All those lights. All those symbols of hope and comfort. They'd guided sailors home in days gone by; they would lead her home one day too. She had to believe it.

⚓

Jenny and Pip were huddled in the shed on a glacial November night. The windows were opaque with ice, and freezing rain drummed on the roof. Pip wore fingerless gloves and a black beret rammed down over his ears. Jenny had tied an old scarf round her head and had dressed in a long-sleeved blouse and her thickest jumper under her old winter coat.

As usual, Pip was listening to the BBC news, his pencil racing across the paper in a looping scrawl as he transcribed the newsreader's words. Jenny was trying to decipher his writing and translate into Spanish. When the transmission had finished, he turned to her, grinning. 'Did you get all that?'

'Not yet.' She frowned. 'Your writing is becoming more and more illegible. You need to translate it into recognisable English for me before I can translate it into Spanish.'

'Sorry.' Pip drew his hand through his hair. 'But it's great news, Jenny. The Eighth Army has secured the Middle East and Egypt at El Alamein. Good old Monty. That will really cheer up the Spaniards too.'

'Good old Monty indeed,' echoed Jenny. She blew on her numb fingers, then folded them into the sleeves of her coat. She'd taken on more work recently: helping Robert organise the safe houses, and devising coded messages to labourers in hiding. It was thrilling to be involved in the war effort, and her new responsibilities kept her from worrying so much about Alice.

'You know,' said Pip, 'we could still win this war.'

Jenny smiled at his optimism.

They turned back to their work, but after a few minutes, Jenny heard a car engine and caught the flash of headlights.

'Quick,' she said. She seized the radio from Pip, switched it off and eased it deftly into the book, while Pip extracted the headphones and placed them in the flowerpot before inserting the false bottom. Then they both pressed their pages of notes into seed trays and threw compost on top. It was a routine they'd practised from time to time and they'd got it down to a fine art. By the time footsteps approached, they were sitting at Dad's old workbench calmly repotting geraniums.

Jenny turned a puzzled face to Pip at the soft knock at the door. It was too timid to be a raid, and neither Mum nor William would have knocked.

Pip shrugged and went to investigate. It was Stefan, dressed in grey slacks and a navy Breton jumper, with a beret pulled low over his forehead, hiding his blond hair. Apart from his height, there was nothing to distinguish him from an islander. Pip ushered him in.

Jenny's heartbeat slowed a little at the sight of him. She peered over his shoulder, but there was no one with him.

'Excuse me for interrupting, but I've come to warn you,' he said, looking worried.

Jenny glanced at Pip in alarm.

'We have some search parties out hunting for escaped Russian slaves. The men are inspecting barns and remote farmhouses. I am worried for Rebekah.'

Jenny struggled between gratitude to Stefan and panic for her friend. Panic won.

'Do you have another safe place we can take her?' asked Stefan.

Jenny noted the 'we'. He obviously intended to use the car to help them. She looked at Pip, but he shook his head. 'I doubt if we can organise anything at this short notice,' he said.

'Then she'll have to come here,' Jenny said. 'She can sleep in Alice's bed.'

Anxiety sluiced across Pip's face. 'It's a big risk.'

'Well, perhaps only for a couple of days until we can find somewhere safer.'

Stefan nodded. 'I think it will work,' he said. 'At the moment we are conducting searches far outside the town. Rebekah should be safe at your house for a while.'

'Good,' said Jenny. 'It will also do her good to have some company. I've felt so guilty about her sleeping on her own in the barn each night. And I think Mum will understand.'

'Come on,' said Pip. 'We need to hurry.'

They ran out of the shed, piled into Stefan's car and sped off into the night.

* * *

Rebekah was startled to find the three of them rushing into the barn, but soon grasped the danger. Pip and Stefan gathered up her stuff and Jenny ushered her into the car. Half an hour later, they were all sitting in Mum's kitchen drinking bramble tea and eating hunks of cabbage loaf. Mum had been shocked to see Rebekah with them and Jenny had seen a flash of fear cross her face, even though she welcomed her warmly enough.

Stefan must have seen it too. 'I will try to find you some extra food for your guest, Mrs Robinson. And William is a growing boy.' He turned to William, who was sitting at the table watching everyone closely. 'I'm sure you could do with more to eat.' He winked at him, and to Jenny's surprise, Will smiled back.

It seemed Stefan was doing all he could to support them after Alice's disappearance. He'd visited them often during the intervening weeks, usually under cover of darkness, and in civvies so he wouldn't be recognised. His appearances still worried Mum, but so far none of the neighbours had said anything.

'Come on, Rebekah,' Jenny said. 'I'll take you upstairs.' She picked up some of Rebekah's things and motioned to her to follow.

As they entered the bedroom she'd shared with Alice for nearly twenty years she looked round it with fresh eyes, as Rebekah might see it: the little window jutting out under the eaves that ushered in the scent of honeysuckle in summer, the faded rose wallpaper that Dad had always been meaning to replace, the dark oak wardrobe in the corner in which Alice's spare uniform still hung. She took in the two beds, separated by a small lamp table, with their pink candlewick covers, and swallowed down a lump in her throat. That was where she and Alice had whispered late into the night, silly stuff about school and friends early on, then, increasingly, their anxieties about the war. They'd always trusted each other with confidences until recently. And when Alice had finally admitted how she felt about Stefan, Jenny had attacked her, urging caution. He'd proved himself a good man, though – all that Alice had believed him to be. But who knew whether they would ever be reunited? Poor Alice. She was so far away from them all now.

'Do you think I'll be safe here?' asked Rebekah.

Jenny frowned. 'It is risky,' she said. 'I don't think we can keep you longer than a couple of nights. Stefan seems to think the German authorities are more interested in tracking down escaped slaves than Jews on the run, but it will get more and more dangerous as time goes on.'

'But what if he's wrong?' asked Rebekah in a thready voice. 'What will we do if they do come here?'

'We'll do all we can to protect you,' said Jenny. 'We've outwitted them so far. The Germans have taken so much from me; I'm not going to let them take anyone else I care about.' She reached under her bed and pulled out the trolley Dad had made for their feasts all those years ago. 'We'll devise a signal,' she said, 'and you can hide here.' It was a good job Rebekah was so slight and that Dad had built the frame deep to allow for under-bed storage. 'You lie down on it and cover yourself with these blankets to suggest an innocent collection of spare bedding, then push yourself back under the bed and drag the counterpane down. You won't evade a thorough search, but you'll be safe from a cursory glance.'

Rebekah's face was white with worry. She nodded. 'All right,' she said. 'But I hope it doesn't come to that.'

Jenny put her arm round her shoulders. 'Me too.'

When they came back downstairs, Jenny was surprised to see Pip with her volume of Shakespeare under his arm. She raised an eyebrow at him.

'Is it okay if I borrow this for a while, Jen?' he asked. 'I know you never use it.' His expression was deadpan. 'Dad has asked me to read some bits of *Henry V* to him in the evenings, so I thought you wouldn't mind.'

'Of course,' replied Jenny. 'Borrow it for as long as you want.' She glanced at Stefan, who luckily was staring out of the window. He was of course an ally, but they didn't need to implicate him in their resistance work any further than necessary. The wireless would open up all sorts of uncomfortable questions about what they were using it for, and the less Stefan knew, the better, however trustworthy he might seem. She wondered what Pip intended to do with it. Surely he wouldn't consider keeping it in his own house given Mr Marett's position on the island. They would both get into trouble if it was found there.

'Ah. William Shakespeare.' To Jenny's horror, Stefan had turned back from the window and was now peering with interest at the book under Pip's arm. 'I studied *Macbeth* at school.' He gazed into the middle distance, no doubt trying to remember some lines, then intoned:

Tomorrow, and tomorrow, and tomorrow,
Creeps in this petty pace from day to day . . .

Pip was looking completely blank, although Jenny saw in the tightening of his jaw and the way his fists were balled against his sides that he was fearful too.

Stefan reached out an arm to take the book. 'I forget what comes next,' he said.

She stepped forward, took a deep breath and declaimed:

To the last syllable of recorded time;
And all our yesterdays have lighted fools
The way to dusty death.

He beamed. 'You know the speech.'

'Indeed I do.' Thank heavens Mrs Heald had made them learn it by rote. She doubted she'd have been able to recite much else.

Stefan nodded, seemingly satisfied. 'They are powerful words. He knew a lot, your William Shakespeare.'

'We need to go,' said Pip, still white-faced. 'It's getting late.'

'Of course,' said Jenny. She caught his look of relief.

Once Stefan and Pip had said their goodbyes, Jenny sensed the tension easing a little. But she felt the precariousness of their situation keenly. None of them was safe, and having Rebekah with them took the peril to an even higher level.

⊥

It was much colder in Biberach now. Alice had woken one morning to a bright, clear light and the first snowfall carpeting the ground. The cold penetrated deep inside her body until even her bones were chilled. And the weeks of meagre food had played havoc with her digestion. Even though she was ravenously hungry, the sight of the ersatz bread and glass of cloudy water that passed for breakfast had her stomach surging until sometimes she had to run to the latrine and dry-heave until she could face eating anything. As she sat on the hard bench, taking deep breaths to quell the nausea and force herself to eat a morsel of bread, a sour-faced woman sitting to her right turned to her and muttered, 'Morning sickness?' her epiglottis sliding up and down her scrawny throat.

Alice recoiled and voiced her denial vehemently. She was conscious of Clara, to her left, staring at her. 'I'm just going to go back to the dormitory to comb my hair,' she muttered.

'All right. I'll stay on to finish the rest of our feast.'

Normally she would grin wryly at Clara's sarcastic words. They used humour all the time to offset the awfulness of camp life, but on this occasion she could only nod. If she opened her mouth, she'd be sick.

As she crept back to the dormitory, trying to buy some time to compose herself, she started to count in her head. She had slept with Stefan back in September. It had been an instinctive decision, a reassurance before a dangerous undertaking, and a need to be as close to him as she possibly could. If something went wrong, at least they had consummated their love. As it was, it had turned out to be a premonition. She'd never regretted it. In some strange way she felt it validated their relationship as much as a marriage ceremony would. It had only been the once, but in the passion of the moment, they hadn't taken precautions, and she hadn't had her monthly since. She'd put it down to the stress of the camp and the meagre diet, but what if it were something else? Surely she couldn't be pregnant.

Part Three

January 1943–September 1945

27

Jenny was in the kitchen with Mum one cold January afternoon, making blancmange from potato flour and carrageen moss. The food stocks had become more scant than ever lately, and were it not for Stefan's occasional generosity, they'd have been desperate. Mum tipped the moss into a bowl and added hot water from the kettle. Jenny went to the larder to find some vanilla extract, noticing how bare the shelves were. Before the war there would usually be a cold joint wrapped in muslin, the remains of a pie, a big bowl of dripping, and gleaming jars of jam and marmalade, not to mention a huge jug of milk. Now they were down to their last few desultory tins and a few rubbery vegetables.

William opened the back door and entered the kitchen. His nose was red and his eyes watering with cold. Mum ushered him over to the stove so that he could warm his hands.

'Did you have a good day at school, Will?' Jenny asked.

'*Ja, danke*,' he replied.

Mum stopped stirring. 'What did you say?'

'*Ja, danke*,' he repeated.

'Will, you do realise that's German, don't you?' said Jenny. 'Why on earth are you using those words?'

William flinched.

'You haven't been talking to German soldiers, have you?'

asked Mum. 'I've told you to stay away from them. If I can't trust you, we'll have to go back to collecting you from school like we did when you were little.'

William shrugged off his satchel and put it on the kitchen table. Mum immediately placed it on the floor. 'William?'

He pulled out a new exercise book. *Deutsche Grammatik*, it said on the cover.

'Why d'you have a German grammar book?' asked Jenny.

'We have to learn German now,' said William. His face was creased up as though he was about to cry.

'Those bloody Jerries,' said Mum. 'Not content with starving us all to death, they're now corrupting our children.'

'Poor Mr de Carteret,' said Jenny. Mr de Carteret was the headmaster. He'd been there in Dad's day too. A disciplinarian with a heart of gold. 'I don't suppose he was given a choice.'

Mum banged a glass of milk down on the table. 'All right, William. I'm sorry I was cross with you. I didn't know about the new ruling. I expect you'll be good at German. Jenny's got a flair for languages, haven't you, love?'

Jenny thought about her work translating the BBC news into Spanish. 'It would seem so,' she replied. Mum still didn't know about her and Pip's secret work in the shed. Or if she had her suspicions, she never asked. Jenny ruffled William's hair and he ducked his head. 'I'll help you if you need it,' she said.

He nodded.

Mum carried on stirring the moss with renewed ferocity, muttering to herself.

They all jumped at a loud knock on the front door. Jenny glimpsed the outline of uniformed figures through the hall window, and her heart plummeted. 'Mum, I think it's German soldiers,' she whispered. She couldn't believe they had been so preoccupied with William that they hadn't heard them arriving. 'You stall them, I'll warn Rebekah.'

'All right,' replied Mum, white-faced.

Jenny bounded upstairs. They'd long since agreed on a secret signal, but it wasn't necessary. There wasn't a sign of Rebekah when she got up there.

'Rebekah,' she whispered, conscious that the soldiers would be inside any minute. 'Are you all right?'

There was no answer.

'Rebekah?'

Still no answer.

She could hear voices downstairs and didn't dare say any more. She just had to hope Rebekah had heard the men approaching and was already in the hiding place. She took one last look around, straightened Rebekah's bedspread, then hurried back down to the kitchen, trying to keep her breathing level and her expression calm.

She arrived to find William trying out his new language on two German officers while Mum hovered anxiously in the background.

'Good afternoon. How may we help you?' Jenny asked. She certainly wasn't going to speak to them in German, even if she could.

One of them held out his hand. 'Captain Hans Schneider. Pleased to meet you. We have been speaking to your brother here. It is good to hear he is learning German at school.'

The other man followed suit, introducing himself as Lieutenant Kurt Meyer. He was tall, with close-cropped fair hair. The low winter sun slanting through the kitchen window glinted on his brass buckle and the revolver at his belt.

'Are there any other members of your family?' Schneider asked. His expression was not unpleasant, but there was an intensity in his blue eyes that had triggered another swoop of fear in Jenny's stomach.

'No. We are all here,' she said. 'My older sister Alice is in a camp in Germany, and my father was killed over two years ago.' She tried to keep her tone neutral.

'That is unfortunate,' said Schneider. 'My condolences for the death of your father.'

Jenny inclined her head. She didn't dare look at William, but she could sense the bewilderment on his face. *Don't mention Rebekah, please don't mention Rebekah, Will*, her brain screamed. They'd rehearsed this scenario with him many times, stressing again and again that he must not give Rebekah away, but there was always a little bit of William that was unpredictable. You never quite knew how he might react.

Schneider nodded. 'All the same, you do not mind if we check?'

'Of course not,' said Jenny. She sensed Mum stiffening. 'But may I ask what you're looking for?'

'We have had reports of a Jewish nurse going absent from the hospital. We are checking all her old colleagues to see if she has taken refuge in one of their houses.'

Damn. They must have found out. She had hoped the initial confusion of the deportations and all the comings and goings from the hospital had been enough to keep the Germans off the scent – as it had seemed to originally. It had been months now since Rebekah had escaped, but clearly the cat was out of the bag now. Someone must have talked. Perhaps one of the local hospital staff had mentioned Rebekah, assuming she'd been in one of the deportations, and then they'd worked out that Alice had gone instead. Whatever had happened, once the Germans had discovered Rebekah was missing, it was obvious the trail would lead to them.

Jenny was furious with herself. How could she have put them all in danger? The weeks had gone by, with Rebekah being so good with William, and Stefan and Pip smuggling in extra food, and it had seemed easier to keep things as they were. Besides, no one had ever come looking for her. Until now.

She clamped her palms to her sides to stop her hands from shaking. 'It was my sister who was the nurse,' she said. 'And as I said, she is in Germany. We're not friends with any of her old colleagues, and even if we were, we certainly wouldn't consort with Jews.' She tried to spit out the last word. Lieutenant Meyer looked at her sharply.

The two men clattered round the kitchen, peering into the larder, the cupboards and even the oven, although goodness knew what they expected to find there. When they moved on to the rest of the downstairs, Jenny finally looked at William and put a finger to her lips. He gave her back a blank look.

She heard them checking the bookcase, and she inwardly breathed a sigh of relief that Pip had taken the wireless, still in the Shakespeare.

Her pulse accelerated as the men stomped upstairs. She darted a glance at Mum, who was clutching at her neck, rigid with shock. She grabbed a few carrots from the larder and placed them on the table, together with a small knife. 'Keep busy, Mum,' she whispered. 'It's important that they don't suspect anything.'

Mum nodded faintly and picked up the knife.

Jenny forced herself to fill a pan with water and place it on the stove. Above all, she must look unconcerned. Any suspicion of guilt or fear would have the Germans investigating further.

For what seemed an age all she could hear was the stomp of jackboots on the upstairs floorboards and the sound of doors being opened and shut. She shut her eyes, bracing herself for the rumble of the trolley being yanked from under the bed . . . Rebekah's scream . . . a terrifying thud . . .

She tried to breathe through the tightness in her chest, her ribcage squeezing the air out of her lungs. *Keep calm, keep calm*, she told herself. What else was there to do? She looked round the kitchen. Mum was still chopping carrots like an automaton. The water was coming to a boil on the stove. She darted into the larder and started moving tins around on the shelves.

Suddenly she heard the sound of a chair scraping. She whipped round to find William rushing out of the kitchen. She exchanged a terrified glance with Mum, then charged after him. To her horror, he ran down the hall and up the stairs.

'Will,' she called from the bottom of the stairs, trying to keep her voice calm. 'Come back down, please. Mum needs you in the kitchen.' But there was no answer. She went up, her heart in her mouth.

A pale-faced, wild-eyed William was in Mum's bedroom, staring at the soldiers as they searched. Jenny felt a moment's pity for him.

'*Schnell*,' he kept saying, clearly having remembered the word from his German lessons. Every time one of them moved to a different place in the room, he went and stood behind them. Poor Will, he was so fond of Rebekah and obviously trying to do his bit to help, but his presence was clearly annoying the men.

Captain Schneider flicked him an irritated glance. 'Please remove your brother,' he said to Jenny. 'He is impeding our search.'

Jenny swallowed. 'Of course. Will, come downstairs now.' She grabbed his arm to pull him out of the room, remembering too late that it was the worst thing she could have done.

He wriggled free. 'No,' he shouted. 'No-no-no-no-no.' Jenny's heart was beating so hard she felt as if it might break through her chest wall. 'Please, Will.' She tried to keep the panic out of her voice, knowing it would increase his agitation, but she was desperate to lure him away.

The soldiers clattered out of the room and made for the bedroom Jenny shared with Rebekah. To Jenny's consternation, William followed them. 'Come downstairs, Will,' she begged again. He threw her a manic look. His cheeks were flushed, his hair plastered with sweat. There was no knowing what he would do in this state.

Jenny was helpless to intervene as Lieutenant Meyer strode over to the wardrobe, shoved the clothes aside and rapped his knuckles against the wooden panel behind them. He must be checking there wasn't a false back. Despite her intense state of panic, Jenny felt a second's relief that they hadn't created some sort of hiding place for Rebekah there. But her heart rate accelerated again as Captain Schneider turned his attention to the beds, ripping back the eiderdowns and thrusting up the mattresses to feel underneath.

Her legs were so weak, it took all of Jenny's efforts to remain standing. It was only a matter of seconds before he looked underneath the bed and discovered Rebekah. The poor girl must be petrified.

Out of the corner of her eye, she saw William sprint across the room to the wardrobe. '*Schnell, schnell,*' he barked again. Then he opened the door, pushed his fist inside and started punching the wooden panel in a deafening rhythm.

'*Hör auf, das reicht!*' shouted Schneider, whipping out his revolver and pointing it at William. Jenny couldn't understand the words, but their meaning was clear enough.

There was a rapid tattoo of footsteps and Mum arrived in the room, panting, her expression desperate as she took in the scene in front of her.

'Please don't shoot him,' she whispered. 'He can't help himself. You're frightening him. Have some compassion, I beg you.'

Captain Schneider continued to point the gun at William.

She stepped forward, her arms in the air. 'Shoot me instead.'

Jenny couldn't believe how calm Mum sounded. She herself was too frozen with terror to look at her.

Several seconds of silence followed. Jenny said nothing, but her mind was screaming at William to stay still. Any movement from him could cause the officer to fire.

'Mrs Robinson.' Captain Schneider was stern-faced. His eyes glittered.

'Yes.'

He lowered the gun. 'We won't be searching your house any longer.'

Mum's head sagged.

Jenny took a deep calming breath. 'I will show you out.'

'We will use the back door,' said Lieutenant Meyer. 'So we can search the garden. Goodbye.' He bowed his head.

Jenny followed them outside as they tramped through the vegetable plot and ransacked the shed. She heard the sound of Dad's flowerpots being smashed, and silently thanked God again that the wireless set was now back with Pip.

Eventually they seemed satisfied and marched off down the drive.

When she went back into the kitchen to report that the men had gone, Mum slumped into a chair. Jenny wound her arms round her. 'It's all right, Mum,' she whispered. 'We're all safe for now.' Mum put her face in her hands, her shoulders shaking with relief.

Jenny darted a glance out of the window, then rushed upstairs. As she entered the bedroom, the bedspread twitched and Rebekah emerged shakily from her hiding place, shedding the pile of blankets she'd hidden under, just as they'd practised.

'Thank goodness you acted quickly,' said Jenny, giving Rebekah a hug and dusting down her jumper.

'Thank goodness for your childhood food stashes,' replied Rebekah.

Jenny thought of all those times she and Alice had pulled out the trolley for their midnight feasts. Little had they realised then how important the hiding place would become. How she wished she could tell Alice and Dad what a lifesaver it had been.

28

In the early spring sunshine, Alice waddled along one of the paths that criss-crossed the camp. Her ever more protruding belly strained against the seams of even her roomiest skirt until she worried they might rip. The opening of her blouse gaped against the pressure of her enlarged breasts. The guards had taken her off the heavier duties and she no longer had to help the other women from her barrack room collect wood to feed the black pot-bellied stoves, or trek down to the village with Clara to barter for food with the locals. She was dividing her time between first-aid duties at the camp and working in the stores. Today she was helping to unpack the contents of a recent consignment of food parcels. The deliveries had made such a difference. Now they could supplement their measly meals with delicious luxuries. Thank God for the Red Cross.

As she walked past the barracks, the strains of 'You Are My Sunshine' poured out of one of the rooms and threaded through the warm air. After the intitial months at camp when the inmates were subject to strict regulations, the Germans seemed to have realised they could be trusted and started to relax the regime. Now the prisoners were allowed to operate the camp in their own way, subject to a few conditions. Clara and the others with Jewish connections continued to be separated at night-time but could still wander freely during the day. A few people had acquired gramophones. Their musical selection was limited, though, and this song was a frequent favourite. Alice smiled to herself as she heard the familiar refrain:

You are my sunshine, my only sunshine;
You make me happy when skies are grey;
You'll never know, dear, how much I love you;
Please don't take my sunshine away.

She caressed her stomach and sang along under her breath to the baby cocooned there. She'd been horrified to discover her pregnancy last winter, wondering how on earth she'd be able to nurture a baby when she could hardly look after herself, but now it was a comfort, providing some hope through the dark days. The fear of never seeing Stefan again was always there, but at least she had a part of him now, even though it was daunting to contemplate bringing up a baby in a prison camp.

Clara had been so supportive, as usual. She'd confided in Alice that she and her husband had been trying for a baby since just after they were married. There'd be no chance of starting a family now. It must have been hard for her watching Alice's pregnancy advance. There were children at the camp too – often whole families had been deported together. Sometimes Alice caught Clara's wistful expression as she watched a ragged group of lads kicking a football, or a couple of girls sitting on the wall plaiting each other's hair. Poor Clara. Everywhere she looked there must be reminders of her own childlessness.

Alice wondered if Samuel was even still alive – not that she'd told Clara her fears. She wouldn't have chosen to have a baby out of wedlock, with all the stigma it brought, but she was lucky to have the promise of new life. Clara might never have that. In fact, as time went on, she became so emaciated that even if she and Samuel had been together in this hellish place, and even if she'd miraculously conceived, Alice doubted her body could have sustained a pregnancy.

A few petals of pink blossom detached themselves from the branches of the cherry trees alongside the path and drifted on the air, bringing with them the faintest scent of rose and lilac, and reminding her of their garden at home. It was the smell that would greet her when she opened the back door on a spring morning – no doubt that was what Dad had intended when he'd planted those bushes all those years ago. She snapped off the memory: it was best not to think too much about Jersey, or Mum, Jenny and Will. Those thoughts were too distressing; she had to keep strong for the baby, concentrating on the here and now – or even the future, when she could finally hold him in her arms.

She stopped to look at a small kitten sitting beside the store hut. Someone must have given it a saucer of watered-down condensed milk, and it was lapping at it with its tongue, emitting tiny meows of pleasure. She imagined her own baby pulling on her nipple with his small mouth, drawing sustenance from her, enjoying their shared closeness.

She entered the large building that housed the Red Cross store, reassured as usual by its network of strong iron girders and struts. They'd heard a few Allied planes roaring over in the last few weeks; it would be darkly ironic to be bombed by their own people. But the building looked strong enough to withstand an attack.

'Morning, Alice. There's a new delivery just arrived. Can you check the contents?' Mr Matthews, the store overseer, kept his eyes fixed firmly on her face. He'd never commented on her pregnancy in all the time she'd worked there, and she certainly wasn't going to bring it up.

'Of course.' She walked over to the table on which lay a number of oblong boxes made of heavy-duty cardboard, each stamped with the Red Cross symbol and the name of the Biberach camp. She picked up a pair of scissors that Mr Matthews must have put out earlier, and cut through the strands of cord, opening the first box and inhaling its sweetness. Even when she returned to their dormitory, her clothes would still carry the delicious cloying scent – cruder than the cherry blossom, but just as hopeful.

The contents of the box were cushioned in thin strips of multicoloured cellophane. She delved in and drew out a jar of strawberry jam, followed by a tin of condensed milk, a small bar of chocolate and a tin of powdered milk with the word KLIM on the side. Mr Matthews had laughed at her puzzled enquiry when she first saw one of the tins. 'It's "milk" spelled backwards,' he'd told her. 'Ingenious, eh?' Alice had smiled back but secretly wondered if she should be secreting tins of Klim for the baby. But she didn't want to get Mr Matthews into trouble. She'd just have to hope she had enough of her own milk when the time came.

She liked working in the Red Cross stores, even though she saw less of Clara now. Her nursing training had made her quick and deft with her hands, and she knew Mr

Matthews appreciated her tidy ways. Jenny might have created a more ingenious system, and maybe saved them hours of work, but at least Alice obeyed instructions and didn't question decisions.

More items followed: biscuits, corned beef, rice pudding, salt, pepper, cigarettes and soap. As she unpacked them, Alice liked to imagine the delight on the recipients' faces. The rice pudding and beef were filling and nutritious – they would satisfy hungry bellies and fuel growing limbs – but sometimes it was the little luxuries that made a difference: being able to have a proper wash with scented lather instead of just cold water; seasoning one's food; having something to smoke – cigarettes made a huge difference to many of the inmates. Some of the men had tried to use the ground acorns left over from making coffee to create cigarettes, but the real ones were much better.

After a couple of hours, when she stopped to rub her aching back, Mr Matthews looked across at her. 'Have a rest, my dear. There's a couple of extra packets of Lyons tea here. I'll make you a cup.'

Proper tea! Alice could scarcely believe it. They hadn't had real tea in Jersey for years. She, Mum and Jenny had been drinking bramble or parsnip tea, and neither of them was palatable. How strange that as prisoners in Germany, they were still afforded some luxuries such as this.

She heaved herself onto a chair while Mr Matthews filled the kettle and assembled cups and saucers. 'Did you know Jersey is the tea-packing centre of the world?' he asked her.

'I had no idea,' said Alice.

He poured the steaming water into the teapot. 'Yes.

Horniman's have a factory over at First Tower. Tea doesn't take up much space, so they import it from South America, then pack it up and distribute it all over.' He gave the teapot a stir, then filled the cups.

'Why Jersey?' Alice took her tea gratefully. To be honest, she'd never taken much interest when Dad had embarked on one of his long explanations about Jersey's trading history, but she had more time now, and it was kind of Mr Matthews to talk to her.

'Tax avoidance!'

'But if we have so much tea on Jersey, how come the islanders can't buy any?'

He sighed. 'The Germans confiscated all the stocks.'

'Typical. Well, here's to the Red Cross.' She raised her teacup in salute, and Mr Matthews followed suit.

They both looked up as Sarah Mauger appeared in the doorway. She was from Alice's barracks, a thin woman who sniffed a lot and was known for making barbed comments. She'd had a field day when she'd discovered Alice was pregnant.

'Alice, love, do you have any box cord?'

'Probably.' Alice made to stand up, but Mr Matthews stopped her.

'I'll go, my dear.' He glanced across at Sarah. 'What do you want it for?'

Sarah arranged her features into a suitably earnest expression. 'My sandals have broken. I can make some new ones with the rope.'

Alice looked at the softened mouth and beseeching eyes and turned away. She'd seen Sarah in far less humble pose: teeth bared in anger when she thought someone was stealing from her, or face flushed with hostility if she felt they had more than their share of food.

'All right.' Mr Matthews went off to the storeroom, where Alice had deposited the rope earlier after carefully winding it into balls.

'Give us an extra packet of choccy, Alice,' Sarah hissed.

'I'm sorry, Sarah. All supplies have been accounted for. I'm not allowed to give you anything.'

Sarah bristled. 'Bet you smuggle some out for Clara, though, don't you?'

'I do not.' Alice felt a flush of anger travelling up her face. She wasn't lying. If she'd been allowed, she'd have slipped some extra treats to her friend, who was looking thinner by the day, but they'd both have got into trouble if she did. She had to content herself with donating some of her own rations. Clara often said she wasn't hungry, though, and Alice suspected she was denying herself in order to allow her more nutrients for the baby.

'Well, you're not above receiving more than *your* dues!' Sarah nodded towards Alice's cup.

'Mr Matthews made me the tea. You can finish it if you want.'

'Ta!' Her eyes never leaving Alice's face, Sarah reached out for the cup, hawked up some saliva, then spat into it. 'There you are, dear,' she said, smiling sweetly as she replaced it in the saucer. 'Cheers!'

Alice said nothing. She couldn't think what was keeping Mr Matthews.

'So what do you have to do for these favours?' asked Sarah, picking up a packet of biscuits from the open box on the table, sniffing it, then putting it back.

'I've told you, I don't get any favours.'

Sarah ignored her. 'Do you open your legs for Mr Matthews like you did for that German? You Jerrybag scum.'

Alice bit her lip. How had Sarah found out about Stefan? If she'd seen them together on the island, surely she'd have said something earlier? Someone as nasty as her wouldn't have been able to keep quiet. She'd get to the bottom of it eventually, but it was probably best to say nothing at this stage.

'Here you are, Miss Mauger.' Mr Matthews advanced down the room with a bundle of box cord in his hand. Alice couldn't be sure if he'd heard the exchange, but he must have realised from her burning face and Sarah's disdainful expression that something was up.

'Oh, thank you so much, Mr Matthews,' Sarah said in a sugary voice. 'I really am very grateful.'

Mr Matthews nodded. 'All right. Now off you go. We've work to do.'

She departed meekly, but as she walked past the outside of the window, she flashed Alice a V sign. And it certainly wasn't for victory.

'Was that girl bothering you?' Mr Matthews asked, picking up her teacup and frowning at the contents.

'She was just accusing me of secreting extra items for myself and my friend.' Alice didn't tell him about the other accusation, the one that hurt a lot more.

'Well, that's nonsense, and I'll tell her so if I see her again,' he said.

'Thank you,' Alice replied quietly, and resumed her unpacking.

* * *

Maybe it was her imagination, but over the next few days, Alice became convinced that Sarah had been gossiping about her and Stefan. When she queued for the latrines, she thought she saw other women draw away from her or turn their backs to strike up conversation with someone else. If she caught somebody's eye, they would look the other way, and sometimes, when she entered the barrack room, all talking would stop, as though she was the subject of the conversation. It was a far cry from that day at the harbour when her fellow deportees had offered her their own clothing to make up for her lack of belongings. Yet she was the same person as she had been then, wasn't she?

Their current treatment of her — imagined or otherwise — hurt. She had to admit that in some ways they were right. She had slept with a German soldier. Technically she *was* a Jerrybag, although she hated to be identified with those women who openly paraded themselves with German soldiers, flaunting their cigarettes and nylon stockings, looking down on honest islanders who refused to consort with the enemy and suffered deprivation and hardship as a consequence. Her love for Stefan was real and heartfelt; she hadn't been using him, or he her, but in others' eyes she was no better than a prostitute.

She'd long since told Clara her story, and to her friend's credit, she hadn't offered a word of condemnation, unlike Jenny and Rebekah's initial mixed reactions. Alice didn't know how Sarah Mauger had found out about her relationship with a German — perhaps she'd overheard her talking to Clara. However the news had got out, it was clear that Clara was now her only friend left in the camp, not that she'd been that close to anyone else. More than once she'd defended Alice against spitefulness, and Alice suspected she'd done even more to protect her behind her back. 'Just ignore them,' Clara had said. 'They're not worth it.'

She was right. Thank goodness for her and kind Mr Matthews.

Over at the wall-building site, Pip checked that no one was watching, then leant backwards to raise his arms over his head and interlock his fingers. His bones creaked. It felt good to stretch. He tipped his head back until he could see the bright blue sky. Spring at last. It had been a tough winter, the Germans constantly tightening restrictions. In February there'd been another deportation: two hundred islanders this time, including Jacob De Gruchy and Jack Vautier, who he'd been at school with.

Alice was still incarcerated in Germany. The Robinsons had had a Christmas card from her, and there'd been a few letters. Jenny had shown him one. Camp life sounded monotonous, and it was clear that Alice was missing home, but other than that she seemed in good spirits, and had made some friends. Whether this was an accurate account, or kept deliberately vague for the censors, it was hard to tell. Pip wondered if she'd ever return, but he didn't relay his fears to Jenny.

It was difficult to know how the war was going. In the first two months of the year, the Russians had seemed to be over-powering the Germans, but in March, the Germans had destroyed the Russian Third Tank Army and a few days later recaptured Kharkov. By the end of the month they'd managed to push the Russians back a hundred miles on the south-eastern Russian front. Pip found himself increasingly tense when he listened to the wireless, desperate to hear of Allied victories.

He'd long since resigned himself to not playing an active

part in the war. His actions were more subversive: the wireless transcripts, which were still being smuggled to the Spaniards; helping the Robinsons to look after Rebekah; and recently, a new gesture of defiance. He smiled to himself as he gazed down the length of the wall. Every few yards there was a slightly altered configuration of stones. They would be almost invisible to a casual observer, but he could see them: little V signs made up of stones that were a slightly different colour to those surrounding them. A modest memorial to his resistance.

V for victory. Surely it couldn't be long now. There'd been small acts of rebellion all over Jersey. People had been painting Vs over German signs and on walls. The JCP members used the Morse code for a V – three dots and a dash – when they knocked on the Sand Street door. It sounded like the opening bars of Beethoven's Fifth Symphony. How ironic that it was composed by a German! But the one that amused him most had been a couple of years ago, when the artist Edmund Blampied had designed a banknote that, when folded in a specific way, revealed a V symbol. Wonderful.

There was still no one around. Pip checked in every direction, then set off quietly towards the storeroom. The basket was in the corner as usual. He seized a brioche roll and an apple, shoved them deep into his pockets, then strode back to the wall to resume his work. The sense of satisfaction lasted for several hours. More food to take to the Robinsons. The anticipation of Jenny's smile of gratitude warmed him for the next few hours.

⚓

Jenny was upstairs with Rebekah when she happened to look out of the window and saw a figure coming up the drive. Her heartbeat started to accelerate. After the visit of the German officers, and their near-discovery of Rebekah, her anxiety about unexpected callers had increased even further. But as she took in the familiar face, she relaxed again.

'It's all right. It's Stefan,' she said.

Rebekah slumped back on the bed.

'I'll go down to see what he wants. Do you want to come with me?'

'No, I'll stay up here, thanks.' Since that terrifying episode with the Germans, Rebekah seemed to have shrunk in on herself, her face white and pinched, her dark hair lank, her nails bitten almost to the quick.

Jenny squeezed her friend's shoulder, half registering how bony it had become. 'I'll see what he wants, then pop back up later.'

Rebekah nodded, her eyes huge and wary.

Jenny ran downstairs to find Mum in the kitchen already talking to Stefan. She still wore that guarded expression she adopted whenever he came round, but her words were friendly enough. 'You're very kind. Thank you. It's so thoughtful of you.'

There was a small sack of provisions on the table.

'Hello, Stefan. Is this from you?' Jenny gestured to the sack.

Stefan bowed his head. 'We've had a new delivery, more than we need. I thought you may be able to use these.' He opened the sack and placed two tins of cooked ham, a packet of macaroni and a large bag of flour on the table. Finally he drew out a small package.

'Coffee!' said Jenny, pulling it towards her and sniffing it excitedly. 'We haven't had proper coffee in months!'

Stefan smiled. 'From France.'

Jenny didn't like to ask how he had come by such a feast,

but it couldn't have been easy; he was clearly determined to help them.

Mum set about making them all some coffee while Stefan and Jenny talked. As usual, he was eager for news of Alice. Jenny rummaged in the drawer to find Alice's latest letter. It didn't say much. She was never sure if her sister's apparent optimism was to stop them worrying about her or because of censorship. Perhaps both.

Dear Mother, Jenny and William,

I hope this finds you well. I'm fine. The weather is much warmer now and we are permitted to go out for walks. Biberach is beautiful in spring: the Bavarian Alps lit up by the sun and the sight of blossom everywhere. I miss the sea, but the air is fresh and pure here and probably very good for us.

We've had another delivery of Red Cross parcels, so there is plenty of food to go round. As well as a few nursing duties, I am still working with Mr Matthews in the stores. I am lucky as the work isn't too arduous.

I hope you are getting enough to eat and that you are in good spirits.

Please give my love to my friend.

Yours,

Alice

At the bottom was a tiny drawing of a lighthouse. Jenny could never look at it without a pang. She passed the letter over to Stefan, who scanned it quickly, then placed it on the table and stared into the middle distance.

'She sounds well.'

'Yes. And sends her love.' The reference to 'my friend' was obviously meant for Stefan. It was painful that she couldn't write to him directly, nor he to her, but this was the next best thing.

Stefan took a final gulp of coffee, rinsed the cup, then said his farewells. 'I'll be back with more food when I can.'

Mum shook his hand. 'We are so grateful,' she said. For once her features were relaxed, her mouth softened, her eyes confirming the sincerity of her words.

Stefan smiled at her sadly, then followed Jenny down the hall to the front door. She watched him as he walked down the drive, his head bowed, his shoulders hunched. He disappeared round the bend, but Jenny still lingered, enjoying the softness of the spring evening. Dusk was falling, the sun no more than a wash of orange in the sky and the pewter clouds backlit with gold. It had been kind of Stefan to come over, and he was clearly as worried about Alice as they were. Poor Stefan. Poor Alice. She hoped against hope they'd one day be reunited.

When she returned to the house, Mum had washed up the coffee cups and was putting away Stefan's provisions.

'That was kind of him,' Jenny said, picking up the bag of flour from the table and taking it to the larder.

'Yes, he's looked after us well.' Mum didn't expand any further, but Jenny could tell she was warming to Stefan. He could so easily have left them to their own devices after Alice had gone, and he was bringing the food at some risk to himself.

Jenny was just about to draw the blackout on the kitchen window when she heard scuffling from the garden. It was unlikely to be Stefan returning, and anyway, he'd surely approach from the front door, as he had before. Perhaps it was a badger. There was a sett in the nearby copse, and recently she'd been convinced one was responsible for the holes that had appeared in the lawn. Not that the lawn bore any resemblance to the pristine patch it had been when her father was alive. Now it had dark areas of moss and was sprinkled with daisies. Pip popped in to mow it for them from time to time, just to keep the grass down, but Dad's precious garden was no longer something to be proud of.

At first she thought it was indeed an animal she was looking at. A large, shaggy figure was crouched in the middle of the vegetable plot, digging up the potatoes she and Pip had planted earlier in the year. She raised a fist to knock on the window and shoo it away. But when she looked closer, she realised it was a man, clothed in rags, with wild hair, scrabbling in the earth as if his life depended on it. Her stomach lurched. They'd never felt vulnerable living out in the countryside when Dad was at home. But now they were three women and a child, in wartime, and they were more exposed. It was too bad Stefan hadn't stayed longer.

She rattled the back door to check it was locked. There were only the two of them downstairs. Rebekah was still in their room, and William was making something complicated from Meccano on the landing. She beckoned Mum to the window. 'Look over there,' she said, pointing at the hunched shape in the twilit garden. 'Who d'you think that is?'

Mum peered out. 'Bloody cheek,' she said, 'stealing our vegetables.' She grabbed the carving knife and made for the door.

'Mum!' shouted Jenny. 'Don't be daft. He could be armed.'

Mum retreated. 'I suppose you're right. But I'm not letting anyone rob our food from under our noses.'

Jenny looked again. The man was squatting on his haunches, a dirt-encrusted potato in his hand. 'I'm sure it's not a German,' she said. 'They don't need to steal our spuds.'

'No,' sniffed Mum. 'The bloody Krauts can lay their hands on anything they want.'

Something twisted in Jenny's heart at the way the man was eating. 'He's starving, Mum,' she said. 'I reckon he's an OT worker. Look how thin he is. I don't think he'd have the strength to attack us. I'm going outside to speak to him.'

Mum handed her the knife. 'Don't take any chances,' she said.

Jenny slipped quietly out of the back door and stood in the shadow of the house. The man was darting little glances round the garden in between bites of raw potato, the whites of his eyes the only brightness in his sallow face. She approached softly. 'Are you all right?'

He froze, then jerked upright as though to run.

She made a calming motion with her hands. 'Do you speak English?'

The man shook his head. His eyes were like caverns. '*Ruský*,' he said.

'Ah . . . Russian.' Of course. Now that food was so scarce on the island, it was becoming harder and harder to secure provisions for the slave workers. The Russians in particular were suffering terribly. Their rations were deemed the minimum necessary to get a day's work out of them, but in practice they were starving. No wonder they stole food from local farms and gardens. They were allowed out of the camps outside working hours, which was probably why this man was foraging now.

Jenny thought quickly. 'Come with me,' she said, beckoning him across to the shed. He looked wary, but limped after her. She motioned him to the chair Pip normally sat on to listen to the radio, and mimed fetching food and clothes.

As the man smiled his thanks, she saw tears glistening in his eyes.

She sped back into the kitchen, where Mum was waiting anxiously. 'It's all right. It's as I thought. He's one of the slave workers. Poor chap's frozen, and very hungry. Can we let him have some of Dad's old clothes and some of that ham Stefan brought?' She felt sad and frustrated that the resistance workers were no longer providing resources for the labourers, but at least she could do something to help this man.

Mum blanched and put her hand to her chest. Damn. Jenny hadn't meant to be so thoughtless. It wouldn't be easy for Mum to give away anything of Dad's. Jenny put her arm round her. 'Maybe just the ham, then.'

Mum took a deep breath. 'No, your father would tell me off for hoarding his clothes when someone was in need. There's a jumper I still haven't packed away. I've been sleeping with it under my pillow, but I'll have to do without it eventually. Might as well be now.' She went upstairs to fetch the item while Jenny retrieved a tin of ham from the larder, opened it, and carved a few slices. It was probably safer to leave the man in the shed than invite him in. William could come down at any time and react badly to finding a stranger in the house. She and Pip were always careful to remove any signs of their illicit transcription work. There was nothing he could steal apart from a few of Dad's old tools, although instinctively she trusted him.

Once Mum had returned with the jumper, Jenny suggested

she stay inside and listen out for William, while she herself saw to their guest.

When she returned to the shed, the man was still sitting on Pip's chair, leaning over the bench, his head in his hands. Jenny held out the jumper and the ham.

'Thank you, thank you,' he said. He pulled on the jumper, stuffed the ham in his coat pocket, and stood up, extending a thin hand.

Jenny shook it. 'Jenny,' she said, pointing to herself.

'Alexei.'

There wasn't much more she could do, and the man – Alexei – seemed content to go. She mimed that she would leave some more food in the shed the next day, and she thought he understood.

She stood by the back door as he limped off down the garden, through the bottom gate and into the field beyond. It had been a shock to see such deprivation and suffering at close quarters. She watched his thin figure until it blended into the darkness. There was a camp over at Westmount. Perhaps that was where he was headed. At least his belly would be a bit fuller and his body a bit warmer thanks to her and Mum. It wasn't much. If he'd been Spanish, they could've had a conversation – maybe make a regular arrangement for provisions. He wasn't a big man, Pip would have lent him some clothes, she was sure. She'd start putting things by in case he came again. At least now she could put one name to the faceless hordes of Russian slaves on Jersey: Alexei.

29

Jenny hadn't been into the office to help Mr Marett for a while, so it was a relief to sit at the tidy desk, sorting invoices into date order. Everything was so uncertain at home. They still lived on edge, dreading another knock on the door. Jenny had tried to reassure Mum and Rebekah that the Germans wouldn't return, having seemingly not come across anything suspicious, and Stefan had confirmed that the authorities assumed Rebekah had now left the island. The concern had abated slightly, but there was still the gnawing anxiety about Alice.

Jenny missed her sister more than she'd ever imagined she would. She'd recently come across another old note from her in a book, when she was trying to find something for Rebekah to read. *I'm sorry I hurt you*, it said in a childish scrawl. *Can we be friends again now?* There was a crude drawing of a lighthouse on the bottom, the same symbol Alice used in her letters from Germany. Jenny kept the note under her pillow; it somehow felt as though she was keeping Alice with her too. How she wished they could rediscover their past closeness. She'd give anything to have her back now.

Alexei had visited several times after that first night. Jenny had dug up more potatoes and boiled them, so at least she could give him a hot meal, and Mum had ransacked the case

314

in the loft for more of Dad's clothes. Alexei had been pathetically grateful. It was strange to sit with him in the shed while he ate, knowing that was where Pip listened to the news and she translated it for other OT workers. She'd never met any of the labourers they continued to support in any way they could, but somehow, meeting Alexei helped her to imagine them all more clearly as individuals, putting a specific face to all that she was risking for them.

But after a few days, he stopped coming. Whether it was because he didn't want to presume too much on their kindness, or there was a more sinister reason, Jenny didn't know. She told Pip about him, and one night they even went over to Westmount to see if they could find him, but they weren't allowed into the camp and there was no sign of him in the fields and lanes around the area. Jenny suspected that whenever she saw a group of Russian slaves, she'd always be searching their faces to find one that was familiar.

Mr Marett greeted her warmly as usual, taking her coat from her and hanging it up on the stand in the corner, then insisting he make her a cup of proper tea, even though the office tea caddy was almost empty. He was treating her almost like a daughter-in-law now.

They chatted for a bit. As ever, Jenny was economical with the truth. It would be dangerous for him to learn of their illicit resistance activities, and she was anxious to protect him. She and Pip had taken a rare walk out to Le Haguais the other day, and she cheered the elderly man with talk of all the signs of spring they'd seen on the way: primroses clinging to the banks, the maples budding, and the sight of red-tailed hawks on their long flight back from the south.

'The war seems to be going better for the Allies,' she said, as she approached his desk to slide back a drawer of the filing cabinet and tuck in a pile of newly arranged papers.

Mr Marett put down his fountain pen. 'Yes, looks like we're winning in North Africa now. Let's hope the Krauts surrender over there soon.'

Jenny returned to her own desk. 'Didn't Winston Churchill call it "the end of the beginning"?'

'He did, my dear. All we can do is hope.' He picked up his pen again.

Jenny resumed her filing, wondering if they really could allow themselves some optimism. Could she imagine a world where Alice returned from Germany and they all got on with their lives? The desire to go to Cambridge was still strong, stronger perhaps now that she'd had to wait so long. She'd have been grateful for the opportunity three years ago, but now she'd bite their hands off if she was offered a place.

They worked in companionable silence for half an hour until it was broken by the ringing of a telephone. Mr Marett reached for the receiver.

'Yes? . . . Oh, good morning, sir.'

Jenny looked up. Must be the bailiff. He was the only person Mr Marett would call 'sir'.

She tried to keep busy during the call so as not to look as though she was listening in. It was impossible to deduce the nature of the discussion from Mr Marett's reactions anyway. The bailiff was clearly doing most of the talking, and Mr Marett just nodded or gave monosyllabic replies. The phone call was a short one, and after a few minutes he put the receiver back on its cradle.

'You don't have a wireless set, do you, Jenny?'

Jenny shuffled some papers on her desk, trying not to let her hands shake too much. 'No, I don't.' Thank God she could answer that question with perfect honesty now. But she felt a lurch of dread for Pip.

'Good. It appears the Germans are having another crackdown on radios. They've given the islanders one last chance to surrender them.' He reached for a sheet of foolscap from a pile on his desk. 'I'll get something put in the *Evening Post*. I've got the editor's number here somewhere.' He pulled out a drawer and delved inside.

'Is there anything I can do to help?'

'Not really, dear. Just spread the word, though, will you? If anyone *is* caught harbouring a wireless, I think the penalty will be much harsher this time.'

Jenny nodded, then bent her head quickly to stop Mr Marett noticing that her face was flushing with apprehension. What if the Germans started wide-scale searches for radios and came across Rebekah this time? Or they searched the Maretts' house and discovered Pip's hidden wireless?

The afternoon passed in an interminable procession of tasks. Her usual enjoyment of the work had evaporated, and all she could think of was the need to warn Pip and Rebekah. A couple of times Mr Marett gave her a sharp glance when she handed him the wrong document or slopped hot water on his desk as she put down his cup. It was so hard to concentrate.

'Are you all right, my dear?' he asked her after she had to tear open an envelope that she'd already sealed, having realised she'd put the wrong letter inside. 'It's not like you to make so many mistakes.'

Jenny massaged her forehead, grateful for the excuse to stop. 'I'm sorry. I have a bad headache. I think it might be turning into a migraine.' It wasn't altogether a lie. There was a sharp pain above her left temple and she felt feverish with worry. An image flashed into her mind of Dad's brown glass bottle of headache pills. Had they thrown them away? Normally she'd have asked Alice if she could get her some painkillers from the hospital. Perhaps she could pick some feverfew leaves on the way home and ask Mum to boil them up for her.

'Right. That's it.' Mr Marett stood up, retrieved Jenny's coat from the stand and held it out for her. 'I'm sending you home before it gets worse. Time is of the essence with these things.'

Jenny hadn't set out to deceive him, but it was probably better she did go home before she made any more errors, and it would give her a chance to warn Pip sooner rather than later.

She stood up, thrust her arms into the coat sleeves and turned round to do it up. 'Thank you. I'll try to pop back tomorrow to make up the hours.'

'Only if you're better, my dear. You need to get properly well first.'

She flashed Mr Marett a guilty smile as she hurried out of the office.

Once she'd unclipped her bicycle from the railings outside, she decided to ride out to Grouville, rather than going home as she'd originally intended. It was best she warn Pip first, then they could decide what to do about Rebekah. Mum wasn't expecting her back for ages, and perhaps the fresh air would do her good. Mr Marett would never know she wasn't

318

going home to lie down in a darkened room as he probably imagined.

She cycled quickly down the street and headed north-east. It would be nice to surprise Pip, and already the act of pedalling and steering had helped calm her mind after the worrying news. The sun was warm on her back as she cycled up Longueville Road, watching the lambs frisking in the fields and enjoying the blackthorn fizzing in the hedgerows. The higher she climbed, the more the wind buffeted her hair, until she realised that the headache had disappeared completely.

She got within sight of the sea and dismounted. The grass was too bumpy up here to cycle, especially as, like most people by now, she'd had to fill her inner tyre with sand. She pushed the bike towards the headland and very soon saw Pip by the wall. He had his back to her, and there was a pile of rocks by his side. He was picking each one up, turning it round to check the shape, then wedging it in place.

Jenny had never seen him at work before. Watching him from afar felt as though she was seeing him for the first time. Despite the food shortages, he'd filled out over the last two years, the physical labour building up his muscles and broadening his frame. His face was permanently tanned from the sun and wind. They spent so much time in the shed these days, listening to the wireless and transcribing the news reports, that she thought of him as an indoor person, forgetting the hours he'd spent sailing before the war, his love of the elements and nature. It explained why he seemed to enjoy the wall-building despite the physical effort involved, and despite essentially working for the Germans. And of course it was another act of subversion. If he appeared to work willingly, they'd be less inclined to suspect him of anything untoward.

'Pip!' Her first attempt to call him was borne away by the wind. His back remained towards her; he was still engrossed in his task, frowning as he rejected a badly fitting rock and replaced it with another one. She walked a few more yards, propped her bike up against a nearby shed and approached him quickly. 'Pip!'

This time he did turn round, his smile instinctive at the sight of her. Then he glanced left and right as though to check whether anyone was watching. Jenny noticed another figure, about a hundred yards away, involved in the same activity as Pip, but he didn't seem aware of them.

'What are you doing here?' He put down the rock he was holding, took off his gloves and kissed her cheek quickly. His face was flushed with exertion. At least Jenny hoped that was what it was — not embarrassment at her appearance. She'd taken a bit of a risk coming up here; she didn't want to get Pip into trouble with his overseer, although thankfully there didn't seem to be any Germans around.

'It's not a social call,' she said.

Pip raised an eyebrow.

'I was in the office this morning. Your father took a call from the bailiff while I was there. Apparently the Germans have issued another demand that people hand in their wireless sets.'

Pip frowned. 'Well, I'm not handing in mine.'

Jenny had anticipated this reaction. 'Do be careful, Pip,' she said. 'Your father thinks there'll be much harsher penalties this time. Perhaps even imprisonment or deportation. Isn't there somewhere else you could hide it, less risky to both you and him?'

Pip looked out to sea. Jenny tried to imagine what he was thinking. When he turned back, his face was composed but his tone determined. 'There are chaps over there risking their lives for their country.' He ran his fingers through his hair. 'And you expect me to hand in a wireless set in order to save my skin?'

She put up her hands. 'All right, all right. You're certainly no coward, Pip. I love that about you. But it was only fair to warn you.'

'I know. Thank you.'

'And you're jeopardising your father by having the wireless set in the house.' The Shakespeare book was now lodged in Pip's bedroom. He brought it over to Jenny's in an old brief-case whenever they were working on the transcriptions.

'I might have to move it again.' He traced a shape on the ground with his foot. 'I can't take it back to yours. You're doing enough still hiding Rebekah.'

'What about the cottage in Sand Street?'

'I'm not sure. There's enough illicit material there already. Krauts would have a field day if they raided the place.'

'Well, it needs to be out of your house. There's too much at stake.'

'I'll have a think. Thanks for the warning, anyway.' Pip reached inside his pocket and drew out an apple. 'Here, I found this in the storeroom this morning.' He nodded towards the shed where Jenny had propped up her bike. 'Can you take it to Rebekah?'

She took the apple. 'Of course. So that's the shed you're stealing food from.'

321

He shrugged. 'The Germans have plenty. No one seems to notice.'

Jenny darted a kiss on his cheek. 'Be careful, won't you?'

'Of course. See you later.' He gave her a mock salute, then turned and picked up the stone he'd dropped earlier.

Jenny saluted back, but before she set off, she noticed that the figure further along the wall had stopped and was watching them keenly. The knot of anxiety in her stomach tightened. It lay there all the way home.

Alice went into labour during the night as she lay on the straw-filled sack that served as a bed in the crowded barrack room. She woke to a dragging pain low in her pelvis. Conflicting emotions rushed in: excitement that she might soon meet her baby, but fear of the conditions she was bringing him into and the agony she'd have to endure. She'd known women whose labour had lasted several days, and had witnessed their distress and exhaustion. She lay for a while feeling the contractions ebb and flow. The pain came in waves, like breakers forming far out to sea, building momentum until they reached a crescendo before rolling, tamed and exhausted, up the beach. At its peak the spasms were almost unbearable, then they suddenly subsided and all was calm again. Her child had been conceived by the sea. Now she was far inland, but the powerful forces inside her body transported her back to the ocean.

She wrapped her arms round her abdomen, trying to convey as much love as possible to the life cocooned there. 'We're in for a fight, little one,' she whispered, 'but we're going to win.'

She'd spent the last few weeks buoyed up by the anticipation of finally meeting the child that she and Stefan had created.

She thought of the people she'd lost: Pip, her father, Stefan. But this baby would be hers for ever. Despite the constant worry about giving birth in a prison camp, she was determined to give this child the best life she could, even though her own future was so uncertain.

It was amazing how strongly her body was reacting: the fierce involuntary surges that pulled and softened, setting in motion the age-old birth process. Yet yesterday the baby had been so still; she'd barely felt a movement as she'd sat in the Red Cross hut sorting parcels until Mr Matthews insisted she left. She'd wandered back in the June sunshine, savouring the scented air and enjoying the distant views of the Bavarian Alps shimmering in the haze and the forest-clad hills below them. Perhaps her child was garnering strength, content to rest in the warmth of her womb, conserving the energy he'd need for his long journey. Looking back, it was obviously the calm before the storm.

A sudden restlessness gripped her and she sat up. She felt the urge to pace, to pound the corridors in an attempt to get away from the pain. Wrapping the blanket carefully round herself, she swung her legs over the bed until her feet came into contact with the bare floorboards. She couldn't face rooting around for her shoes. Even the thought of bending over to put them on made her grimace. So instead she padded out of the room in bare feet, clutching the blanket.

It was dark outside, although the air was already warm, promising another hot day. Over to the east, the sky was slashed with pale blue nearer the horizon. She watched as the streaks brightened, the blue turning to pink then fading into yellow as the whole sky became lighter. She was dimly aware of a skylark singing insistently, its song unbroken and high-pitched.

The pains were closer together now. She had to stop whenever a contraction overtook her, bending over and gripping the wire fence that encircled the compound until her breathing became easier and she could walk on slowly. For months she'd blocked out any thoughts of the birth, but now she couldn't delude herself any longer. She'd seen babies delivered at the hospital and knew what was involved. There was so much that could go wrong, particularly in these conditions. It was terrifying to contemplate giving birth on her own. She needed expert help.

The camp was coming to life: she heard the piercing reveille whistle and the clanging and clattering from the kitchen block. A thread of acridity wound through the air. Someone must have burnt the porridge.

The sky was brighter now, the sun a white ball haloed by gold, the air gauzy and a fine mist rising from the grass.

'Alice!' Clara was running towards her, her face full of concern. 'Are you all right?'

Alice tried to smile, but her face contorted with pain. 'I think the baby's coming,' she said. It was an effort to speak calmly. All she wanted to do was shout and scream to drive away the fierce contractions.

Clara looked alarmed. 'I must have had a premonition that something was about to happen.' She appeared exhausted just from the short distance she'd run, and Alice felt a stab of worry for her. Her hollow chest was heaving; her face was grey in the early-morning light. Even the slightest effort seemed to tax her now. 'Stay there. I'll go and find someone.' She took a deep breath, as though to summon some energy, and hurried off again.

Alice pulled the blanket more tightly round herself, dimly

conscious of her flimsy nightdress – donated by a woman who'd grown too thin for it – and her bare feet. But another onslaught overtook her and all she could think of was the tightening grip on her body. She sank to her knees.

At length Clara returned with Dr Braun, the camp doctor, who helped her to her feet. An image of Stefan's caring face flashed into her mind. Why couldn't it be him delivering their baby? She gritted her teeth and allowed herself to be led to the medical block, assisted by Clara's gentle arms on one side and Dr Braun's firm support on the other.

Once in the hospital, Clara was sent packing. Alice watched her departure with regret. She longed for her friend to be allowed to stay and hold her hand. If she'd given birth at home, Mum would have been there for her, wiping her forehead, offering her sips of water, whispering encouragement and advice. She wouldn't let herself imagine Mum cradling her first grandchild, Dad hovering proudly in the background, Jenny and William waiting to greet their niece or nephew. It was too painful to contemplate.

At least she could lie down on the scratchy grey blanket of the sanatorium bed. The doctor examined her, then beckoned to a nurse, who placed an ear trumpet to her tummy. She whispered something to the doctor, who frowned. Alice wished she could hear their conversation. It was hard to know from their reaction whether something might be wrong. A ball of dread formed deep in her belly, further intensifying the vice-like grip of the contractions, and she submitted herself to another deluge of pain.

30

Pip hoisted the rucksack onto his shoulders and began the long trudge home. The sun was lingering longer now, and he still felt its warmth on his back as he pounded the tarmac along the Longueville Road. He'd been building walls for months and his body had got used to the work. His muscles no longer ached from leaning over to wedge the stones in place, and although he still wore gloves, his skin had hardened underneath; he rarely got blisters now.

It had been good to see Jenny earlier. They had little leisure time these days, now that the extra daylight hours meant he could no longer leave work early. Jenny was either helping her mother, queuing endlessly for food, or in the office with Dad. Of course, there were still their resistance activities, but those didn't afford them time for themselves.

He was deeply grateful for her rushing straight over to let him know about the Germans cracking down on wirelesses, although he meant what he'd said – he had no intention of relinquishing his. But she was right. He could no longer keep it in his bedroom; it wasn't fair on Dad. He'd make some enquiries later.

He was nearing the town now. As he rounded the bend at Bagot, he looked across at the sea, gleaming in the evening sun. It would have been a perfect evening for sailing, and he longed to be on the *Bynie May*, ploughing through open water under full sail with nothing but screeching gulls for company. It was a while since he'd checked on her. Maybe he could persuade Jenny to come down to the harbour at the weekend, and they could recoup some of that precious leisure time. As far as he knew, the Germans hadn't requisitioned the boat. Although he wasn't allowed to sail her, the *Bynie May* was still his, waiting for whenever he might be able to do so again.

But as he approached the house, he saw an unfamiliar car in the drive with a German soldier at the wheel, and realised that he was too late.

He opened the front door, entering a house that felt heavy with suspicion and unease. He dropped his rucksack in the hall and walked into the lounge. It was as he'd feared. Two German officers were sitting in armchairs, with a white-faced Dad, his lips in a firm line, facing them. One of the officers held Pip's wireless on his lap. The Shakespeare volume lay on the floor.

Something icy inched up Pip's spine. He was done for. There was no doubt about that. But he had to protect Dad at all costs.

'Good evening, Officers,' he said, smiling broadly and trying to project a nonchalance he didn't feel. He held out a hand. 'I see you have my wireless. You beat me to it. I was about to surrender it to the Feldkommandant, only I had to finish my work first.' He surreptitiously wiped his palm down the side of his trousers. 'I've been building walls up at Grouville, helping you defend the island from the Allies.' If the Germans believed he was cooperating, he might just get away with it.

The officer holding the wireless smiled back. The smile was

genial enough, but his eyes were cold. 'That is interesting, Mr Marett,' he said. 'So can you tell me why the wireless was concealed in a volume of the plays of William Shakespeare?'

Pip kept his gaze level. He tried to remember if the book had Jenny's name in it. What idiots they'd been. But she hadn't been impressed with the prize. Knowing her, she wouldn't want to claim something she felt no affection for. Yet it was vital he put the Germans off the scent or she would be in danger too.

'Oh, that's just a convenient means of carrying it,' he said. 'Keeps everything together. Stops the wires trailing on the ground. I can't bear Shakespeare. I was made to spend hours studying him at school, so it felt like revenge to gouge the pages out for the wireless.'

The officer smirked. 'You *can't bear* your most famous English playwright? That's not very patriotic, Mr Marett.'

Pip shrugged. 'I never enjoyed English literature. I always preferred geography.'

'And what have you been using this wireless for, Mr Marett?' The German's eyes bored into him.

'Concerts mainly. You know, big-band stuff . . .'

'And do you listen to the music with your father?'

Pip didn't dare look at Dad, although he could hear his ragged breaths. 'No, my father had no idea I had a set. I listen on my own in my bedroom.'

'I see. So why didn't you hand the set in when wirelesses were first requisitioned, nearly a year ago now?'

Pip tried to look shamefaced. 'I'm sorry. I know I should have. I just couldn't bear to lose out on my music. I didn't think it would do any harm.'

'And you the son of a prominent member of Jersey's ruling body.' The man shook his head theatrically and tutted.

Pip was aware of Dad's sharp intake of breath. He still didn't dare look at him.

'Very well,' said the German. 'Even if we ignore this transgression, there is another matter we would like to discuss with you.'

Pip's heartbeat, which had started to settle, accelerated again. What on earth had they found? They'd obviously searched the house thoroughly before he'd arrived. Poor Dad. Such an affront to his dignity. And he must be wondering what on earth Pip had been involved with. There'd be an almighty row later. If he was still around to face it.

The officer held out his hand. 'May I see your rucksack, please?'

Pip went back into the hall to retrieve the bag from where he'd left it. He gave it to the officer, who undid it and tipped its contents on the floor: a black wallet, a pair of worn gardening gloves, a spare jumper, a cap and a copy of John Buchan's *The Thirty-Nine Steps* that he was reading at lunchtime, if he was allowed a break. What a relief that he'd given Jenny the apple for Rebekah earlier. It was hardly incriminating – he could say he'd brought it from home – but it might seem strange to appear not to have eaten it when everyone was so hungry.

The German shook the empty rucksack, then felt in all the pockets. Pip felt a slight jolt of satisfaction at the man's frustrated expression.

'We have had reports of food being stolen from the supplies hut over at Grouville. Do you know anything about that?'

Pip shrugged. 'No, I don't.' There were quite a few people who could have reported him, but he'd put money on that blasted Peter Dewe; he'd definitely looked at him furtively a few times. Once again, though, he seemed to have escaped punishment. Fate really did seem to be on his side. His pulse slowed again, and he started to look forward to an evening with Dad. There'd be the inevitable inquisition, of course, but Dad would mellow after a while. There was still some whisky in the decanter they were saving for emergencies, and Pip reckoned this constituted one. He could almost taste the fiery liquid burning his mouth and scorching his throat. Then the feeling of relaxation oozing through his limbs as he revelled in the relief that the Germans had failed to pin anything on him. He just had to get through the next few minutes.

The officer picked up his hat, which he'd placed on the coffee table, and made as if to go. Then he suddenly turned back. 'Oh, just one more thing, Mr Marett.' He motioned to the other German, who'd remained silent throughout the proceedings. 'Kapitän Schmidt, would you mind showing our friends here the document you found behind Mr Marett's chest of drawers?'

Pip's stomach lurched. He'd been so careful. Destroying all his notes and transcriptions as soon as the leaflets were published, checking his room again and again for incriminating evidence. How could he have let something slip? Trust the Germans to be so thorough that they'd even pulled out his chest of drawers. So stupid of him not to have anticipated that.

The other officer held out a page torn from an exercise book, covered with Pip's spiky handwriting. It was a set of notes he'd made from listening to the news. The one thing he was determined the Germans should never find. The one thing that would do for him once and for all.

'Please come with us, Mr Marett. We would like you to explain to Colonel Knackfuss why you have been transcribing the contents of the BBC news, an action expressly forbidden according to our order of the thirteenth of June 1942, and punishable by up to five years in prison.'

Pip swallowed and finally allowed himself to look at Dad as he was led out. His father's face was a mask of anguish and horror.

Time had stopped. Alice had no idea if she'd been in labour for hours or days. All she knew were the relentless pains that forced all her attention inwards as she tried to fight the waves of agony that took her closer and closer to the abyss. Occasionally the doctor would come and press on her belly, inflicting further torture, mutter with the nurse again, then disappear.

Alice thrashed around the bed, desperate to escape her own skin. The nurse restrained her gently. She tried to stay still after that, biting her lips so as not to cry out, driving her fists into her legs to stop herself from moving.

The twisting, dragging and pulling felt as if her abdomen was trying to squeeze out all its contents. There was a searing pain in her lower back and a stabbing to her stomach as though she was being attacked on all sides. Then the onslaughts came so fast she couldn't even draw breath between them.

Just as she felt she couldn't go on any longer, she was overcome by a primitive force that had her on her knees, grunting and pushing, intent on the compulsion that drove her body, every part sweeping her downwards. She felt a warm gush of liquid, then the baby was expelled from her in a slithering rush. The nurse cut the cord without a word, wrapped the baby in a blanket, then dashed with it out of the room.

The silence flowed back as Alice lay there wondering what on earth was happening.

Before long the midwife returned to deliver the placenta. Then she was joined by the doctor, his features wreathed in sadness.

'I'm sorry, my dear. Your baby was born dead,' he told Alice, looking at her pityingly. 'He was not meant for this world.'

Alice's head tipped back against the pillows as a wave of misery engulfed her.

'A boy?' she whispered.

The doctor nodded. 'Please accept my deepest condolences.' Then he and the midwife left the room, leaving Alice to contemplate her tragedy alone.

Jenny was back home when the call came. Mum took it and returned to the kitchen with her disapproving face on.

'Who was it, Mum?' asked Jenny, laying the table. She averted her eyes as usual from Dad and Alice's places.

'That was Mr Marett. Apparently Pip has been arrested.'

'Oh no!' Jenny jumped and a fork clattered to the floor. 'But I went over to warn him about the wireless.'

'What wireless?' Mum bent to retrieve the fork and handed it to Jenny, her expression still stern.

There was no point hiding the truth, although she could gloss over her part in it. 'Pip had a set concealed in his bedroom. He was using it to listen to the BBC news.'

'I see. I always thought that young man was foolhardy. We're not even allowed to *have* wirelesses, let alone listen to anything in English.'

'I know. He was just trying to ascertain how the war's going. You know his father wouldn't let him fight, so he couldn't find out first-hand.' Jenny's explanation sounded flimsy even to her own ears.

Mum sighed. 'Just as well. He'd have done even more daft things.'

Jenny ran the fork under the tap and dried it on a tea towel. '*Brave* things, Mum.'

Mum shrugged. 'What's the point? The Jerries will get us all one way or another.'

'That's not true. The Allies have been doing so much better lately. Look at North Africa.'

'I don't know how this war will end. If it ever does.' She turned to prod at something in a saucepan that was bubbling on the stove. 'And what was your part in this, Jenny?'

Jenny gnawed at a bit of ragged skin by her fingernail. 'I listened with him occasionally.'

Mum shot her another steely glance. 'Aren't you putting us in enough danger shielding Rebekah?'

'I'm sorry, Mum. I should have thought. We might have to take Rebekah back to Farmer Picot's barn for a while, until the wireless searches have died down.' She'd been thinking about this on the way back. She'd seen enough of the Germans' modus operandi by now to know they'd have a big crackdown for a few days then move on to something else. They could always bring Rebekah back then. 'I'll go and tell her.'

Rebekah listened white-faced to the news about Pip. 'That's terrible,' she said. 'Do you think he'll be deported?'

'It depends how much they have on him. Mum was a little vague on details. I think I'll cycle over to Mr Marett's tonight and see if I can find out more.' Jenny didn't want to confide her deepest fears about Pip to Rebekah when her friend's position was so precarious, but underneath she was terrified for him.

Rebekah nodded. 'He might get off with a caution. Or a fine. It will put paid to your resistance activities, though.'

'We'll see,' said Jenny, her anxiety turning to anger. 'I'm not giving up without a fight. Pip's arrest has made me even more determined. Thankfully, I don't think they know about me, so I can carry on under the radar.'

'That's the spirit.'

'I'm sorry, Rebekah. You must be even more worried for your own safety now.'

Rebekah gave her a wan smile. 'I'm always at risk. Ever since Hitler decided to round up Jews. But what about you and your family? Are you worried that you've become more vulnerable?'

Jenny explained about her plan to move Rebekah back to the barn for a few days.

Rebekah smoothed the bedspread. 'I can be ready tonight,' she said.

'All right. I'll phone Farmer Picot now.' She ran downstairs to make the call.

Mercifully, Farmer Picot was willing to take Rebekah, and

even better, he offered to collect her in his truck as soon as it was dark. He would come over on the pretext of delivering straw for Binkie, and smuggle her back hidden under tarpaulin. It was a risk, but it was the best they could come up with in the time-scale, and probably safer than keeping her where she was.

Jenny hugged her goodbye and cycled over to Mr Marett's, anxious to know more about Pip and sensing the old man needed company after such an awful shock. He seemed pleased to see her, although he greeted her at the door with his hair standing on end as though he'd run his hands through it many times.

She accepted his offer of Scotch, despite hating the stuff, as she suspected he needed some and was too polite to drink without her.

'Pip's still in jail,' he told her, handing her a glass. 'The charge is illegally possessing a wireless set and using it to disseminate the BBC news.'

Jenny took a sip of the whisky and tried not to shudder. 'Will he be allowed to defend himself?'

'I don't know. I have a lawyer standing by in case. Article 53 of the Hague Convention definitely does *not* give the German authorities the right to confiscate wireless sets or any other form of personal property.'

'That's hopeful,' said Jenny.

'Maybe. He's also expressly disobeyed orders to listen only to German stations. But it's circulating news bulletins that they'll get him for. And I have a feeling they'll want to make an example of him, seeing as he's my son.'

Jenny glanced at Mr Marett's face. His skin seemed more lined than earlier, the folds deeper, the eye bags more pronounced. Poor man. It would break him if he lost Pip. 'This must be such a shock to you,' she said.

He leant his head back and tipped the remains of his whisky into his mouth, then stood up. 'A drop more?'

Jenny shook her head. She forced herself to take another sip. It still tasted disgusting, but she was beginning to feel the effects of it now. Warmth spread through her body, taking the edge off her fear.

'I had no idea this was what Pip was up to. The brave idiot. Presumably you did?'

'Yes, I'm sorry. Pip thought it was better you didn't know about the wireless, as it would have put you in a difficult position.' She decided to keep quiet about her part for the same reason.

'Well, it's certainly put me in a difficult position now.' Mr Marett slammed his glass down on the coffee table beside him, then looked across at her. 'I'm sorry, my dear, you must be frightened for him too.'

Jenny bit the inside of her cheek. 'Yes, I am.' She didn't like to speculate in front of Mr Marett what the Germans would do to get the truth out of Pip. She tried to snap off the image of him being tortured, his face black with bruises, perhaps even his fingernails ripped off. He was brave, there was no doubt about it, but everyone had their breaking point. She took another sip of Scotch, and this time found the taste to be more anaesthetising than burning.

'We'll just have to hope and pray,' said Mr Marett. 'Thank you for coming, Jenny. I'm grateful. We should know more tomorrow. I think I'll go into the office. Try to keep things as normal as possible. I'll let you know if I hear any more.'

Jenny stood up. 'I'll be in tomorrow too,' she said. She also needed to keep busy. And that way she would be on hand when any news came through.

Mr Marett came to the door to say goodbye. Jenny hugged him warmly; she had a feeling the bottle of Scotch would be empty before the evening was out.

31

Jenny grasped the handle of the Gestetner machine and turned it anticlockwise with a firm motion. She'd created the stencil earlier by typing up the latest news translated into Spanish, and now the machine was churning out copies with its familiar clattering sound, while the smell of ink filled the air. Later she would run off English copies too, which would be distributed around the whole island. She and Robert had been extending their area of influence lately, determined to spread the news as widely as possible.

She glanced at the first sentence as the sheets rolled off the press:

Ha llegado el día D. Bajo el mando del general Eisenhower, las fuerzas navales aliadas, apoyadas por fuertes fuerzas aereas, comenzaron a desembarcar esta mañana los ejércitos aliados en la costa del norte de Francia.

At the same time, she translated it back to English in her head: *D-Day has come. Under the command of General Eisenhower, Allied naval forces, supported by strong air forces, began landing Allied armies this morning on the northern coast of France.*

It was hot in Stan Hamon's attic, and she stopped briefly to wipe a slick of sweat from her forehead. At least she was still contributing to the war effort. With Pip no longer around, and his wireless out of action, she relied on Robert Durand to transcribe the news for her these days, although she still did the translation, and now the copying. She was determined more than ever to carry on with the work she and Pip had started. It was all she could do for him now.

The summer of 1943 had turned into a long, hard winter of cold and deprivation. Now it was June 1944 and still no word from Pip. At his trial he'd been sentenced to fifteen months' internment in Germany. Mr Marett had been right. They'd made an example of him on account of his father's role, and the penalty had been harsh. Jenny had exchanged one despairing look with him as he was led out of the court-room. He'd been stooped and beaten, his face livid with bruises, confirming her worst suspicions and causing her fears for his future to soar. She hadn't seen or heard from him again.

She tried to keep an image alive in her mind of him listening to the wireless. It was the activity that had got him arrested, but she still loved the memory of his eyes shining with excitement, two bright spots of red on his cheeks. Sometimes she visualised him on the *Bynie May*, the boat under full sail in the blazing sun, his hair blown back, his features vivid with excitement. The other image, the one of him slumped in a corner of a filthy cell, with only rats and cockroaches for company, his face pale and his eyes hollow with despair, was one she tried to banish, although sometimes it came to her in the night, and she'd wake up shaking and bathed in sweat.

There were so many people to worry about: Alice in Germany, Rebekah now back with them and still in hiding,

Mum, William . . . Everywhere she looked was risk and responsibility.

Better to focus on the job in hand. Something practical. Something she could achieve. The other things were too huge to cope with. She lifted the pile of copies from the machine, wiped her face again, and set about folding the papers. Since Pip's departure she'd poured all her energies into resistance work, taking on all the responsibilities she was offered. Anything to sabotage the Germans' actions.

News reports were still being smuggled into the camps by whatever means they could find. And the war news was so much better these days. The Allies had done well in North Africa and the Russians were driving the Germans back, reclaiming more and more territory. But today's news was the best yet. Surely the Allies would reclaim Europe now?

Yet despite the good news from abroad, things were even harder on the island, and she and Mum were finding it increasingly difficult to feed everyone, including Rebekah. Sometimes Jenny feared that they'd all starve to death before the war was over. Although on a sunny morning such as this one, glimpsing a piercing blue sky through the window and listening to the distant sound of gulls, she could almost believe in hope.

'Are those done, Jenny?' Robert's head appeared at the entrance to the attic, at the top of the ladder.

'Yes, I've just finished.' Jenny gathered up the papers and moved the Gestetner machine to the bottom of the cupboard before locking the door and pocketing the key. If a visitor was determined enough, they could still break in, but at least a cursory glance round the attic would reveal nothing suspicious. They'd deliberately not cleared away the old suitcases festooned with cobwebs, a battered trunk with the initials S.A.H. on the cover, and a few old tin toys huddled in a desolate group in the corner. The room appeared as it had been before the war: an old attic housing a few ancient possessions. No one would have guessed it was the headquarters of the Jersey Communist Party.

'Time for a cuppa?' Robert climbed back down the ladder and Jenny followed him down the stairs and into the kitchen. 'You can have nettle or dandelion.'

'What a choice!' said Jenny. 'Nettle, please.'

Robert took a bowl of brown liquid from the larder, tipped it into a pan, and started to heat it up on the stove. Jenny delved in the cupboard for cups and saucers. The JCP kept a few food items and some crockery in Stan's kitchen. Stan didn't mind, and they always divided up what they had. Not that there had been much to share lately.

Robert poured the tea into a cup and Jenny sat at the kitchen table with him, sipping the earthy liquid. It could have done with some sugar, or even a spoonful of honey, but there was no chance of that.

'So, what do you think of this latest news?' she asked.

Robert frowned. 'It's potentially exciting,' he said. 'If the Allies can push back the Jerries in Europe, then the war will be over. But it's a big if.'

'You don't sound too optimistic.'

'I am hopeful. It's just that it's such a huge undertaking. The Germans are weakening, that's for sure, but I don't trust Hitler an inch. And I'm worried what this means for the Channel Islands.'

'Do you think the Germans will be even tougher on us now?' asked Jenny, thinking of Pip's punishment.

'Maybe. We'll just have to see. I think things will get a whole lot worse before they get better.'

Jenny looked at Robert's thoughtful face. He had dark eyes, floppy brown hair and a permanently intense expression. At one time she'd wondered whether he wanted more than friendship, but she'd made it clear she wasn't interested. He seemed content with that, and after a while she heard he was walking out with Suzanne Machon from the hairdresser's in Roseville Street – although it didn't look as though he'd let her scissors near his hair recently. Nevertheless, it was nice to know they could work together as comrades. It had been Robert's idea to support the labourers and Jenny had been glad to help him, despite the ever-present dangers. He could still be hot-headed at times, though, and even now she didn't completely trust him.

They finished their tea and she washed up the cups while Robert checked that the cottage was secure. Then they went their separate ways: he to take the copies to their distributors at the Spanish camp and she to return home and help Mum. Sometimes she wished their roles were reversed.

A few days later, as soon as Mum could spare her, Jenny went into the office to put in a few hours' work. Mr Marett welcomed her warmly as usual, but he'd aged dramatically since Pip had been taken. His hair was almost white now, and folds of skin hung under his eyes. Jenny suspected he didn't sleep well. She noticed his hands were shaking slightly as he took her coat. She wished there was some way she could make his life better. If they had any food, she could have invited him over for a meal. Theirs was hardly a happy household, but at least there were more people to talk to. But then again, she didn't want to risk him finding out about Rebekah. It was too dangerous. The best she could do was to keep him company at the office from time to time.

She let him tell her about the Allies landing in France. She didn't want him to suspect she was still getting news from England. In theory they weren't supposed to know anything, although Mr Marett, with his connections to the bailiff, knew more than most.

'It's very good news,' he said. 'If our lads can beat the Jerries back, this could be the beginning of the end.' Two bright spots of red appeared on his cheeks, and Jenny suddenly saw the likeness to Pip.

'That's wonderful,' she said, smiling at him as she drew a ledger towards her.

'And of course that means Pip could be released very soon.'

Jenny smiled again. She had been secretly wondering about this too. 'I hope to God you're right,' she said.

'Yes, it's what keeps me going, seeing my boy again. And you must miss him too, my dear.'

She breathed in slowly. 'Very much,' she murmured. In truth, she yearned for him far more than she'd ever imagined. She had always kept him at bay, thought of him as a brother and close friend, but since he'd left the island, her dreams were of Pip before the war: the boy who adored her, who was always telling her of his plans, or organising trips on the *Bynie May*. Why had she taken him so much for granted? Why had she never told him how very dear he was to her? She'd been so fixated on Cambridge and a glittering future, she'd neglected to realise that the best prize was right in front of her. Please God she'd have the chance to show him how much she loved him. Those were the two things that drove her now: seeing out the war and being reunited with Pip. And both seemed to be coming closer.

When the phone rang a few minutes later, Jenny was still deep in thought. She raised her head as she heard Mr Marett's voice.

'Good morning, sir . . . Yes, I see . . . Worrying news . . . I will indeed . . . Thank you for letting me know . . . Goodbye.' He replaced the receiver. 'It's as I feared. There won't be any supply ships making it across to us now. The Allies will try to starve out the occupying forces. There are currently around twenty-five thousand soldiers on the islands. They won't be able to join their comrades defending Europe, and they won't be able to get access to food here. It's a question of whether we can all survive long enough.'

Jenny nodded grimly. Robert had said as much earlier. Mr Marett had been so caught up in the possibility of Pip coming home that he'd neglected to consider whether they'd be alive to welcome him. And of course, if they were starving on Jersey, Pip and Alice were quite possibly starving – or worse – in Germany. It was going to be a terrible wait. She just hoped their nerve would hold.

By the time she left the office, St Helier was a hive of activity. A number of German soldiers were erecting more barbed-wire barriers and lugging sandbags over to the bunkers. Jenny saw new machine guns placed along the side of the road, their barrels trained on the beach. Guards were in position outside the gasworks and the electricity station. When she popped into

344

Rimmington's to see if there'd been a milk delivery, she heard a group of people talking in the queue. One said she'd heard the telephone exchanges had been shut down, a second claimed she'd seen guards outside the gas works and electricity power stations and a third reported that huge concrete posts were being erected in the fields to prevent glider pilots from landing. Everyone was in agreement: the Germans were preparing for invasion.

Alice called the baby Karl. But only in her head. It was hard enough being branded a Jerrybag by her fellow islander prisoners; she didn't need to add fuel to the fire by advertising her son's half-German origins. But in her imagination he was little Karl, her golden boy, who'd grow up to have blond hair and blue eyes like his father.

The first few days after her birth they let her stay in the sanatorium, her full breasts leaking milk into the pillow, her body sore and bleeding. But the physical pain would go; the mental torment was far more damaging.

Eventually they encouraged her to get up. She began to walk around the ward; she got dressed; she ate desultory meals on her own; she responded to the nurses' questions in low monosyllables. After a week, she went back to the barracks.

'I'm so sorry,' whispered Clara. She must have seen Alice trudging away from the hospital, her hand resting on her still distended stomach, and had rushed across to greet her. She hugged her tightly, her eyes full of sympathy. 'They wouldn't let me come into the hospital to see you. I was in agony wondering how you were.'

Alice grimaced. 'I wouldn't have been much company. I think I was half mad for a while.'

'You poor, poor thing. It must have been devastating to lose the baby.'

'The worst thing ever.' Clara had told her about the miscarriages she herself had suffered; the spiralling hope and plummeting grief that accompanied each pregnancy. She'd never carried a baby to term, as Alice had, but the result was the same: a crippling sense of loss and an aching need to cradle a small, warm body in your arms.

Alice leant her head against Clara's shoulder and they walked slowly back to the dormitory.

After a few more days of rest, Alice went back to sorting out Red Cross parcels in the hut with kind Mr Matthews, who touched her arm gently, his eyes full of sadness, then left her alone to her grief. But she could feel his frequent glances of anxiety when he didn't think she was looking, and every so often, a cup of tea or even some chocolate would appear by her elbow. She drank and ate mechanically, her attention still focused inwards on the film that replayed constantly inside her head: the waves of pain, the slithery, slippery birth, the awful silence, the bleakness of the doctor's expression, then the announcement that her baby was dead. If only they'd let her look at him, hold his cooling body for a few minutes, stroke his head, marvel at his tiny hands, then perhaps the image of his lifeless form would supplant the others, but she hadn't even been permitted that comfort.

Apart from the support offered by Clara and Mr Matthews, Alice's imagination was her main solace. At night, when she awoke cold and cramped, she fancied she heard his plaintive cries, and drew her ghost child to her, feeling him root blindly at her chest until he latched on, drawing and pulling at her nipples with satisfied little moans until he was sated. She rocked him in his cot, singing him imaginary lullabies, then gazed at his sweet little face, purple-lidded eyes closed in sleep, his mouth twitching in his dreams. During the day, he was strapped to her back; she felt the phantom weight of him as she walked. As the months passed, he rewarded her with little smiles, then gurgles, then full-blown laughs when she blew raspberries on his tummy or tickled his palms.

Now it was summer again, a full year since his birth, and she imagined his lurching steps until, increasingly confident, he started to follow her around the camp, his little feet tap-tapping after her.

Apart from Clara, her fellow inmates continued to shun her: at first it was her relationship with a German that had drawn their censure, but now, she suspected, it was her grief that repelled them. None of the other women spoke to her, no eyes met hers in recognition, no mouths turned up at the sight of her, no friendly words came her way. But she had Karl, her secret child, to sustain her. That and the promise of being reunited with Stefan one day.

But even Alice was jolted out of her reveries by the increasingly frequent sound of planes flying overhead. 'Lancasters and Wellingtons,' Mr Matthews told her knowledgeably. 'Our brave boys giving their all.' His eyes welled up. 'The tide is turning, Alice. There are more Allied planes flying in than German ones flying out.'

'But won't there be reprisals?' Alice pushed a strand of hair behind her ear. 'If our lot are killing German civilians, what will the Germans do to us?' There'd been rumours of forced marches further east to camps far more terrible than Biberach. And even in their camp, the food supplies were dwindling, the conditions becoming harsher. Occasionally Alice would be called on to put a sling on an injured arm or bathe a bloodied nose. The normally respectful guards were increasingly lashing out in frustration. Everywhere the fear was palpable.

Mr Matthews frowned. 'I don't know, dear. All we can do is hope and pray that the war ends soon. Perhaps we'll be released before we know it.'

Alice wondered if Clara would ever be reunited with her husband. As time went on, her kind friend was looking even more agonised, and Alice suspected she feared Samuel was dead. They became even closer, united in shared grief: two women without their men, two mothers without children.

Yet Karl lived on in Alice's imagination. Increasingly she dreamt of sailing back with him to St Helier harbour, to a newly freed Jersey, and introducing him to Mum, Jenny and William at the quayside. She had no idea what would happen to Stefan if the Allies won the war, but she allowed herself to hope that she'd be reunited with him too. And somehow that hope was represented by the image of a lighthouse that flickered in her mind, its sturdy form stolidly resisting all that the sea and sky could throw at it, beaming its light across the darkness, guiding her back to love and safety.

32

'I'm not eating this.' William spat a semi-masticated brown lump onto his plate.

'Please try, William. I spent hours picking it from the beach this morning.' Mum passed her hand over her forehead. There were dark circles round her eyes and her skin looked white and pinched. 'I risked being blown up by a landmine to get it.'

Jenny shivered. 'Come on, Will, it's not that bad.' She speared a small amount of the bladderwrack onto her fork and placed it in her mouth, trying to ignore the strong seaweedy taste.

William was stroking Binkie, who sat on his lap as usual, eyes closed in bliss. Mum had long since given up insisting the rabbit remain outside in his hutch; they tolerated him, knowing he kept Will calm. William held out some of the seaweed to the creature, who sniffed at it then turned his head away. 'You see. Even Binkie won't eat it.'

Mum gazed at him wearily, then her expression sharpened. 'Well, that's Binkie's loss,' she said.

Jenny tried one more time. 'William, you have to eat. There isn't anything else. If you don't eat this, you'll become weaker and weaker and starve to death.'

William's mouth dropped open and his eyes filled with tears. 'I can't,' he whispered.

'All right,' said Mum, grabbing his plate and standing up to put it in the sink. 'Have it your own way. But don't come to me saying you're hungry.'

One of the tears slipped down William's cheek and he buried his head in Binkie's soft fur.

Jenny poured a small amount of milk into a cup and handed it to him. 'Here, drink this,' she said. 'It will help to keep up your strength.'

Mum firmed her lips but said nothing.

They started at the sound of someone coming up the drive. Jenny peered through the window. Stefan. She went to open the front door.

Stefan bowed his head. 'I am calling to see if you have heard from Alice recently.'

Jenny opened the door a little wider, glancing over his shoulder to check he was alone. 'Would you like to come in? I'm afraid we have nothing to offer you.'

Stefan sighed. 'And I have nothing to bring. We have had no food deliveries for many weeks.'

Jenny nodded. 'We're all starving,' she said. She led him into the kitchen and pulled out a chair for him. He looked in a worse state than they were, his jacket hanging off him, his face gaunt and hollow. Jenny handed him Alice's latest letter. He took it eagerly, his eyes already devouring the words. Eventually he sat back, a half-smile on his face.

'I think Alice probably has more food than we do,' he said.

Jenny's mouth twisted wryly. 'I think you're right. She sends her love.' There'd been the usual greeting for her 'friend'. And the familiar lighthouse sketch at the bottom.

Alice hadn't said much. She never did. Ever since the first

letter with a German postmark had arrived, Jenny had tried to read between the lines, but it was impossible really. At least the camp appeared to be in lovely countryside and Alice seemed fit and reasonably well fed; certainly well enough to write. Jenny wondered if any of the Allied planes were flying over Biberach. Things had definitely been stepped up recently. But sometimes she seriously wondered whether they'd starve to death before the war was over.

'How are you, Stefan?' asked Mum, joining them at the table. She'd become progressively less defensive with him as his steadfast concern for Alice became more and more evident as time went on. He was good with William too.

'I am well, thank you, Mrs Robinson, if a little hungry.' He reached out to stroke Binkie's back and smiled at Will. 'And how is William?'

'I'm fine apart from the stinky seaweed.'

Stefan laughed.

'Are you busy at the hospital?' asked Jenny.

He smoothed down his jacket. 'I am no longer at the General,' he said. 'The new underground hospital has been finished. I work there now.' He massaged his forehead. 'We have had many German casualties since the Allies landed in France.'

Jenny nodded. 'That must be very difficult for you.' It seemed years ago that Alice had told her about the accident over at St Lawrence, and the terrible murder of all those OT workers. It had been the underground hospital they'd been working on. The slaves had continued to build it and now it was operational. Briefly she remembered Alexei and wondered if he'd been involved.

Stefan's face had a haunted look. 'It is an eerie place to work, especially at night. The wards have no windows, so there is no natural light in the building.' He screwed up his eyes.

Jenny tried to imagine the shadowy corridors, screams of pain echoing in the darkness. She closed her eyes too.

'Stefan,' said Mum, 'would you mind coming outside with me a minute?'

Jenny glanced at her face, but her expression was inscrutable.

'Of course,' said Stefan. He got to his feet and followed her out into the garden.

Jenny reached out to stroke Binkie, wondering what Mum wanted Stefan to do.

They reappeared after a few minutes. 'I must go,' said Stefan. 'I'll see if I can track down some meat for next time. Please tell Alice when you next write that her friend sends his love back.'

'Of course,' replied Jenny.

He turned to go, then stopped. 'And have you heard anything from Pip?'

She shook her head, not trusting herself to speak. There was still no news. It had been over a year now. At least Alice was able to write. There'd been nothing but silence from Pip.

'I'm sorry.' Stefan bowed his head again and set off back down the drive.

'What was that about?' Jenny asked Mum as she came back into the kitchen.

'Never you mind,' said Mum. But as she picked up the kettle to boil water for yet more dandelion tea, her expression was one of quiet satisfaction.

* * *

A week later, Jenny arrived home from a long day helping Mr Marett in the office to a wonderful meaty aroma filling the kitchen. Mum was laying the table, humming to herself. There was even a jam jar of roses on the red-checked oilcloth.

Jenny gave a low whistle. 'What's going on, Mum?'

Mum glanced at her. Was it Jenny's imagination or did she look a bit embarrassed? 'Stefan brought us some meat, as he promised,' she said. 'I dug up a few onions and carrots from the garden and I've made a stew. If we eke it out carefully, it should last us a few days.'

'How wonderful,' said Jenny. 'Good old Stefan. I must write to Alice and let her know how kind he's been. I'll have to choose my words carefully, of course, to evade the censor, but I'm sure I can get her to understand. It's a shame she isn't better at crosswords or I could have written even more cryptically.'

Mum smiled. 'You and your crosswords.' She drew a casserole out of the oven and carried it triumphantly to the table, then lifted the lid and stirred the contents. The sumptuous aroma grew even stronger. 'Can you call for William – and why don't you ask Rebekah down too, just this once? I think we can chance it.' Jenny normally carried a tray up to Rebekah in her room rather than risk her coming downstairs, but Mum was right, it would be nice for her to join them on what was clearly a special occasion.

She went to the bottom of the stairs and called up. William came down straight away, but Rebekah failed to appear. Jenny ran up to her room to investigate and caught Rebekah in the act of pulling out the trolley. She must have startled at being invited downstairs and thought she was in danger. Poor Rebekah. Their lives were bad enough, but hers was so much worse. She had virtually no freedom, and every unusual event triggered a terrified panic that the house was about to be searched again. In the early days she'd risked going out for walks at night, but since the soldiers' visit she hadn't ventured beyond the garden. Such a limited existence.

'It's all right,' said Jenny. 'There's no one else here. It's just that Mum has made a stew. We thought you might like to join us for the banquet.'

'Thank you,' said Rebekah, clutching at the bed frame to steady herself. Her face was very pale.

Jenny led her down and showed her to her place at the table. Mum spooned some of the food onto her plate, then served William.

'Real meat,' said Rebekah. 'I can hardly believe it. Where did you get it?'

Mum didn't answer, so Jenny explained that Stefan had brought it.

The next few minutes passed in silence as they all gave the meal their undivided attention. The stew was delicious, savoury and succulent, and even the vegetables tasted good after having been steeped in the rich gravy. Jenny couldn't remember when she'd last had such enjoyable food. It was good to see the others tucking in as well. They'd all looked so gaunt recently. The memory of the feast would sustain them for weeks. Unless Stefan came up with any more offerings.

'What kind of meat is it?' she asked. She was glad for Rebekah's sake that it wasn't pork. It tasted a bit like chicken, but more intense.

'I'm not sure,' replied Mum, avoiding her eye.

That was strange; surely Mum could have identified the

animal from the carcass, but maybe Stefan had presented it to her already butchered.

'Have you heard from Alice recently?' asked Rebckah.

'Yes. Just this morning.' Jenny went over to the dresser and retrieved the new letter that had arrived a few hours earlier. As usual, there wasn't much information. Just that she was well and missing them. Descriptions of the weather and the scenery. She seemed to still be working in the Red Cross hut. Jenny assumed her life was as dull and routine as theirs were. Apart from her friend Clara, and Mr Matthews who worked in the stores, she never mentioned anyone else. Jenny hoped she wasn't lonely.

There was still no communication from Pip, and Jenny wondered, with her usual lurch of anxiety, how he was. It was hard to face the lack of news day after day; the constant fears that circled her brain each night; the bleak look on Mr Marett's face every time he greeted her. They'd given up asking each other if they'd heard anything. Each knew the other would get in contact as soon as they did.

Mum started clearing up the plates, and Jenny and Rebekah helped her pile them into the sink.

William stood up too. 'Mum, were there any vegetable peelings? I'm just going to feed Binkie.'

Mum didn't turn round. 'I didn't peel the vegetables,' she said in a low voice. 'I just scrubbed them. More roughage that way.'

'Well, I'll see how he is anyway.' William opened the back door and disappeared outside.

Mum started to wash the plates, her shoulders sagging, while Jenny went to find tea cloths for her and Rebekah to dry up.

William was back in under a minute. 'Binkie's gone!' he said.

Jenny went to comfort him. 'Oh Will,' she said. 'He must have escaped. Are you sure you fastened his cage?' She hoped to goodness a fox hadn't got him.

Will nodded mutely, tears swelling in his eyes.

'Why don't you leave a little bowl of milk in his cage?' suggested Rebekah. 'He might come back when he's hungry.'

'That's a good idea,' said Jenny, smiling at their friend. Rebekah was so practical, just like Alice. It would help keep William's distress at bay, as well as keep hope alive a little longer. They bustled around the kitchen finding a bowl and pouring in a small amount of their precious milk.

But by the time William went to bed, Binkie still hadn't returned. All night the meat churned uneasily in Jenny's stomach as she pictured Mum's expression of triumph mixed with embarrassment. She'd long since guessed where their meal had come from; she just hoped William would never work it out for himself. Without Binkie to calm him, his tantrums might become more frequent; he'd be more of a risk to himself and others. In the short term their hunger had been assuaged, but in the long term they might be storing up more problems for themselves. She hoped they wouldn't come to regret Mum's actions.

33

By the spring of 1945, Alice and Clara were still at Biberach. Karl would have been nearly two by now. As they walked round the camp, Alice imagined a tiny hand in hers and heard the pitter-patter of small feet. The sky was often filled with planes these days, so in her mind, she squatted down and pointed out the distant shapes of de Havilland Mosquitos, all bearing the distinctive RAF roundel, all promising hope from abroad.

Sometimes she tried to picture Stefan with them. There was so much she didn't know about the father of her child. Was he good at sport? Would he have kicked a football with his son? Or preferred to sit him on his lap and read him a story? Karl would have been half British, half German. A unification of two nations at war. And an emblem of peace, perhaps, in a bright new future when harmony reigned once more.

Alice had been ten when William was born. Old enough to hold him after Mum had fed him. She could still remember the little head nestling against her neck as she rubbed his back to wind him, and his bright brown eyes trying to focus on hers as she pushed him down the lane in his pram in an effort to get him to sleep. He'd screamed a lot too, she remembered, strange, anguished sounds that made Dad grow red in the face. 'Will someone please hush that baby?' he'd shout at Mum, only making William worse. Then Mum would nod to Alice, who would scoop Will from her arms and take him into the garden, pointing out the flowers to him in a soothing voice until he calmed down.

Alice remembered the conversations, too. 'There's something wrong with that child,' Dad would say. And Mum would shake her head and come out with one of her usual platitudes: 'He's just tired' or 'He's just a difficult baby.' But after a while, she ran out of excuses. Will didn't seem to want to kiss or hug them as other children did. He just sat on the floor lining up his train sets, roaring with rage if someone dislodged the arrangement. He took a long time to learn to speak, and when he did, for ages he'd just repeat what they said to him. 'If only he'd call me Mummy,' said Mum sadly, 'I'd feel he wanted to belong to me.' But he never did. He didn't call her anything until he was six, and then he just said 'Mum' like Alice and Jenny.

Perhaps Karl would have been like Will. She would have known how to treat a little boy who was different. Whatever traits he might have had, the child who only existed in her mind was perfect, the beautiful son who would never leave her.

One chilly April morning, Alice was last into the washroom. She and her roommates had been woken up at seven as usual, but for some reason her limbs were heavier that day, her head muzzy. It was so hard to rouse herself. She'd been dreaming of Karl. They were walking hand in hand down the beach, towards the frilly edge of the sea as it whispered up the sand. She'd picked up a small stone, its wave-worked surface smooth, held it between her thumb and first finger, then bent back her wrist and flicked it forwards, just as Dad had taught her and Jenny when they were children. In her dream, Karl shrieked with delight as the pebble skimmed the water.

When the reveille whistle penetrated the thick air of the barrack room, she'd rolled over and buried her head in the pillow, desperate to hang on to her young child and the sun-drenched beach. But her dream was pushed back by the moans and grunts of her roommates, until it faded into the faintest memory of joy and warmth. She'd sat up, swung her feet off the bed and reluctantly entered the day.

Everyone was leaving the washroom as she went in. There was only time for a lick and a promise, as her mother used to call it, or she'd be late for roll call. She made for the open half-culvert that ran along one side of the roughly plastered wall. The basins always reminded her of the metal troughs Jersey farmers used to provide water for their cattle.

Just as she was trying to coax more than a thin trickle from the tap in order to wash under her arms – there wasn't any soap – she heard her name being called in a scathing fashion from the doorway, followed by a tutting sound. Sarah Mauger. It would be. Just as she was late already.

Sarah had largely left her alone after Karl had been born. Even she had some grudging respect for Alice's grief. But now she obviously thought Alice was fair game again.

'Tarting yourself up, Jerrybag?' she asked.

Alice stiffened. She felt particularly vulnerable standing half naked at the basin, her nightdress pulled down to her waist, her limp breasts exposed. The nurse had bound them after Karl had been born. They'd felt like molten rocks on her chest for days until her milk supply dried up. Another reminder of her loss.

She grabbed a threadbare towel from the hook and dabbed at herself quickly before drawing her nightdress over her shoulders again and doing up the ties at the front. Only then did she turn to face the other woman.

'I'm late, Sarah. You will be too.' Sarah was already wearing the grubby skirt and grimy blouse that had become her uniform, so she was much further on in getting ready than Alice, but Alice didn't want her to hang around.

'Why don't I wait for you? We could go down to roll call together?'

'No, you go on,' muttered Alice. 'I still have to get dressed.'

'Well, let me help you then.'

She had a sudden vision of Sarah handing her a succession of garments, doing up her buttons, brushing her hair, eyes glinting like some malevolent lady's maid from days gone by. She shuddered inwardly.

'I'm fine, thank you.' She turned and marched back to the barrack room, hoping the woman would take the hint.

But Sarah followed and stood in the doorway as Alice went over to the rail at the end of her bed and grabbed her clothes.

'There've been more planes coming over lately. Have you heard them?' she asked. She jabbed a finger into her bird's-nest hair and teased out a few strands with her nail.

'Yes.' Alice did up her greying brassière and reached for her blouse. 'Allied aircraft.' There was obviously something big brewing. Mr Matthews was convinced the end was very close now. But what was Sarah getting at, and what did she want from her now? Alice kept her guard up and waited to see what more she would say.

Sarah twirled the strands of hair round her finger. 'Have you heard the rumours?'

'What rumours?' Alice did up her blouse, trying to keep her suddenly rubbery fingers on the buttons.

'About what the Germans will do with us if they're defeated?'

'Well, they'll let us go, surely? They'll have to.' Wasn't there some sort of convention about how prisoners of war should be treated? Dad would have known. She hoped she wasn't just trying to convince herself. The alternative was too unbearable to contemplate.

'Of course they will.' Sarah smiled sweetly. 'These soldiers are pussycats really.'

Alice frowned at the sarcasm and thought of all that they had suffered under their guards in the camp. The sight of Clara, who was little more than a walking skeleton now, was what tortured her the most. But the non-Jewish inmates also had a lot of freedom, considering they were in an internment camp. They could go for walks, the children could play outside, and despite the Red Cross deliveries having dried up lately, most of them had enough to eat. Alice was still slipping Clara as much food as she could – angry that the Jews were treated so appallingly – but she suspected Clara shared it with others in her hut. She certainly wasn't looking any better nourished. But maybe more of them were being kept alive because of her.

Sarah took a step forward. 'The Biberach guards are different to the Nazis, of course.'

A tendril of unease started to coil through Alice. What was Sarah hinting at? What were these rumours? She stepped into her skirt, slipped on her shoes and went to the mirror to run her hands through her hair. But she couldn't play for time any longer. She kept her back to Sarah but watched her sly expression in the mirror. 'What do you mean?' she asked.

Sarah examined her nails, which were blunt and cracked, just like everyone else's. 'I think there are plans for your Jewish friends.'

Alice whipped round. 'What have you heard?' Her heart started to thud.

'Apparently they're thinking of shooting all those in the huts.'

All those in the huts. Alice swallowed down a surge of nausea.

Sarah shrugged. 'Either that or they're going to blow the whole camp up before they leave. At least that would be a bit more democratic.' She gave a hollow laugh. 'How about we hold hands when the time comes, Alice? Go up in a puff of smoke together?'

Alice tried to compose herself. 'How about we just focus on certainties?' she replied. 'If we don't make this roll call, we'll be doomed anyway.' She strode out of the room, leaving Sarah trailing in her wake.

But inside she was terrified. She'd lost her father, Stefan, Karl, and she would probably lose Clara. And now, just as they might be on the verge of being rescued, she could be about to lose her own life too.

Two weeks later, the roll calls were still going on. It was hard to believe they were expected to attend them. Rumours had accelerated over the last few days that the war was nearly over; the larger number of Allied planes in evidence and the increasingly bleak expressions on their guards' faces all confirming that the hearsay was true. But Alice couldn't ignore her growing sense of dread that something terrible might be about to happen. They were all on edge awaiting it.

Yet despite Sarah's dire predictions, the Jews remained in their huts, and Alice saw no sign that the guards might try to blow up the camp. The Germans seemed far too busy saving their own skins now. Perhaps, precise to the last, they were trying to leave neat records of inmate numbers for the camp liberators and deflect any reprisals that might be made against them for the brutal treatment of prisoners.

Whatever the reason, Alice marched obediently down to the parade ground with the others from her barrack room, ready to stand in the all-too-familiar row to be counted. She glanced idly round for Clara, but couldn't see her. The poor woman could barely put one foot in front of the other now. It seemed to take her longer to reach the parade ground each time.

Alice stood ramrod straight while the counting took place. She'd learnt from bitter experience over the years that it didn't do to talk or fidget. As long as her body was obedient, her mind could run free. But she'd barely allowed herself to indulge in her usual fantasy about building sandcastles with Karl, or visiting Portelet Common again with Stefan, when she was jolted back into consciousness by the sharp sound of the whistle.

'Not again,' muttered Sarah Mauger, who was standing further down the line. She'd left Alice alone after her frightening speculations that day in the washroom, although she wasn't above darting her the odd disdainful glance.

'It appears a prisoner is missing,' rasped a guttural voice from the front. 'We will count you again. Please maintain your positions.'

There was a collective slumping of shoulders, though Alice wasn't too bothered by the recount. The sun was shining and a warm breeze threaded through the crowd. Things could have been a lot worse.

But just as the roll call began again, a guard rushed over from the Jewish area of the camp, saluted the Kommandant, and muttered something that Alice was too far away to catch.

Her chest tightened. What was he saying? And why hadn't Clara yet appeared? Her heart started to thrum.

The sun was hot now, and an older woman beside her swayed as though she was about to faint.

'Are you all right?' Alice asked, glancing quickly across at her.

The woman nodded, her lips pale, her forehead glistening with sweat. It must have taken all her strength to remain upright.

Finally, another announcement: 'The missing prisoner is accounted for. You may all leave.'

Alice waited impatiently until her row was dismissed, then rushed over to Clara's hut as fast as she could. But no one seemed to have seen her friend.

In the early days at the camp, when they'd both been relatively fit and well, the two women had usually met in Alice's dormitory. It was more spacious than Clara's cramped hut, and apart from Sarah, the other women had been friendly enough. But in the last few weeks, Clara had had to reserve all her strength for the roll calls, so Alice had taken to going to the Jewish barracks. As usual, she tried not to recoil as she made her way into the shadowy room. The hut was situated near some tall trees at the back of the camp and rarely seemed to get the sun. The air was thick with disease and despair.

As her eyes became used to the gloom, she realised that Clara's bed was empty, her blanket and sheets neatly folded. Where on earth was she? Had she been moved into the hospital?

She rushed out of the room and into the path of a straggly line of people making their way back to their huts.

'Has anyone seen Clara?' she shouted.

The woman at the front, wearing a pinched expression, looked at her through haunted eyes. 'I'm sorry,' she said. 'Clara died this morning. She just couldn't go on any longer.'

Alice's legs gave way and she sank to the ground in anguish.

She was so consumed by Clara's tragedy that the next few days passed in a terrible blur. But she still had to work. She was making her way to the Red Cross hut like an automaton when she heard a sound that broke through the fog of despair.

'What the hell is that?' Sarah Mauger was running towards her.

'I don't know,' replied Alice. Loud mechanical juddering noises were coming from the town. The two of them ran to the edge of the compound that overlooked Biberach.

'Tanks!' Sarah shouted. 'Lots of them.'

Alice peered down the hill. In the distance, a line of brown vehicles were lumbering along the road. She could just make out French flags streaming from the bonnets. Sarah waved and called out, but the tanks kept going.

'We're too far away,' Alice said, 'but it must be a good sign, surely.' She tried to feel elated, but she was still too numb from Clara's death.

Sarah nodded, all venom suspended, and rushed off to spread the word.

Alice went to tell Mr Matthews, but before she got there, she was conscious of other sounds, and frenzied activity around the camp. German officers were swarming round the compound carrying cases and boxes and loading them into vans. It looked like they were leaving.

Alice entered the Red Cross hut, where Mr Matthews was peering out of the window.

'Have you seen what's happening?' she asked him.

'I was just wondering what all the noise was.'

She told him about the tanks, and the Germans leaving.

'This must be good news,' he said, beaming at her. 'The Germans have obviously caught wind of something. I reckon the French are liberating the town. They'll come for us soon. They must.'

Alice suddenly felt choked up. If only Clara had survived a few more days, she would have been free. They could have returned to Jersey together and Alice could have nursed her back to health at Mum's.

'I tell you what,' he continued. 'This is too important a day to waste. Let's lock up and see what's happening.'

'All right,' said Alice, and followed him back towards the camp.

As they approached the barracks, another frenzy of activity greeted them. Men and women were rushing out of their huts, white garments fluttering in their hands. Alice looked around, expecting German soldiers to apprehend them at any minute, or even now to be lighting the fuses that would blow up the camp as Sarah had predicted, but they all seemed to have departed. It looked like the prisoners were on their own. She and Mr Matthews watched as people draped cloths over the barbed wire or attached them to flagpoles. A memory fluttered in her mind of the Jersey islanders hanging out white sheets of surrender and Mum rigging up that pair of Granny's bloomers. Now another group of people were capitulating. But this time it wasn't to the Germans, it was to their liberators. Or so she hoped.

'Surely it's only a matter of time,' said Mr Matthews. His eyes were glassy.

Alice placed her hand on his arm. 'I think you're right,' she said, her voice suddenly hoarse with a mixture of grief and anticipation.

'Do you know what day it is?' he asked her.

She shook her head.

'The twenty-third of April. St George's Day.'

A faint memory of an English lesson at school drifted back to Alice. 'Isn't it Shakespeare's birth date too?'

Mr Matthews laughed. 'I have no idea,' he said.

'I think I'm right,' replied Alice. 'Good old Shakespeare. Jenny would be thrilled.' She smiled sadly at his baffled expression.

34

Jenny was in the kitchen helping Will with his homework when Robert Durand telephoned her.

'Can you come to a meeting of the JCP tomorrow night? We're meeting at Leslie Huelin's flat in Peirson Road. Number nineteen.'

Jenny only hesitated for a moment. Initially she'd carried on with the translation work for Pip's sake, but as time had gone by, her more active involvement in the Resistance had helped channel her fury against the Germans. She didn't always trust the party members, or believe in their politics, but at least she was fighting for Jersey, the island she and Pip loved so much.

So the following evening, she cycled over towards the seafront until she reached Peirson Road. It was a shadowy late-April evening with an icy chill in the air. Despite the cold, early bluebells were beginning to haze the woods and a robin was chirping somewhere overhead.

They'd made it through another winter, thank God. Just after Christmas, the SS *Vega* had chugged into St Helier harbour, bringing with it thousands of food parcels from the Red Cross. Almost every adult islander had gone down to the quay to queue for their allocation in order to prevent the Germans intercepting them. Mum had exclaimed over the chocolate, biscuits, cigarettes, sardines and corned beef. There was even a small bar of soap. The *Vega* had visited the islands several more times, and everyone was starting to look better nourished. It had probably saved their lives. Mum passed the cigarettes and some of the chocolate on to Stefan. It was only fair when he'd given them so much.

And the war news was better still. Last night, Jenny had translated another BBC transmission and discovered that all resistance in the Ruhr had ended, and that 370,000 German prisoners of war had been taken. Surely Alice and Pip would be returning soon? A burst of joy shot through her body as she freewheeled down the hill, her hair streaming in the wind. She tried to imagine a future when the war was over, Alice was back home, and she and Pip were reunited. What bliss that would be.

When she got to Leslie's flat, she propped her bike up against the wall as usual, padlocked it carefully and let herself in. Pausing in the kitchen to get herself a glass of water, she heard voices coming from the living room.

'A people's democracy is exactly what's needed,' Robert was saying. 'We just need to get rid of the pesky administrators first.'

She walked into the room and everyone stopped speaking. Four faces turned towards her.

Robert swallowed. 'It's all right, chaps,' he said. 'It's only Jenny.' He drew out a chair for her. 'Any news from Pip?'

She shook her head and sat down. 'What are you all talking about?'

It was Paul Mühlbach who answered; a slim man with close-shaven blond hair and sharp features. Jenny knew him vaguely.

He was a former German soldier, now a deserter, in hiding on account of his anti-Nazi position. He had fought in the International Brigade in Spain, but had been captured and sent back to Germany. There he'd been given the grim choice of Dachau or the army. He'd chosen the latter, but remained determinedly anti-fascist.

'We're planning a mutiny,' he said.

Jenny could feel her mouth slacken. 'What?'

'For tomorrow,' said Leslie Huelin, 'International Workers' Day.'

'What are you intending to do?' asked Jenny, her heart pounding with shock. Subversive activities were one thing, but a full-scale coup was quite another.

Paul cleared his throat. 'The German soldiers are starving,' he said.

'We're *all* starving,' Jenny replied.

'Yes, but you've had the benefit of Red Cross food parcels. Nobody sends those to the enemy.'

Jenny looked at Paul's haggard face, the thin wrists protruding from his shirt, his trouser legs shaking. He was right. Stefan was starving too. The Germans were desperate.

'Many of my ex-comrades are ready to revolt,' he said. 'They're demoralised and worried about the Red Army advancing on their homes back in Germany and the Allies bombing their cities. If Jersey Communist Party members start a mutiny, they'll join in.'

His words did nothing to slow Jenny's heartbeat. 'What do you plan to do?' she whispered.

'We've arranged for the commander of Elizabeth Castle, Oberst Linder, to fire a cannon from its ramparts at ten o'clock tomorrow,' said Leslie. Built on a rocky islet in St Aubin's Bay, the castle had defended Jersey for more than four hundred years. The battlements dated back to the 1590s. 'I know he's a Kraut, but he's sympathetic to the cause. Mühlbach vouches for him.'

Paul nodded.

'That will be a signal that the revolt is about to begin,' Leslie continued. 'When they hear it, the soldiers will turn on their officers, disarm them and then surrender the island. Once Jersey is in our hands, we can go ahead with our plans to set up a Marxist utopia.' He examined his fingernails. 'Of course, we'll have to clear out the old guard first. But I predict it won't be long before the red flag will be flying over the States of Jersey building.'

There was a pause as the group members contemplated that ideal. Jenny looked at their naïve faces, all bearing the same hopeful expression.

'So what will you do with the *old guard*?' she asked. That would include Pip's father, surely?

'Oh, they'll have to be imprisoned,' replied Leslie nonchalantly.

Jenny realised she'd been holding her breath. She tried to let it out slowly.

'So, are you with us, Jenny?' he asked.

She thought rapidly. If she turned them down, they'd realise she was a risk and it could put her and her family in danger. But if she accepted, she'd be party to a potentially violent coup on the island. What on earth was she to do? Whichever decision she made could have momentous consequences.

She decided that it was best to go along with them for now.

She licked her lips, which had become suddenly dry with apprehension. 'Of course,' she said, beaming at them all.

'Great.' Robert smiled back. 'We were hoping you'd join us. I'll let Leslie explain the proposed course of action.'

Leslie stood up and positioned himself in front of her, clearly about to make a speech. 'We'd like you to report to First Tower School tomorrow morning. When the signal cannon fires, you're to go into the school, approach the headmaster and tell him to keep the children inside in case they're hurt in any ensuing action.'

Jenny felt a clutch of worry. But at least she wasn't being asked to bear arms. She supposed she could do that. But what about Mr Marett and the others? She'd have to find a way to protect them. She'd sleep on it first, and try to come up with a plan before morning. There was still time.

But she couldn't settle that night: there were too many worries circling in her brain. An image of those men storming the town, taking over and imprisoning Mr Marett – or worse – haunted her.

At three o'clock, Rebekah sat up in bed. 'What's the matter, Jenny?'

Jenny sat up too. 'Sorry. Did I wake you?'

'It's all right. I haven't slept much either. What's on your mind?'

Jenny stumbled her way through a description of the meeting, her fears for what Robert and his comrades might be about to do.

Rebekah seemed to hold her breath as she took it all in. Then she exhaled slowly. 'The mutiny will happen with or without your involvement. At least you're protecting the children.' It was hard to see her face in the darkness.

'I know, but how can I be aware of the danger to Pip's father and the others and not warn them?'

'But if they find out it's you, they'll probably shoot you.'

Jenny wiped her eyes with the back of her hand, then placed it on the counterpane to stop it shaking.

'What would Pip's dad tell you to do?'

'I think he'd probably tell me to do what I could to safeguard them without endangering myself.' She could almost imagine Mr Marett saying the words: 'I'm an old man, Jenny. I've lost my wife and I may have lost my son too. You have all your life ahead of you. You need to think of yourself now. And if Pip does come home, he'd never forgive me if you saved me to sacrifice yourself.'

But did that make it right? She wished her own father were here to advise her. But then again, she probably wouldn't have told him about the peril she was in. She'd protect Mum and William for the same reason.

Rebekah sighed. 'Could you go to Mr Marett and warn him?'

Jenny wiped her palms down her nightdress. 'Yes, that's what I'll do. I'll go over first thing, and we can talk it through and decide what's best to do.'

'Good decision.' Rebekah rolled over onto her side.

But Jenny lay on her back, her eyes wide open in the darkness, her pulse still throbbing.

She was up early the next morning. She dressed quietly, trying not to wake Rebekah, then tiptoed downstairs. Mum hadn't surfaced either: the kitchen was pitch black. Jenny didn't bother with breakfast; she opened the back door carefully and went out into the garden, noting with a pang Binkie's empty cage, collected her bike from the shed, then cycled off down the lane.

She decided to go to Pip's father's house first. It was only seven; he didn't get into work until eight thirty, so she doubted he'd have left yet. It was still cold, a sharp wind blowing into her face, and she wished she'd dressed more warmly. She tried to keep focused on the difficult conversation ahead of her. It was vital that she persuaded Mr Marett to protect himself without allowing him to alert the bailiff too soon. What if, like her, he felt he had to act on the knowledge? And what could the bailiff do anyway? His only possible course of action would be to inform the Germans and prevent the rebellion, but then he would be personally betraying his own people, resulting in certain imprisonment and possible death for many of them. The terrifying possibilities surged through her head as she gripped the handlebars tightly.

But when she got to Mr Marett's house, there didn't seem to be anyone in. She went round the back to check all the windows, and searched the garden, but the house was in darkness and there was no answer to her frantic knocking. Eventually she gave up and decided to go on to work.

It was the same story at the office: silence and darkness. Where could he be? Her stomach lurched at the awful possibilities. Had the mutiny been brought forward? She stood staring at the front door, at a loss as to what to do next.

35

It was getting late. Jenny had to be at First Tower before the cannon went off, as Robert had instructed, and ensure that all the children were kept safely away from any violence that might be about to erupt. Finding Mr Marett would have to wait. She remounted her bike and set off.

By the time she got to the school, snow flurries were whirling through the thin air. She took up her position on the street corner opposite, having leant her bike against the railings, and stood there trying not to look too conspicuous. It really was bitterly cold. She wiped away an icy drip from her forehead, then blew on her hands to keep warm. It was ridiculous weather for early May – much more like winter than spring.

She glanced at her watch. It was nearly ten o'clock now, the time she'd been told the cannon would go off. She tried to think how she would persuade the headmaster to keep the children inside. What if he refused to listen to her and insisted they went out to play? Would other deaths be added to her conscience? And then there was Mr Marett. Where on earth was he? She was almost paralysed with fear.

She checked her watch again. Five past ten. Why hadn't she heard the cannon? She tried to imagine Oberst Linder lighting the fuse, then standing back . . . the fire travelling along the cord until it met the gunpowder . . . powerful flames spurting out of the mouth of the gun. Surely she would hear the explosion from across the bay?

She waited for another ten minutes, alert to every sound, but all she could hear was birdsong and the distant sound of childish voices. More terrors sluiced through her. Had the revolt begun without her knowledge? Had the mutineers been captured already? Had the Germans got wind of the event? Perhaps even now, enemy patrols were on their way to arrest her.

At twenty past ten she decided she couldn't wait any longer. She remounted the bike and cycled shakily back to Peirson Road. There was no sound from inside. No one arrived and no one left. She pushed open the door and entered the revolutionaries' lair.

Leslie, Robert and the others were sitting in silence in the fug-filled room. Robert was staring at the ground; Leslie had his head in his hands. No one met her eyes. She'd expected the place to be crackling with energy. Something must have gone badly wrong.

'What's happened?' Her nose was starting to drip now she was in the warm. She blotted it on the edge of her coat sleeve.

Leslie raised his head. 'Bloody Linder refused to fire the shot.'

'Scuppered all our plans,' added Robert. 'I knew we shouldn't have trusted a Jerry.'

Jenny grabbed the back of a chair for support, her legs suddenly weak. 'So the mutiny didn't go ahead?'

'Well, we wouldn't effing well be here if it had, would we?' Leslie's eyes were bloodshot.

'All right, Huelin. It's not Jenny's fault,' said Robert.

Leslie put his head in his hands again.

Jenny sat down, her whole body trembling with relief. 'I'm sorry,' she said. But inside she was elated.

As soon as she felt strong enough, she stood up and left the room. No one tried to stop her. She had to find Mr Marett.

She cycled through the streets of St Helier, her feet pounding the pedals and her hands gripping the handlebars. The bike was heavy with all that sand in the tyres. Her thighs and calf muscles burnt. When she got to the office, she threw the bike to the ground and rushed in.

Mr Marett was sitting at the desk, his expression one of utter incredulity. Oh no. Had he caught wind of the plans and discovered her part in the aborted mission? She was already breathless from the cycle ride, but now her chest was so tight she could barely inhale.

'Are you all right?' she managed to ask.

'Mmm?' He didn't sound angry. Just shocked.

'Has something happened?'

He finally registered her presence. 'I've just returned from the bailiff's office. I can't believe what I've just heard.'

So that was where he'd been this morning. Jenny's heart started to pound again. 'Please tell me!'

'Coutanche had a telegram from the War Office first thing and wanted to pass on the news.'

'What news?'

Mr Marett blew out his cheeks. 'Hitler's dead. Apparently he shot himself.'

'Blimey.' Jenny lurched towards the desk.

He grabbed her hand. 'Surely the war has to end now, doesn't it? And Pip will come back.'

'Yes, he will,' she said. Tears stung her eyes as Pip's joyful face appeared in front of her. 'He will.'

✦

At Biberach, each day brought new freedoms. French soldiers came into the camp bringing with them extra food, and milk for the children. Alice and her fellow inmates, who'd lived on ersatz bread and rotten meat for the last few months, in the absence of new Red Cross parcels, seized on the extra supplies. Soon afterwards they were visited by US servicemen distributing sweets and chocolate. Children were hoisted onto their jeeps and lorries and given rides round the camp. Alice blinked away the image of Karl sitting with them, his little legs swinging, his face lit up with smiles.

At last, towards the end of May, they were finally advised to pack up their possessions and be ready to move out at a moment's notice. It didn't take Alice long, not having had much to start with. She stuffed her scant belongings into the backpack she'd been given on the quayside in Jersey, cast a last look round the dormitory, and went to stand outside the barracks ready to board the French army vehicle that was to take them to the US air force base at Mengen.

As she sat on the back of the lorry, she gazed back at the camp with mixed feelings. It had been appalling, and sometimes terrifying, to be taken away from her family and incarcerated in Germany. She didn't know how she'd have coped without Clara. She still felt bereft without her friend. But it was comforting to know that she was living in the land of Stefan's birth. And she'd had Karl here, the child of their

378

love. She'd never found out what they'd done with his little body, but he was there somewhere. He'd been so real to her all the time she'd been in camp. Would she still be able to imagine his presence once she was back on Jersey?

And then there were the worries about her homecoming. It was an open secret that she'd been pregnant by a German soldier, and although people were sorry for her by the end, as a result of her obvious grief, she still heard the word 'Jerrybag' whispered in the dormitory and the refectory. How could she bring such shame on Mum, Jenny and William? Would she ever be accepted back home as Alice Robinson, the competent nurse, or would she just be the 'horizontal collaborator'? And what about Stefan? Would she ever see him again?

There were some administrative delays at Mengen, but before long they were loaded onto Dakota aircraft. There were no seats on the plane; they just sat on metal floor plates with heavy canvas belts to strap themselves in. Alice couldn't see out of the window from her uncomfortable perch, so had to imagine the fields, woods and mountains that sped away below them, taking her further from Karl and from the country Stefan loved.

When one of the crew announced on the loudspeaker that they'd just crossed the English Channel, everyone cheered. Alice smiled. Somewhere down there were her family. The few letters from them that had got through to her had been a comfort during her time in the camp, and she'd particularly cherished Jenny's little drawings of lighthouses. They had all seemed well enough, if struggling to find food. She just hoped they'd still be glad to see her when they heard her news.

They landed at Hendon, and were taken to a reception centre at Stanmore in Middlesex, where they were deloused. Then they were each given a pound and driven to Victoria railway station, from where they travelled to Portsmouth and then on to Jersey by boat.

As Alice sat on the deck, gazing out at the choppy sea, her stomach churned with nausea and nerves. She caught sight of the Corbière lighthouse, rising up out of the water as white and proud as when she'd last seen it from the *Bynie May* with Pip. Her father's explanation to her and Jenny when they were children drifted back to her: *It acts as a guide and warning. It keeps sailors away from danger and leads them safely home when they return.* 'Look, Karl,' she said to the small form she felt sitting next to her, his eyes transfixed by the churning waves. 'That big white thing there is called a lighthouse. It means we're coming home.'

⚓

Jenny waited with Mum and William on the jetty for Alice to arrive. As she peered across at the horizon, she willed the ship to appear. She suddenly felt nervous about how Alice might behave towards her, and thought of all the sharp words and misunderstandings between them before Alice had been so suddenly taken from their lives. She just wanted her sister home safe. She was sure the hospital would have kept her job open, and Alice would be overjoyed to find Rebekah alive and well. They'd managed to protect her friend for the duration of the war, after all that Alice had sacrificed for her. Rebekah had moved back to her old house since VE Day, and Jenny missed her more than she'd expected.

But there was still no news from Pip. Every day Mr Marett

shook his head sadly to her question. There'd never been a letter from him, or even a 'capture card'. Just an appalling silence that lengthened with every day that passed, as the knife in her stomach twisted tighter and tighter.

Jersey was free again. They'd all poured into Royal Square at three o'clock on the ninth of May for Churchill's announcement. Someone had connected a wireless to the loudspeaker system, and the prime minister's voice came across loud and clear. Jenny had stood with Mum and William and listened to him announcing, 'Our dear Channel Islands are to be freed today.' The rest of the speech was drowned by cheers, although there were a few mutterings to be heard.

'So he's remembered us now, has he?' said one man. 'Taking his share of the credit when he bloody ignored us for five years.'

His neighbour nodded. 'Yes – we weren't his "dear Channel Islands" when he demilitarised us and let the Krauts walk all over us, were we?'

A woman turned round. 'That's enough. Churchill did his best. And he won in the end, didn't he?'

One of the men spat on the ground.

Jenny tried to ignore them. Instead she concentrated on the bunting hanging from every building, the Union Jacks fluttering overhead, the broad smile on the bailiff's face as he confirmed that they were free at last. *Come home, Pip, please come home*, she begged inside her head as the band struck up. He should have been here to share this day with her. They'd both played their part in the victory: all those long evenings translating, the endless trips over to Sand Street, rescuing Rebekah, the prospect of the terrifying coup. Her heart heaved with sadness. Pip had surrendered his freedom for the cause; maybe – she could hardly bear to think about it – his life. How could she have taken him for granted when they were together? What if she'd realised too late that he was the only man for her? She felt tortured by regret.

'All right?' Mum's expression was anxious.

Jenny swallowed. 'Fine. Such a proud day.'

Mum nodded. 'The last time we were here in Royal Square, Alice and Pip were with us.'

'I know. And Dad had just been killed.' It'd been five years since they'd lost him. Five hard years of grief and deprivation and anxiety. But they'd got through it. Jenny felt for Mum's hand and gave it a squeeze.

And now the three of them were together again on the quayside, hopeful that they would soon be four.

'There's the ship,' shouted William. He pointed at a faint shape on the horizon.

Jenny looked out to sea. There indeed was HMS *Beagle*, steaming towards them. She turned to Mum. 'Not long now,' she said.

Mum smiled back.

The ship took an age to arrive and disembark the passengers, but eventually there was Alice. Thinner, paler and with lank hair reaching to her shoulders, but definitely Alice. Her face lit up when she saw them. She had a small bag in one hand, and the other arm was outstretched as though she was tugging something.

William ran up to her first and gave her a big hug, causing Alice to step back in surprise. He took her free hand and led her to Jenny and Mum, who embraced her too.

Mr Marett had been kind enough to drive them over in the

car, and he was waiting to take them all home. He took Alice's bag from her and stowed it in the boot, then held the door open for Mum to sit in the front while the three siblings piled into the back.

Alice didn't say much on the journey home, just stared out of the window. It was a beautiful June day, cow parsley frothing in the hedgerows and a sea of pink thrift lining the roadside. The sky was a brilliant blue with a few wispy clouds.

Jenny felt a rush of affection for her sister. Kind, loyal Alice. If only Pip could make it back safely too, then life might truly be good again.

Once they were home, Mum set about making Alice some acorn coffee — the real stuff hadn't yet arrived back in the shops — and cutting up slices of cabbage loaf. There was even a scraping of butter they'd saved from their rations.

Alice asked after Rebekah, and they assured her that they'd kept her friend safe. She told them about what had happened to Clara.

'That poor, poor woman,' Mum said. 'We're only just hearing about how Jewish people and their families have suffered. Thank God Rebekah wasn't discovered. I dread to think what they'd have done to her.'

Alice smiled sadly. 'It'll be good to see her again.'

'She'll be over later. She didn't want to intrude on your time with us, but I'm sure she can't wait to see you either.'

Alice took a sip of her drink, then pushed back a strand of hair that had swung in front of the cup, and looked intently at Jenny. 'And what about Stefan? Have you heard what's happened to him?' Her words were casual, but Jenny saw the desperate longing in her eyes.

She told Alice how good Stefan had been to them during the war, how he'd kindly brought them food until he had less than they did.

Alice's face brightened at her words. 'And is he still here?' Again the searching glance.

Jenny shook her head. 'I'm afraid not. The Allies rounded up all the remaining German soldiers and took them to England. He's no doubt imprisoned over there. I don't know any more details.'

Alice gripped the table, her fingers whitening. 'How can we find out?'

'I suppose I could ask Mr Marett. He might know.'

Mum placed a plate of buttered bread in front of Alice. 'What will you do now, dear?' she asked. 'Go back to the hospital?'

Alice looked blank for a moment, then massaged her forehead. 'I suppose so,' she said. 'Eventually.'

'There's no hurry,' said Jenny. 'You've been through a terrible ordeal. You need to spend some time recuperating. Gathering your strength. Food supplies are beginning to trickle back through now. We'll feed you up in no time.'

Alice looked at her through haunted eyes. 'You don't know the half of it,' she said.

36

One September day, when Jenny came into the office to do some work, there was the usual fruitless enquiry as to news about Pip. Afterwards she lingered by Mr Marett's desk.

'Was there something else, dear?' he asked.

She fiddled with a chain round her neck. Pip had given it to her years ago. It had once belonged to his mother. She always wore it now.

'I was wondering if I might have a week off in November.'

'Of course. Are you going away?'

'Sort of. Just a few days in Cambridge.'

'Cambridge? That's a long trip at this time of year.'

Jenny tucked her hair behind her ears. 'I've decided to take the university entrance examination.'

Mr Marett picked up a fountain pen from his desk and unscrewed the lid. 'Yes, I remember that before the war there was talk of you going to Cambridge. Maths, wasn't it?'

'It still is. I've always loved the subject.'

'I would imagine you're very good at it. You can certainly add up a column of figures faster than anyone I know.'

Jenny smiled. 'My father was keen I follow in his footsteps, and for years, all I dreamt of was studying maths at university.'

Mr Marett hovered the pen over the inkwell, released the catch on the side, dipped in the nib and drew up some ink. 'And then the war came along.'

'Yes. And for a while my resistance work with Pip took over. That and trying not to starve. My ambition to study faded into a distant dream, one that belonged to a life before any of this.'

'Well, you certainly did your bit. Both of you.' His mouth twisted.

Jenny reached out to squeeze his hand. 'My priority is still Pip,' she said. 'I thought I'd take the entrance examination just to see if my maths is up to it, but in the meantime, I'd like to carry on working for you, if I may?' She still enjoyed being at the office, and it was nice to work alongside Pip's father. In a way, it brought her closer to Pip. 'I thought I'd wait until we hear any news, then make a decision.'

She didn't add that she needed to find out if Pip was dead or alive first; it sounded too bald, too callous to say it out loud. But in essence, that was what she planned. If they got Pip back, however badly damaged, she'd devote herself to caring for him and making him well. Cambridge could wait. If he didn't come home, then perhaps she would study, if she was offered a place. It was the not knowing that was the worst. It was hard to do anything when she was in limbo. In the end, it was Mum who had persuaded her to apply to Cambridge. 'It's what your dad would have wanted. And I think deep down you want it too.' Jenny had nodded. And for the first time in ages, she'd gone to bed thinking of algebra and geometry rather than Pip.

Mr Marett doodled on the blotting paper on his desk. 'Let me tell you something, Jenny. When I was a lad growing up here, I had a good friend, Albert Pearce. We were in and out of each other's houses all the time after school. At weekends

386

we went off on cycling tours round the island, sometimes camping overnight. I'd have done anything for Albert and he for me.' He broke off to look into the middle distance.

Jenny tried not to fidget. It was hard to know where this was going, and she had a lot of ledgers to get through. She wondered how long Mr Marett's reminiscence would take. She'd only intended to ask him for a few days off, then get on with her work.

'When war broke out in 1914, we both decided to enlist. Albert was put in the Wiltshire Regiment and I joined the Duke of Cornwall's Light Infantry. I ended up at Ypres; Albert was sent to the Somme.'

Jenny tried to imagine a younger version of Mr Marett in army uniform, eager-eyed and pink-cheeked. Had something happened to him in the last war? Was this another reason why he'd been so reluctant to let Pip fight?

'I was one of the lucky ones. I survived the war in Belgium and returned to Jersey sound of limb and mind. I met Pip's mother soon afterwards, and we had two happy years together before we lost her giving birth to Pip.'

Pip had told her as much as he knew of his mother. Jenny had always wondered how different things would have been for him had she lived. Maybe Mr Marett would have been less protective, but then again, perhaps it was his very attempts to stop Pip fighting that had driven Pip to join the Resistance. He might have been safer in the navy, returning unscathed as his father had, and even now would be in the office laughing and chatting to them. Jenny tried to summon a lively, active Pip into the room, but there were too many doubts and shadows in her mind. He failed to appear.

'But I never saw Albert again,' Mr Marett continued. 'His poor parents waited years for a letter or a telegram, but no one seemed to know his fate. I tried my hardest to track him down – even went over to France once to look for him – but he'd disappeared without trace.' He broke off to pull out a handkerchief and wipe his face: whether his grief was for Albert or for Pip it was hard to tell. 'When they installed the tomb of the Unknown Warrior a couple of years after the war in Westminster Abbey, I went to London to pay my respects. I stood at that tomb and thought of Albert.' The tears were running freely now. 'I wonder whether I'll go there again and think of Pip.'

Jenny leapt up, knocking over the chair in her haste, and put her arms round him. 'Please don't give up hope,' she murmured. They'd tried all the obvious channels: the bailiff, the Red Cross, the Foreign Office – Jenny had even written to all the major newspapers – but no one had any information. The war might have ended, but the world was still in chaos. So many people were looking for missing loved ones. Frustrating though it was, they just had to be patient.

Mr Marett smiled at her weakly. 'I'll never give up hope,' he said. 'But I have to be realistic. I may never see Pip again – or find out what happened to him.'

Jenny's legs started to buckle. She squeezed his arm and sat down again. Sometimes when she woke up in the middle of the night she thought about the possibility of Pip never being found, but by morning had put it out of her mind. It was still early days. There was always the prospect of news. That one day he'd jump off a ship, wander down to the harbour to check on the *Bynie May*, then saunter into the office with a wide smile and a long list of adventures to recount. He'd come back after Saint-Malo, hadn't he? He'd gone missing then, and they'd all been anxious, but he'd returned safe and sound. Surely the same could happen this time.

Mr Marett took a deep breath. He seemed a little more composed now. 'You can't wait for Pip for ever. Even if he does come back, I don't think you'll be fulfilled unless you study. There is too much going on in that sharp brain of yours for you to be content being a housewife.'

Pip had tried to persuade her all those years ago how perfect they were for each other, but she'd been so determined they could only be friends she hadn't entertained the thought. How she wished now that she'd listened to him. He'd been right all along and the knowledge was killing her. 'Yes, I suppose so,' she said.

'It's your life, not mine,' Mr Marett told her, 'but if you'd take some advice from an old man, I think you're right to sit the exam. If you get in, you can still come back to the island after you've done your degree. And if Pip doesn't return . . .' he broke off to clear his throat, 'then those years won't have been wasted.'

Jenny blinked to stem the swell of tears. 'Thank you,' she said.

Part Four

September–December 1946

37

Jenny took a thick wool jumper from her drawer and folded it carefully before placing it into her suitcase. Mum had been knitting the garment all summer, despite the heat, and Jenny intended to cherish it. She'd unravelled an old pullover of Dad's to make it. It was kind of her, and it was lovely to take something of Dad's to Cambridge too. Almost as though he was there with her. She'd been told Cambridge was much colder than Jersey, especially in winter, when a cruel east wind blew across the fens. She'd be glad of it then, and it would always remind her of both her parents.

She still found it hard to accept that she was actually going to England. The flame of ambition to read maths at Newnham had been ignited when she was younger than William. It had been dimmed for most of the war, but now it burnt so strongly it almost consumed her. The conversation with Mr Marett last year seemed to have rekindled something – almost as if she'd needed his permission to dream again. She'd gone up to Cambridge last November to take the exam, and heard just after Christmas that she'd been accepted.

She'd be following in illustrious footsteps. Millicent Fawcett had drawn up her campaigns for women's suffrage at Newnham; her daughter, Philippa, also an alumna, had become the first woman to obtain the top score in the maths Tripos.

But any excitement she felt was muted. There was still no sign of Pip or any word from him. Mr Marett had a permanent stoop and a shuffling gait now. His eyes were always red-rimmed. Jenny thought he was the embodiment of sadness. Day after day she went to the office hoping to hear some news, and day after day he informed her there'd been none. Despite petitioning all the authorities he could think of, again and again, he always drew a blank.

In the end Alice went back to work at the General. She needed to stay busy to keep her mind off her losses, and her salary was essential now that Jenny was no longer working for Pip's dad. Karl didn't usually accompany her to the hospital. It was as if he sensed this was her territory, not his. Even had he lived, he wouldn't have come to work with her. She supposed she'd have left him with Mum, and later he'd have started at the Rouge Bouillon infant school she and Jenny had gone to all those years ago. She pictured him in little grey shorts and jumper, a cap on his head and a brown leather satchel slung over his shoulder. She'd have listened to him read after school and bathed his scabby knees if he'd fallen over in the playground. Would he have been picked on for being the child of a German? She hoped not.

It seemed everyone knew she'd slept with a German soldier. She saw the glances between nurses when she came on the ward, or sometimes caught a patient whispering to a relative when they thought she wasn't within earshot. Of course, others had returned from the camp who knew about Karl, and word would have got out. She'd intended to tell Jenny and Mum the day after she'd returned from Biberach, but Jenny had wheeled it out of her that evening.

They'd been in their room getting ready for bed. Karl had scrambled under the covers ahead of her, and she'd leant over to stroke his hair while he drifted off to sleep. When he'd finally settled, she turned to see Jenny looking at her strangely.

'What are you doing, Alice?'

Alice sighed. Perhaps now was as good a time as any. 'Sit down, Jenny,' she said, 'I have something to tell you.'

Jenny looked at her, appalled, as it all came out.

'You poor, poor thing. Having to deal with all that on your own. It's almost unimaginable.'

Alice blinked back the nightmare of Karl's birth. 'It was terrible. I don't think I'll ever get over it.'

Jenny reached over and took her hand. 'Will you tell Mum?'

'Yes. In the morning.' She couldn't face Mum's reaction yet. Telling Jenny had been hard enough.

'Poor Mum. A grandson.'

Alice took a juddering breath. 'He would have been. Your nephew, too. And William's.' She ran her hands through her hair. 'We've both lost so much.' No one could ever bring Karl back, though. Or Dad.

'Will you go to England to track him down?' asked Jenny.

'I don't know if I could do that to Mum and William right now. I've only just got back. If it wasn't for them, though, I'd go to England like a shot. I'm desperate to find Stefan. But I think I probably need to go back to the hospital for a bit.'

'You can't live your life trying to please others. You must do what's best for you. We've been given chances others haven't. We have to take them.' Jenny's expression was determined.

'Are you still hoping to go to Cambridge?'

'Yes. I think I am. Although I'd abandon that ambition in a second to have Pip back.'

'I know. Would you have married him?'

Jenny smoothed the counterpane with her palms. 'If he'd asked me, yes. But I seem to have realised that too late. What about you and Stefan?'

'Absolutely. No question.'

Jenny smiled. 'Do you know, I've put together a little stash again, now there's more food in the shops.' She pulled out the trolley and opened the box. 'Apple?'

Alice laughed. 'For old times' sake. Yes, please!' Perhaps they could still be the lighthouse sisters.

38

Jenny pulled out her chair and sat down at the old mahogany bureau in her college room. It had a drop-down writing surface and a number of tiny drawers where she kept her pens, compasses and set squares. She'd never had a desk of her own. When she'd been at school, she'd done her homework on the kitchen table, trying to shut out the sound of Mum banging cupboard doors and muttering to herself as she cooked, or perched awkwardly at the small dressing table she shared with Alice, having pushed aside the combs, brushes and jars of cold cream. There was never enough space there to spread her books out properly. Having a whole room and desk to herself was such a luxury.

She ran her hands over the bureau's smooth surface and wondered, not for the first time, how many others had used it before her. Had Cecilia Payne-Gaposchkin perched on this same chair, pondering the secrets of the universe? Or one of the brilliant Fawcetts? She just hoped she'd live up to all her dazzling predecessors.

The desk was pushed up against the window, from where there was a view out over the garden. Gowned figures hurried round its edges: students laden down with books, intent on arriving at a seminar on time, or dons off to give lectures. A sharp wind riffled through the grass of the manicured lawn and rustled the yellowing leaves of the mulberry trees. Jenny shivered. Her room was freezing. She'd barely known cold like it, not even at the end of the war, when the gas supply was cut off and they'd run out of firewood. She pulled down the sleeves of the jumper that Mum had knitted for her. The wool no longer smelt of Dad, but she still felt as though a part of him were there with her.

It wasn't university work that she was about to engage on, but an important communication to Alice. She pulled one of the desk drawers open and took out a sheet of paper and an envelope. Then she filled her fountain pen from the inkwell, stared into space for a bit and began to write.

Newnham College
Cambridge
Sunday 13th October 1946

Dear Alice,

Well, this is the life! I can't believe I have my own room in the college. It's really big, with a shared bathroom just along the corridor. It's wonderful to sleep all night without having to listen to you snoring! Sorry, sis. That was just a joke. I really miss you actually, but hope you're getting on well at the hospital. Do write when you get time, although I expect you're very busy. I try to write to Mum once a week too, with a separate letter for William. I tell Mum about the friends I'm making and the food I eat. I keep all the maths stuff for Will. He seems to be getting on really well in school. Who knows, he might read maths himself one day?

She smiled at the thought of William studying at Cambridge. He'd fit in well here. Nobody would think he was odd or laugh at his strange behaviour. They would just see his clever brain. He'd be accepted. Perhaps for the first time in his life.

She carried on with her letter.

It's wonderful to be finally realising my dream. Sometimes it feels as though those six terrible years never happened and I've just gone straight from school to university. The work is really stimulating. I can get lost for hours in algebra: so fascinating and challenging. I really feel this is where I'm meant to be, and although there will always be a hole in my heart while Pip is still missing, it is much better to keep busy here than pining for him back on Jersey and having to see the sadness on Mr Marett's face day after day. I found that almost unbearable.

She paused to think of her ex-employer. Poor man. She wondered how he was coping. Perhaps she'd write to him too, later. But she had to convey her latest news to Alice first.

Something strange happened the other day. I got chatting to a girl next to me after a trigonometry lecture. Like me, Joan seems a little older than most of the other students. It turned out she'd spent the whole of the war doing some sort of clerical work at a place called Bletchley Park in Buckinghamshire. She was a bit evasive about it, actually, which I thought was strange.

Anyway, she asked me about my family, so I told her about you and Stefan. She said she had some contacts at the Home Office from her days at Bletchley and could probably find out where he's held. I'm hoping she might be able to find something out about Pip too.

I don't want to get your hopes up, dear, but I really think she wants to help. So stand by for more news soon.

Much love for now,

Jenny xx

She ended the letter with a little sketch of a lighthouse.

Was it Alice's imagination, or had the hill back from the hospital become steeper since she'd been in Germany? At the end of a long day's shift, her calves ached as she trudged back home, longing for a hot bath and the oblivion of sleep.

It'd been hard to pick up the threads of her old life at the hospital. So much had changed: regimes had been altered, new staff had appeared, old colleagues had left. Those who'd remained told her what a struggle it had been to keep the hospital going during the war. Apparently the electricity had been cut off in the spring of '45, apart from in the theatre during operating hours. Patients couldn't be X-rayed, and there was no lift to take them to the top of the building. At night they'd used candles donated by the Red Cross. The boilers hadn't been able to operate – linen was washed in cold water, as were the patients.

And she'd changed too. She wasn't the eager young nurse she'd been in the early years of the war. She'd had a relationship with a German and had borne his child. Disillusionment and dejection coloured her being. She no longer believed in a bright future; all her energies were brought to bear dealing with the daily drudge of the present.

She opened the back door and smiled wearily at Mum. 'Cuppa?'

'Yes, please.' She unfastened her cape and draped it over her arm. Food supplies were still rationed, but packets of tea had started arriving back in the shops, and it was such a treat to drink the real article instead of the wartime ersatz versions.

Mum poured her a cup and handed it over. 'There's a letter for you from Jenny.'

'Oh good. I'll read it upstairs.' Alice removed her shoes, placed them on the rack by the back door, and took the cup and the letter up to her bedroom.

As she sat on the bed, sipping tea and catching up on Jenny's news, reading the promising last paragraph again and again, Karl appeared beside her.

'Dadda,' he said.

Alice smiled. 'Yes, Dadda, Karl. Maybe he's still alive. Maybe I can see him soon. She waited until her heartbeat settled before taking some paper and a pen from her dressing table drawer and composing a reply.

St Helier

Jersey

Friday 18th October 1946

Dear Jen,

I'm so pleased it's all working out for you in Cambridge. Dad would have been delighted.

You are right that life is busy in the hospital, and I'm keeping myself occupied. It's hard to rediscover my earlier love of nursing, though. Sometimes I feel I'm just going through the motions. Thank God for Rebekah. She wants to spend a lot of time with Tom of course, and we're all so relieved he returned safely, but we still go on cycle rides together, and of course it's lovely having her on the wards with me. I can't complain.

I do admire you for getting on with things and trying not to think about Pip too much. I wish I could forget Stefan. I have no idea if we have a future together, but I'm determined to try and find him. It is wonderful to hear that your friend might be able to help.

Write to me the minute you hear anything. I'll try not to get my hopes up too much, but I will await news with bated breath.

In the meantime, much love,

Alice xx

She sketched the now customary lighthouse at the bottom, then took the letter downstairs to find an envelope and stamp in Dad's old bureau in the sitting room.

'Just out to post my reply to Jenny,' she told Mum, who was still drinking her tea at the kitchen table.

'That was quick. I thought you were tired.'

Alice smiled. 'I feel fine now,' she said, and let herself out of the back door. Karl's small hand found hers, and he trotted off beside her along the pavement.

A return letter arrived from Jenny a week later.

Newnham College
Cambridge

Wednesday 23rd October 1946

Dear Alice,

I have news! My Bletchley friend informs me there's a Dr Stefan Holz registered at a prison camp for German soldiers on Dartmoor. Apparently he was born in August 1919, which makes him the right age. Alice, I'm pretty sure we've located your man!

What will you decide to do about this? Cambridge is about three hundred miles from Dartmoor, so although I'd love you to stay with me while you look for him, I don't think it would be practical. Apparently the nearest hospital is Barnstaple. Perhaps you could apply for a transfer or temporary placement there. It would be wonderful for us both to end up in England, although hard on Mum and Will, of course, but you mustn't let that stop you. If I knew where Pip was, I'd be over there like a flash.

Write as soon as you can and let me know what you intend to do.

Much love,

Jen xx

As usual, Alice had taken the letter upstairs when Mum handed it to her after her shift, but now she ran down to the kitchen.

'Mum, I've something to tell you.'

Mum turned from the stove, wiped her hands down her apron, and went and sat at the table.

403

Alice joined her and relayed the contents of Jenny's last two letters.

'I see.' Mum twisted her wedding ring round her finger.

'I agree with Jenny that I need to go across,' said Alice. 'I have to do everything I can to find Stefan.'

Mum stretched out her fingers and examined her nails. They were cut short, and her fingers were red. Small age spots had appeared on the back of her hands. 'Do you really think this is a good idea?'

'What d'you mean?'

'Well, there's no guarantee you'll be able to find him, and it could be years before he's released. And . . .' she examined her nails again, 'you'll come up against a lot of prejudice on account of his nationality.'

'Don't you think I know that?'

'Yes.' Mum sighed. 'But how much time did you actually spend with him? He might have changed beyond recognition. Isn't it better to stay on at the General? You never know, you might take up with a nice island doctor.'

Alice massaged her forehead. 'I love him, Mum,' she said. 'There'll never be anyone else for me. I have to give this one last shot. And I need to tell him about Karl.'

Mum stood up and returned to the stove. 'Then you'd better book some leave, hadn't you?' she said.

39

Alice sat on a bus as it rumbled its way out of Barnstaple towards Bideford, then meandered through quaint little villages with names like Frithelstock and Milton Damerel. She loved the Devon names: you used different parts of your mouth to say them, unlike the softer French-sounding towns on Jersey. The bus was bound for Holsworthy, which according to Jenny's friend was the site of Stefan's camp. It was just over an hour away from the hospital where she now worked.

She hadn't intended to ask for a transfer, but a job had come up at the North Devon Infirmary and she'd decided to apply. If she did manage to track Stefan down, she would want to be on hand, and if she didn't, it would still give her the opportunity to get away from Jersey and have a new start – something she increasingly felt she needed. She had to serve out her notice at Jersey General, of course, and there was quite a lot of paperwork to secure her post and accommodation, but by mid November she was Sister Robinson of the North Devon Infirmary, in charge of men's medical – a promotion as well.

The job part was fine – she enjoyed her new responsibilities – but it had been much harder than she anticipated to leave home. She'd not long been reunited with her family, and now they were apart again. It was particularly heart-wrenching to leave her mother, with Jenny over in England too. Thank goodness Mum still had William. And Rebekah continued to pop round often. Jenny had done so much to protect her during the war. There was a time when Alice would have been resentful of her sister's closeness to her friend, but now she was just so very grateful. Jenny had been a treasure, there was no doubt about it.

She gripped the seat in front of her and gazed out of the window at the corduroy squares of ploughed fields and the occasional farm building, trying to distract herself from worrying how she'd feel when she reached the camp. Would Holsworthy remind her of Biberach? A knot of fear formed deep in her stomach. What if she was arrested? Fraternisation between the local population and the prisoners of war was strictly forbidden. She'd have to avoid being seen by the guards.

It had taken her a while to find out how to get to Holsworthy, and, if she were honest, to pluck up the courage to go. She had no clear plan in her head. She knew that the number 85 bus stopped near the camp: she'd found that out by making casual-sounding enquiries of local nurses, and poring over bus timetables at Barnstaple library. All she could think of was to walk round the perimeter and see if she could spot Stefan on the compound. Jenny's friend had explained she needed official permission to visit. She'd applied on compassionate grounds, but the paperwork was taking an age, so she'd decided to take matters into her own hands.

She opened her handbag and drew out the envelope with Stefan's name on it. She doubted if she'd actually see him – there were reputed to be hundreds of prisoners at the camp – but perhaps there'd be someone who could find him. She had to tell him how she felt. That she'd thought of him constantly while she was in Biberach and had never given up on them having a future together.

Karl appeared on the seat beside her, swinging his legs and looking out of the window. His eyes were bright and his face was flushed. Alice put her arm round him and snuggled him close. 'You will find my daddy,' he said. The knot of fear loosened a little at his comforting words. He always seemed to know when she needed him most; perhaps he could predict the future too. Wouldn't it be wonderful if he was right?

The bus dropped them off at Kingswood Meadow, the nearest point to the camp. Alice got off, Karl still with her, then headed north-west towards Exhibition Field, where she'd been told the camp lay. As they walked along Foresters Road, she saw men in coarse jackets and baggy trousers working in the fields. Some of them had flat caps on. They were hoeing the soil with energy, despite their gaunt frames. Alice imagined they were prisoners of war. But none of them looked familiar. Stefan wasn't among them.

Eventually she reached the camp, a large compound consisting of low huts built on grass, surrounded by wooden posts and barbed wire. Her heart rate increased again. The camp was more rustic than Biberach, the buildings makeshift in comparison to the Bavarian solidity of Alice's quarters, but it was still a prison. And it still brought back terrible memories. Karl's little hand squeezed hers.

There was a huge metal gate blocking the entrance, with armed guards either side. An Alsatian prowled up and down, barking whenever someone approached from within the camp. Alice's chest tightened and she took a painful breath.

She made her way across some rough undergrowth, giving the entrance a wide berth. Karl grizzled a bit as he stumbled on the bumpy soil, and once he cried out when a bramble tore at the soft flesh of his lower leg, but Alice rubbed at it and kissed it better, and he marched on. 'You're a brave boy, Karl,' she said. 'Just like your daddy.' And she had to be brave too.

She pointed towards the distant figures in the camp, some jogging, some walking around the compound. Even from far away, she could see how emaciated they were. There was something ashamed-looking about the slouch of their shoulders, the way some of them stared at the ground rather than across at the view. She remembered the proud, upright young men who'd marched through the streets of St Helier in immaculate uniforms. Such a contrast.

As soon as she was out of sight of the sentries at the entrance, she approached the boundary. Her legs were so weak she could barely walk. She told herself just to put one foot in front of the other.

One of the prisoners had his back to the wire fence, and was watching a game of football that some of his fellow inmates were playing.

'Excuse me,' she whispered, her mouth almost too dry to speak.

The man turned round, then raised an eyebrow. He had close-cropped dark hair and purple shadows under his eyes. His cheeks were hollow.

'I'm looking for a German soldier. His name is Stefan Holz. I don't suppose you know anyone of that name, do you?'

'*Mi dispiace*,' said the man.

'Do you speak English?' she asked him, conscious of the stiffness in her voice.

He smiled sadly. *'Io non parlo inglese. Sono italiano.'*

She caught the last word. *Italiano.* Of course, there were Italian prisoners at the camp as well as German. Just her luck to meet one who didn't seem to have a clue what she was talking about. She tried one last time. 'German soldier: Stefan Holz.'

The man shrugged. *'Mi dispiace,'* he said again.

Alice passed over her letter, trying to stop her hand shaking. What if he kept it? Or gave it to the authorities? It was such a risk, but what else could she do?

The man took the envelope, tucked it into the breast pocket of his coat, and walked off.

It had been silly to come here; she knew it was a fool's errand, yet to have Stefan so close and not be able to see him was too much temptation. But at least she knew where he was now. If the paperwork didn't come through soon, or the letter didn't reach him, perhaps she'd chance her luck another time.

She pointed at the compound. 'Your daddy is somewhere over there,' she told Karl. She tried to conjure Stefan's shy smile and steady blue eyes. It seemed a world away when he'd last kissed her, but the memories of their time on the island kept her going. She still loved him and hoped he loved her too. They might still have a future together. She wouldn't give up on him.

They traipsed back to the bus stop.

She felt wiped out after another long bus journey spent fruitlessly looking out for Stefan in the farms they passed, but despite her exhaustion, she sat down and wrote to Jenny as soon as she arrived at the nurses' home, begging her to speak to her friend again. A letter came back by return, assuring her that Joan would make enquiries about her case. All Alice could do was wait anxiously.

Fortunately, hospital life kept her busy. Now that she was a ward sister, there were more reports to write and more staff to be responsible for. She thought back to the early days at the General, when she and Rebekah were probationers. How naïve and young they'd been then, and how much they had to learn. It felt like a lifetime ago now.

But as she hung up her uniform after another long shift, relieved to be free of the stiff collar and starched cap, she acknowledged that nursing alone wasn't enough for her. Sometimes the uniform felt too rigid, life on the wards too full of rules and regulations. She'd always thought she'd have a husband and a family eventually. Surely a nursing career shouldn't be the biggest achievement of her life? She needed Stefan.

A few days later, Alice was coming onto a late shift when she saw an ambulance outside the hospital. Bert, the driver, was just shutting the doors, the occupants having been discharged.

'Afternoon, Sister,' he said.

Alice loved the way people spoke in Devon, kind of rolling the 'r' sound around their mouth. 'Hello, Bert. What's happened here?'

'Nasty one,' said Bert. 'A truck carrying munitions collided with a lorry. Bloody incendiary device exploded. Truck were blown to smithereens. All four of the buggers thrown out.'

'How terrible. What are their injuries?'

410

'One open fracture of the tib, two with concussion and the fourth with some burns on his leg. Second degree probably. They was all foreign. Couple of Italians and two Germans. One of the Krauts spoke English. He seemed to take charge. He'd even put a splint on the tib chap by the time we arrived.'

Alice felt a surge of hope at the mention of an English-speaking medic, but she quickly suppressed it. There was work to be done and surely it was too much of a coincidence to imagine it might be Stefan. She thought quickly. The burns and the concussions would probably end up on her ward; the fracture would go to men's surgical. 'So there was an explosion, you say?'

Bert rubbed his nose. 'That's right, Sister. Funny thing was, it was probably one of their bombs in the first place. There was a bit of a raid on Barnstaple back in '42. Chap aiming for the gasworks, I reckon, but must have gone off course. Might have been the device that blew up today. Probably contravenes the Geneva Convention making them prisoners move munitions around, but I expect they 'ad it coming to them.'

'Where were the men from?'

'That PoW place just east of Bude.'

'D'you mean Holsworthy?'

'That's the one.'

Stefan's camp. She really mustn't get her hopes up, but her pulse was racing now. 'Thanks, Bert. I need to go.' She walked briskly into the hospital, heading for the emergency room. Three of the bays were occupied. She looked into the first one. A doctor was examining the man who'd fractured his leg. The patient's face was grey, his eyes closed in pain. Harsh sounds came from his mouth.

The doctor turned. 'You don't speak German, do you, Sister?'

'A little,' said Alice. She'd meant to go straight on to the next bay – this man wouldn't be one of her patients – but she couldn't ignore the doctor's request. 'What would you like me to tell him?'

'Can you explain that we'll take him into theatre to fix his leg? He doesn't need to worry. He'll be in good hands.'

Alice translated the doctor's words and the patient nodded, clenching his teeth as though to brace himself against the ordeal of surgery.

One of the concussion patients was in the next bay. A nurse was checking his vital signs. A quick glance at the man's face showed it wasn't Stefan. Alice's heartbeat slowed a fraction.

She peered into the other cubicle. No Stefan there either. She made her way upstairs to the ward. There was no reason why he would have been one of the injured – perhaps she'd let herself get carried away – but she couldn't stop herself searching for him.

The staff nurse was just going off duty. 'Afternoon, Sister.'

Alice picked the day log up from the table. 'Everything all right?'

The nurse quickly filled her in with reports of the regular patients. 'Oh, and there's a new man in bed ten. Burns casualty from the accident over at Holsworthy. Nurse Ridd is seeing to him now.'

'Thank you. I'll go and check.'

'All right, Sister. If there's nothing else, I'll be off.'

'Yes, thank you, Nurse.' Alice snapped on a smile, then hastened down the ward.

She moved the screen aside and watched as Nurse Ridd applied a Bunyan bag to the patient's leg, then gently inflated the cushion containing the heated saline solution. She was a kind girl, a little anxious at times, but took her work very seriously. Patients usually thrived in her care. The patient was lying on his front; the burns must be to the back of the leg. He was a tall man, with matted blond hair.

'Well done, Nurse. You're doing a good job.'

Nurse Ridd blushed. 'Thank you, Sister.' She finished fastening the bag.

'Would you like me to help you turn him?'

'Yes, please.'

Together they rolled the patient onto his side, then paused to check he was stable before completing the turn. The man's head lolled back against the pillow as he groaned in pain. When Alice glanced at him, her breath snagged in her throat. His face was much thinner than when she'd last seen him, and there were new lines either side of his mouth and a small scar near his hairline. His eyes remained shut, but there was no doubt that it was Stefan.

'I'll come back when he's awake,' she told Nurse Ridd, her emotions see-sawing between joy at finding him there and horror that he'd been injured.

Nurse Ridd nodded.

She returned an hour later to find Stefan sitting up, grinning broadly at her.

'Alice! Tell me I'm not dreaming.'

She drew the screen around his bed, then hurried to his side. 'I can't believe it either. I was frightened I'd never see you again.'

413

He took her hand. 'I've missed you so much. I never stopped thinking about you.' Despite the pain etched across his forehead, the tenderness in his eyes was the same as that night on the common.

She had that feeling of wholeness again, and realised that all the time she'd been away from him, she'd felt that a part of her, somewhere deep inside, was missing. 'Nor I you. Did you get my letter?' She'd poured out all her longing on paper. It was much more eloquent than she could afford to be now, a ward sister standing in front of her patient.

'Yes, I did. But I wasn't allowed to write back. There was nothing I could do to contact you.'

'Perhaps it was a blessing in disguise that you were injured. Otherwise how would we have found each other?'

Stefan frowned. 'We should never have been asked to transport munitions.'

'I know. The ambulance driver said as much. Something about contravening the Geneva Convention.'

'He was right.' Stefan released her hand to wipe a slick of sweat from his forehead. 'I did my best to look after the other casualties.'

'Bert said you'd done a good job.' The accident at St Lawrence flashed into Alice's mind. He'd been a tower of strength there too.

He nodded and leant back on the pillow again.

'Are you in pain?'

'A little.'

'I'll get you some APC.' She went over to the medicine cabinet, which she unlocked with the key that hung on her belt. She took out a bottle of tablets and tipped out two. Then she replaced the bottle and relocked the cabinet before returning to Stefan. 'Here you are.' She poured a glass of water from the jug on the bedside locker and handed him the pills.

He tilted his head to swallow them, then took a long drink. 'Thank you.'

'I really ought to get back to the ward.' She felt a sudden jab of resentment. All she wanted to do was stay with Stefan.

'Of course. See to your other patients. I will try to sleep now.'

She longed to kiss him properly, especially as the bed screen protected them from prying eyes, but she was still on duty. She contented herself by pressing her lips to his forehead.

Her mind was a blur as she went through the usual routine: accompanying the doctors on their evening rounds, administering medications, replacing drips, supervising the evening meals. How she managed to perform all her duties she'd never know. All she could think about was whether she should tell Stefan about Karl. It was so joyful to see him after all these years, but how on earth could she shatter his world with the news of their tragedy?

She checked on him from time to time. He slept for a bit, and managed to eat some supper. She sent Nurse Ridd to take his pulse and temperature and was relieved to hear that both were normal. No sign of an infection as yet. As soon as her shift was finished, she rushed to his side.

She gave him a sanitised version of her time at the camp, and he told her about the end of the war and how the Germans had been taken off Jersey and sent to England. After a while, his speech slowed and his face grew pale.

'You're getting tired,' she said. 'I'm going to pop home to get some sleep, but I'll be back as soon as I can.'

Stefan nodded, his eyes already closing.

Alice tiptoed out and collected her outdoor clothes from her locker. She'd been right not to tell him about Karl. It would be cruel to burden him with the terrible news when he was so vulnerable, and she didn't want to risk delaying his recovery. She'd tell him when the time was right. Sleep was the best medicine now, and she knew that Sister Taylor, who'd just come on duty, would keep a close eye on him.

She spent a sleepless night, alternating between fear and elation, and was back at the hospital well before her shift was due to start, eager to hear how Stefan was. She popped into the cloakroom before entering the ward. Sister Taylor was there, getting ready to go off duty.

'How's bed ten?' Alice asked.

Sister Taylor pushed a strand of hair under her cap. In the mirror, her eyes met Alice's. She shook her head.

'What?' Nausea surged in Alice's throat. 'But he was fine last night.'

'No.' Sister Taylor put her hand on Alice's arm. 'He's still fine. So well, in fact, that he's been sent back to Holsworthy.'

'I see.' How could she have been so stupid? In trying to stay professional, she'd failed to confide her relationship with Stefan to any of her colleagues. As a result, no one had thought to warn her he was being discharged.

'Wait a minute. There's something in the desk for you.' Alice followed Sister Taylor into their shared office. 'Here.' She rummaged in a drawer then handed over an envelope. 'From Dr Holz. He badgered me into finding some stationery for him. He wanted to leave you a message. Seems you left quite an impression.'

416

Alice smiled weakly. 'Thank you,' she said.

She read the letter in the toilet after Sister Taylor had left. In it, Stefan said all the things he hadn't been able to tell her yesterday. He still loved her. He still wanted her. And as soon as he was released, he'd come and find her. But it didn't stop her being worried to death.

⊥

Jenny turned off Sidgwick Avenue and down Newnham Walk towards the elaborate wrought-iron gates that marked the entrance to the college. The gates had been erected in Victorian times to keep out men, although she doubted the delicate flowers that adorned them would have deterred a determined suitor.

The porter lifted his hat. 'One minute, Miss Robinson, I have a letter for you.' A little jolt of pleasure went through her: first the fact that the porter now recognised her and knew her name, a sure sign of her acceptance at Newnham, and second that someone had written to her.

He handed her a small envelope with familiar loopy handwriting on the front. How lovely, a letter from Alice. She would read it in her room after making some tea – still a treat – and indulging herself by lighting a fire. She hadn't got used to the wind that swept off the fens – or straight from the Russian Urals, as some would have it – and seemed to blow right through her. And it was even chillier now that it was November.

She thanked the porter and set off for her room. Thankfully there was no one in the corridor wanting to chat, so she was able to light the fire and make the tea straight away. Finally, a cup in her hand and her black-stockinged feet stretched towards the warmth, she opened Alice's letter.

When she'd finished reading, she put the sheets back into the envelope and gazed out of the window. Alice sounded so happy. She could feel her excitement jumping out of the page. But she was right too that Mum would be worried that she'd found Stefan. Jenny knew all too well how devastating it was not to know the whereabouts of someone you loved. She'd been determined to help Alice for that reason, and clearly she'd been successful. But part of her hoped the relationship would fizzle out, that Alice would meet an English doctor at the Barnstaple hospital who'd put all thoughts of Stefan out of her head. The Robinsons had grown fond of Stefan and they owed him a huge amount. He certainly hadn't deserved his fate. But Alice would face a hard future if she married a German; it would be difficult to find acceptance among the locals, and only the strongest relationship could survive their disapproval. And then there was the baby. When Alice had told her, Jenny had been horrified at what her sister had been through. She couldn't stop thinking about that poor little boy – her nephew, Mum's first grandchild. Poor Karl. And poor, poor Alice. She'd suffered enough.

Yet a tiny bit of her was envious too. At least Alice had found the courage to express her love for Stefan. Jenny's relationship with Pip had never become physical. She'd not given him anything to hold on to, and that haunted her now he was missing. As the weeks and months rolled on, it was becoming less and less likely that he was still alive. Would she ever know what had happened to him?

She put the letter down. The room was snug now, the air tinged with the smell of burning coal. She went and sat at her desk, then pulled one of her mathematics books towards her: *Method of Fluxions* by Isaac Newton. If she concentrated on Newton's findings from all those years ago, and took herself back to the shadowy realms of the eighteenth century, perhaps she could shut out her fears about Pip.

A few days later, Alice arrived back at the nurses' home after a long day on the wards to find an envelope with Jenny's handwriting in her pigeonhole. Her heart started to beat faster. She picked it up, went to her room, threw herself on the bed, and opened it straight away.

Newnham College
Cambridge
Friday 29th November 1946

Dearest Alice,

I'm afraid this comes with some bad news, so I hope you're sitting down when you read it. My friend with contacts at the Home Office has told me that most of the prisoners from Holsworthy have been repatriated. I'd imagine your Stefan is amongst them. Only a remnant remain at the camp, and they'll be going soon.

The letter fluttered to the floor. How could life be so cruel? She'd left her home to work in England and waited patiently to see Stefan all these long weeks, only to have him taken away from her once again. Surely he would find some way to get word to her? She took a deep breath, then leant over the bed to retrieve the letter.

I'm so sorry, Alice. The only good thing to come from this is that Stefan must be a free man now. I could ask my friend to track down his address in Germany and perhaps you could visit him. You must have some leave saved up – and some money. I'll find out all I can.

Thinking of you. All love,

Jenny xx

Alice folded the letter again and again until she'd turned it into a tiny square. It was only when Karl appeared, stroking her back with his little hand, that she allowed herself to cry.

40

Jenny went back to Jersey in mid December. Christmas 1946 was a slightly less frugal affair than Christmas 1945 had been. After Dad had died, Mum hadn't the heart to buy a tree, and there hadn't been any to spare in the latter war years. Jenny helped Will to make paper chains out of old newspaper, both of them enjoying the precision of measuring, cutting and sticking the thin strips. Will was fifteen now. He still didn't like to be hugged and he still wouldn't allow food items to touch on his plate, but he was much easier to talk to.

'I've ordered a chicken from Lidster's,' said Mum. There were no turkeys to be had, of course. 'It'll probably be an old boiling fowl, but it's better than nothing.'

Jenny thought back to the formal Christmas meal at Newnham in the grand dining hall. There'd been turkey there, with plenty of roast potatoes and bread sauce, and rich plum pudding to follow. She wondered how the cook had obtained the supplies. She'd eaten well at Cambridge, as her thickening waist and fuller face testified, but Mum said the extra weight suited her. She just wished Alice would eat better.

'How was Alice when you saw her in London?' asked Mum, echoing her thoughts. She took the kettle over to the sink and filled it with water.

They'd managed to meet in early December and had a

pleasant afternoon shopping in Oxford Street. There was still rationing, of course, but there was a little more choice in the shops now, and they both bought some lipstick and face powder for themselves along with presents for the others. Alice had looked pale and seemed quiet, although she'd brightened when she'd managed to find a new blouse for Mum and some more Meccano for William. Jenny had promised to take them across with her when she went home a week later. In the evening, they went to the Victoria Palace to see *Sweetheart Mine*, although afterwards Jenny had wondered if a show about an old married couple was the best choice for two spinsters. They'd stayed at a cheap bed and breakfast overnight, and the next morning she'd insisted on seeing Alice off at Paddington, as she had a much longer journey.

Jenny thought of her sister's tight smile and gaunt frame. 'She's fine, Mum,' she said.

'I do miss her.' Mum lit the ring on the stove, placed the kettle on it, then sat down at the table, where William was bent over a copy of *Biggles Fails to Return*, mouthing the words to himself and licking his finger every time he turned a page.

'I know,' said Jenny. They'd had Christmases without her before, of course, when she was in Germany, but that was in wartime, when everything had been different. 'I'm sure she'll come next year. We just need to give her time.' She got up to fetch the cups and saucers from the cupboard.

Mum sighed. 'I never thought I'd have two unmarried daughters well into their twenties. There should be husbands and babies round this table.'

'Now, Mum. You know I can't move on until I know what's happened to Pip.' Jenny had been over to see Mr Marett the day after she got back. His voice quivered now and he was quite unsteady on his feet. Poor man. How she wished for a happy ending for them both. But still no word of Pip. Not even her Cambridge friend had been able to help track him down. She'd never give up looking for him, though, even if it took the rest of her life.

Mum nodded. 'It seems so cruel that you've both lost your young men.'

Jenny pressed Mum's hand. 'There's still hope,' she said. 'And in the meantime, you have two career women. Alice is heading for a matron's role one day, and I'm going to be a brilliant mathematician.'

Mum gave a watery smile. 'Your father would have been so proud,' she said.

'Yes, he would.' Jenny wiped Mum's cheek with her hanky, then saw to her own. 'And he'd want us to have the best Christmas we can, too.' She put her hand over William's book, causing him to look up from his page. 'Come on, William, let's hang up those chains.'

⚓

On Christmas night, Alice sat at the desk in the shadowy ward, a shaded lamp pooling light on a sheaf of patient charts in front of her. The air was permeated with the soft breaths and occasional snores of the supine bodies. Outside the window, snowflakes twirled, adding to the thick white drifts that had already formed. It had been a bitter winter so far. Karl sat next to her, building a complicated structure from wooden bricks. He would have been three now, perhaps destined to be practical and clever like his father. The bricks would have been her Christmas present to him. She seemed to remember

William having similar ones, endlessly lining them up in precise rows, and throwing a tantrum every time someone moved them so much as a fraction.

She wondered what Mum, Jenny and Will had done for Christmas. She missed them badly, but it had been the right decision to stay here. She'd have only been a spectre at the feast at home, and someone needed to be on duty. It might as well be her. Besides, she couldn't leave if there was a chance Stefan might still try to get in touch.

They'd given the patients as good a Christmas as they could. The kitchen staff had rustled up a roast lunch, and some of the junior nurses had spent hours making crackers. The visitors had started to arrive early in the afternoon, bringing gifts, tins of mince pies and Christmas cake. For a while the ward was noisy with chatter and goodwill.

But now everyone had gone and the place was hers again. She looked around at the tawdry decorations. Someone had cut out the letters to spell HAPPY CHRISTMAS and strung them along the wall. The last S had come loose and drooped at the end.

She tried to shut off thoughts of home. They'd all be in bed by now. Perhaps they'd spent the evening playing games or listening to the radio. There'd probably have been a walk too, after lunch, maybe down to the sea. She'd spent all day trying not to picture them eating their Christmas meal. If Dad and Karl had lived, there'd have been six of them at the table.

What else would she have bought Karl for Christmas? Perhaps she'd have knitted him a little jumper with a train pattern on the front. She'd seen some Dinky toys when she and Jenny had been shopping together in London, but had resisted buying them, even though he'd have loved the model of an American Jeep she'd seen on display. Jenny would have said she was going mad, and she didn't want to worry her. But she'd thought about it that night when they'd stayed at a guest house, imagining Karl's face lighting up at the sight of it, and how he'd spend all day pushing it up and down.

And what would she have given Stefan? She could have knitted him a scarf perhaps, or saved up for a nice watch. She tried to imagine him back home in Germany, sitting round the dinner table or opening presents with his family. Did he think of her constantly, as she thought of him? The ache in her heart was almost unbearable. She'd do everything in her power to track him down, then apply for time off to visit. After all they'd been through, she wouldn't let him go without a fight.

But there was no time to dwell on that now. She had a job to do. She stood up stiffly and walked down the ward to check on her patients. That was where her responsibilities lay.

Everyone was quiet, worn out by the festivities. She stood by one elderly patient's bed, noting with satisfaction his bright cheeks and regular breaths. The poor man had been admitted a week ago after a stroke. Until recently, Alice had been worried about his grey pallor and listless manner. But a couple of hours with his family had done him the world of good. Nurses and doctors could help to mend bodies, but the company of loved ones mended spirits.

Further down the ward, a young man was turned on his side, his fingers still clutching a copy of *All the King's Men*. Alice prised it gently from him and placed it on the bedside locker. He'd have plenty of time to read it tomorrow.

As she crept back up the ward, she heard a sudden disturbance behind the closed double doors at the entrance and made out two faint figures through the glass.

She looked at her watch. Eleven o'clock. Visiting hours had long since finished, and she hadn't received notification of any late admissions. She hurried to investigate.

The closer she got, the more familiar one of the shapes looked. Her heart started to thrum.

Two people stood at the door. One was an elderly man with a clerical collar and a benevolent expression. But it was the other figure that drew her attention. A lean, upright frame, a shock of blond hair, and a smile as broad as the ward.

'Stefan!'

'Shh.' He laughed and held his arms out wide.

Alice flew into them, luxuriating in his vivid, wonderful closeness, the strength of his hands, his shoulders still firm despite his gaunt frame. She stretched up to kiss his cheek, savouring his warmth and the familiar smell of him.

'*Mein Liebling*,' said Stefan, again and again.

Much later, as they sat in the staff canteen eating a meagre breakfast after Alice's shift had finished, Stefan told her his story.

Most of his fellow prisoners had been sent home to Germany back in November, as Alice had discovered. But a few had been left in place to finish off the farm work over the winter, Stefan amongst them. Some of the local church members had invited prisoners into their homes to celebrate Christmas with them, and he had spent the day with the elderly Methodist minister and his family. Over supper, he'd told them about Alice, and the minister had insisted on driving him to the hospital then and there. It had taken them some time to get through the thick snow and worsening conditions, hence their late arrival.

'I can't believe you've been here all this time,' said Alice, blotting her cheeks with her handkerchief.

Stefan caught hold of her fingers and drew them to his mouth. 'I thought of you all the time. I knew that somehow there'd be a way to find you, but we were never allowed out and we were kept so busy during the day. I was frightened I'd be sent back to Germany before I could see you again.'

Alice nodded. 'I'm so relieved you weren't. I've been trying to track down your parents' address so I could come and visit. But you're here after all. And how kind of the minister to invite you for Christmas.' Her eyes brimmed again.

'Yes, a wonderful man.' Stefan's face was wind-tanned, his chin dark with stubble, and his hands were scarred and chapped. No longer the nimble doctor's fingers she'd once held. But he was Stefan. Her Stefan. And they were properly together at last.

Their tea and toast were ignored as she told him the full story of her internment at Biberach, and then, word by painful word, the birth and death of Karl. And all the time she felt the small presence next to her, his little eyes watching her intently, his quick breaths in the thick air.

Stefan was visibly shocked at her account; his face blanched and his eyes became glassy. 'We had a son,' he whispered.

Alice took a deep breath. 'I've imagined him with me all this time, his little body growing and changing. He'd be three by now.' Karl turned curious eyes towards Stefan, and Alice fancied that father and son smiled at each other.

Stefan took her hand again. 'You've suffered terribly. We both have. But soon I'll be a free man. I may even be able to get a job at the hospital, if they'll allow a German doctor to work here. We can make a future together.'

Alice nodded, her heart too full to speak.

Epilogue

November 1996

Jenny stands on the quayside, trying to ignore the chilly gust that knifes through her woollen coat and whips her scarf against her face. She turns her head to escape the wind's force, and looks across to the harbour. They've built a smart new marina now, where millionaires' yachts loom majestically. A far cry from the little *Bynie May*, moored by the south pier for the whole of the war. She imagines that the boat saw more action than all those swanky ships, though, and for a moment the ghost of Pip hovers at the edge of her consciousness, his eyes gleaming, his skin bronzed from the sun, life and energy leaping from every pore.

She wipes a mittened hand across her face. She honoured her promise to track him down. Eventually she was contacted by a Cambridge academic who was researching the whereabouts of Jersey resistance heroes and had come across some new archive material. Pip's name was on a list of prisoners at Naumburg, south-west of Berlin. Her beautiful brave boy had died of dysentery. She visited his grave at Halle, and placed on it three images: a photograph of herself, a painting of Jersey and a picture of the *Bynie May*. The three loves of his life.

Mr Marett died a broken old man, consumed with loss and defeat, never knowing his son's fate.

But they're all old now. Alice and Stefan have a live-in carer. They spent a lifetime tending to others; now it's their turn to be looked after, although their family visit often.

The band tune up, then launch into a repertoire of wartime songs: 'We'll Meet Again', 'The White Cliffs of Dover', and 'There'll Always Be an England'. Time contracts and she's back in 1940, when she stood on the same quay waiting for the boat to take her to England, then changed her mind at the thought of leaving. It was the right thing to stay; she and Pip did their bit for the war, both of them – Pip sacrificed his life to it – and now, today, he will finally be honoured.

It's strange how her life has come full circle. The very lighthouse that she and Alice visited as children, when they were the lighthouse sisters, has been moved to St Helier, where it now stands as a memorial to those who lost their lives during the war. As she gazes up at its solid white structure, she sees again the two little girls running down the steps, full of excitement and curiosity. So different and yet so close. Just as they are now.

Their father's words drift back over the years: *It acts as a guide and warning. It keeps sailors away from danger, and leads them safely home when they return.*

But it never led Pip home, did it?

She murmurs the familiar words of Laurence Binyon's poem: *They shall grow not old, as we that are left grow old: Age shall not weary them, nor the years condemn . . .*

⛵

Alice fumbles behind her for the remote control and turns on the television. There's a click and a silence before the picture spreads across the screen. She checks her watch: just before half past one. The weather forecast is starting, then it'll be *South Today*. Jenny assured her the memorial service would be covered on the BBC local news. She calls for Stefan to join her.

As Stefan pulls up a chair, Alice sits forward in her seat, willing the early items to be dispensed with quickly. At last the newsreader announces that they'll be going live to St Helier, where an important ceremony is taking place. She delves inside her cardigan sleeve for a hanky, knowing she will need it. Stefan reaches for her hand and she smiles at him. His strength will see her through. It always has.

The commentator is standing on the quay, his back to the large crowd. Alice sees a tall, fair-haired figure amongst the throng. She can't make out his features, but it looks like their son. He promised them he'd attend the service. Jenny will be somewhere there too, near the front, probably, as she's taking part. Alice listens to the wartime songs being played by the band. She remembers how the crowd sang 'There'll Always Be an England' when she left for Germany. She could still hear the words as the boat chugged its way across to Saint-Malo. That was the worst time, so far from home, missing her family and Stefan desperately . . . then giving birth to Karl. She glances up at the wall, to where she always imagined their son's picture would have hung. But God has compensated. They've had three beautiful children since, a lifetime of happiness and laughter. And enough memories to sustain an old couple in their twilight years.

It's strange how things have turned out. She always thought Jenny was the one destined to be married. But she never met anyone who measured up to Pip. She stayed on at Cambridge

431

and built a brilliant career there, becoming a professor before she retired. Dad would have been so proud. He'd have been proud of them all: Alice a lifetime of service as a nurse, and Jenny and William at Cambridge. William is a lecturer there too now. Mum was eventually left alone on the island she loved, but she visited all three of them often in England, so happy that her daughters were close again and both still doting on their brother.

Alice's attention sharpens. The band has stopped and the bailiff is giving a short speech about the islanders' pride in those who gave their lives for their countrymen in the fight against evil and oppression. Then he invites an imposing figure to step forward.

'The ambassador of Israel is going to present the Righteous Among the Nations award to Professor Jennifer Robinson, for the risks she and her family took to prevent a Jewish nurse from being deported to the Continent, keeping her safe on Jersey during the occupation.'

Alice holds her breath as Jenny steps forward to receive her honour. She bows her head, then shakes the ambassador's hand. As she returns to the crowd, a hunched but still recognisable figure approaches her. Rebekah. After all these years. The two women hug. Alice presses her hanky to her face and feels Stefan's anxious glance.

'Professor Robinson.' The bailiff's tone is polite but insistent. Jenny kisses Rebekah's cheek and turns away. Rebekah returns to the crowd. 'We'd also like to present you with a posthumous Médaille de la Résistance for Pip Marett, in respect of the work you both did in informing the foreign prisoners of news from Britain during those long war years, an act of courage for which Pip paid with his life.'

Jenny steps forward to receive Pip's honour.

The camera lingers on her glistening face, then pulls back to show the whole quayside, before finally closing in on the lighthouse, tilting slowly up the tower. And as Alice stares at the building that for so long has blazed its bright rays of hope through the darkness and across the troubled sea, the tears run unchecked down her cheeks.

Author's Note

For twenty-three years I lived with a surname I hated: Marett. It was difficult to spell, easy to mispronounce and it seemed to cause everyone asking me for it to immediately acquire a hearing problem, forcing me to repeat it, and so further increasing my embarrassment. When I got married I was only too happy to take on my husband's surname and ditch my maiden name.

So it was with some surprise I discovered, on my first visit to Jersey, that the name I'd disliked for its rarity in England had many listings in the Channel Island phonebook.

I thought the name might mean something nautical (the first four letters of my name, Mare, are Latin for 'the sea'), so it seems appropriate that my ancestors lived on an island. It was comforting to know that there were others who might have shared my name, and when I researched my family tree several years later I discovered there were several illustrious Maretts on Jersey, whose histories I won't bore you with here.

Suffice it to say that by the time I came to write this book, I had made peace with my former surname, and by then my beloved father, who gave me the name, had passed away, so it became linked with my precious memories. When my husband first suggested I bequeathed one of my characters my maiden name, I initially baulked, those feelings of embarrassment surfacing, but then I realised he was right (I have to admit he often is) and Pip Marett has become a favourite protagonist.

I've tried to maintain historical accuracy as far as possible, but there are a couple of events I have to confess to inventing for the sake of the story: one is the shooting of Russian slaves at St Lawrence, the other is the poor treatment of the Jews at Biberach, although both are consistent with atrocities of the time.

I was going to have Jenny track Pip down at the end of the novel, but then I realised a far worse outcome was never to know what happened, never to have that sense of closure, to plan a funeral or tend a grave. Such was the fate of some islanders who never discovered their loved ones' whereabouts. There is a short documentary about this here: https://vimeo.com/229688437. I have taken the liberty of suggesting that the research of 'a Cambridge academic' takes place at the end of the twentieth century, as it better fits my story, although in reality it was the beginning of the twenty-first century.

In the past I've written about events that fascinate me, but have had no personal connection with – apart from the fact my novels are set around World War Two, a war my own father fought in. So it is with some relief I can say that I *do* have a family connection to Jersey, and for that reason this story is particularly close to my heart. I hope you've enjoyed reading it as much as I've enjoyed writing it.

Acknowledgements

When I first came up with the idea of writing a novel set on Jersey during World War Two, I imagined myself spending many days on the island, carefully researching its history and visiting key people and locations. But this was early 2020 and before I could make any plans, the global pandemic hit. Travelling became impossible so any visits had to be virtual ones, and all knowledge had to be gleaned remotely. This was both terrifying and heart-warming: terrifying because I know how well Jersey people know their history and I was anxious about getting all the details right; heart-warming because so many kind people responded to my requests for information and advice. I am particularly indebted to the following:

Anne Williams, my ever wise and wonderful agent.

The amazing Sherise Hobbs and the team at Headline, especially Bea Grabowska and Alara Delfosse.

Jane Selley, for her attention to detail during the copy-editing.

Stephanie Norgate and Jane Rusbridge for their generosity and support.

The National Meteorological Library and Archive, particularly Mark Beswick, the Archive Information Officer, for helping me ascertain the weather conditions on Jersey in June 1940.

Rhys Perkins of the St Helier Yacht Club for his very helpful advice on sailing and his patience in answering my many questions.

Andre le Quesne and Doug Ford for kindly providing information on the Saint-Malo evacuation.

David Worsford for generously sharing with me the draft chapters on Saint-Malo from his now published book: *Operation Aerial: Churchill's Second Miracle of Deliverance* (Sabrestorm Publishing, 2021).

Michele Leerson and Jersey Heritage for so helpfully facilitating my research at a time when I couldn't visit the island due to Covid restrictions.

Gary Godel for his expert help with information on Operation Haddock, featured in chapter two of the novel.

Anne Hudson for farming insights and for kindly checking my Devon scenes.

Jeannette Hardiman, Wendy Falla and Mike Entwistle for helpfully supplying local knowledge.

Sue Thomas for her expert help with all things maths related.

Emily Kinder for checking my Cambridge scenes and for her helpful insights into life at Newnham College.

Clare Tredinnick for kindly giving me permission to use the name of her late father's boat, the *Bynie May*.

Rosie Millar, Nuria Baso Hernandez, India Phillips and Sue Greenhalgh for help with Spanish and Italian translations, and Adam Duce for advice on conveying the Devon dialect.

I am also indebted to John Alexander for his expert advice on filming techniques.

Any unintentional mistakes are my own.

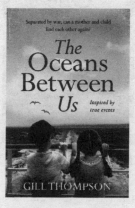

**TO SAVE HER CHILD, A MOTHER MUST MAKE
AN IMPOSSIBLE CHOICE.**

Prague 1939. Young mother Eva has a secret from her past.
When the Nazis invade, Eva knows the only way to keep
her daughter Miriam safe is to send her away – even if it
means never seeing her again.

But when Eva is taken to a concentration camp, her secret
is at risk of being exposed.

In London, Pamela volunteers to help find places for the
Jewish children arrived from Europe. Befriending one
unclaimed little girl, Pamela brings her home.

Then when her son enlists in the RAF, Pamela realises how
easily her own world could come crashing down . . .

Available to order

REVIEW